SAVAGE VICIOUS HEIR

DUET FOUR

HEIRS OF ALL HALLOWS'

CAITLYN DARE

Copyright © 2024 by Caitlyn Dare

All rights reserved.

No part of this book may be reproduced in any form or by any electronic or mechanical means, including information storage and retrieval systems, without written permission from the author, except for the use of brief quotations in a book review.

Editing and proofreading by Sisters Get Lit(erary) Author Services

Cover by Sammi Bee Designs

SAVAGE VICIOUS HEIR: PART ONE

1

ABIGAIL

Rain pelts down on the umbrella someone holds over me, the wind howling around us.

It's a miserable day.

Cold. Dark. Bleak.

But it matches my mood. The endless stream of tears rolling down my cheeks. The angry storm battering my insides.

I feel like I haven't taken a breath since I heard the words.

He's gone.

My father. The one person I had left in the world.

I always knew this day would come—sooner than it should have because of his ill health—but I didn't know.

I didn't—

"Abi," Raine gently squeezes my arm. "It's time."

"W-what?" I blink at her. Empty. Hollow.

Numb.

"The rose." She motions to the open grave. The dark black hole they lowered my father's casket into.

I take a step forward, and another. "Goodbye," I

whisper, throwing the lone stem into the abyss, watching as it disappears.

"We should get you inside," she says, wrapping her arm around me. "This storm isn't going to pass anytime soon."

I nod, letting her lead me away.

Wondering when the pain will stop.

Wondering how I'll ever piece myself back together after this.

I don't know how long I've been sitting here, hiding in my bedroom. But eventually, a knock pierces the silence. My sanctuary.

"Abigail?" a soft voice calls. "It's me." Olivia slips inside. "There you are." She offers me a sad smile. "We were worried."

"I... I can't."

"I know, gosh, babe." She hurries to my side and takes my hand in hers. "I know. Can I get you anything? Something to eat? Drink?"

Something to take it all away, I swallow the words.

She would never do that though. Maybe her boyfriend's friends Theo and Oakley would. Give me a pill to tamp down the pain. But not Liv. Not Tally or Raine.

My friends.

The only people I have left expect Maureen, my father's carer. And now he's gone, I suppose she'll—

I shove down the wave of grief before it consumes me fully.

After losing my mum in the accident that left me scarred and ruined, I thought I knew pain and loss. But this feels different. Even though I've had years to prepare, losing my father has broken something inside me. Fractured me apart in ways I can't even fathom.

It wasn't time.

We didn't have enough time.

Yet, he's gone.

He left me.

And now I'm alone.

"You're not," Liv says, and I realise I must have said that last part aloud. "You have me and Tally and Raine. The boys too. And Elliot—"

I go still at the mention of his name.

Elliot Eaton.

The boy I've spent weeks fantasising about. Falling for the idea that there could be something between us, that maybe the strange tug I feel in his presence was reciprocated. That, maybe if, one day, I was brave enough to pull on that tether, he would pull back.

He didn't.

And I should have known. I should have known that someone like me wouldn't be the kind of girl Elliot Eaton wants.

At least if one good thing came from all of this... this hurt, it's that we can pretend it never happened.

We can pretend I didn't kiss him that night.

"Abi?" Liv gently nudges my arms, pulling me from my maudlin thoughts. "Tell me what you need."

"I want to sleep," I whisper over the hoarseness of my throat.

"But the wake—"

"Tell them, I'm sorry. But I can't. I can't go down there."

"Do you want to stay here? I can take you back to my house or—"

"It's fine. I'm fine." The lie turns the air thick and heavy. But she doesn't argue.

Instead, Liv helps pull back the covers and gets me settled. "I'll stay with you," she says, but I shake my head.

"Alone. I want to be alone."

Another lie.

But one I need to tell to shore my defences, to protect myself. Because while she might be my friend, while they all might be my friends, one day, they'll leave.

Just like everybody I love does.

"Abigail, I'm so very sorry for your loss," Mr Porter says.

"Thank you. Is my room ready?"

"Abigail, I—"

"Please, Mr Porter, I can't stay in the house. I can't... be there." Panic floods my voice as blood roars in my ears.

It's been two days since the funeral. A week since my father passed. And I can't spend another second rattling around in that big empty house.

He's everywhere, in everything. Haunting me.

When the headteacher of All Hallows' doesn't answer, I add, "Please, I'm begging you. Money isn't an issue, you know that."

Ironic really, that my father, as a well-respected judge, earned more money than we could spend. But it couldn't save him.

It couldn't cure the disease addling his body.

"Fine, yes. Of course. You can move into the dormitories."

"Thank you. Thank you." Relief sinks into me as I wipe my eyes.

I'm surprised I have any tears left to fall. It's all I've done for days. Cry and sleep and cry some more.

After the wake, the girls wanted to stay with me, but I didn't want them too. I couldn't bear it. The pity in their eyes, the utter hopelessness.

Besides, I don't want them to know that I'm slipping. Falling into old habits and dark places. And I definitely don't want Elliot to know. I don't want him to try and intervene and play that big brother role that I so obviously mistook for something more.

I inhale a shuddering breath, thanking Mr Porter again. "When can I move in?"

"As soon as—"

"Today," I blurt out. "I already have my things."

"Okay, okay." He concedes. "Mrs Danvers will get you settled. Let me call her."

He does and I wait. Desperate to get to my new room—my new home I suppose.

The house is legally mine now as are most of my father's money and assets. But I can't think about that yet. Can't deal with any of it.

All I want to do is sleep and forget. Just for a little while. Until the pain recedes and I feel like I can breathe again.

"She'll be right over," he says, standing. "As for your class schedule, I'll speak to your teachers. See if we can make some allowances, maybe look at coursework extensions."

"Thank you."

He gives me a small nod. "Your father was a good man, Abigail. His absence will be felt by all of us."

There's a small knock on the door and I'm saved from having to say anything else when the dorm aunt Mrs Danvers appears.

"Oh, Abi." She rushes over to me and takes me by the shoulders. "I'm so very sorry."

"Thank you."

"Come on, let's get you settled. I have a lovely quiet room for you in the Bronte Building."

"Take good care of her," Mr Porter says.

He's never been an easy man to deal with, but his words seem genuine.

People liked my father. An intelligent and revered man, they respected him. Even if he didn't always make the right choices. Like trying to secure my future by marrying me off to Reese Whitfield-Brown.

I suppress a shudder.

It was an act of desperation. To make sure I had someone to take care of me when he was gone. But Reese and I weren't right for one another and when I realised he had fallen in love with Olivia, I begged my father to change his mind.

And for a while, I thought that maybe Elliot would—

No.

I shut down those thoughts.

I was wrong.

I misread everything. Every glance and touch and whisper between us.

While I was looking at him like he might be the one to keep my heart safe, he was looking at me as nothing more than a sister. A friend. An obligation.

I follow Mrs Danvers out of the building and across campus toward the dorm buildings. All Hallows' is a beautiful place steeped in history and tradition. But it also houses some dark secrets. Whispers of secret societies and twisted games. It's no surprise though, when some of the richest, oldest families in Oxfordshire send their children here.

Lawyers, businessmen, politicians, they are the country's future leaders.

I never cared before, happy to hide in the shadows and avoid people's stares. But then I befriended Olivia Beckworth, and she pulled me into her life. Their lives.

The Heirs of All Hallows'.

But the rumours and gossip do Reese, Theo, Oakley, Elliot injustice. Entitled and arrogant and dangerous, they are. But they're also loyal and strong and protective. And if you're welcomed into their inner circle, you're one of them.

You're family.

But after making the vital mistake of kissing Elliot the night I discovered my father had passed, I fear everything is ruined now.

He's the last Heir standing.

The only one of them not in a relationship. And when he does finally meet someone, there'll be no room for me in their circle of eight.

So it's better really; better that I cut myself off and accept my fate now.

I'm not one of them, not really.

And I never will be.

But it was nice to pretend, for a little while, that I belonged.

"Your room is at the end of the hall and around the corner, next to the fire escape. So you'll have plenty of space."

"Thank you."

We slip through the door separating the main hallway and small hallway where my new room is. She's right, it is out of the way. Almost in its own annex.

"Here's your key." I take it from her, and she offers me a sad smile. "If you need anything—"

"I'll be fine, thank you." I unlock the door and push open the door.

"It's a little bigger than most of the rooms but given the circumstances…" She trails off, understanding glittering in her eyes.

"There's no guidebook for this kind of thing, Abigail. But you have people who care. If you ever need to talk, you can come to me or Miss Linley. And I'm sure the girls are all eager to help in any way they can."

I nod too weary to reply.

"Okay, well, I'll leave you for now. Take all the time you need."

"Thank you."

She hesitates but doesn't say whatever is on her mind. So I step further into the room and close the door behind me. It's a nice, bright space, daylight pouring in through the window overlooking the campus grounds but it feels all wrong.

I throw down my bag and march toward it, lowering the blinds first, and then yanking the heavy curtains shut, plunging the room into darkness.

Turning, I walk over to the bed and fall down onto it, curling myself around one of the pillows.

Then I close my eyes and pray sleep finds me.

2

ELLIOT

"She was meant to be here today," Olivia says as I join our table for lunch.

Concern knots up my stomach, but I refuse to let it show. My grip on the tray in my hand tightens momentarily before I throw it down on the table and drag my chair out, making it screech loudly against the ancient parquet flooring beneath our feet.

"Christ, who pissed in your Rice Krispies this morning?" Oak asks, studying me closely.

"I don't eat fucking Rice Krispies," I mutter, reaching for my fork and stabbing a tomato as if it personally offended me.

"You know, if you did, it might help you lighten up a little," Reese suggests, slinging his arm around his girl and tugging her into his side.

Turning his attention from me, he whispers something into Olivia's ear which makes her cheeks turn almost as red as the tomato I just stuffed into my mouth.

Shaking my head at them, I take in the other two

couples surrounding me. Theo and Raine, Oak and Tally. And then my eyes land on the empty chair.

My stomach twists up tighter as her absence eats at me.

It's been the same way since the night she discovered her father died.

She's seen the girls and they have trickled down the basics of how she's coping, but it's not enough.

I'm sure the guys probably know more. But it's not like I can ask without raising suspicions.

They already give me enough shit about my interest in the quietest member of our little group. I don't need them digging any deeper into it. They already have a few too many ideas about what might exist between us.

And so does she if what happened at Raine's birthday party is anything to go by.

My lips burn just thinking about it.

I've seen a few different sides to shy, meek Abigail Bancroft over the past few months, but fuck me if she didn't knock me sideways with her forwardness that night.

I didn't think she had it in her.

Despite everyone around me thinking that I'm oblivious to Abigail's interest, I'm not. I'm aware of everything that happens around us. They should know me better than that by now.

But as much as her obvious interest might make my heart beat a little faster, I can't do anything about it.

I might be an arsehole. But I'm not that big of an arsehole. I would never willingly bring a girl like Abigail into my life.

She's too good for it.

Hell, I wouldn't even bring a bad girl into it.

No one deserves to be a part of the life I'm forced to live.

The guys know more than anyone else. Well, anyone

who hasn't lived inside the torturous four walls of the Eaton mansion. But even their knowledge is limited to what I've allowed them to know.

The last thing I need is anyone—namely, Abigail—attempting to peel back my hardened layers and attempting to discover what's hiding beneath.

It's not pretty, and certainly not something I want to share with her.

She deserves a boy next door type. A nice lad who will take care of her. Someone who belongs to a happy, loving family, not a twisted, corrupt one who doesn't care about anything but money and power.

And now she's lost the only parent she had left, she needs my poison in her life less than ever.

She needs the girls. They can give her what she needs right now.

Whatever the fuck that is.

I mean, really. What the hell do I know about comforting a girl who's lost their terminally ill parent?

I can barely look after myself and my boys most days.

"Have you called her?" Tally asks, dragging me back to the conversation they were having before I sat down.

"Yeah, just goes to voicemail," Olivia says sadly.

"Same."

"Well, let's just blow off classes after lunch and go to her house," Raine suggests. "I knew it was a bad idea not to go and get her this morning."

"She was adamant she wanted to do it alone," Olivia argues.

"Yeah. And look how well that turned out. Besides," Tally adds. "She's not at her house."

My breath catches and my eyes jump up from focusing on my lunch to fully focus on Tally. "Where the fuck is she then?" I bark, earning myself more than a couple of amused looks from the guys.

Fuck.

"Didn't they tell you last night?" Olivia asks. "She moved into dorms."

A deep frown wrinkles my brow. "Why the fuck would she do that?" I bark, instantly regretting my outburst.

There aren't many people in this world that can make me lose my grip on reality, but the shy, petite redhead is certainly one of them.

Actually, she might be the *only* one.

"She couldn't be at the house any longer," Tally explains. "So she begged Mr Porter for a room."

"You lot helped her move though, right?"

I don't need a verbal answer, the sadness on their faces says it all.

"She's not making it very easy to help her right now."

"Then you need to try harder," I argue.

"Maybe you should give it a go," Reese suggests. "You might be able to get through to her in a way the girls can't."

"I doubt she'll want to see me," I reason, my heart rate increasing and my blood heating as I briefly think about what happened the last time we were close enough to have a conversation.

I might have attended the funeral, but I didn't get anywhere near her. Instead, I remained in the shadows, hoping that my presence alone would be a support to her while I watched her any chance I got.

I knew if the guys caught me, my life wouldn't be worth living. So I kept it discreet.

I'm pretty sure I was so discreet that she had no idea I was even there.

I've second-guessed that decision since the moment I

stepped out of the church. Maybe going to her and letting her know I was there would have helped.

But why would it?

I'm not her friend, not really.

Sure, we've hung out a few times. Broke into the school offices and stole Raine's transfer papers together—something I did not think she'd be up for, let alone instigate—but that's where our relationship ends.

Or at least it did until she kissed me...

No. That's where it ends.

I can't go there.

"She doesn't want me turning up at her door," I mutter, dropping my eyes to my lunch again.

It suddenly looks a whole lot less appealing than I did when I got it. That doesn't mean I won't eat it though. I need it. My body needs it. The rugby season might be coming to an end, but that means that exam season is starting. And if I stand any chance of breaking away from the life and the shackles that have been placed around me since birth, then I need to do better than Scott.

A bitter laugh bubbles up in my throat as I think about that ever happening.

There is nothing I could ever do that would make me better than Scott Johnathon Eaton in the eyes of those who look down on me on a daily basis.

One day though... one fucking day everything I've been through is going to have been worth it.

Fuck knows how, but thinking any other way isn't an option. Because if I did then... where the fuck would that leave me?

"Or maybe you're the one she's waiting for," Oak adds with a smirk. "A nice little dorm warming with her favourite Heir."

"Oak," Tally chastises.

"What? Something tells me that your girl needs a little spice in her life right now. Eaton could be just the thing."

Panic shoots through me. "Trust me, that's the last thing she needs."

"But how do you know?" Theo asks, finally joining in.

"Because I do, okay?" I snap.

Sensing my quickly souring mood, the conversation around the table turns to the upcoming Easter Break. The last chance to enjoy ourselves before the hard work really starts.

Talk of going away for the week floats through the air. And while the thought is a tempting one, there's no way any of us could leave right now with Abigail suffering. The girls would never go for it, not unless they could convince her to go.

Different locations get thrown around, but I don't pay any attention to them. There are more important things to worry about right now than a holiday in the sun, no matter how good a break from this place sounds.

We're on the cusp of the next big stage in our lives.

While the guys and I spent our childhoods dreaming about finally taking claim of the Chapel and becoming Heirs, it seems to be speeding by faster than I ever thought possible.

Before we know it, we're going to be Scions at Saints Cross U and once again, we'll be under the control of Scott.

A place I'd happily never be again.

But I have no choice. Being a Scion was written into my life plan the second my parents discovered I was a boy. It doesn't matter what I want.

What do I even want?

All I've ever done was what I was told, what was expected of me. The opposite was never an option.

Eventually, the bell rings, signalling the end of lunch. Oak, Theo, Raine and Reese take off in the direction of their next class, leaving me behind with Olivia and Tally. Both of them look at me with pleading eyes, and my heart bottoms out, knowing exactly what's going to happen next.

I want to help, I do. But I doubt my efforts are going to be worth it.

"Would you just go and see if she'll talk to you?" Tally asks.

"She promised us she'd be here today," Olivia adds. "We're doing everything we can, but we're not getting through to her."

"And you really think I can?"

Olivia shrugs. "Honestly, I have no idea. But we've got to try. She's doing her best to shut us out, and that's the last thing she needs right now. She's alone, Elliot. Totally alone."

Understanding washes through me. None of the people around me on a daily basis might believe it, but that's a feeling I'm more than familiar with.

"I've got classes all afternoon then training," I argue weakly.

There is a part of me desperate to go and find her new dorm room right this second and kick the door in so I can get to her. But there is another that wants to take a step back and allow her to deal with this her own way.

"What if she genuinely does just want to be alone?" I counter.

Both of their chins drop as they stare at me.

"You don't really mean that, surely," Tally says. "You care about her just as much as we do. She's your friend, Elliot. And she needs us right now."

My teeth grind as I once again discover that I've done a really shit job of covering the soft spot I have for Abigail.

I've let my guard down with her—with all of them—one too many times and now they're going to use it against me.

Sucking in a shaky breath, I dump what's left of my lunch into the bin and throw my bag over my shoulder. "I'll think about it," I say before stepping into the flow of students who are heading toward their afternoon classes.

"She needs you, Elliot." Tally calls, making guilt coil tightly around me. "Please don't let her down."

Fuck's sake.

That's exactly what I'm worried about.

3

ABIGAIL

Knock.
Knock.
The noise barely penetrates my mood.
Numb.
Detached.
Listless.

It's been two days since I moved into the Bronte Building.

Two days in which I've barely had enough energy to drag myself out of bed and brush my teeth let alone take a shower.

But I can't seem to crawl out of the abyss. The dark desolate void that threatens to consume me every time I think about the fact that my father is gone, and that I'm all alone.

People keep telling me that it'll pass. That time will help.

But it's a lie.

Something people tell each other to ease the heavy pauses and awkward silences.

I know because I've already walked this path before.

Losing my mum was difficult. One of the most painful things I've ever experienced. But I had my father. I had someone to share my grief with.

Sure, he was never the same after we lost her. Consumed with securing my future and making sure I would be okay when the day came that he also left me. He became even busier at work. Distracting himself with one high profile case after another.

My father loved me, but in the days and weeks and months and years after the accident, he didn't always show it.

But I'd take a lifetime of having him here cold and detached and unsure of how to reach me over a lifetime of being alone.

My eyes sting as I fist my chest, trying to rub away the constant ache. But nothing works.

Beyond sneaking out to find some strong alcohol or sleeping pills, I've resigned myself to broken sleep.

Knock.

Knock.

I almost forgot somebody is at the door. Reluctantly, I slip out of bed and pull on my All Hallows' Saints hoodie. It swamps my small frame but feels like a layer of armour as I burrow deeper.

Pulling the door ajar, I peek out into the hall.

"Thank God," Tally exclaims. "I've been standing out here for almost five minutes."

"You have?"

Huh. I don't remember hearing that many knocks.

I blink at her, trying to focus my bleary vision.

"You didn't hear me?" Concern crinkles around her eyes.

"I... I was asleep." The lie barely thaws the ice in my veins.

"You didn't show up for class."

"I'm not ready."

"And I get it, I do. But you won't come hang out with us. You won't talk to Miss Linley. You won't return our texts. We're worried, Abs."

"I'm fine. I just need some space."

"Did something happen? With you and Elliot?"

"What? No! Why? Did he say something?"

"He didn't say anything but from how skittish you're acting, I'm inclined to think something did happen. If he hurt you—"

"Stop." I sigh. "He didn't hurt me. Elliot would never hurt me." At least not in the way she is thinking.

Relief skitters across her expression, and I want to scold her for even thinking Elliot would do something like that.

But then I remember that he did hurt me, so I swallow the words.

I need to let go of my silly little infatuation with him. I let myself get carried away. Saw signs that weren't there. Wanted things he never wanted to give me.

"You can tell me, Abs. If something did happen..."

"It didn't."

"But he hasn't come to see you?"

"I... What?"

"Elliot. He hasn't come to see how you're doing?"

"No, why would he?"

"Come on, Abs. I know the last week or so has been rough. But you're not stupid. Elliot cares about you. He—"

"I'm really tired," I rush out. "Can we pick this back up another time?"

"I'll stay with you, I don't mind."

"No, it's fine. I don't need a babysitter. I'm sure I'll feel a bit better after I've had a sleep."

"But—"

"Thanks for coming." I herd her away from the door. "I'll speak to you soon."

Tally regards me, her brows knitted together. "I'll check on you tomorrow," she says.

I nod because what else can I do?

It isn't that I don't want her or the girls to check on me. I just can't pull myself out of it. It's too raw. Too painful.

She has Oakley, and Olivia has Reese, and Raine has Theo, and I'm happy for them, I am. To have found that kind of unconditional, unwavering love. But I'll never have that. I'll never know—

I shove the thoughts out, giving Tally a small wave as she backs out of my room.

"Please, Abs. If you need anything..."

Another nod.

Another false promise.

She gives me a weak smile and I close the door, sealing myself off from her. From reality.

It's better this way.

Better to hide—something I've spent the last five years of my life doing.

But as I get back into bed and pull the covers up around me, I can't help but replay her words over in my head.

Elliot cares about you.

He does, I know that.

Just not in the way I hoped.

I miss an entire week of classes, but I can hardly find it in myself to care.

Mrs Danvers and Miss Linley both came to check on me, to make sure I'm looking after myself. But it's the girls who finally pull me out of the black hole I've found myself in.

"Come on, Abs," Tally calls as I delay the inevitable.

They turned up at my door ten minutes ago, insisting that I get out of my room and get some fresh air with an impromptu trip to Dessert Island, our favourite bakery in town.

I don't want to go but I also know I can't wallow for much longer before they stage a more serious intervention.

"Coming," I yell back as I grip the sink and stare at myself in the mirror.

I look so... so different.

I've always shied away from my appearance, ever since the accident that left me permanently scarred. But now I barely recognise myself. My skin is paler than usual and my eyes seem vacant. The scar marring my cheek stands out. Taunting me.

Blinking away fresh tears, I quickly plait my hair into a loose braid over my shoulder to hide the silvery line and return to the girls.

"There she is," Olivia says with an encouraging smile.

"Sorry I took so long."

"You're ready, that's all that matters."

"Come on," Raine adds. "The girls promised me a morning of sugary goodness." She takes my hand and tugs me toward the door.

Fear takes hold as I step over the threshold and out into the hall.

"Abi?" she asks, concern heavy in her voice.

"I'm fine."

Fine.

God, I hate that word.

I'm not fine—I'm barely holding on.

But I can't let them see the true depths of my despair. The utter helplessness and loneliness I feel.

The fear.

They bundle me into Liv's car and head for town, talking about the upcoming Easter Break. But I barely hear them, watching the countryside roll by.

"What do you think, Abs? It might do you good."

"Sorry, what?" I meet Tally's gaze.

"I asked if you might want to come away with us? It's not definite yet but the boys are talking about it."

"Oh, I don't know. I'm not exactly good company right now."

"No, but you're our friend. You're one of us. It wouldn't be the same if you didn't come."

There's no way I can go with them. Not if Elliot goes, which he will.

I don't want to see him again, to look him in the eye and see the rejection there. It was enough the first time around. And maybe if my father hadn't left me, if the cruel, unforgiving disease wrecking his body hadn't taken him, I would have been able to move on from the kiss.

I would have been able to turn off my unrequited feelings and accepted a friendship with Elliot.

But everything is different now.

That night will always be entwined with the second to worst day of my life.

By the time we arrive at Dessert Island, I feel sick to my stomach. But I put on a brave face, opting for a peppermint tea and an oatmeal and raisin cookie, which I pick at as the girls tiptoe around me.

"It's okay," I say. "You can talk about normal stuff."

"We just don't want to overwhelm you." Liv squeezes my hand. "We know how hard this is for you."

They don't, how could they?

Liv might have lost her mum when she was little, and Raine might have grown up in foster care, but it's not the same. Because they found their place. They found their tribe. They found their person.

Tally's phone vibrates and she smiles at the incoming message.

"Oakley?" Liv asks, and she nods.

"They're in town."

Dread snakes through me. "They're not—"

The door chime tinkles as Oakley, Theo, and Reese pour inside, shaking off their jackets from the downpour.

"What are you doing here?" Liv asks, keeping one eye on me.

"We were passing through and wanted to say hi." Oakley glances in my direction. "It's good to see you up and about, Abs."

I manage a weak smile, clutching my mug as if it's my life raft.

"I know we've said it already but we're so fucking sorry about your dad," Theo adds.

"Thank you."

I should be relieved that Elliot isn't with them. But when Tally asks where he is, the atmosphere changes.

"He, uh... he had a thing." Oakley's gaze darts from me to the boys and back again.

"A thing?" Tally frowns. "What thing?"

"Nothing important." He dismisses her, pulling a chair up to the table.

Reese and Theo follow suit, each sitting beside their girlfriends. Making it perfectly obvious that I'm the spare wheel.

The spare wheel that Elliot obviously wanted to avoid.

Disappointment curdles in my stomach.

"Did the girls ask you about our Easter getaway?" Oakley grins. "It'll do you good to get out of town for a bit."

"It's sweet of you to invite me but I don't think I'm ready."

"Come on, Abs, it'll be—"

Tally elbows him in the ribs. "Don't push her. There's still time for her to change her mind. Right, Abs?"

"Right." I offer them a tight smile.

"Will you be back in class next week?" Raine asks.

"Maybe."

"You know we've got your back, Abs." Reese gives me a small nod. "No one is going to say anything or upset you."

"I know and I appreciate it, I do."

It's not that simple though. I'm used to being the brunt of people's whispers and stares, I've lived it for years.

But just when I was finally finding my inner strength, my confidence to step out of the shadows, everything went to hell and once again, I've been swallowed up by the darkness.

And this time, I'm not sure I'll be able to pull myself back out.

4

ELLIOT

I sit in class with my eyes locked on the empty chair in the row in front of me.

Concern for the girl who should be sitting there courses through my veins as the teacher drones on about something I really should be listening to given that exams are right around the corner.

Nothing distracts me from studying, from thoughts of my future and my determination to succeed. But it seems that Abigail Bancroft might just be the exception to the rule.

Ever since she started hanging out with us, I've found my focus drifting to her in every class we share. Thankfully, it's only a couple. I'm not sure I could cope if it were more. And this is the only one where she's close enough to interact with, should I choose to.

But with her not here, I'm even more distracted than usual.

The girl's request for me to go and check on her nags at me. Guilt that I haven't done it already knots up my stomach. But not going is the right thing to do.

She won't want to see me, let alone hear anything I have to say.

I might have been the one to pick her up after she got that phone call that night about her dad, but I can't forget the reason she was running in the first place.

She was running from me.

Running from my reaction to her when she reached up on her toes and kissed me.

Without realising, my fingers lift until the tips are pressing against my lips as I remember just how soft hers were against mine.

So soft.

And so fucking tempting.

The need to return it, to take everything I'd been craving in the weeks that had passed burned through me. But I knew it was the wrong thing to do.

Kissing her would have been selfish. And I couldn't do it to her.

You did the right thing, my voice of reason confirms for the millionth time since that night.

But no matter how often I hear it, it doesn't stop me from regretting it.

The lesson passes agonisingly slowly with her unignorable absence. Thankfully, the rest of the day is full of classes we don't share so I'm able to push thoughts of her aside—even if slightly—so I can focus.

Easter Break is right around the corner, and while it might be our last chance to chill out before exam season starts, it's also the last chance we all have to make sure we're on top of everything.

The guys keep talking about going away, jumping on a plane, and spending the time at the beach. But as welcome as the prospect of sun is, I'm just not sure I can do it.

I need to be studying. I need to be focusing, not frolicking around in the sea with three lovesick couples.

I mean really, what were they even thinking of inviting me in the first place?

Third wheel much?

Jesus.

I slump lower in my chair and continue working on the exam question we've been set. But my mind is never fully on it.

I haven't seen her since the funeral.

It's been over a week now.

It's my own fault, though.

I could have just manned up and gone to Dessert Island with the guys the other day instead of making a bullshit excuse.

I told myself that I was doing it for her, that she wouldn't want to see me.

But really, I was being a selfish prick.

I knew the second I looked into her eyes, I was going to drown in regrets.

"Right, time is up. Hand your sheets in on your way out and I'll have them marked for you for next lesson. All your work for the break has been posted online but if you need anything, you have my email. I'll be checking daily," the teacher says, bringing the class to an end.

I stare at my answer, cringing that I've barely even got to the point I was trying to make.

"Fuck it," I mutter under my breath, snatching it up and dropping it on the desk on the way out, pretending that everything is right in my world.

As is usually the case, people move out of my way, letting me out of the room first.

There are some benefits that come with having Eaton

as a surname—with being an Heir. Although, if I'm being honest, I'm not sure they're entirely worth it.

My grip on my bag tightens as I make my way down the hall that will lead me in the direction of the locker room to get ready for practice.

It's the only place where everything makes sense right now. Once I'm out on the pitch, the rest of the world falls away. My family, the expectations placed on my shoulders, my future that's been mapped out for me, my regrets and stupid decisions. It's just me and the ball, my only focus is scoring and coming out on top.

I'm about to shove the double doors open that will lead me outside when a flash of red catches my eye off to the right.

"Red," I call before my brain can catch up with my mouth.

Suddenly, a classroom door opens, and a flood of kids emerge, chatting, laughing, relieved that another day at All Hallows' is over.

"Shit," I hiss, stretching up to see if she's still here. Hell, if it was even her.

Her hair might be unique, but she's not the only redhead that roams these halls.

Just the only one I have any interest in.

By the time the crowd has thinned out, there's no sign of her.

Ripping my eyes from the hallway, I look out the doors to where I'm expected to be for practice in less than ten minutes.

My head tells me to go one way, my heart... Well, that's on a completely different page.

She won't want to see you.

With a sigh, I continue forward, toward where I'm meant to be, where I'm needed.

I barely make it through the door before it becomes obvious that someone was waiting for me.

"Eaton, a word?" Coach asks, loitering in the doorway to his office.

"Sure," I mutter, following him inside. "Everything okay, Coach?" I ask, dropping into the chair in front of his desk that I've spent many hours in over the years.

We might now have a state-of-the-art student welfare department now with outstanding therapists and counsellors, but this right here, it's all I need.

The scent of leather, mud, and sweat and the concerned stare of a man who pins all his hopes of success on a bunch of rich, spoiled arseholes every year.

"Everything is great. The team is looking solid in the run-up to our final games. That isn't the reason I called you in."

"Oh?" I ask, already dreading what the next words out of his mouth are going to be.

He holds my eyes steady before he lands the blow I've been expecting. "I've had your father on the phone."

"Of course you have," I murmur.

"Your time here at All Hallows' is coming to an end, and naturally, he wants to ensure you go out as strong as possible," he explains.

Although something tells me he's rephrased my father's actual words and softened them a little.

"I'm more than aware of that, Coach. Trust me, I'm doing my best to stand up against Golden Boy's legacy."

"Elliot," Coach sighs, rubbing his jaw.

"It's fine, Coach. Really. I'm more than used to his bullshit."

"Son, I—"

"Seriously. Everything is under control. My grades are

good, great actually, and as you said, the team is looking promising. I've got this in the bag."

He assesses me ominously. He knows as well as I do that anything I achieve will never be good enough for the infamous Johnathon Eaton.

His Golden Boy set the bar very high during his time here. It doesn't matter if I shatter that bar into smithereens, it'll never be good enough. And that is something I just have to live with.

One day I won't have to live up to the impossibly high standards he holds me to, and I won't have to constantly compete with Scott despite knowing that I'll only ever fail.

One day...

One fucking day.

"Is that all, Coach?"

His eyes bounce between mine, I fear seeing more than I'm willing to let anyone see. "Something isn't right with you, Eaton. I can sense it."

"Coach," I complain.

He holds his hands up in defence. "I know. I know. I just... I'm here, okay? Whatever it is. I'm here."

"I know, Coach. And I appreciate it more than you know."

With an almost genuine smile, I let myself out of his office and continue down toward the locker room. It's already in chaos when I walk through to find my spot beside Reese, Oak and Theo.

"Where the fuck have you been?" Theo barks.

"Meeting with Coach," I explain, toeing off my shoes and pulling my tie free so I don't have to stop and think about what he just said.

He's right. Something isn't right with me. But then, what's new there?

Something has been wrong with me since the day I was born.

My surname.

Practice is exactly what I need. Coach works us until my legs can barely continue. It's cold, and the rain is torrential, battering us. Most of my teammates hate it and spend the entire session bitching. But I love it.

I never feel more alive than when I'm covered in mud, raindrops drip from my hair, my heart beats so hard I can barely catch my breath. It's heaven. Or as close as I'll ever get.

"Plans tonight, boys?" Oak says once the four of us are standing in the showers. Something we get to do alone thanks to us being Heirs.

Everyone else on the team has to wait their turn. It's pretty fucking sweet.

"Taking Liv out for dinner," Reese answers first.

"Ugh," Oak complains. "If I have to hear any more about your bullshit anniversary, I'm going to puke. Who celebrates four months together anyway?"

"It's five, thank you," Reese states proudly.

"Is it, though? Are you sure? Don't want to fuck that card up, bro," Oak taunts.

"It's fine. I can write whatever I want in a card. My dick and all the orgasms it delivers will more than make up for it."

Oak starts gagging at the thought of Reese railing his twin sister.

They really need to get over it.

It's been four... maybe five months now. They're practically brothers-in-law as well as stepbrothers.

"You okay, man?" Theo asks as my brain melts with my previous thoughts. "You look like you're having an aneurysm."

"I'm great," I lie.

"So you don't have another night with your textbooks planned then?" Oak asks with a smirk. "You really are living your best life right now. Eaton."

"Exactly," Theo agrees. "You're the last man standing, man. You've got your pick of every Heir chaser. Hell, you could have multiple at once. They're so desperate these days. But here you are wanking over an exam paper every night."

"That is not what I'm doing," I argue, unable to get the visual out of my head.

"Of course it isn't. You're still tugging that tiny thing over a certain redhead. You grown a pair and gone to visit her yet?" Reese chips in.

"Fuck off," I grunt, unable to come up with anything more intellectual to respond with.

"Well, you should. She might be very grateful for it and make it worth your while," Theo suggests, wiggling his brows suggestively.

My fists curl with the need to lash out on her behalf. I'm about to throw the punch I'm desperate for when Oak places his hand on my shoulder.

"He's joking. Aren't you?" he says, glaring at Theo.

"Sure. Totally," he says insincerely.

Tosser.

"You should totally go and check in on her, though," Reese adds.

Their advice stays with me as we dress and then go our separate ways. They've all got plans with their girls. And they're right, I plan on locking myself away in my room and studying.

I emerge from the building, the rain just as torrential as it was during practice. But I don't bother pulling my coat on. Instead, I let the ice-cold droplets hit me, punishing me for all the things I've fucked up recently.

My legs move on autopilot, but I hesitate when I reach a fork in the path that will either lead me toward the Chapel hiding on the outskirts of the All Hallows' campus or the girls' dorm.

She doesn't want to see you, that voice pops up again.

But what if she does…

5
―――
ABIGAIL

The knock on my door startles me, and I close the textbook I've been staring blankly at for the last thirty minutes and climb off my bed.

Another knock renders me frozen in place.

There's something different about this. More urgent and insistent.

More demanding.

I don't know how I know it isn't Tally or Liv or Raine standing on the other side of the door, I just do.

"Come on, Red. I know you're in there, open up."

My heart ratchets.

Elliot's here.

He's here.

Any other time, I might have felt a trickle of excitement at the knowledge he came to see me. But I only feel the heat of embarrassment staining my cheeks.

He knocks again, and I remain deathly still, listening. Waiting to see what he will do.

Another knock, and he mutters something inaudible

before leaving, his heavy footsteps growing quieter and quieter.

He came.

Confusion wars inside me. He made it clear he doesn't feel the same about me when I kissed him. So surely he'd want to keep his distance.

The girls probably insisted he come check on me. I'll have to tell them not to do that again.

I don't need Elliot's pity.

I don't need anything from him.

As if on cue, my phone bleeps and I grab it off my desk, scanning the text.

> Tally: He just wanted to see how you were.
>
> Abigail: I don't need a babysitter, Tally.
>
> Tally: Abs, come on. We're worried.
>
> Abigail: I just need time.
>
> Tally: Yeah, I know. You know where I am if you need me.
>
> Abigail: Thanks.

Getting back into bed, I clutch the covers to my chest and stare up at the ceiling.

Maybe I should have let Elliot in. But seeing him again, after everything... it would only serve to remind me of that night.

I can vividly remember answering Maureen's call, crumpling to my knees as her words hit. Elliot's strong arms around me, the concern in his eyes as tried to figure out what was wrong.

Why?

Of all the boys in All Hallows' for me to develop feelings for, it had to be Elliot Eaton.

Leader of the Heirs.

One of the most untouchable and formidable students in the sixth form.

What the hell was I thinking?

Except, I wasn't thinking.

Because it caught me off guard—*he* caught me off guard. His patience and protectiveness. His ability to make me feel seen. The way he's always so gentle with me and my feelings.

A weary sigh rolls through me as I toss and turn, desperately trying to get comfortable. To banish the depressing thoughts from my head.

But I can't help but think I didn't only lose my father that night.

I lost my friend too.

"Are you sure you don't want to come?" Tally asks for the third time since her and the girls turned up at my door an hour ago.

"I told you, I can't."

"Abs." Liv squeezes my hand. "It might do you good. You've barely been out of your room."

True.

But after the trip to Dessert Island the other day, I realised I wasn't ready to be in the real world.

Not yet.

Everything is different now.

The colour is leached from everything. The joy. I don't want to burden them with my grief, my pain. Not when they're all so sickeningly happy and in love.

"You don't have to worry about me," I lie. "I'm going to catch up with some coursework and revision. I won't wallow, I promise."

Liv studies me a little too closely, as if she knows I'm lying. But to my relief, she doesn't say anything.

"We'll check in, every day," Tally adds. "Yeah, you'll be sick of us."

"You don't need to do that."

The heavy weight of shame presses down on me. Shame that I'm not stronger, that I can't shake off this utter hopelessness I feel.

They'll go on holiday. They'll have an amazing time. They'll come back and be full of stories and inside jokes, and that's how it'll go now.

They'll do more and more things together and gradually, I'll fade into the shadows. I'll become nothing more than a memory to them.

A pang of sadness goes through me.

"I just want you all to know," my voice cracks, "that I appreciate everything you've done for me over the last couple of weeks."

"Of course, Abs." Tally flashes me a concerned smile. "You're our friend."

Friend, I might be.

But one of them, I am not.

Raine watches me from the chair, offering me a small sympathetic smile.

She was there that night.

The night I kissed Elliot.

It was her words that had spurred me on and given me the confidence to approach him. To take that scary leap of faith.

Does she know?

Does she look at me and know what happened? That

my father's death wasn't the only thing that crushed me that night?

"I hope you all have a great time," I say, ignoring the lump in my throat.

"I don't know who is more excited. Us or the boys," Tally says. "We've rented this gorgeous villa overlooking the ocean and... are you absolutely positive you can't come? There's five bedrooms, so you and Elliot would have your own room each."

"Tally," Liv hisses.

"What? I'm just saying, it isn't like they'd have to share."

"Maybe next time." I force my lips into a smile.

"We'll hold you to that." Tally smiles.

"When do you leave?"

"Friday as soon as classes get done. Our flight isn't until eight. But we've booked a lounge at the airport."

"Exciting."

I've never been out of the country before. Dad was always too busy for extended family vacations and Mum... well, I can't think about her right now.

Not without feeling like I might break apart.

"Take lots of photos," I add, and I mean it.

Everyone's lives don't have to stop just because mine has.

"We'll miss you," Tally adds.

"It's only ten days. I'll be fine."

God, I hate that word.

I hate it so much.

Because I am anything but fine.

But they don't want to hear that I can't sleep because my skin feels too tight, or the shattered pieces of my heart feel like they might explode out of my chest.

They don't want to hear that sometimes I am so

overcome with a sense of fear and loneliness that it paralyses me. That sometimes I wonder if it would be better for me to just not exist.

They don't want to hear any of that.

So I keep it locked away. I shove it all down inside myself and paste on the best fake smile I can muster and tell them I'm fine.

Because lying is better than the truth.

Lying is the *only* thing that's going to get me through this.

"Okay then, if we can't persuade you otherwise..."

"Go." Brittle laughter spills out of me. "Go pack and repack and pack some more. And text me when you arrive."

"We'll text you tomorrow, silly. Or you could try and come to class." Liv holds my weary gaze, but I give her a little shake of my head.

"I... I can't."

"Okay, okay." She stands, giving my hand one last squeeze before releasing it. "Remember, if you need anything—"

"I know."

"Try and get some sleep, Abs." Raine gives me a small wave and disappears into the hall.

"Bye." Tally follows her.

But Liv lingers. "Abi, I—"

"I'm fine. I've got this, I promise."

"I can stay with you—"

"No, absolutely not. It's ten days. I'll be fine."

We both know it's a lie. But she respects my decision.

"You're going to get through this, babe. I promise."

"I know."

I would get through it.

Eventually.

Somehow.

I just wasn't sure I'd be the same when I finally crawled out the other side.

"Abigail, you came." Maureen sweeps me into her warm embrace, squeezing me tightly before holding me at arm's length to look at me. "How are you?"

"I'm fine."

"I wasn't sure you'd want to do this yet but I didn't want—"

"It's fine."

It wasn't.

The last thing I want to do is sift through my father's things and sort out what is to be donated to charity and what is to be discarded. But Maureen has a life outside of my family's affairs, and her position with a new family starts after Easter, so she wants to get a head start.

It was nice that she thought to include me but I'm not ready to do this.

I'm not sure I will ever be ready.

Inhaling a shaky breath, I give her the best smile I could muster and say, "Shall we get started?"

For the next two hours, we work side by side to empty his wardrobe and chest of drawers. Maureen is efficient and meticulous, her pile of clothes for donation growing by the second. I, on the other hand, mull over every shirt and every suit jacket, silent tears streaking down my cheeks.

"Maybe I should do this," she offers, taking a navy-blue jacket from my hands.

"W-what?" I blink up at her.

"It's too much, too soon," she says softly.

"No, I'm fine."

"Abigail, don't do that. Don't pretend you're fine when you're clearly not."

"I am, it's just..."

"It's still early days. The grief is raw. I'm sorry I burdened you with this."

"No, no. I should be here." A fresh wave of emotion crashes over me and sobs wrack through me.

"Why don't we go downstairs, and I'll make a fresh pot of tea. Then I'll finish what I can up here, and we can talk about how you want to proceed with the rest of it."

"Okay."

I let her lead me out of my father's bedroom and downstairs. Maureen pulls out a chair for me and gently shoves me into it. "Oh, Abigail. I should have realised..."

"I'm fine," I mumble, unable to stop the tears.

"Sweetheart, you are not fine, and that's okay. It will take time. Is there somebody at school you can talk to? A counsellor? Or teacher?"

I nod, the numbness spreading over me, saturating every inch of me until I'm trembling.

"Tea, we need tea." Maureen flusters as she sets about making a fresh pot of tea. She knows her way around the kitchen, this house, almost as well as I do.

"Your father was a good man, Abi. One of the best. I'm going to miss him tremendously. But I want you to know, just because I won't be here anymore, doesn't mean you can't call or text me, okay? I will always make time for you. I promised him that."

"Thank you."

Exhaustion creeps into my bones as she slides a mug of tea in front of me.

"Do you want me to call someone? I'm not sure I like the idea of you going back to campus in this state."

"I'm fine." I inhale a sharp breath, trying to shake off the clutches of hopelessness. "I'll be fine."

"Are you sure, sweetheart?"

"I promise."

I can do this.

I have to do this.

I have to find a way to endure.

Because I'm alone now. I'm all alone and I only have myself to rely on.

I can do this.

Maybe if I repeat the words enough, they'll eventually come true.

6

ELLIOT

"She hasn't left, not even once?" I ask, horrified.

"Nope. Not that any of us have seen," Kara, one of the more trustworthy girls who lives in Abi's dorm tells me, wearing a concerned frown.

When Abi didn't answer her door to me a few days ago and then still didn't return to school or agree to go on the holiday the boys planned last minute, I figured I needed to do something.

She didn't want to see me. Fine. I could deal with that. But I wasn't leaving her here alone without some kind of monitoring.

I had to pick my spy carefully. I couldn't ask any of the Heir chasers. They'd agree to anything if they thought they had a chance with me.

That might sound arrogant as fuck, but it's true.

I'm not stupid or deaf. I've heard the gossip floating around All Hallows' since Theo got with Raine.

I'm the last Heir standing, and there is a one hell of a prize at stake.

At least there is, according to them.

My stomach knots as I think about being nothing but a pawn in their games. Sure, I've had my fair share of fun exploiting the chaser obsession with us. But as soon as the others started settling down, it all began to lose its appeal.

We were meant to be wild together. And we were... for...

Fuck, who am I kidding, we never were.

Reese fucked off almost the moment we got the key to the Chapel last summer, and then no sooner had he come back was he fucking Liv. Oak fell for Tally not long after. And for a while, Theo and I got to enjoy life as single Heirs, yeah. But that didn't last.

As the least likely member of our group to settle down, I thought I was pretty safe having him as a wingman. But apparently, even the wildest bachelor can be tamed by the right woman.

Raine is awesome. Hell, all the girls are. I can understand how it's happened. But fuck. That doesn't mean I don't feel completely left behind.

And I don't just mean literally.

They're all sunning themselves on the Amalfi Coast, and I'm sitting here in Kara's dorm room while the torrential British weather hammers against her window.

It's my own fault, I'm more than aware of that.

I could be with them right now.

I should have been with them right now. I had the fucking ticket booked.

But I couldn't do it.

I couldn't leave knowing she was struggling.

So I came up with some bullshit excuse that my dad needed me over the break. I'm not entirely sure they bought it. But fuck it. They left. I'm still here. And more importantly, Abigail is still locked in her room.

"She must come out for something to eat and drink, though, no?" I ask hopefully.

"Not that we're aware of."

"Shit," I hiss, scrubbing my hand down my face before marching over the window and looking out. Not that I can see fuck all. The rain is so hard it makes everything a little blurry.

You could be in paradise right now...

"Just go and see her if you're so concerned. We all know you have a master key."

I still at her words.

"That's not the point."

"So it is true," she murmurs. "There was a part of me that hoped the rumour most of the girls here go to bed in their best lingerie in case one of you randomly chose to make a twilight appearance was bullshit."

"I've never done that," I snap, my hackles rising.

"If you say so."

I spin around, my chin dropping ready to snap back again, but then my eyes land on Kara's face. She's not one of them. She isn't a shameless chaser.

She's decent. Not trying to bc something she's not.

"Why did you agree to help me?" I ask, curious as fuck.

She shrugs. "You looked..." She pauses and looks away.

"I looked?" I prompt.

"Desperate, okay. You look desperate and I took pity on you."

"Wow," I breathe. That's a fucking first. I'm not sure anyone has ever taken pity on me before.

"So, are you going to go up there and see her or what?" When I don't answer, she continues, "It's not very Heir-like to hide away from your problems or be scared of a girl. Especially one as damaged as Abigail Bancroft."

My teeth grind. I might have asked her because she was different, but I forgot that she has zero concern about the hierarchy of this place and will say exactly what she thinks.

Exactly what I don't need right now.

"I'm not scared of her. I'm concerned and—"

"So go unlock her door and see with your own eyes. You can sit and wait for us to catch a sighting as much as you like but she's not making it easy."

She stares at me, waiting for me to make a decision, say something or... fuck knows what.

"Fuck. FUCK," I bark before storming toward the door and throwing it open with a lot more force than necessary.

"Good luck," Kara calls after me.

I take the stairs two at a time, glaring death at anyone who dares to try to talk to me until I march down the secluded corridor where Abigail's new dorm room is.

I can only assume they put her down here to give her peace and quiet. And while I might agree that she needs it, it also makes it really fucking hard for anyone to keep an eye on her.

Her door taunts me.

I've stared at it more than I want to admit to in the past few days.

She knows that I've been here the two times I've knocked. But there have been more instances where I decided against it. Convinced myself that she's okay, that she really just needs space. That she doesn't need me.

I stand there for the longest time just staring at the brass number on her door, debating what to do.

She doesn't need you in her life...

"Fuck. Fuck." Lifting my hand, I curl my fist and rap my knuckles against the door so softly, I almost can't hear it.

My heart races as blood rushes past my ears. I've never been this indecisive about anything in my life. But then, Abigail has never fit neatly in any of the boxes I divide my life up into.

She's never just been another girl at school. Nor has she really fallen into the friendship category. Sometimes, it's like she's one of the boys. But she doesn't really fit there either.

She's like a bright shining star who refuses to fit into any of my dark squares.

With a sigh, I knock again, louder this time. I'm hardly surprised when nothing happens.

"Red?" I call, hating the quiver in my voice.

This isn't who I am.

Or at least, it isn't anymore.

It's been a lot of years since I was weak and unsure of myself.

Eatons aren't weak.

We are the best, and you need to start acting like it.

You are above everyone else. Not beneath them.

Anger shoots through my veins as I hear my father's voice in my ear as clearly as the way he shouted those words at me.

"Red, it's me. Open up. Please." I shout, resting my palm on the door as I step closer, as if that'll help her hear me.

Nothing.

The master key Kara mentioned burns red hot in my pocket.

I've been carrying it around with me since the girls first asked for me to check on her. I knew she wouldn't willingly open the door to me. And that has nothing to do with her recent loss and everything to do with how I acted when she kissed me a few minutes prior to her getting that phone call.

I freaked out. There is no other way to explain what happened the moment she reached up on her toes and brushed her lips against mine.

I wanted it.

Fuck me, did I want it.

It's all I've thought about for weeks. Months even.

Abi has entwined herself into my life in a way that no other has before. And I allowed it, willingly.

She's been in my room. Fuck. She slept in my bed. No girl ever sleeps in my bed. Yet I let her and I took the fucking couch like an idiot.

Whenever she's around, all I want to do is pull her into my arms, feel the warmth of her body against mine. Take her beautiful face in my hands and brush my lips against that scar that runs down her cheek, trace it with my tongue.

She hides it. Maybe not so much since she's become friends with the girls, but it's still obvious that she's embarrassed by it. But it's beautiful.

She's beautiful.

Strong.

Breathtaking.

And you are standing out here like a fucking pussy.

Digging my hand into my pocket, I pull the master key free. Before I change my mind, I tap it against the panel and watch as the light turns green.

My stomach knots, but I don't back out. Not this time.

Pushing the handle, I crack the door open. The second I do, her sweet, addictive scent floods my nose. It's the encouragement I need to push the door even wider.

"Red?"

But there is still no answer.

The room is dark, the curtains closed. I can only just about make out the shapes of the furniture.

"Red?" Stepping further inside the room, I quietly close the door behind me and move toward the bed.

My eyes adjust to the darkness, allowing me to see the lump in the bed.

Nervously, I move closer. I'm sure the last thing she wants is for me to wake her. But I figure that if I see her sleeping peacefully and looking like herself then it'll settle my concern over her well-being and I can leave happy that she's looking after herself.

But when I get there, I don't find her red hair fanned out over the pillow. Reaching out, I gently press against the lump and quickly discover that it doesn't belong to a person; instead it's just more pillows.

Fumbling with the light on the nightstand, I flick it on and flood the room with light. My breath catches as I look around. It doesn't look like anyone is living here. There is one bag sitting inside the open wardrobe. But that is it. There's nothing on the desk, the shelves, the windowsill.

The only sign of life is a bottle of water and an empty box of tissues on the nightstand.

My concern for the girl living—existing—inside this room only grows.

Why didn't the girls tell me things were this bad?

This isn't the room of a girl who's dealing with her grief and trying to find a way forward. This is the room of someone who is drowning.

My eyes land on the closed bathroom door, and my heart jumps into my throat.

She's hiding.

By the time I get to it, my hands are trembling as images of what I might find inside race through my head.

Memories threaten to assault me, and I fight to shove them deep inside the lockbox they belong in.

She wouldn't.

I have to believe she wouldn't do something like that.

Fear makes me move faster, and the second the handle is in reaching distance, I twist it and throw the door open, unsure if I'm prepared for what I will find inside.

All the air rushes from my lungs as the girl I haven't stopped thinking about for the last few months finally comes into view.

I don't know what I was hoping for.

But she's not in her doing her hair or makeup. She's not fighting against her grief and the darkness.

She's drowning.

And she's going down fast.

7

ABIGAIL

My eyes connect with Elliot's but the horror in his gaze barely touches the ice around my heart.

"What the fuck?" he rushes out, storming toward me.

Cold water beats down on me still, but I no longer feel the sting of it against my skin.

I've been in here too long.

"What the fuck happened?" he grits out, reaching in to turn off the shower. It's only then, with him looming down on me, that a shiver runs through me.

He's... furious.

"Red, talk to me. What happened? What the fuck are you doing?"

I climb shakily to my feet, aware that my thin pyjamas are stuck to my body. But if Elliot notices, he does a really good job of hiding it.

Because he doesn't want you like that, the cruel little voice whispers in my ear.

I screw my eyes shut and inhale a steadying breath. He wasn't supposed to find me like this.

When I open my eyes again, they dart from his thunderous gaze to the mirror above the sink. Or, at least, what's left of it.

Shattered glass litters the sink and vanity, a pile of shards on the tiles. A trickle of red blood leading into the shower cubicle.

"You're hurt," he says, softer this time.

"I'm fine." I go to pull a towel off the hanger but he beats me to it, wrapping me up and staring down at me.

"Talk to me, please."

"I... I'm fine."

His teeth grind together, his jaw working overtime as I shut him out.

But I can't do this.

I can't—

"Red, look at me." Elliot slides his big hand to my jaw and tips my face up to meet his. "What. Happened?"

"I-I... I broke the mirror." The feeble lie spills out of me in a rush of breath.

"You broke the mirror." His brow arches, his doubt swirling around us.

He sees through the half-truth, of course he does.

It's Elliot. He sees everything.

But I can't tell him what really happened.

I can't.

Shame burns through me like acid.

"It was... an accident," I whisper, unable to look him in the eye.

Elliot has always made me feel stripped bare. Understood and seen. But everything feels different now.

Now that my father is gone.

Now that I know Elliot doesn't feel the same.

His jaw tics again but he doesn't argue. Instead, he gently shoves me out of the bathroom into my room.

"You need to get out of those wet clothes," he says gruffly.

"I... yeah," I sigh. Because what else can I say?

Tension crackles around us as he grabs my All Hallows' hoodie off the back of my chair and thrusts it toward me. "Can you manage?"

"I'm quite capable of dressing myself," I snap.

His brow lifts again in that smug arrogant way of his.

I can't blame him. I'm a mess, and he's... he's Elliot Eaton. He doesn't lose control. Ever.

God, what must he think of me.

Then something occurs to me.

"Why aren't you in Italy?"

"Something came up," he replies.

"Oh. And breaking into my room, what was that?"

"You weren't answering anyone's messages. The girls were worried."

The girls...

Of course they were the ones to send him here.

"Well, as you can see. I'm fine. You can go now."

"I'll give you some space to get dressed. Pizza good?"

"Pizza?" My brows furrow.

"You need to eat—"

"I'm not hungry."

"Tough shit. Get dressed and I'll order." He marches back into the bathroom, and I stand there, gawking after him.

This is bad.

Really bad.

I make quick work of stripping out of my soggy pyjamas and change into a set of clean clothes, forgoing the hoodie Elliot gave me.

A fresh wave of shame builds inside me as I take in the state of my room. It's a mess.

Just like me.

I blink back the tears pooling behind my eyes.

"I didn't know what you liked so I ordered something with meat and something plain."

My gaze snaps to Elliot standing in the doorway, watching me. Assessing me like I'm an opponent he wants to take down.

Before everything happened, that look in his eye would have sent a small thrill through me.

Now I feel nothing.

"You didn't have to do that." I wrap my arms around my waist, holding myself together. "Like I said, I'm fine."

"I cleaned up what I could in the bathroom," he says. "I'll get maintenance to stop by and replace your mirror."

"Don't," I blurt before I can stop myself.

He stares at me with unforgiving intensity.

"It's fine," I stumble over the words. The lie. "I have another mirror out here. I don't want to put anyone out."

The look he gives me makes me wither inside.

"I'm tired."

"It's the middle of the day."

"What are you doing, Elliot?" A weary sigh rolls through me.

"You're shutting everyone out. It's been weeks. You can't—"

"Don't tell me what I can and can't do. Not right now. Not while—" I heave a deep breath, trying to push down the wave of grief.

"Shit, Red. I'm sorry, okay. I'm not good at this. But hiding away in your room, pushing everyone away, it isn't going to help."

"I just want to be alone."

"I found you sitting under an ice cold shower—"

"I don't want to talk about it."

"Fine."

"Fine." Elliot glares at me.

Turning my back on him, I march toward my bed and rip back the covers, climbing inside.

I can't deal with him right now.

Or ever for that matter.

Because being close to him, having to look at his annoyingly handsome face only reminds me of everything I will never have. And it kills something inside me.

Ignoring him, I burrow under the covers, close my eyes, and murmur, "Turn the light off on your way out."

Somewhere in my dreams, a door clicks shut.

Wait a minute, that wasn't—

I crack an eye open, searching the dimly lit room for—

"You," I breathe, my gaze landing on Elliot sitting in my desk chair with a pizza box in his lap.

"Yours is on the bed."

The rich smell of tomato and garlic wafts through the room, making my stomach growl.

I can't remember the last decent thing I ate—or kept down.

"You're still here."

"Got nowhere else to be." He shrugs.

"I don't need a babysitter."

"The state of your room would suggest otherwise."

My stomach sinks at his cruel words. But maybe it's a blessing in disguise, a reminder of who and what Elliot Eaton really is.

An Heir with no heart.

"Eat," he orders.

"I'm not hungry."

"I'm not fucking around, Red. You look like you've lost at least half a stone. You need to eat. Please," he tacks on.

"Fine." I sit up and snatch the pizza box up, grabbing a slice and methodically eating it.

I don't taste anything as my stomach churns. But I swallow it down, hoping that the sooner I placate Elliot, the sooner he will leave.

I can't stand him here, in my space, acting like he cares. Like he isn't only here because the girls sent him.

When I've managed to eat a whole slice, he goes back to watching whatever show he's got playing on my small TV. I throw the box back down and turn over, giving him my back.

I don't want to face reality yet.

I don't want him or anybody else to try and drag me back in the real world.

I like it in here where it's safe and dark and isolated. Where I can wallow and cry and breakdown without risk of anyone seeing me.

I hadn't meant to smash the mirror earlier. It just happened.

One minute, I was staring at myself, replaying every bad memory in my head, and the next…

My chest tightens, my fingers curling into tight fists against my bedsheets as the intense emotions war inside me. Grief. Shame. Loneliness. Anger. There's a maelstrom raging, and I don't know how to stop it.

I don't know how—

"I'm sorry," his voice cuts through the air but I don't glance back to look at him. "About that night. I didn't want to hurt—"

"It doesn't matter," I rush out, unwilling to hear his reasons.

"Abi, come on. Don't be like this. We're friends, aren't we?"

Friends.

Bitter laughter crawls up my throat, but I trap it. He's seen enough. I can't give him anything else—I won't survive it.

"Red?"

"Sure, Elliot," I murmur, still refusing to look at him. "We're friends. I'm really tired."

"I'll stay for a little bit. You can sleep."

"No, that's—"

"Fuck's sake, Abi. Just sleep. I got you."

But that's the thing.

He doesn't have me.

He never will.

When I wake up the next time, Elliot is gone, and my room looks ten times cleaner and tidier than it did before.

Shame pricks at my chest but I shove it down. I didn't ask him to do that. I didn't ask him to do anything.

Desperate to pee, I push back the covers and gingerly climb out of bed. The one slice of pizza sits heavy in my stomach, but I feel no desire to purge it like everything else I've eaten the last few days.

On my way to the bathroom, I notice a note on my desk.

I'll be back tomorrow.
Try not to break anything else.
E

A small huff of indignance leaves me. He's such an overbearing idiot. Maybe if I text the girls and reassure them I'm okay, it'll get him off my back.

Or maybe I could just end things right now and save everyone the trouble.

The intrusive thought hits me so out of left field, I clutch the doorframe and inhale a ragged breath.

I don't want to die.

I don't.

But the thought of living—*of surviving*—without my father, without any family, feels so overwhelming right now.

When the thought passes, I head into the bathroom, ignoring the broken mirror. Sure enough, Elliot cleaned up in here too. But I'm too exhausted to find it in myself to care.

I have no idea what time it is, how many hours have passed since he left, but it doesn't matter.

All I want to do is sleep. To close my eyes and fall into the darkness. At least there, nothing is real. Nothing can hurt me. Even the monsters that haunt me in the shadows.

After flushing, I wash my hands. Something glints in the light, and I discover a shard of glass behind the taps.

Elliot must have missed it.

Carefully, I pick it out and hold it up.

It would be so easy...

I drop it and stumble back, hit by a wave of shame that makes me retch.

Falling to my knees, I manage to shove my head into the toilet right as the pizza makes a reappearance.

8

ELLIOT

Sweat beads my brow as I scrub the bath. My head spins and my back aches like a bitch but it's not enough to stop me.

Every single inch of the Chapel has been cleaned. All the shit the guys left around the place has either been tossed in the bin or thrown back into their rooms, the doors slammed quickly behind me so I didn't have to see the state they left them in.

I don't want to clean up after them, I really fucking don't. But I need to do something. Anything to squash the feeling of being totally out of control.

A feeling that I hate down to my bones.

I've never felt it so keenly as the moment Abigail's bathroom door opened and I found her in the shower shivering and sobbing.

Looking up, I stare at the tub and see a vision of her curled up in it.

My grip on the sponge in my hand tightens sending a rush of bubbles down the side. "Fuck," I hiss, starting the scrubbing all over again.

My skin prickles with unease, my muscles burning from the awkward angle.

But it could be worse.

I focus on the pain, letting it feed the mania that's racing through my veins.

When it has been cleaned within an inch of its life, I fall back on my arse. A huge rush of air spills from my lungs as I pull my legs up to my chest and wrap my wet arms around them.

My heart races and my chest heaves.

It's not good enough, a little voice nags in my ear. *You are not good enough.*

"FUCK," I roar, able to unleash fully seeing as the Chapel is empty. "Fuck. Fuck. Fuck."

Emotion burns at the back of my throat as visions of Abigail continue in my head.

She looked so small, so frail, so... sad.

The need to try and fix her is all-consuming.

But she doesn't want me.

She told me to leave.

You shouldn't have listened...

But if I didn't, then what would I have done? Just sit there and continue to watch her sleep.

At least you'd know she's okay.

Alive.

Not hurting herself.

Lifting my arm, I stare at my watch. I might see the hands of the clock, but the time doesn't actually register.

I just watch the second hand as it ticks around.

Everything is moving around me, the world continues to turn. I should be out there making the most of it, dragging Abigail along with me to prove that there are so many better ways to deal with all this than to lock herself away and hide from the world.

But it would make me feel like nothing but a hypocrite because hiding is exactly what I do when life gets too much.

A bitter, self-deprecating laugh falls from my lips.

Just look at me now. I'm sitting in the middle of a sparkling clean bathroom surrounded by the scent of bleach.

Twisting my hand around, I stare at my skin. Red and raw. The edges of my nails are sore. The urge to pick at them, to make them bleed burns through me.

But while I might allow some of my vices to slip through every now and then, that's something I know I need to keep a hold on.

I'm still sitting in the exact same position fuck knows how long later with a numb arse when my phone starts vibrating in my pocket. With a pained sigh, I pull it free, praying I'm not going to find my father's name staring back at me.

Talking to him, even if it is through a phone, is the last thing I need right now.

Relief floods me when I discover who it is, although I'm not exactly happy because I know exactly what they're about to ask.

Sucking in a deep breath, I drag my mask on and get ready to pretend that everything is fucking rosy. "Hey, how's paradise?" I ask, cringing at the tone of my voice.

"Fucking awesome. We're missing you though, bro," Reese says.

"I know. It sucks. I'm gutted." It's not a total lie.

Would I like to be lying on a white sandy beach right now with thoughts of home, school, exams, and reality a distant memory? Hell yes.

But it was never going to happen. Not with Abigail still here suffering.

She might not have been my excuse, but I'm pretty sure they all know the one I gave was bullshit.

They know me better than I want them to sometimes.

It's annoying as fuck.

But then, I guess that's what best friends are for. Annoying the shit out of you.

"You want to say that like you actually mean it?" Reese suggests.

"I do mean it. The weather fucking sucks here. And I've spent all day cleaning up after you messy fuckers."

"That's on you, man. We made sure everything was presentable when we left. No our fault it's not up to your exacting standards."

My teeth grind at his words.

"Sounds like you're living your best life right now, mate. Well done."

"Fuck off. Did you actually want anything?" I mutter. "Or did you just call to brag?"

"If I wanted to brag, I'd be telling you all about the view I've got right now. Clear blue skies and girls in itty-bitty bikinis."

"Careful, Liv or Oak will have your balls if they hear you mentioning girls in bikinis."

"Bro, it's my girl I'm staring at right now. She bought this little red—"

"Spare me," I grunt, not wanting him to paint me a picture of his girl—one of my closest friends—in a bikini. I've already seen enough since they got together. Pretty sure Oak has too.

"Jesus, Elliot. You really should pull that stick out of your arse every now and then, mate."

"What did you want?" I mutter, really not in the mood for a dressing down from him.

Especially when I'm sitting in the middle of the bathroom like a loser.

It really isn't necessary.

"Promised the girls I would check in to make sure you're holding up your end of the bargain."

"I'm not a glorified babysitter or a stalker," I sneer.

"I don't know, I think you could totally pull off the stalker thing. You're pretty good at moving around in the dark unnoticed."

"Whatever."

"But she's okay, yeah?"

Shuffling back across the spotless tiles beneath me, I rest back against the wall and tip my head to the vaulted ceiling above me.

"Yes, Abigail is fine."

"Did you want to say that in a way that actually makes me believe that you've seen her?" Reese suggests.

"I have seen her. And she's..." Drowning. Not coping in any sense of the word. Torturing herself. "Fine."

"Fine? That's not exactly— Babe, what are you—"

"Tell me she's better than fine," Liv demands down the line, having stolen it from Reese.

"She's okay."

"That's not any fucking better, Elliot. She still isn't answering our calls, and all her replies to our messages barely contain more than one or two words."

"I don't know what you want me to say, Liv. She's struggling, but she's fighting it."

Barely.

I know that I should probably tell them the truth. But what good will that do? They'll all worry and regret leaving her. And that would only pile extra guilt onto Abigail.

"Is she making any kind of progress?" she asks too fucking hopeful.

"We had pizza together." Okay, so it's not entirely true but it's all I've got.

"Okay, good... That's good."

"Just enjoy your holiday, yeah. I've got this."

I definitely do not have this.

"I can't help it," she says. "The last time we saw her before we left, she looked so... broken."

"She'll be okay," I assure her. The words hold much more confidence than I feel.

Nothing but Liv's heavy sigh fills the line. I feel her concern right down to my soul.

"I really hope so. This holiday was a mistake."

"Or it might be the time she needs without the three of you mothering her."

"Elliot," she warns.

"Trust me, yeah. I've got this."

"Can you get her to call one of us, please? If we could just talk to her then—"

"I'll see what I can do," I promise. "Go and enjoy yourself."

"Okay, okay. Although, it's not the same without you both here."

"I'm sure you've barely noticed I'm missing," I say, trying to ignore the stab of pain to the chest my words cause.

"Don't be silly. No one is cleaning up the villa behind us."

"Ha, you're funny."

Liv shrieks down the line. "Gotta go, Reese is—"

The line goes dead but I don't immediately lower my phone from my ear.

Indecision wars within me.

Maybe I should have gone and left this place behind.

I shake my head, thinking of her again. Not that I've

really stopped since the moment I walked out of her dorm room yesterday.

Yeah, I was never going anywhere.

Well, not unless Abigail went with them.

Pushing to my feet, I pick everything up and place them in the cabinet under the basin before washing my hands and splashing my face.

Lifting my head, I stare at myself in the mirror, hating the reflection that stares back at me. Evidence of my lack of sleep is right there, the shadows I spend most of my days fighting are beginning to encroach, darkening my eyes.

There's only one way I know that will help banish them. I've just got to hope that by the time I get to where I need to be that something a little more positive will greet me.

I throw myself in the shower, trying not to obsess over the fact I'll leave water stains on the glass and soap suds around the drain as I dress and attempt to fix my hair before heading out of my room.

The Chapel is quiet. Too fucking quiet. So quiet it allows the voices in my head to get louder, and that is never a fucking good thing.

Grabbing an apple and bottle of water on the way out, I brace myself for the wind and rain that is still assaulting campus as I jog toward the Bronte Building.

There's no one around, and campus is almost empty with most kids heading home—or somewhere exotic—for the Easter Break.

I don't see anyone and as I let myself into the Bronte Building, it doesn't get any better. The place is deserted.

Running up the stairs, I make a beeline for Abigail's room, leaving a trail of water behind me.

Unlike yesterday, I don't second-guess knocking. I'm over that after the state I found her in in the bathroom. If anything, this is merely a polite gesture to ensure she's ready for a visitor. Not that finding her half-dressed would be a bad thing in any way.

Reining myself in, I call out, hoping that this time she might just invite me in herself. I told her I was going to come back so she should be expecting me.

"Red, I'm coming in whether you answer the door or not."

Nothing.

"Fine. Let's do this the hard way then, shall we?" I mutter to myself before pulling the keycard from my pocket and repeating my actions from yesterday.

However, when I swing the door open, thankfully, I find her sitting in the middle of the bed. But that's about the only positive I find.

The curtains are still shut despite it being mid-afternoon, and the place is in darkness.

"Hey," I say softly, studying her the best I can. "How are you doing?"

Silence.

"Red, you're going to need to talk to me. Have you eaten anything today?"

I catch sight of the pizza box I left her with yesterday. Lifting the top, I find that the only slice that is missing is the one she ate in front of me.

"Red," I warn.

"I'm not a child, Elliot," she snaps.

"Never said you were," I say, closing the lid and straightening the box up on the desk alone with a couple of books that have been knocked.

"I don't need you looking after me."

"No, so who's going to do it then because right now, it doesn't seem to be you."

9
———

ABIGAIL

Elliot Eaton is the most arrogant, infuriating person I've ever met.

I glare at him as he slips into my room and closes the door behind him, leaning back against it.

Damn him, coming here again. Pretending he cares. Pretending he—

Stop. Just stop Abi.

He cares. I know that. He just doesn't care enough. Not in the way I wish he did.

I huff out a resigned sigh, and he arches his brow.

"Did the girls tell you to come?"

"Something like that," he mutters, making a beeline for my desk chair. He lowers himself down but not before pulling a packet of biscuits out of his hoodie pocket.

"Eat." He throws them onto the bed.

"I'm not hungry."

"I swear to God, Abi..." He runs a hand down his face.

"Fine." My stomach gives a little growl as I tear into the packet, and I feel his knowing gaze on me. But I refuse to look at him, to give him the satisfaction.

The biscuit feels like ash on my tongue as I chew and swallow, forcing it down over the permanent lump in my throat.

"Water?" he asks, and I nod.

Elliot gets up and goes to the small mini fridge next to my desk and grabs a bottle of water. "Here." He hands it to me. "You need to get out of this room. Get some fresh air."

"No, I really don't."

"Red, come on—"

"Please, don't call me that."

It's too intimate. It hurts too much.

He releases a heavy sigh, sinking back into the chair. "Tell me how to help you."

"Leave me alone."

"And risk you starving yourself or worse."

"What's that supposed to mean?" I spit, anger swarming my chest.

"Nothing," he concedes. Too quickly. Too easily. "It means nothing. But I'm worried. We all are."

Worried enough that they all left to have fun in the sun, I trap the bitter words.

I don't blame them. I don't even resent them. I'm no fun to be around, and the truth is I don't belong with them.

I never did.

Something that's become increasingly obvious since the night I kissed Elliot.

To think, I actually let myself believe I was one of them. One of the pretty girls. The strong, confident girls like Olivia and Tally. Even Raine arrived at All Hallows' and made it clear she wouldn't take crap from anyone, least of all an Heir.

I've never been any of those things. I'm too shy. Too quiet.

Too weak.

A rush of emotion burns up my throat, but I force it down, taking a gulp of water.

Elliot makes everything worse by being here. The intensity in his eyes as he watches me, the air of disapproval in his expression.

"I don't know how many times I have to say it, I'm fine."

"You're fooling nobody but yourself," he says quietly. But I catch the hint of anger there.

The frustration.

"My father died," I snap. "He was all I had left. He's gone, Elliot, and now I'm alone. Is that what you want to hear? That I'm barely hanging on?" My fingers twist into the bedsheets as I inhale a shuddering breath. "He's gone, so forgive me for trying to come to terms with my new reality."

"You're wrong."

"What?" I ask incredulously because how dare he.

How bloody dare he?

"You said you're alone. You're not."

"Semantics." I shrug, the burst of fight I felt mere seconds ago already seeping from my body, leaving me exhausted.

"You have people, Re— Abi. You just need to open your eyes and see that."

"Because everyone loves having me around so much?" I cut him with a scathing look. "Let's face it, I'm only in your inner circle because the girls took pity on me."

"That's not—"

"I think we both know it is. And it's fine. I know my place in the social hierarchy, Elliot. And it's not with the Heirs and their girlfriends."

He studies me for a second, rubbing a hand over his

chiselled jaw. "How is it you can fight me on this, but you don't even have enough self-preservation to eat?"

Snatching another biscuit from the packet, I hiss, "I'm eating, aren't I?"

Anger consumes me as I bite into it, barely tasting the slight hint of ginger. But I know it's not only directed at Elliot and his insistence on barging my life. I'm angry at myself. For letting my guard down and allowing myself to believe that maybe I could walk in their world.

I have money, sure. I have more money than I know what to do with. My life is privileged and even if I never figure out what I want to do post-college, I'll never want for anything. But I've never truly lived in that world.

Their world.

The parties and charity events and country club lunches.

I've been too focused on looking after my father, on hiding myself away from the world, to be interested in all that.

"You've got it all wrong," he says quietly and my gaze cuts to his.

I don't want to do this.

I don't want to listen to him try and placate me.

I'm not one of them. I'm not—

"If we didn't want you around, you wouldn't be."

A small unconvinced huff leaves me. Maybe I'm not being fair to them. Maybe my own pain and suffering is clouding my judgement on everything. But I've spent years—*years*—alone. With no friends. With nobody in my corner. Suddenly having them all, only to lose them again soon feels too much to bear.

It's better this way.

Better if I sequester myself away and deal with this on my own.

"I don't need you, Elliot. I don't need anyone."

The lie hurts, makes my heart recoil, but I have to be strong.

I have to keep him at arm's length. He made it perfectly clear where he stands on there ever being an us.

You shouldn't have done that. The words he said to me that night echo through my mind.

"I'm not going to just leave you here to rot." Frustration coats his voice.

"That's not—"

He pins me with a hard look, the kind he reserves for the students at All Hallows' who dare to cross his path.

It's a look I'm not all too used to seeing from him, one I might have once cowered at. But nothing but an overwhelming streak of irritation sparks inside me.

"I'm not scared of you." The words land like a blow and I'm not sure who is more surprised—him or me.

But something flickers in his icy expression. Something besides the blatant surprise. I can't decipher it though. I'm too annoyed. Too weary.

"There." I twist the top of the biscuit packet and thrust them towards him. "I ate. You can go now."

Elliot narrows his gaze. "Come out with me."

"What? No!" Absolutely not.

"Come on, Red. We'll go for a drive. Go to that dessert place you all love so much. Just... get out of this room for a bit."

I can't. The words lodge in my throat.

"Just for an hour," he goes on, "It'll do you good."

"Do you know what I want, Elliot?" I force myself to look at him, really look at him. He waits and I take a steady breath. "I just want to be left alone to deal with things how I want to deal with them."

I'm sure hurt flickers over his face but that can't be right.

"That's really what you want?" he asks coldly. I nod, and the muscle in his jaw clenches. "Fine." He stands. "Have it your way."

And he storms out of my room, taking every bit of air with him.

Elliot didn't come back.

Not that I blame him.

I made it clear, I don't want or need his help. I don't need a babysitter. I need...

God, I don't know what I need. All I know is relying on Elliot Eaton isn't it.

Another day passes. Another day of ignoring the girls' calls and texts. I manage to reply to Tally to placate them enough not to send Elliot back. But for the most part, I stay cocooned in a ball of grief and sadness and anger.

Elliot wasn't wrong. This isn't healing. It's wallowing. Drowning in the emotions suffocating every inch of me. But I don't know how to shut it off. And with every minute, every hour that passes I slip deeper and deeper. So deep I can't breathe.

I shove back the covers and stumble out of bed, trying desperately to suck in air. To fill my lungs and make them work again. But the band across my chest constricts, tightening to the point of no return.

I can't breathe.

I can't—

I crash into the vanity, gripping the edge and trying to force my heart rate down. Breathe in and breath out slowly.

Count steadily to five. Close my eyes and focus on my breaths.

Over and over, I repeat the cycle, waiting for the panic attack to pass.

Eventually, it does, and my eyes flicker open as I finally feel in control again.

Except, I'm not.

A restless energy simmers under my skin, desperate for release. I need to get it out.

I need to not feel this... this sheer desperation. This hopelessness and utter, utter loneliness.

Before I can stop myself, I reach for the shard of glass, the one I concealed behind the taps, where I originally found it.

It feels dangerous in my hand. Sharp and jagged. But something else unfurls inside me.

A yearning.

Until a wave of shame hits me, so strong I sink to the tiles, my back hitting the shower cubicle. Tears stream down my face as I stare at the piece of glass, an internal war raging inside me.

I don't want to die.

I don't.

But I do want to cut out the pain living inside of me. To carve it from my chest, out from under my skin.

Drawing my knees up, I tip my head back and inhale a sharp breath. My hand drops between my thighs as I let the emotions consume me once more.

I can't do this.

I can't fight it.

I'm not Olivia or Tally or Raine. I'm not a bad ass girl who can fight for herself and what she wants.

I'm broken and scarred and terrified of what my future holds.

I'm a mess.

Only this time, there's nobody to pull me out.

This time, there's nobody to watch over me and tell me it's going to be okay.

I sob harder as the tip of the glass shard cuts into my thigh, as I drag it along my pale skin.

And in that moment, I hate myself.

I hate that I'm not stronger.

But underneath all the shame and hatred is another feeling. One that I cling to as blood trails down my leg, dripping onto the tiles.

Relief.

10

ELLIOT

My skin is itching, concern knotting at my stomach.

I shouldn't have left her.

But I didn't know what else to do.

My instincts told me to scoop her off the bed, throw her over my shoulder and bring her back here. But I couldn't do it.

Abigail didn't want me there. She certainly didn't want to be here with me watching her every move.

But there was a little voice that said it was exactly what I should do no matter how much she would hate me for it.

I find myself gazing at the front door picturing myself storming through it with Abigail in my arms. The vision excites me more than I think it should.

Closing my eyes, I remember vividly how she looked curled up in my bed not so long ago. She had no idea that I didn't leave after she passed out. That instead, I slipped into the shadows so she wouldn't spot me immediately if she did wake again. That the sight of her twisted up in my sheets, searching for me in her tipsy sleepy state.

She looked so beautiful. Her red hair against my dark sheets was so striking, so mesmerising. The temptation to crawl in with her and pull her into my body was strong.

My need to protect her, to wrap her in my arms and stop anyone from hurting her is becoming a need almost too much to bear.

It's been three days since I walked out.

I've heard nothing from her since, not that I was expecting too. And I've had nothing but grief from the girls about her lack of communication and my apparent inability to keep tabs on her.

My fists curl on top of the dining table, my short nails digging into my skin as I remind myself of the way she dismissed me the last time I visited.

As far as I know, she hasn't left her room since I walked out. The girls in the dorm haven't had anything to report. I have to trust that if there were something wrong that they'd alert me.

Is that a cop-out from going back and facing reality? Probably. But I don't trust my ability to look into her eyes and not do the exact opposite of what she's asking of me.

Slouching lower in the seat, I let my head hang back. The Chapel is in silence. I thought I'd like the peace and quiet without my boys here. But it's becoming obvious very fast that being here alone isn't half as relaxing as I hoped it would be.

Sure, the place is nice and tidy. I don't get up in the morning to a sink full of washing up or random pieces of dirty laundry strewn around the place. There's also no risk of walking in on any of them doing something they really shouldn't be in a communal area. But fuck, I miss them.

Of course, I have no intention of telling them that though. It would only go to their heads. And their egos are already big enough.

Blowing out a long breath, I startle when a loud knocking starts on the front door.

"Fuck's sake," I mutter before shoving my chair back to see who it is. Although, it soon becomes apparent it was not necessary.

My stomach drops into my feet as the door slams closed and my father strides into the vast space as if he owns the place. He looks around with his top lip peeled back.

He made it very clear on his first visit here after we got the key that he didn't approve of our chosen décor. But fuck him.

I was so over living in a sterile box like the home I was forced to grow up in. The Chapel's days of being cold and unwelcoming ended the moment Scott's reign was over.

We couldn't rip this place apart fast enough.

"Father," I greet, sounding about as thrilled as I feel about his sudden appearance. "You should have said you were coming." I'd have locked the door.

"I had a meeting with Mr Porter," he explains, finally turning his eyes on me.

He assesses me just like he has my home. And it's clear that what he finds pleases him just as much as my interior design skills.

Grey sweats and a hoodie never have been a part of Johnathon Eaton's approved wardrobe. The only casual item of clothing allowed is a rugby jersey, and only during a game.

"We were discussing the next academic year. Your successors," he adds.

If he's hoping to spark some interest with that comment, then he's going to be bitterly disappointed.

"Right," I mutter.

I probably should care about who's going to take over

this place once our year is done. But honestly, it's the least of my concerns right now.

"We're concerned that they're not ready."

"Then you should probably be talking to their fathers instead of me," I point out.

Being an heir is a tradition passed down for generations. If Toby Middleton and his boys aren't prepared, then that should fall on their elders shoulder for not preparing them properly.

Each of us have spent our entire lives preparing to rule All Hallows' as Heirs, and then Saints Cross U as Scions.

Fuck learning to ride bikes or playing out in the woods or anything else normal kids get the pleasure of doing. We were too busy learning the way of our world while those above us threw their weight around because apparently, they've earned the right to.

"I will be. But the current Heirs have a responsibility in the next generation as well." He quirks a brow. "You should be more than aware of this, Elliot. Scott did everything he could to ensure you were ready for this position."

I only just about manage to hold in my scoff of disgust.

Yeah, that motherfucker sure did whatever he could to ensure my life under his reign was nothing but pure hell.

"I'm aware." I've still got the fucking scars to prove it.

"You have a term left to ensure they're ready. It'll reflect badly on you and your reign if they're not."

I stare at him, hearing what he's really saying.

It'll reflect badly on me.

"Your brother and I haven't worked as hard as we have during the Eaton reign for it to be—"

His words fade off into the distance as my phone starts vibrating in my pocket.

I ignore it, although it pains me to do so.

I don't care who it is, it could be a telemarketer, I'd prefer to talk to them than listen to my father explain all the ways he thinks I've failed during the past few months.

His deep voice continues to rumble around the Chapel, but none of the words register as my phone rings off, but almost immediately starts up again.

My heart picks up speed.

Whoever it is really wants me.

Abigail.

My stomach knots. I already know it won't be her ringing me. She's too damn stubborn for her own good. But it could be about her.

Before I know what I'm doing, I pull my phone from my pocket.

Millie.

Shit.

Even if it isn't about Abigail. Theo's little sister calling me while he's away can only mean one thing.

I really need to answer but—

It's only then I realise that my old man has stopped talking.

Swallowing thickly, I risk looking up. His eyes are narrowed, his lips pressed into a thin line as irritation comes off him in waves.

"I'm sorry, was I boring you?" he seethes.

My teeth grind. I could explain about Millie needing me and Theo being away. But what's the point?

"Do you have something more important to do other than discuss how to recover your reputation?"

"I have a study session," I say simply. It's the only excuse that would ever get me out of a Johnathon Eaton dressing down.

His teeth grind as he glares at me. "This conversation

isn't over," he concedes. "Scott is coming home this weekend. We need to sit down and—"

My phone starts ringing again. "I really need to go before I'm any later."

Marching toward the front door, I shove my feet into my trainers, throwing my bag over my shoulder, pretending it's got something useful in it.

The second he steps out of the Chapel, I slam the door behind us and take off toward the school.

His eyes burn into my back, but my focus isn't on him as I pull my phone free and return Millie's call.

"What's wrong?" I bark without any kind of greeting.

"Uh..."

"Spit it out, Mills. You haven't been blowing up my phone for fun."

"Yeah. I know. I just... I don't know if..."

"Millie," I growl.

"Crap. Yeah. So... some of the girls saw Abigail sneaking down to the kitchen last night for first aid supplies."

"What? Why?" I bark, my feet moving faster.

"I don't know. No one asked."

"But—"

"Kara told me you told her to tell you if she saw or heard anything. That's all I know."

"So why are you telling me, and she isn't?" This is exactly what I wanted to avoid, dragging Millie into my bullshit when she's already been through enough.

"I don't know, I guess she's scared of you or something. Scared what you might do if..."

"If what, Mills?"

"If Abi hurt herself on her watch."

"Shit," I hiss, dread sitting heavy in my stomach. "I'm coming to check on her now," I explain.

"I'm sure she's fine. She probably just—"

"Call me if you hear anything else, yeah?"

"Of course."

"Thank you, Mills," I say before hanging up and digging the dorm master key from my bag.

I have the door open only a second later and I'm heading toward Abigail's room. It's a route I've taken numerous times in the past few days. But something feels different this time.

I don't hesitate when I get to her door, instead, I unlock it and throw it open. Her room is still in darkness, and once again it's empty. But I know where she is this time.

Storming toward the closed bathroom door, I don't bother warning her that I'm coming.

I don't give a shit if she's mid-pee.

The door swings open, revealing the girl I've come for sitting with her back against her wall and her bare, pale legs spread out in front of her.

Any other day, the sight of so much of her skin on display when she usually hides would be enough to stop me in my tracks.

But not today.

It's the sight of the bright red blood running down her thigh and dripping on the floor that makes my heart stop.

"Abigail," I growl dangerously.

She's holding what looks like a massive shard of glass—

Motherfucker.

It's a bit of the mirror I must've missed cleaning up.

I left her here after she smashed that and she—

"You need to leave," she says weakly, without so much as looking up.

"You've got the fucking kidding me. There is no fucking way I'm leaving you here now."

"Please," she whimpers, her voice wrought with emotion.

I don't realise I've moved closer until I suddenly drop to my knees before her and wrap my hand around hers.

Her skin is cold, and it sends another shot of concern through my veins.

"You need to stop," I beg, attempting to pull the glass from her clutches without causing her any more damage.

My skin itches as I stare down at the cuts she's caused.

My heart rate picks up as understanding washes through me. But as much as I might empathise with her need for release, I will never accept her causing herself pain, making her pretty skin bleed.

She gasps as I finally uncurl her fingers from the shard. It's my first clue that I didn't manage to remove it without hurting her. The rush of blood down her arm is the second.

I stare at the trail of blood in a daze as it races toward her elbow.

Fuck.

Reaching my hand out, I cup her jaw and give her no choice but to look up at me. Wetness from her tears coat my fingers, making my chest ache. But that has nothing on the moment her eyes find mine.

All the air comes rushing from my lungs as I finally fully understand just how many lies she's told over the past few weeks.

"From here on out," I warn quietly. "We're doing this my way."

She swallows, her throat rippling against my fingers but she doesn't argue.

Instead, she remains silent as I scoop her body into my arms, clutch her to my chest, and do what I should have done days ago.

11

ABIGAIL

"Sit," Elliot commands as he places me gently down on his bed. "I'll be back."

His heavy gaze lingers for a second, dropping from my face to my thighs, the dried blood there.

I flinch, hating how much his disapproval, his blatant anger, affects me.

I didn't want him to see me like this.

I didn't want anyone to see.

Shame snakes through me as I sit on his bed. Lost and alone. And so—

"Let me take a look." Elliot approaches, dumping a first aid kit on the bed beside me, and lowers to his knees.

"It's nothing." I try to cover myself, but he gently pries my hands away.

"It's not fucking nothing. You were..." He audibly swallows, his eyes shuttering as he inhales a ragged breath.

When his eyes open again, his gaze pins me to the bed. Paralyses me and makes me wish I could shrink into nothing.

"Elliot, I—"

"Why?" he grits out. "Why the fuck would you do this to yourself."

"You wouldn't understand," I whisper, dropping my gaze, refusing to look at him.

Refusing to face the truth.

"You think I wouldn't... Of course you do." Bitter laughter spills out of him but I'm too weary, too broken to care.

The silence is deafening as Elliot begins to clean my thighs. He's careful; methodically wiping the tiny cuts with an antiseptic wipe before covering them with a small dressing.

When he's done, he grips my chin and forces me to look at him. "Promise me you won't do this again."

"I... I can't," I breathe, the truth a glacial wall between us.

His eyes darken, making my heart tumble in my chest. He looks terrifying. Beyond angry.

"It wasn't like I was trying to kill myself or anything." My voice cracks. "I just... I needed it to stop. I needed..." I swallow the words. Because how can I possibly explain everything?

He's Elliot Eaton. An All Hallows' Heir. He would never be so weak, so desperate that he had to hurt himself the way I have.

Another wave of shame rolls through me, curdling in my stomach.

"I want you to stay here," he says.

"What? No, that's not—"

"I wasn't asking, Abigail. Clearly, you can't be trusted to look after yourself." He lets go of my chin and stands. "I'll ask Millie to pack up your things and bring them over."

"Elliot, I can't move into the Chapel, it's not... I can't."

"The girls will be back soon. When they find out about this—"

"What?" I bolt up. "You can't tell them. You can't... No, Elliot." Panic floods me as I glare at him. "This has nothing... *nothing* to do with them. Nothing. Please."

"Shit, Abs. Calm down. Just take a fucking breath, yeah." His arms come around me and he gathers me into his chest, but I can't stop crying.

I can't stop the tears from pouring out as I curl my fingers into his hoodie.

I've imagined being in Elliot's arm so many times, spent my days wondering what it would be like to be the centre of his world. But not like this—never like this.

The thought is like a bucket of ice-cold water, and I instantly step back out of his hold, frantically drying my eyes. "I'm sorry," I say, forcing myself to meet his narrowed gaze. "I'm a mess, I know. But it's not your problem, Elliot. I'll speak to Miss Linley, get some help. I'll—"

"No."

"No?" My brows furrow.

"You can stay here until you feel... better."

As if it's that simple.

"I'm not sure that's a good idea."

"We're friends, aren't we?"

Friends.

He might as well have driven a stake through my already broken heart.

Friends.

But even that word is a lie. Because Elliot and I are not friends.

We never were.

He watches me. The way a person might watch a cornered animal. Cautious. Hesitant.

Scared.

"Please stop looking at me like that," I quietly seethe.

"Like what?"

"Like you pity me."

"Fuck, Abi, that's not... You scared me today."

"What?"

"When I found you like that, you scared me. I'm not used to that... that feeling."

"You weren't supposed to find me." My voice is barely a whisper.

"Just stay here a while. Until the girls get back. Until you're in a better headspace. Can you do that for me?"

"Where will you stay?" I ask, glancing round his room.

It's not the first time I've been in here and I'm dreadfully aware of the fact that I'm one of the very few girls who've ever seen inside Elliot Eaton's inner sanctuary.

I thought it meant something then.

I know different now.

"I'll figure something out." He shrugs.

"I can't stay here," I reiterate, although it sounds less convincing this time. Because the truth is, the thought of going back to my dorm room alone terrifies me.

"Have you eaten today?"

"What?" I stare blankly at him.

"I'll get you something. Make yourself at home." Elliot marches out of the room without a backward glance and I stand there, wishing things were different.

Wishing I was different.

My eyes flutter open only to be met with darkness. I push up onto my elbow and scan the room.

Elliot's room.

A sliver of moonlight illuminates the place, casting shadows around the functional, clean, and tidy space.

After bringing me a sandwich and a packet of crisps, he sat and watched me eat. I didn't like it. But I was tired. Bone-deep exhausted.

I'd barely finished half the sandwich before Elliot pulled back the covers and helped me into his bed and left me to sleep like a small helpless child.

The shame still lingers but it's swamped by the grief, the endless heartache.

Slipping my hand beneath the covers, I run my fingers over the dressing on my inner thigh, wincing. But pain and shame aren't the only things I feel when I think about how it felt to cut myself.

I shake off the unwanted thoughts, desperately trying to fight the urge to run into his bathroom and find something sharp enough to give me that moment of release.

Of sheer and utter relief.

Fear prevents me from even getting out of bed though. If Elliot ever catches me doing that again... I don't want to think about what he might do or who he might tell.

I blink away the tears burning the backs of my eyes as I roll onto my back, my gaze snagging on the clock on the wall.

It's late. A little past ten. I wonder what Elliot's doing.

Before, I might have gone to find out. But I'm not that girl now.

Now he's made it clear where we stand.

I can't ignore the urge to pee though, so with a gentle huff, I shove back the covers and lean over to switch on the lamp.

Standing, I—

"Dear God, you scared me," I blurt, taking in Elliot as

he runs a hand down his face. "What the hell are you doing?"

"What does it look like?"

"When you said you'd figure something out, I didn't think you meant you'd sit and watch me like a stalker."

"I'm... That's not what I was doing."

I arch a brow not buying it for one second. "You don't trust me," I say, realisation hitting me dead in the chest.

"I just wanted to make sure you were okay."

"I need to pee." I wave him off as I drag my weary body into his small bathroom.

The second the door clicks shut behind me, I let loose a breath.

This isn't going to work. I can't stay here with Elliot watching my every move.

But he has a point.

Elliot doesn't trust me.

And the hard truth is, I don't trust myself either.

Inhaling a sharp breath, I make quick work of peeing before washing my hands.

Much like his bedroom, Elliot's bathroom is clean and tidy and decorated in the muted tones he seems to favour. One wall in here is a deep bluish-grey colour that reminds me of his eyes, the storm permanently swirling there.

God, what am I doing here?

I need to shore up my defences against him. Not let him rescue me at every turn.

His white-knight routine confuses me. Makes my silly foolish heart flutter wildly in my chest. But I must remember the truth. Elliot isn't helping me because he cares like that. He's helping me because he feels obligated to do so.

I'm a burden to him, a responsibility he feels he must bear.

I suck in another shaky breath as I grip the edge of the vanity.

"Abigail." His gentle knock sends my pulse skyrocketing. "Everything okay in there?"

"Y-yeah. I'll be right out."

It's an effort to go to the door and open it, to meet his steely gaze.

"I was peeing, Elliot." A sigh escapes me as I brush past him and sit on the bed. "When do they get back?" I ask, trying to break some of the tension between us.

"In a couple of days."

I nod, hands fidgeting in my lap.

"Do you need anything?" he asks.

"I have water." I tilt my head toward the fresh bottle on the bedside table. One he must have put there earlier.

"If I go downstairs, do I need to be worried?"

A stone plunks my chest. "I'm not going to hurt myself if that's what you mean."

He studies me for a second then nods. "Get some sleep. I'll see you tomorrow."

Elliot walks out of the room and closes the door behind him.

I flop backward, huffing out a little breath but my eyes flicker over to the door. To where I wonder if Elliot waits on the other side to see if I'll do something reckless.

He's such an enigma. A closed book who guards his secrets. It seems ridiculous now that I ever had the notion that I might be the girl to get under his skin and discover the boy beneath the cold exterior.

I almost can't believe I let myself think I could.

He's an Eaton. A future Scion. In September, he'll go off to Saints Cross University and rule there with an iron fist, just as his older brother has done before him. He has a name to uphold, a reputation.

His has his entire future mapped out if the rumours are to be believed.

There's no room at his side for a girl like me.

So how can I stay here?

How can I let myself accept his charity... his pity?

The truth is, I can't—I shouldn't.

Yet, I'm not sure I'm strong enough right now to walk away.

12

ELLIOT

I grunt as I shift on the sofa for the millionth time since I forced myself to walk away from Abigail earlier.

She doesn't think I trust her.

She doesn't think I understand.

I shouldn't be surprised.

I know the image I show the rest of the world. I know what the population of All Hallows' thinks of me.

I'm Elliot Eaton.

Second in line to the Eaton empire.

The powerful son of Johnathon and Julia Eaton.

Grandson of John Eaton.

A bitter laugh spills from my lips.

No fucking pressure, right?

Since the day I was born, every set of eyes in this town have been on me.

The only person more under the spotlight than me is Scott.

A place that he just fucking loves to be.

Any chance he gets to look better than me. Or more so,

make me look worse he jumps on without a second thought.

He's the oldest. The true heir.

He's good at it too. A cold-blooded, sadistic fuck just like our father.

I bet he hasn't had a day in his life where he's second-guessed his place in the world, his position in his town, and the weight that comes with it. Let alone lose himself to the pressure. To the knowledge that no matter what, you're just never going to be good enough. Never going to stand up to the impossible expectations placed on your head.

But I guess you don't have to worry when you're the family's Golden Boy.

My fists curl at my side, my nails digging into my palms until just a bite of pain shoots up my arms.

Squeezing my eyes closed, I try not to think about how Abigail would have felt as that shard of glass pierced her skin. How strong the relief would have been as the first drop of blood spilled free and ran down her porcelain skin.

My mouth waters as a craving I haven't succumbed to for a long-time surges back full force.

I focus on my breathing, forcing myself to think about the here and now.

I've got her here.

She's in my bed.

Suffering.

Hurting so badly that she's causing herself physical pain to try and deal with it.

I've felt pretty fucking useless most of my life. But I can honestly say that I've never felt more out of my depth than I do right now.

Previously, I've been letting down my parents. Scott. Myself. I can deal with that. It's pretty fucking normal, if I'm being honest with myself.

But I can't let her down.

The girls trust me to keep her safe. And I've already failed.

Maybe if I'd acted sooner. Brought her back here when I first saw her in that shower, drowning in her own grief.

Maybe...

Maybe...

Maybe...

None of those thoughts will help me.

Focusing on all the ways I've let her down will only lead to pain.

But then the relief...

I sit up with a start, my chest heaving, my breathing erratic and my skin prickling.

"Fuck," I hiss, jumping to my feet so I can begin pacing.

My head screams at me to do it.

To give into the pressures and fall back into old habits.

But my heart... that tells me something very different.

Refusing the former as an option, I take the stairs two at a time toward something—someone—who can distract me from my own issues.

I move through the Chapel silently in the hope I don't wake her.

She might do nothing but sleep right now, but I figure she must need it. Only, the second I crack my bedroom door open, silence doesn't greet me. Instead I'm met with loud, gut-wrenching sobs.

A huge, messy ball of emotion crawls up my throat as I rush inside.

"Red," I breathe, forgetting all about her request for me to stop using it, and before I know what I'm doing, I'm standing with my knees pressed against my mattress, trying to decide what to do next. "Shit," I whisper.

As my eyes adjust to the darkness, I discover that she's not even aware that I'm here. She's too lost in her grief.

Her head is in her hands, and her entire body is trembling.

Without thinking, I crawl onto the bed and wrap my arms around her tiny frame. She startles. Her entire body freezing as my warmth surrounds her.

"No," she whimpers, finally dropping her hands from her face so she can attempt to fight me off.

Her tiny palms press against my chest, but she hasn't got anywhere near the strength she'd need to make me release her.

"Stop, Red. Just stop. It's okay," I whisper, my lips beside her ear.

The fruity scent of her hair fills my nose, turning my previous cravings in an entirely different direction. But just like the relief I wanted earlier, I won't allow myself to have this either.

"No," she cries. "Nothing is okay."

"Shush," I soothe, shifting our position and lifting her onto my lap.

She fights again, but it's pointless, and a couple of seconds later, she gives in and tucks her tear-soaked face into the crook of my neck.

I fucking hate feeling them, the evidence of her pain, almost as much as I love them.

Locking down my own needs, I focus on her.

"I've got you, Red. Everything is going to be okay."

She shakes her head, refusing to believe my words but she doesn't say anything else.

"I'm sorry for leaving you," I whisper.

It was a risk. There are plenty of things she could use as a weapon against herself in both my bedroom and bathroom. But I didn't think she'd do it again. Not so soon.

Her shame was palpable when I first found her and then cleaned her up. I was confident she wasn't going to repeat those actions any time soon.

But following her wishes and leaving her alone hurt. And knowing that she's been sitting up here crying her heart out slices mine into tiny pieces.

She deserves so much more than this.

She's beautiful, both inside and out.

She shouldn't have to deal with the kind of pain she's suffered in the last few years.

It's cruel.

She's suffering and my father and Scott are running around town, throwing their weight around and getting everything their sick, twisted hearts' desire.

They should be the ones to experience a little pain. Not this sweet, innocent young woman who has the rest of her life just waiting for her.

So fucking cruel.

She continues to cry for the longest time, but as the seconds pass, I notice her hold on me tighten.

I go from a person she tries to push away to a lifeline she clings to.

I shouldn't fucking like it. But I do. Too fucking much.

Eventually, her sobs ease and her violent trembles soften.

I breathe a sigh of relief that the worst is over, but I don't release her.

I can't.

With her in my arms...

Fuck. I'm addicted.

Although obviously slimmer than I've ever known her, her body feels soft and pliant against mine.

She might be covered in a large All Hallows' hoodie, but I just know that her skin beneath will feel like silk.

I felt it when I cleaned up her thighs.

Fucking hell, I need to get a grip.

I squeeze my eyes closed tighter and try not to let my head go there. The flash of the white cotton knickers she was wearing, her sweet scent, her warm, soft skin.

Something tells me it could well have been the most intimate she's ever been with anyone… and it was with me.

She doesn't show off her body. She doesn't reveal her skin.

I think back to that cabin we all visited when she refused to even put on a swimsuit to get in the hot tub. We all know that she's hiding scars. But is she hiding more than just the aftermath of that car accident?

Is there more to this than any of us know?

Her breathing gets deeper, and steadier, her body getting heavier in my arms.

"Red?" I whisper, testing to see if she's cried herself to sleep.

Nothing.

Not wanting to spend the rest of the night sitting in the middle of my bed with Abigail in my arms, I gently lean back, taking her with me.

The movement brings her to and she holds me tighter, mumbling "No, don't let me go."

My heart swells.

Maybe I can do something right in my life.

Lying down on my side with my head on my pillow, I do something I've never done before.

I fall asleep with a girl in my arms. In my bed.

If only she could understand just how massive this moment is for me. But the reality is, everything she's going through right now trumps it by a mile.

I wake more than a few times over the next few hours.

Having another body in my bed is bizarre. But not as weird as having them wrapped around me like a koala. Still, as uncomfortable as I might have been, I never tried to move her or let her go.

I couldn't.

The fear that she'd wake up and shove me aside, regretting all of this—assuming she's even aware—is very real.

If this is all I'm ever going to get of this incredible young woman, then I'm going to take it.

She can even pretend it never happened in the morning if she wants.

I'll remember though.

It'll be enough.

It has to be enough.

I wake before sunrise after a few hours of fitful rest with Abigail still sleeping beside me.

As much as I want to stay here and experience her reaction when she wakes, my need for the bathroom makes it impossible.

Gently as I can, I slide my arm from beneath her body and tuck the duvet tight around her as I roll away, leaving her alone in my massive bed once again. Without looking back, I pad across my room, peeling my sweaty t-shirt and sweats off as I go.

I take a piss before turning the shower on and quickly jumping in.

As much as I hate to wash her scent off me, I don't need the reminder of something I'm never going to have again.

Last night was a one-off.

It's better for all of us that it is.

I can't have Abigail.

Not the way I really want her.

It wouldn't be fair to her.

With my skin red from the almost unbearable heat of the water, I towel off and brush my teeth. I pause at the bathroom door with my hand on the doorknob, second-guessing myself.

There's a part of me that wishes she's awake and will invite me back into the bed, but there is a bigger part that knows that's wishful thinking.

With a sigh, I pull the door open and slip out. The room is still in darkness, and there is an unmoving Abigail-sized lump under the covers in the middle.

With just one quick glance, I walk over to my dresser and pull out a clean pair of boxers and sweats. Forgoing a t-shirt, I leave the damp towel in a pile on the floor—something that physically pains me to do—but my need to get out of the room and breathe some air that's not laced with Abigail's scent is too much to ignore.

The second I'm out of the room, my chest deflates and my shoulders lower.

But as much as my heart begs for me to turn around, or at least look back over my shoulder, I don't. I fight it and think of her.

You are not what Abigail needs. Not really.

Walk away, Elliot. Before you cause her even more pain than you already have.

13

ABIGAIL

My heart gallops in my chest as I lie there, still and silent, pretending to be asleep while Elliot takes a shower.

Part of me wants to glance at the bathroom door, to see if he shut me out, the way I've shut him out more than once since he brought me to the Chapel.

But I don't.

I don't move.

I can't.

Waking up in his bed, with him right beside me, was a shock. One I hadn't expected, not even after the way he comforted me last night. He was so gentle with me, handling me like fragile glass while my heart splintered over and over.

But it doesn't change anything—I'll always be me and he'll always be him. And the truth of it is, Elliot will never want me the way I want him.

Wanted him.

Because I'm empty inside now. Hollow and broken.

The bathroom door clicks open, and Elliot comes back into the room. I resist the urge to look at him, forcing myself to maintain the ruse that I'm sleeping.

If he catches me awake, I don't know what I'll say—what I'll do.

I hear him getting dressed, feel his intense stare lingering on me. But then, he's gone. And I feel like I can and can't breathe all at the same time.

I don't want to rely on him. I don't want to need him. But the dark thoughts circling my mind swoop in, increasing the constant heaviness on my chest, and I'm terrified—so bloody terrified—of what I might do.

What I want to do.

Rolling onto my back, I stare up at the ceiling, forcing myself to inhale and exhale slowly. Grief isn't a new emotion to me. I've lived with the pain of loss for over five years. But losing my father has irrevocably broken something inside me. Even though I knew this day would come, even though we'd both prepared for it as much as we could, it's here, and I'm not ready. I'm not—

Panic surges through me, coiling around my heart and squeezing until the edges of my vision begin to blur.

Breathe, Abi. You have to breathe.

I repeat the mantra over and over as I grip Elliot's soft bedsheets.

Inhale. Hold. Exhale.

Inhale. Hold. Exhale.

Finally, my heart rate steadies and my breathing returns to a normal pace. But I'm left feeling weak and unsettled.

I wish Elliot were here. I wish I was wrapped in his arms, listening to his soothing words. I can't afford to let myself lower my guard again though.

Because he might be here for me now, but he won't be here forever.

Despite all the tears I've cried in the last twenty-four hours, the urge to pee hits me and I quickly climb out of his bed and head into the bathroom.

My weary gaze lands on the shelf with all his products. Anti-perspirant, expensive aftershave, designer hair gel. All little clues to the lifestyle he leads.

Like so many kids in Saints Cross, Elliot is a trust-fund baby. Set to follow in his father's footsteps and become a successful businessman.

He might rule the halls at All Hallows', but I can't imagine him putting on a suit and playing chief executive of Eaton Enterprises.

After peeing, I wash my hands and tiptoe back into the bedroom. I have every intention of climbing back into bed, but my stomach starts grumbling loudly.

I don't want to eat. I can't bear the thought of it. But I need to eat. I know this.

As much as I know the sky is blue and the grass is green.

My eyes flick to the bedroom door and a deep sigh rolls through me.

Without overthinking it too much, I grab a hoodie off the back of Elliot's door, pull it over my head and slip out of his room to go in search of something to eat.

I've always found the Chapel intimidating. For years, I heard the stories, the whispers and rumours. But it was nothing compared to the first time I came here with the girls, and realised every bit of what I'd been told was true.

The Heirs hold more power than a group of eighteen-year-olds ever should. But that's how it's always been in Saints Cross. Their names mean something. Money. Status. Clout.

The Heirs are untouchable.

But as I tiptoe downstairs, it isn't the Chapel's ominous décor that has my heart racing, it's the Heir I know is somewhere inside.

"Abi?" The quiet desperation in his voice makes me freeze. Elliot sits in one of the wingback chairs, his dark and stormy gaze locked on my face. "What's wrong?" he asks softly.

So softly it throws me for a loop.

"I—I'm hungry."

"You are?" He stands. "I can make you—"

"You don't need to do that. I can get something."

"Yeah, not going to happen, Red." The corner of his mouth twitches. "You sit and I'll make something. Pancakes?"

"Sounds good."

The air turns heavy, something sticky snaking through me. Things are so awkward between us. But I don't know how we got to now. Too much has happened.

"Come on." He motions to the kitchen tucked at the back of the room. The Heirs have a private chef but since the girls moved in, he's around less and less.

I follow, keeping a safe distance between us. If Elliot notices, he doesn't say anything.

"Sit." He pulls out a stool and I climb up. "Did you sleep well?"

The question surprises me given we both know I fell asleep wrapped in his arms.

"Fine." I nod, barely meeting his stare.

Elliot's gaze lingers but eventually he lets out a

frustrated sigh and sets about gathering up all the ingredients he needs. I watch him from under my lashes as he adds flour, eggs, and milk to a bowl and beats the batter with a finesse that should surprise me.

But it doesn't.

Because Elliot is a lot more than the cold, icy exterior he exudes.

"Are you looking forward to seeing the girls tomorrow?"

I lift a shoulder in a half-hearted shrug.

"Things are different," he murmurs.

"They are."

"They're still your friends, you know. Nothing will change that."

My lips purse as I glance away, trying to swallow the ball of emotion in my throat.

"Abi, look at me."

I don't.

I can't.

"Abigail…"

Slowly, I lift my eyes. I don't want to but there's something magnetic about his voice. An invisible thread that tugs on something deep inside of me.

Even now.

Even after he rejected me and crushed my heart.

A beat passes, the air stretching between us. Until Elliot blinks and the moment dissipates.

"I'm fine," I mutter, drumming my fingers against the marble top.

He heats a pan and adds the batter. The silence is uncomfortable, but I don't complain.

I don't say anything.

I barely manage a thank you when he serves me a small stack of pancakes and pushes a bottle of syrup towards me.

My stomach grumbles, but a wave of nausea rolls through me, and I clutch my stomach.

"Okay?"

I nod again.

"Maybe just eat a little. Something is better than nothing." Elliot settles back against the counter, watching me. But the usual ice in his gaze has been replaced with something else.

"Thank you." I take a minuscule bite, struggling to swallow the sugary sweet pancake. But I force it down, knowing I need to eat something.

"Can we talk about it now?"

"About what?" The fork freezes midair, my fingers gripping the handle tensely.

"Red, come on."

"Please, don't call me that."

"You hurt yourself, Abi."

"And I told you, I don't want to talk about it. It was a mistake."

"Ab—"

"No, Elliot," I quietly seethe. "You don't get to ambush me the second I build up the courage to leave your room. I'm not a child. I'm not your problem to fix."

His fist curls against his thigh as he stares me down, but I don't break.

What happened in my dorm room bathroom is my business. Not his. I don't owe him anything.

A ripple goes through the air, fuelled by the anger bleeding from him. But to my surprise, Elliot backs down with a small, pissed off nod.

My brows furrow as two emotions war inside me. Relief... and disappointment.

God, I'm a mess.

I shouldn't want his help.

I *don't* want it.

"There's more if you want it?"

"No, I'm okay."

"I need to go out today," he says. "Will you be—"

"I'm quite capable of looking after myself."

He pins me with an accusatory look that makes me shrink where I sit.

Damn him.

I guess I walked into that one.

"I'll be fine."

"I can ask Millie—"

"Do not finish that sentence." I have nothing against Theo's younger sister. In fact, I like Millie. But I don't need a babysitter. Especially one, five years younger than me.

"Fine." His jaw clenches. "If you need me, I'll have my phone on me."

"Like I said, I'll be fine."

Appetite gone, I push the plate away and slide off the stool. "I'm going to lie down."

"You can stay down here. Hang out, watch TV…"

"I'm tired."

"I don't know how long I'll be," he calls after me as I head for the staircase.

I lift my hand in a small wave, acknowledging him but not really acknowledging. Because what is there to say?

I'm not his responsibility.

I'm not his anything.

And when his best friends get back tomorrow, I'm sure that will become even more painfully obvious than it is now.

I spend the day hiding in Elliot's room.

True to his word, he's gone for hours. By the time I hear him arrive back the sun has sunk behind the perimeter of trees circling the Chapel.

Part of me doesn't expect him to come straight to check on me. But a small part I've tried to hide, to bury, isn't all that surprised when his bedroom door flies open, and he slips inside.

"Abi?"

I pretend to be asleep.

"Red?" He moves closer to the bed, his fingers ghosting over my arm.

A shiver goes through me, but I still don't acknowledge him.

Because what would I even say?

I shouldn't be here. In his bed. In the Heirs' inner sanctuary.

All to appease his guilt. The strange sense of obligation he feels to me and the girls.

Elliot moves around the room, and I think he's stripping out of his clothes. Then the bathroom door clicks shut, and I can breathe again.

It feels like this morning all over again.

Him showering. Me lying here pretending to be asleep.

Minutes pass, each one more painful than the last. Hopefully he'll come out and leave. I don't want to deal with the awkward tension that exists between us now.

But when the bathroom door finally opens again, Elliot doesn't leave. Instead, the bed dips and he moves in behind me.

"I'm sorry," he whispers, tucking his arm around my waist, sending my heart into a free fall.

He pulls me closer, tucking my body into the hard lines of his, and I don't know what to do.

Because this... this isn't right.

He isn't right.

I need to move. I need to shove his arm away and ask him what the hell he thinks he's doing.

But I don't do any of those things.

Because for the first time in what feels like forever, I can breathe.

14

ELLIOT

The moment his name lit up my screen, I knew my day was about to turn to shit.

And it was already shaping up to be a shitshow.

Abigail was pissed at me. That much was obvious. I just had no idea why.

Surely, she wasn't pissed because I held her while she cried; that I allowed her to fall asleep in my arms.

Or maybe she was.

She doesn't want to be here. She wants to be alone without having eyes on her.

I get it. Her need to slink into the darkness unnoticed, to do whatever it takes to lessen the empty hole that's been left in her chest. But I refuse to allow that to happen, even if she hates me for it.

As much as I didn't want to leave her here, I knew I couldn't turn down the demand from my brother.

Life with him gone has been almost bearable. I can just about handle one of them at a time.

But both. And in the same room…

Yeah, I'd rather gouge my eyes out with a fork.

Sure enough, it was every ounce as bad as I was expecting.

By the time I returned to the Chapel, anger burned like a wildfire through me. My fingers cramped from the amount of time I had them fisted, fiery irritation prickled over my skin.

The only thing that made any of it bearable was the thought of Abigail being here waiting for me.

It's selfish of me to want her like this.

To use her to settle everything that's rioting inside me.

But I can't help it.

I tried to stop myself by marching into the shower instead of crawling straight into my bed with her. But it did little to take the edge off the anger and frustration they always stir up within me.

The second I stepped out of the bathroom, there was only one place I was heading next.

She didn't move as I lifted the sheets and slipped in behind her, and the second we collided, I relaxed. But it takes her a lot longer.

Long silent minutes pass as I enjoy the warmth of her body against mine.

I've never needed anyone the way I'm growing to need Abigail. She deserves so much more than what I can offer, but I can't stop myself. I'm falling deeper and deeper into her trap, and she has no idea she's even laid one.

Slowly, her muscles begin to relax, and I breathe a sigh of relief that she hasn't scrambled away from me and demanded to know what the hell I'm playing at.

She stays silent and unmovable, but she's more relaxed, accepting my embrace.

"I had a bad day," I confess quietly, needing to give her a reason for my sudden desire to hold her. "The only thing that got me through it was knowing I was coming home to you."

Her breath catches at my admission. It's the only sign that she's even heard me.

But as much as I might want to tell her more, I know I can't. She has enough of her own shit to deal with. She doesn't need me loading mine onto her shoulders.

"Do you want to talk about it?" she offers after a few more minutes.

Her voice is rough, making me wonder if she spent the whole time I was gone crying.

My grip on her waist tightens as if it'll help squeeze the sadness out of her. "No. I want to forget."

She clears her throat and shifts a little in my arms.

It's an innocent move—I think—but the second her perfect arse grinds against my dick, I have to bite down on my cheeks to stop a groan from spilling free.

Thinking unsexy thoughts, I try to lock down my reaction to her.

But it's hard. Really fucking hard when her curves are right there, and her sweet scent fills my nose.

"Okay," she breathes before falling silent again.

Tucking my face into her neck, I breathe her in, loving the way she shudders in my arms.

It makes me wonder how things could be if I weren't Elliot Eaton.

If I were just a normal boy without more expectations resting on his shoulders than should be possible.

If I had a normal family who would accept her, welcome her in as one of us.

If I had a future that we could carve out together.

But none of that is my reality.

My future is set and my family... Well, the less said about them the better.

But if I could have it just for a little while?

Pretend.

Forget about everything that is wrong with my world and focus on the little bit of light I have right now.

"Can we call a truce?" I ask, making her tense again.

"A truce?" she questions.

"Yeah. No fighting or bickering. Can we just... hang out?"

"You... you want to hang out with me?"

"Yeah, Red. Why is that so hard to understand?"

"I... I don't know."

"We hang out all the time," I reason.

"As a group."

"We broke into the office and stole Raine's file together. That was hanging out."

She laughs. It's like music to my ears.

"We didn't break in," I point out. "You had a key."

"Yeah, well. We still shouldn't have been there."

"Meh, don't you know who I am?" I tease, cringing as the words spill from my lips.

So much for forgetting who I am.

"Yeah, Elliot. I'm more than aware," she says sadly, making me feel like an even bigger dick for the comment.

Her pain ripples through the air, reminding me of why she needs the distraction as much as I do.

"What did you want to do?" I ask.

She shrugs. "I don't know."

"Movie?" I ask, mentioning the first thing that comes into my head.

"Uh... sure."

"I could order us takeout. We can lock ourselves away and just chill."

Finally, she moves, flipping over in my arms. Her breath catches when she discovers that I'm shirtless. Her weary gaze locks on my bare skin for a few seconds before she eventually looks up.

Her eyes are still dark, ringed with shadows. I might be imagining it, but I swear there is more to the darkness than just sadness.

Desire shoots through me and my eyes drop to her parted lips. My fingers clench around her waist, my need to pull her even closer is almost too much to ignore.

Dragging my eyes from her tempting mouth, I find her eyes. She's staring at me as if I hold the answers to all her problems, the salve to her pain.

My tongue sneaks out to wet my lips as the memory of her reaching up on her toes to kiss me at Raine's party all those weeks ago slams into me.

I wanted to kiss her back so fucking badly. Almost as badly as I do now.

"W-what did you want for dinner? Chinese? Indian? Pizza?" I blurt like a moron.

Her eyes shutter before closing entirely, severing our connection the potential the moment had. "U-uh...Ch-Chinese?" she asks.

Lifting my hand from her waist, I reach out to tuck a lock of hair behind her ear. "Whatever you want, Red."

She bites the inside of her lips. I'm sure she's stopping herself from chastising me for using her nickname again or trying to convince herself she doesn't want to kiss me.

The part of me that I'm trying to ignore really wants it to be the latter.

"I'll get my phone. You can choose what we order."

Throwing the sheets off, I push to my feet, keeping my back to her so she can't see how potently she affects me.

Shoving my hand into the waistband of my sweats, I try to discreetly rearrange myself as I snag my phone from the side.

Opening the delivery app, I throw it onto the bed beside her so she can make her selections. "No limit, order as much as you like."

I take a step toward the bathroom, but her heated gaze on my body gives me pause. Her eyes rake down my chest, before following the lines that dip beneath my sweats before focusing lower. I swallow thickly, my dick threatening to make another appearance from just her stare alone.

"I'm just going to take a piss," I say in a rush before darting toward the bathroom.

It would be so easy to cave to what she wants.

Honestly, it would probably be the best way to get her out of her own head for an hour or so.

But I can't.

If I go there... there is every chance I'll never be able to stop.

After lingering in the bathroom for longer than probably necessary—fuck knows what she thinks I must be doing in here—I emerge.

Her eyes immediately find me before she hands my phone over. "I've chosen," she confirms.

Ripping my eyes from hers, I take in what she's ordered, surprised to find a list of more food than I'm sure she's eaten in a week.

It might be positive thinking that she might actually eat a decent amount of it.

She needs it though. As good as her body felt against mine, it was more than obvious how much weight she's lost since her father passed.

Adding a couple of dishes, I submit the order and pocket my phone.

Jumping back onto my bed, she bounces beside me as I

grab the TV remote and open Netflix. "So what do you fancy?" I ask, scrolling through today's top ten options.

"Whatever you want. I'm not bothered."

Glancing over at her, I take in her pale face. My go-to would be some kind of action film, but I'm not sure that's what she needs right now.

Dropping down to the rom-com category, I scroll through until something familiar appears. Selecting it, the opening credits begin to roll.

"*Ten Things I Hate About You*?" she questions.

"What?" I smirk. "You said, whatever I want."

"And you chose this? Do we even know you at all?"

A self-deprecating laugh falls from my lips. "Do you want a drink?" I ask, refusing to go down that road.

"Sure."

It's not until I get to the door that I realise she's paused the TV.

"What are you doing?"

"Waiting," she says, looking over at me with wide eyes that for once aren't full of nothing but pain and grief.

"It's okay, you don't—"

"We're watching it together, aren't we?" she asks with a hopeful lilt.

A smile curls at my lips. "Yeah. We are. I'll be back," I say before ducking out of the room and jogging downstairs.

This whole movie night in my bed screams dangerous, but right now, I'd do anything to keep that lightness in her eyes.

The guys are going to be back tomorrow, and the girls will hurt me if Abigail is still drowning.

I grab as many cans as I can carry and head back up, hoping that a few hours of just being a normal eighteen-year-old will help show her that there is another way to deal with all this grief than to take a blade to her thigh.

When I kick the door open, I find her exactly where I left her with her legs under my duvet and her back resting against the headboard.

She immediately looks over and the second her eyes land on mine the most amazing thing happens.

She smiles.

An honest, wide, beautiful smile.

Something flutters in my chest as my own grin grows, and I'm reminded of just how dangerous this is.

Since the moment Liv befriended Abigail at the beginning of the year it was clear there was something different about her.

And whatever that something is has drawn me in like a moth to a flame.

15

ABIGAIL

I watch Elliot sleeping. The gentle rise and fall of his chest. The way his muscles expand and contract under his t-shirt. The slight flutter of his dark lashes. That little frown that seems permanently etched into his brows.

Elliot Eaton is beautiful. A devastatingly beautiful storm. One that I can't help gravitating toward.

I know it's wrong to watch him like this, but I can't stop myself.

He's so... at peace.

All while I feel like I'm breaking apart from the inside. Piece by tiny little piece.

It was nice at first, watching the movie with him. Pretending that nothing had changed. But as time crept on, the hollow pit in my stomach swallowed any sense of normalcy I felt, until I could barely concentrate on the moving images.

I forced myself to do it though just to avoid anymore of Elliot's unforgiving scrutiny—or judgement.

He's so good at controlling his emotions, but it doesn't mean we all are.

I scratch my arms, trying to relieve the itch, the constant feel of my skin being too tight. Too... everything.

It should be impossible to feel nothing and everything all at the same time. But that's the only way to explain it. Like I'm so numb I'm hyperaware. It's weird and I hate it.

I hate it so much, I just want it to stop.

I want it to be over.

I want to be the girl I was *before*. Before I kissed Elliot. Before my dad died. Before I became this... this broken empty shell.

A girl I barely recognise.

Pushing the covers off, I stumble off the bed and rush into Elliot's bathroom.

If I could just make it stop for a second.

I just need it to stop.

Frustration and helplessness build inside me, rising like a tidal wave I can't escape. Except the wave doesn't break. It just hovers there, taunting me.

I scan the vanity before moving onto the cabinet above the sink. I checked before—and I know Elliot emptied out his razors already—but there must be something.

There must be—

Bingo.

My eyes snag on a small pair of cosmetic scissors tucked away on the back of the shelf.

They're so small and delicate they're practically harmless.

I drop down to the tiles and lean back against the shower cubicle.

Just a little cut.

One little cut to get it out.

The hopelessness. The endless despair. The utter, utter loneliness.

Sliding my forefinger and thumb into the handles, I open and close the scissors a couple of times.

So tiny.

So harmless

And yet...

"What the fuck are you doing?" Elliot growls from the doorway, startling me.

"I-I... I don't know." My voice wavers as my hand hovers between my thighs.

I didn't even realise I'd moved it there.

"Abi, I swear to fucking God. Put the scissors down."

"I... I can't."

"Put. Them. Down." He steps into the room, taking every last ounce of air with him. My entire body vibrates as he glares down at me.

"Abigail."

The scissors clatter to the floor and my heart tumbles, free falling through me. "I—I didn't mean—"

He stalks toward me and crouches down, looking me dead in the eye. "What happened?"

"You were sleeping a-and I... I..." I exhale a shaky breath. "I needed to get it out."

"Get what out?" His expression softens. Just a fraction. Just enough for my heart rate to slow a little.

But I don't give him what he wants, pressing my lips together in defiance.

"Red," he warns.

Silence stretches out between us and I almost cave.

Almost.

"Fine," he hisses, fury flashing in his dark gaze. "Let's try this my way."

SAVAGE VICIOUS HEIR: PART ONE

Without warning, Elliot scoops me and carries me out of the bathroom, dropping me onto his bed.

"Wha—"

"Stay," he demands before marching back into the bathroom.

When he returns he's clutching the scissor in his hands.

"What are you doing?" I shuffle back, eyes as wide as saucers as he drops one knee to the end of the bed and looms over me.

"This is what you wanted, right? You want to hurt yourself?" His free hand grabs my leg and yanks. "You want the pain?" His fingers skim over my knee and along my inner thigh, fingertips dancing over the already marred skin there.

"Elliot," I breathe, my heart crashing wildly in my chest as he snaps open the scissors and angles one of the small blades toward me.

"It'll make it feel better, right?"

"Why are you doing this?" I cry, tears of anguish spilling down my cheeks.

My breath catches as he presses the blade into my flesh, holding it there. It doesn't break the skin, but it will if he drags it.

Do I want that?

Do I want him to do that to me?

"Just say the word, Red. Say the word and I'll give you what you want. I'll make it hurt. I'll make you bleed."

"I..." He starts to move his hand, but I rush out, "Stop. Just... stop."

"Stop?" he asks, and I nod frantically.

"Y-yes."

"You don't want this?"

"I... I don't want this."

I do. At least, some part of me does. But not like this. Not with him in absolute control and me spiralling into complete chaos.

His eyes narrow, the air thinning until I feel like I can't breathe. Like everything is about to come crashing down around me again.

"Elliott, please." My voice cracks and he blinks, the anger in his expression evaporating.

"Abi? Fuck." He drops the scissors, scrambling away from me. "Fuck, I didn't… I'm not… Fuck," he roars, slamming his fist into the wall.

"I'm sorry, okay." Panic floods my chest. "I… I don't know what came over me. You were asleep and I, I needed—"

The broken, desperate look he gives me makes something inside me wither and die.

I thought being rejected by Elliot after I kissed him was the worst thing that could happen between us. But the look he's wearing now comes a very close second.

"Elliot, I—"

"Just go to sleep, Abi.

"You think I can go to sleep after… after that?" Weak laughter bubbles up my throat.

"You should have woken me."

"So you could do what exactly? I told you already, this is my problem, not yours."

"You think I'd just sit by and let you hurt yourself again?"

I drop my gaze and shrug. His hot and cold routine is exhausting.

"Abi, look at me." He moves around the bed until I see his bare feet. "Red."

"You said you wouldn't call me that anymore."

He reaches for me and toys with a strand of my hair. "It suits you."

"What are you doing, Elliot?" I lift my eyes to his, ignoring the flutter of butterflies in my stomach. My vulnerability makes me susceptible to his words, his confusing actions.

The answer I want doesn't come though. He snatches his hand away and suppresses a sigh. "Get some sleep. We'll talk about this tomorrow."

We won't. Because I never want to talk about it.

Elliot moves to the chair and sits.

"What are you doing?"

"Sleep, Abi." He drags a hand down his face, and I hate that I'm the cause of his irritation.

But I didn't ask him to barge into the bathroom and act like my white knight again.

I didn't ask him for anything.

"Fine." Crawling under his covers, I roll onto my side and watch him across the room.

It's weird how quickly I've gotten used to him being here. Or me being here, I guess.

But everyone gets back tomorrow and the little bubble we've created will burst.

I know what I have to do.

When tomorrow rolls around, I have to leave.

I can't stay here and pretend that we're something to each other when he made it perfectly clear we're not.

It isn't healthy for either of us.

"You need to get help, Abi," he whispers, and I squeeze my eyes shut.

He's right.

Of course he's right, and I hate him for it.

But I can't do it. I can't talk to anyone because talking

about it makes it real, and I'm not ready to face the consequences of that.

I didn't do it again.

Elliot saw to that.

And once I go back to my dorm and classes start up, I'll be distracted. I'll have something else to think about.

I can get through this.

I can beat this.

But as I lie there with Elliot's gaze burning into my face, all I can think is…

I'm not strong enough to do this alone.

"Hmm," I murmur as something brushes my hip.

It feels nice, soft and warm and—

"Elliot?" My brows knit as I glance over my shoulder to find the boy in question pressed up behind me.

"What are you—"

"Stop talking," he grumbles, squeezing my hip gently.

My heart practically skips out of my chest at his proximity, the way he continues to touch me.

"When did you…"

"Get into bed?" he asks. "After two hours of trying to sleep in the chair."

"You couldn't have taken the couch downstairs?"

"Didn't trust you wouldn't try to hurt yourself again."

My stomach lurches at that but I manage to choke out, "Oh. We should probably get up. The others—"

"Relax, it's early. They're not due back until lunch time." He snuggles closer, and it is not helping the erratic beat of my heart.

Elliot's mood swings give me whiplash, and I'm not

sure I'll survive another day in the Chapel with him, sequestered away in his room. As if I belong here.

Silence envelops us and I'm almost certain he's fallen back to sleep. But there's no chance of that for me as I reflect on everything that's happened in the last few days.

I almost hurt myself again.

I would have if Elliot hadn't interrupted me.

And it makes me feel so ashamed, so weak to admit that, but it's the truth.

I wanted to feel that momentary release. That split second where I controlled the pain and it felt... good.

A rush of tears burns the backs of my eyes but I blink them away as I lie there, safe in Elliot's arms.

But a noise beyond the door catches my attention. Is that... footsteps?

"Elliot," I hiss. "I think someone is here."

"Not back until later," he murmurs again, barely awake.

"Elliot, I swear to God, I just heard—"

"Hey, fuckface, we're baaaaack."

"Elliot!" I try to twist out of his arms but it's no use. The door swings open and Theo bursts into the room.

"What— Holy shit. Abs?"

"Uh, hi." My cheeks burn as Theo frowns at me in bed with his best friend.

But it isn't his confusion that hurts my heart. It's the way Elliot bolts off the bed and herds Theo out of the room, not sparing me a second thought.

As if he's embarrassed to be seen with me.

16

ELLIOT

With my heart in my throat and regret poisoning my blood, I slam the door closed behind Theo.

My palms stay pressed against it as I hang my head and try to get my sleepy brain to catch up with my body.

They're back.

They're back early.

Fuck.

If only I knew...

If they'd have told me...

Shit.

I never should have let them catch us like that.

They've been trying to convince me to make a move on Abigail for months. Long, painful, agonising months.

Theo's going to be running downstairs right now to tell them what he just found and they're all going to think that their Christmases have come early.

I can picture Reese and Oak's smug 'I fucking knew it' grins from here. I can hear the taunts, the 'about fucking time' and all the other shit they're going to give me for this.

But I can handle my boys.

It's the girls I'm more concerned about.

I promised to look after Abigail in their absence.

They're going to think…

I swallow thickly before letting out a heavy sigh and resting my head on the door.

The only positive I take from Theo's sudden appearance is that I've managed to sink the boner I previously had nicely tucked against Abigail's arse.

I'm not even sure if she was aware. But waking up with her in my arms, feeling her hot little body against mine… fuck. It was messing with me, making me want things I promised myself I would never give into.

But something shifted last night.

Finding her with those tiny pair of scissors in her trembling hand. Knowing that she turned to searching them out instead of turning to me, hurt.

Did I want to hurt her in return? No.

Hell no.

Did I want to scare her? Yeah, maybe just a little bit.

She thinks the pain is going to help. And yeah, for a few seconds, maybe even a couple of minutes, if she's lucky, it will.

But then what?

She's still going to be left with the unbearable grief that kickstarted all this in the first place along with a heap of new scars and stinging regrets.

My skin burns with her attention, and it makes me feel like an even bigger dickhead for the move I just pulled.

I can only imagine what it looked like to her.

She probably thinks that I'm embarrassed or ashamed to be caught in bed with her.

That is so far from the truth, it's not even funny.

I want to protect her, not hurt her, but this is just another example of how I'm royally fucking that up.

Elliot Eaton, just never quite good enough...

My father's voice rings out like a siren in my head making me wince.

Self-hatred rushes through my system.

Why did I think that I could help her? I can barely help myself.

I should have known that this would all end in disaster.

Finally finding my balls, I inhale a sharp breath and turn around.

I instantly regret the move.

Abigail is sitting in the middle of my bed with my sheets clutched to her chest. Her red hair is a mess around her head, her skin is pale. But none of that really registers, it's the silent tears coursing down her cheeks that does.

I fucked up.

I fucked up really fucking bad.

"Red," I whisper, moving closer.

She closes her eyes as if just hearing my voice physically hurts her. "Don't," she whimpers. "Just don't."

"Red, that wasn't what—"

"I said don't—" she hisses. There's more passion and life in her voice than I've heard in weeks, and I hate that it's because of me.

I stand there frozen in the middle of the room as she glares at me.

She looks so tiny, so helpless sitting in my big bed, but at the same time, she holds all the power.

No matter what she tells me to do next, whether it be to crawl back into bed with her—unlikely—or walk out my own bedroom door and never look back, we both know that I'll do it.

SAVAGE VICIOUS HEIR: PART ONE

Her lips part ready to say something, but no words escape.

Lifting her hands, she angrily swipes at her wet cheeks, nothing but pain oozing from her. Her spine straightens, and I prepare for the blow that she's about to deliver when a pounding starts on my bedroom door, saving me from the heartache of what she was going to say.

It's wrong.

I deserve every single word she has for me.

But apparently, now isn't the time.

"Abi?" Liv shouts. "I think we need to talk, don't you?" she teases.

My stomach knots up painfully, if only this was *that* kind of situation.

They probably think I rushed to shut Theo out so he wouldn't see anything good. Unfortunately, there is nothing good here. Only pain, grief, and a boatload of regrets.

Despite her friend being on the other side of the door, Abigail's eyes never leave mine. "You need to leave," she whispers.

My heart fractures in my chest as I take a step back.

There's no point fighting, trying to plead my innocence. She watched my reaction, probably felt it even more viscerally than my touch in the moments before Theo's interruption.

I hold her eyes, hoping that she can read everything I'm feeling but even if she can, she doesn't respond to it.

"I'm sorry, Abi. I'm really fucking sorry." And with those words hanging in the air, I slip out of the room and come face to face with a three-woman firing squad.

"Fuck," I mutter under my breath.

"I swear to fucking God, Elliot Eaton. If you—"

"Raine," Tally hisses, cutting off what I'm sure was going to be a painful threat from Theo's girl.

"I haven't done anything," I confess, but even as the words slip past my lips, I can't help but wonder how true they are.

Something tells me that I may have done more harm than good when it comes to Abigail.

"Are you together?" Tally asks hopefully.

"No," I blurt a little too forcefully than I meant to, making all three of them frown in disappointment.

"But Theo said he found you—"

"It was a mistake. We were watching a movie and—"

"You were watching a movie? In your room? With Abi?" Liv asks, looking totally perplexed.

"Yes," I state. "What about that is so hard to understand?"

She shakes her head. "I... Nothing. Is she okay?"

My breathing falters as I realise that I don't have a decent or convincing enough answer to that question. "She's... She'll be okay. It's just going to take time. Excuse me," I say, slipping past the three of them.

I might be escaping them, but I'm more than aware that I'm about to walk head-first into the next inquisition.

"Can we go in?" Liv calls to me as I descend the stairs.

I want to say no. I never let anyone in my room.

It's my inner sanctuary. The only place where I can truly escape the drama that always seems to surround my life.

But right now, it's not about me and what I want or need.

It's about Abigail.

"Yeah, just... don't fucking touch anything."

"Could say the same to you, Eaton," Liv counters

before the sound of the door opening and then their voices as they disappear inside hit my ears.

I close my eyes, trying to picture what she's doing right now. Has she managed to pull her mask on in an attempt to hide just how much pain she's in, or is she falling apart?

Pain slices through my chest.

I know that what I just did barely scratches the surface of the hurt she's suffering with. But it didn't help.

I promised myself that I'd do whatever it took to help, to support her through this, and all I've done is make it worse.

"Ah, here he is. Mr. Casa-fucking-nova himself," Theo taunts.

"Fuck off," I scoff, making a beeline for the coffee machine. "It's not what it looked like."

I don't look over my shoulder, but I sense them moving closer. Their intrigue over the situation getting the better of them.

"Oh, so I didn't see you snuggled up in your massive bed with Abi wrapped up in your arms then?"

I swallow thickly.

That's exactly what he fucking saw and he knows it too.

"We fell asleep watching a movie," I lie again.

"Sure," Reese adds as a chair is pulled back from the dining table.

"You could have watched a movie down here. Or in her dorm room," Oak says. I don't need to look at him to know he's grinning like a smug motherfucker.

"Yeah, well we didn't. We watched in my room."

"In your bed," Theo tags on.

"Yes. Is there a fucking problem with that?" I snap, finally spinning around to glare at them.

"I don't know, is there?" Reese asks, studying me

closely, as are the other two knobheads. "You seem especially prickly about it."

"She's suffering. She lost her only living parent. Life has been shit. I was just— Fuck it. Do you know what? Think what you like." Abandoning my coffee, I march across the room and throw open the door to the entry hall so hard the door crashes back against the solid stone wall.

Finding my trainers, I roughly tug them on my feet before standing and combing my fingers through my hair.

"Where are you going?" Theo asks.

"For a run. And don't even think about following me."

"Jesus. You'd think he'd be happier after spending the night with a girl," Oak teases, making my teeth grind as I pull the front door open and get blasted by a shot of ice-cold air.

My skin immediately erupts with goosebumps, but I don't double back for a hoodie or a coat. Instead, I embrace the chill, and use it to push me forward.

Without another word, I take off into the morning fog. I cut around the back of the building and jog around the outskirts of the field that separates the Chapel from the rest of the school.

When I'm on the other side, I pause and rest my hands on my knees. My breath comes out in white clouds as my heart pounds.

Once I've caught my breath, I spin around and stare at the imposing building I just ran from. But there's only one place my eyes go to the window right in the middle.

It's the one with the best view of campus. The one I've spent hours gazing out of in the past few months, trying to get everything to make sense.

My breath catches the second I find a dark figure standing at it. I'm too far away to make out any of her features, but I know it's her.

My body knows it's her.

My heart knows it's her.

I've no idea if she can see me, but something tells me that she can. That she's looking right at me.

Hating me.

"Fuck," I breathe, lifting my hands to my head and tugging at my hair until it hurts.

All I wanted to do was help and take that hopeless look out of her eyes.

I failed.

But it doesn't matter because she doesn't need me anymore.

She's got her girls back. They'll help her through this. They can give her everything she needs, say the right words and do the right things.

And I just have to live with the fact that I tried and failed.

I failed the one person I've ever met that I wanted to be different for.

For her.

Abigail Bancroft.

I didn't want to be Elliot Eaton.

I just…

I just wanted to be hers.

17

ABIGAIL

"How was your trip?" I ask as the girls stare at me. The room suddenly feels too small, and my skin feels too tight. So tight, I press my nails into the fleshy part of my thigh, trying to ground myself.

Trying to stop myself from screaming at them all to get out.

"Abs." Tally moves first, approaching the bed with a wary expression. Like she's afraid I might snap.

Is it that obvious?

That I'm barely holding on? Fraying at the edges.

I shove down the destructive thoughts and force my lips into a thin smile.

"I'm fine."

"You're in Elliot's room, Abs," Liv adds, her eyes full of pity. "Theo walked in on the two of you—"

"It was nothing," I rush out. "We fell asleep."

"But you're here… in his room."

"I…" I hesitate, unsure how much I want to reveal to them.

The whole truth isn't an option, but I have to give them something or they'll never let it drop. Because they're right—being here, in Elliot's space, makes a statement. One they're misconstruing.

"I kind of had a breakdown." I offer them the half-truth. "He insisted I stay here until you got back."

"He didn't tell us. He said you were okay."

"I guess he didn't want you to worry."

"Of course we've been worried." Tally perches on the edge of the bed and takes my hand in hers. "We know how hard this all is for you. And we probably shouldn't have left—"

"I wanted you to go."

Needed them to, really. Because if they hadn't they wouldn't have insisted on doing this. Staying with me.

Suffocating me.

"Well, we're back now," she adds. "And if you're staying here we can—"

"I'm not."

"Excuse me?" Her brows knit.

"I'm not staying here."

"But I thought you said Elliot insisted."

"He did. But you're back now and classes start back Monday. I think it's time for me to try and join the land of the living again."

"Abi, there's no rush," Raine says, and I notice she's still hovering by the door.

She's the newest to the group though, the ways of the Heirs and their inner circle.

It takes some getting used to.

Only, I'm not one of them. Not in the way that matters. I never will be.

A fresh wave of sadness goes through me, but I lock it down, refusing to let it sink in its claws and take hold.

They're back now.

They'll check in on me enough that I can go back to my dorm room. Because one thing is for certain, I can't stay here.

I saw how Elliot reacted when Theo walked in on us—heard what he said. Why would I possibly want to stay here and put myself through any more heartache?

"I need some space. You know how Elliot can be," I say quietly.

"He didn't upset you, did he?" Tally asks, still clutching my hand. "Or try anything—"

"No, no. Nothing like that. He was helping me, that's all. It's been... a hard couple of weeks."

"I'm so sorry, Abi." Her eyes brim with unshed tears and I can't stand it.

I can't stand that every time they look at me, they see the same sad weak girl I've always been.

"Well then." I push the sheets back and slip out of the bed. "I'll get my things together and we can be off."

"Abs," Liv chuckles. "You don't have to leave right now."

I look at her with a sad smile, that breaks another piece of my already fractured heart and whisper, "The sooner the better."

It doesn't take long for me to get dressed and pack my things into the small duffel bag Elliot had Millie bring me.

The girls are quiet as we make our way downstairs, watching me with a mix of wary and confused expressions.

"Abs." Theo gives me a little smirk.

"Hi," I offer, trying to resist the urge to flee.

He probably thinks I'm a fool, for clinging to the notion that Elliot would ever return my affections.

"What's going on?" Reese eyes the bag slung over my shoulder.

"I'm going back to my dorm room," I say.

"You're... Does Elliot know?"

"He's not my keeper."

"Whoa, Abs, that's not—"

"Reese, leave it," Liv hisses, stepping up beside me. "We're going to get her settled back in."

"Oh, you don't have to do that."

"We're coming." She marches over to Reese and presses a kiss to his cheek. "See you later. Try and stay out of trouble."

He glances to the door leading to the hallway. "Maybe we should wait for him to get back."

"He left?" she whispers, but it isn't quiet enough, and a sinking feeling spreads through me.

Of course he left.

I don't hear the rest of their conversation, I'm too numb.

Too embarrassed.

They all know how I feel about Elliot. It's not like I've done a very good job at hiding it.

At times, during the constant teasing and encouragement, I actually believed that it meant something.

It hurts that it doesn't.

"Abi, you ready?" Raine asks and I realise she's moved toward the door. Theo is there too, pressed in close beside her. Her protector. Her shadow.

They're lucky. All of them. To have found such unconditional love. To know that they'll always have somebody there to stand beside them no matter what.

"I guess I'll see you around," I say to no one in particular, heading toward Raine and Theo.

"You make it sound like it's goodbye," Oakley jokes. But it's lost on me. Because we all know things are different now.

Even if they don't know the truth—and I hope they never find out—I can't go back.

"You're always welcome here, Abs," Theo adds. "You know that, right?"

"Of course she knows that." Raine squeezes his waist before joining me. "All set?"

I nod, clutching the life out of my bag strap.

Liv and Tally follow behind as we leave the Chapel and step into the brisk weather.

"Are you sure about this?" Tally asks.

"Yeah, I think it's for the best."

"Abi, did something happen? Between you and Elliot, I mean? You can tell us, you know? This is a judgement-free zone."

Liv murmurs her agreement while Raine studies me quietly. My gaze darts away from hers. She was there that night at the party when I kissed Elliot. She had a small hand in giving me the confidence to do it.

Guilt flashes in her eyes as she coasts her gaze over my face. But she has nothing to feel guilty for. She didn't force me to kiss him.

I did that all by myself.

Ugh.

"Nothing happened," I quietly seethe. "He felt bad you were all gone. I know you told him to look out for me."

"Abi, that's not—"

"It doesn't matter." I brush them off. "I need to focus on pulling myself together. Exams are coming up."

"Yeah, but there's no rush, Abs," Tally says. "If anyone has extenuating circumstances, it's you. Mr Porter will—"

"I'm fine. It'll be fine." I just need to focus on putting one foot in front of the other and everything will be fine.

The lie sours on my tongue but I swallow down the aftertaste.

We walk the rest of the way in silence. They want to say more, I know they do. But to my relief, they don't.

When we finally reach my building, I can breathe a little easier. Which seems odd given how much I hated being here before Elliot stole me away to the Chapel.

Tally and Liv go in first, clearing the way to my room. A couple of girls stop and stare, gawking at me like I'm a zoo exhibit. But it's nothing I haven't experienced a hundred times before. The constant stares and whispers. The judgement.

But I can be that girl again. I can slip back into the shadows, keep my head down and out of trouble.

When we reach my door, I inhale a shaky breath.

This is it.

The first day of the rest of my life.

"Abs?" Tally touches my arm, startling me. "You don't have to—"

"Yeah, I do." I offer her a sad smile as I retrieve my key and open it.

The girls follow me inside, hovering. But instead of that easy comforting presence they once gave me, now the air is tense, laced with an awkwardness that makes my heart heavy.

"Do you want to hang out? We could order pizza and watch a film?" Tally asks and Raine adds, "We could bore you with all our holiday photos."

"Actually, I think I'm just going to lie down."

"Already, but it's—"

"Liv." Tally shakes her head. "If Abi wants to rest, we should leave her be. We can check in later."

"Thank you." I manage a weak smile.

"You need anything before we go?" Raine asks, and I shake my head. "You know where we are if you need us, okay?"

"Yeah."

"We'll see you later." Liv and Raine move to the door. But Tally lingers.

"I know things are really hard right now but you're not alone. We're your friends, Abs. I know we're all wrapped up in the boys, but it doesn't change anything, not for me. You're one of us. You always will be." She pulls me into a hug, that I gingerly return.

But the second she steps away, the truth seeps between us.

"I'll text you later."

"Okay."

"If you need—"

"I know, Tally. Go." I flick my head to the door. "They're waiting."

She hesitates. And for a split second, I want her to take it back. I want her to insist on staying with me.

Because although I want some space, I also know the second the door closes and I'm alone, the dark thoughts will rush back in.

And this time, Elliot won't come to save me.

I sleep on and off all day, but it isn't the peaceful, restful sleep I wish it was.

Instead, I toss and turn, clutching a pillow between my

knees as I try to fight the urge to run into the bathroom and—

No.

I'm stronger than this.

Stronger than this poison inside me whispering dark awful things.

Another few days and I can go back to class, that will distract me. It will give me something else to focus on except the gnawing pit growing bigger and bigger inside of me.

By the time dusk falls, I feel emotionally and physically drained. Elliot is right—I probably need to talk to someone.

But I can't bring myself to do it.

I need to be strong. I need to pull myself together and do what I've always done.

Survive.

18

ELLIOT

It's still dark when I let myself back into the Chapel. A cold layer of sweat covers my skin, making my hoodie stick to my back. The warmth hits me the second I step inside the silent building.

It's been the same since they got back, thankfully. No one currently upstairs asleep has discovered my new nocturnal habit. And the longer that I can keep that up, the better.

They're already watching me with curious eyes, waiting for me to crack, or at least react to what happened the day they all got back from holiday.

But while I might look like I'm continuing with my life as normal after Theo found me wrapped around Abi like a snake, on the inside, I'm a fucking mess.

I want to say that I can't remember the last time I got more than an hour of sleep at one time, but I can. It was that night with her in my bed and her warm body snuggled against mine.

Ever since then, my head won't stop spinning and my body refuses to relax no matter how hard I push it.

I run every morning, train with the guys every afternoon before hitting the gym then after studying later at night. But none of it is enough.

Nothing I do can make my brain shut off and push the worry that nags at me every second of the day aside.

She's okay. I know she is.

She came back to school after the holidays, and she's been attending classes.

The girls have been keeping a close eye on her and keeping me in the loop. I haven't asked them to. In fact, I've done everything I can not to talk about her in the hope they'll all forget that I let my guard down and allowed Abi to get closer to me than anyone else has.

I also point-blank refuse to ask about her either. I have other ways to find out the information I need anyway. Sure, their insight is useful, but it's not the only tool I have for ensuring that Abi is okay.

Marching through the kitchen, I make myself a protein shake to set me up for the day before heading up to my room to shower and pretend like I've only just stumbled out of bed to get ready for the day.

I go through the motions of washing up and dressing without any thought. I'm nothing more than a robot, doing what needs to be done.

I should be used to it. It's pretty much how I've lived most of my life.

Shutting down and just doing what needs to be done is easier than thinking too hard about what's to come. It's easier to live in ignorant bliss than it is to think about the expectations placed on my shoulders by those who think they know best.

By the time I pull my bedroom door open again, there's movement and voices. Rolling my shoulders back, I make my way downstairs, pulling my mask on so they can't see how much life is getting to me right now.

Exams are right around the corner. Abi hasn't spoken a word to me since she slipped out of the Chapel while I was out, and my father and Scott are breathing down my neck, piling on the pressure more than ever.

With a sigh, I march down the final few steps and find Reese, Liv, Oak, and Tally in the kitchen. The scent of coffee filling the air.

"Morning, Boss," Reese teases, lifting his hand in a salute.

"Mate, you are way too happy this morning," Oak points out.

"You would be too if Tally did to you what your sister did to me last night."

I roll my eyes as Oak throws a croissant at Reese's head. "Do you fucking have to?"

"You asked," Reese smirks.

"Did I though?"

"Just stop, both of you," Tally hisses, looking exasperated.

"Do you want coffee?" Liv offers as I come to a stop beside the island, considering my options.

"No, thanks."

"You sure, you look like you could do with one," Reese says, his brows pinching as he assesses me a little too closely.

Oakley turns to me. "Or an IV."

"I'm fine," I mutter, taking off toward the front door to grab my coat.

"If you say so," Reese calls after me.

I pause out of sight, waiting to see what they're going to say now I've gone.

"He just needs to go and see her. She's doing better," Tally says, making my chest tighten.

Is she though? Or is she just getting better at hiding it?

Hitching my bag up on my shoulder, I pull the front door open, closing it quietly behind me so they don't know I was listening.

The bitterly cold night has turned into a fresh, sunny spring morning. If things were different, I might even appreciate how pretty campus looks with dewy grass and the first buds of spring poking their heads up. But as it is, I barely see any of it.

The second the Bronte Building comes into view, my eyes climb to the top floor, to the dark window I know she's hiding behind.

Abi might have turned up to classes this week, but she's been far from present. I've watched her in the class we share. She's looked like she's doing the work, but she's acting, pretending that everything is okay.

Just like I am.

I stand there for a few minutes, waiting to see if she's going to appear. But there's no movement or even a light turning on.

The temptation to go up there is strong, but she's made it clear that she's no longer interested in anything I have to offer her.

Ripping my eyes away from the building, I head toward the main sixth form building and then make a beeline for the very back of the library where I can hide and study. Or at least, that's the hope. I've barely been able to focus on anything for days.

The library is deserted, even Miss Sanders is nowhere to be seen.

It's perfect.

Stuffing my AirPods in my ears, I get settled and flip open a book. But despite having lines of text in front of me, things I need to go over in order to even attempt to deliver what Dad expects of me, I don't really see any of them. They might as well be swirling around the page for how easy they are to read.

Hanging my head, I squeeze my eyes closed and try to find some... Well, something.

I don't even know what it is I need right now.

But the second my phone starts ringing, I discover exactly what I don't need.

"Dad," I hiss the second the call connects.

"Well, you sound like a delight this morning."

"I'm studying. Did you need something?"

"Good to hear you're working hard and not expecting those grades to fall into your lap."

I've no clue where he gets the idea that I might even remotely think that. All I've done my whole life is work my arse off to try and be as good at everything as he thinks he should be. Nothing in my life has ever just 'fallen into my lap' as he puts it.

"I'm doing my best," I grunt, his voice making my skin prickle with disgust and irritation.

"Make sure you do. I'm not having you go off to Saints Cross U with anything less than your brother achieved."

I make some intelligible noise in response.

If anyone knows about things falling in their lap, then it's Scott Eaton. Everything he's ever wanted has been handed to him on a platter. And I've had to sit back and watch it happen all the while busting my arse to achieve the same.

"Was that all you wanted?" I ask.

It wouldn't be the first time he's called just to berate me about my life, but there is usually a request for something thrown in for good measure.

"Your presence is required Friday night for dinner."

My heart sinks further with every word he says.

"Where?" I ask.

"Come to the house for eight. See you then." And with that he hangs up, cutting the line dead.

"And what if I don't want to?" I mutter to myself. "Not that it matters what I want."

"Hello?" a soft voice calls before Miss Sander's head pokes out from behind a row of books.

I force a smile at her. "Good morning, Miss. I'm okay here, right?"

"Of course, Elliot. You're always welcome, you know that," she says sincerely.

"Thanks," I mumble.

"I'll leave you to it. I'm tidying up the historical section if you need me."

I smile again and she disappears down the endless row of books.

Ignoring the textbook before me, I turn to stare out the window. The sun has crept over the trees casting the entire campus in a warm orange hue. It should probably make me feel better, but it does very little to warm the ice that's filling my veins right now.

By the time I leave just over an hour later to start my day, I've still achieved nothing other than obsess over everything I don't have the power to change.

This is probably why Scott has always done so much better than me. He doesn't care about anything but his own gain.

If I cared less, then I might just achieve everything that's expected of me.

But I don't want all that.

I'd rather care. I'd rather hurt and experience life instead of just stomping through it and taking what I wanted without a thought for anyone else or how my actions affect them.

The second I pull the library door open to make my escape, I come almost face to face with the one person I care most about.

It's her red hair that catches my eye first. But it's not like it used to be. Instead of being full of life and waves, it's limp and flat.

Something in me dies a little more that she's still not looking after herself.

Abi is too busy looking down at her feet, attempting to hide from the world to notice me standing there right in her way. And it's not until the very last minute that she sees my shoes and attempts to dart around me.

Unlucky for her, I'm faster.

Without thinking, my arm darts out, stopping her from running away from me. She startles and attempts to pull herself from my grasp, but now I've got her, I can't let her go.

Pulling her toward me, I hold tight, indulging for just a few seconds in her sweet scent.

"Let me go," she whispers, still trying to fight. "I don't need—"

"Abigail," I growl, cutting off her argument and commanding her to look up at me.

But she refuses. Her head stays down, hiding from me.

"Red," I warn. "Don't make me—"

She doesn't let me finish my threat.

Her head lifts and for the first time in days, I get a chance to look into her dark and haunted eyes.

I knew what the girls have been telling me was bollocks. But seeing her pain staring back at me just proves that I'm right.

She's still not dealing with any of this properly.

It makes me wonder—and not for the first time—what lows she's been reduced to without me watching over her twenty-four seven.

Guilt threatens to swallow me whole that I've allowed her space to be able to hurt herself.

"Are you—"

"Abs, there you are," Liv calls, giving me little choice but to drop my hand from Abigail's arm. "I thought we were meeting out the front of— Oh hey, Elliot. You cheered up yet?"

I cringe at her question.

"It was cold and—"

"It's all good. Shall we go?" she asks, looking between the two of us as if she expects me to argue.

"Yes," Abigail says without any hesitation. She steps away from me and quickly turns her back ready to walk away.

"Okay, well. Have a good day," Liv says, offering me an unsure smile.

Lifting my hand to rub the back of my neck, I force myself to look at Liv instead of focusing on Abigail and giving myself away—not that I really think I'm fooling anyone with how I really feel about her.

"Y-yeah, you too. See you later, Red. Stay out of trouble, yeah?"

19

ABIGAIL

"Psst," a voice says from beside me.

I glance up from the curtain of hair shielding me from my desk mate and frown.

"Can I borrow a pen? Mine's decided to dry up."

My frown deepens as I try to place him. He's obviously in my class but I don't recognise him, not that I've been paying much attention since classes started back after the Easter Break.

Everything kind of blurs into one lately. The teachers' voices, the constant din of chatter in the hall as I move like a ghost from class to class, the sea of faceless people around me.

I'm barely going through the motions so it's hardly any surprise I can't place the boy currently staring at me with a mix of expectation and mild curiosity.

"So can I?" he whispers with a conspiratorial smirk, and my brows knit tighter. "A pen?"

"Oh, yeah, here you go." Fishing a pen out of my pencil case, I hand it to him.

"Thanks, I'm Ethan."

"Abigail," I murmur, trying to focus on the presentation.

"I know," he replies.

I cast him a furtive glance, a trickle of apprehension going through. But he adds, "I was sorry to hear about your dad."

"I... Thanks."

A fresh wave of grief rises up inside me, but I tamp it down with the breathing exercises I've been trying to implement.

My default setting of late seems to be to panic in the face of my overwhelming and tumultuous emotions. Like they're too big for my body. Too powerful to contain.

I used to do that a lot right after the accident. The memories of screeching tyres and metal crunching and rubber burning would hit me out of nowhere and I would become completely and utterly paralysed. My therapist back then taught me all kinds of breathing exercises. Exercises I haven't done in a long time.

They help a little but a different beast prowls under my skin now. One that requires more than just a few slow inhales and exhales.

"If you ever need to talk..."

I blink over at Ethan, certain I must have misheard him because students at All Hallows' have no interest in being my friend. "Excuse me?"

"It can help to talk," he says as if it's nothing. As if this isn't the strangest conversation I've ever had.

"You don't even know me."

"Abi," he lets out a soft laugh, "we've been in this class for almost two years. You're one of the smartest people here."

"I—"

I really don't know what to say to that. So I gawk at him, confused by the whole interaction.

Ethan flashes me a playful smile, one I'm sure I would recognise if it had been aimed in my direction before.

He's cute. With dark blond hair and blue eyes that exude that classic boy next door charm. And he doesn't look at me like I'm the weird, scarred girl with the tragic past.

So it must be pity then.

He heard about my father, and he wanted to take pity on the sad lost girl in class.

My stomach sinks and I suddenly want to throw my belongings back into my satchel and run from the room. From this godforsaken school.

But I don't, because that would only draw more attention to my way, and I'll probably end up hauled into Mr Porter's office. He's already tried twice this week to remind me that my in-class attendance isn't necessary yet.

He doesn't understand that I need to be here though. Even if I want to claw my skin off. Even if every time somebody looks at me or points in my direction, I want to grab the sharpest object I can find and—

No.

No.

I refuse to give into those thoughts, even though they constantly plague my mind.

Tears burn the backs of my eyes, but I swallow them down, trying my best to ignore Ethan's heavy stare. Because nothing good can come from befriending boys like him.

"Sorry if I overstepped," he says.

I don't reply. I'm not sure there's anything more to say.

He never cared to know me before today, so I'm not interested in him caring now.

I just want to keep my head down. Finish up the last few weeks at college. Figure out what the heck I'm going to do with my life.

And avoid Elliot Eaton at all costs.

I glance behind me as I hurry back to the Bronte Building. I've had the strangest feeling all day—the feeling of being watched.

Which, in some ways, I know to be true.

People *are* watching me.

It felt different today though. Felt different ever since Elliot chased me down and tried to talk to me, an interaction I'm choosing to pretend never happened.

But every time I turn around, I find no one.

Maybe I'm finally losing my mind.

It wouldn't surprise me.

With a frustrated shake of my head, I grip my satchel strap and quicken my pace toward my dorm building.

"Abi, wait up," someone calls after me, and dread pools in my stomach. "Abiga—"

"Hi." I whirl on Millie.

"Hi," she says, a little breathless as if she's been running.

"Were you following me?"

"What? No. I saw you and thought we could talk."

Talk.

She thinks I want to talk.

A flash of guilt goes through me. She's Theo's little sister and she's had it tough too. We have more in common than most, I guess.

Realisation dawns on me. "Did Theo and Raine put you up to this?" I ask.

"What?"

"Talking to me? I don't need a babysitter, Millie."

Hurt flashes in her eyes. "I... That's not... We're all worried, Abi," she admits.

"I'm fine."

Sympathy fills her expression. "I've said that a lot myself over the years. Doesn't make it any truer."

"Please don't do that. I don't want to talk. I don't want to bond over our trauma. I don't—"

"Okay, I get it. You don't want to deal with it yet. There's no textbook for these kinds of things. I just thought you might want a friend. A friend who isn't in the inner circle." The corner of her mouth tips a little.

"You're Theo's sister," I scoff. "I think that makes you part of the inner circle whether you want to be or not."

"So not true and you know it."

My heart tumbles at her words—the truth behind them.

"Crap, Abi, I didn't mean—"

"It's fine," I rush out, wanting this conversation to be over. "I have a lot of coursework to finish, so I need to go."

"Just promise me you won't do anything silly. I know it hurts right now but it won't hurt this much forever."

With a small nod, I move ahead of her and duck into the building, feeling the jaws of shame nip at my heels.

Does she know what I did?

Did Elliot tell her?

Or maybe he told his friends and Theo told Millie.

I'd like to think he didn't. After all, I made him promise that he wouldn't. But they're the Heirs. They don't keep secrets.

At least, they aren't supposed to.

It's all part of their unbreakable bond. The united front they rule All Hallows' with.

At least, it was until they all started to fall in love. Now they have the girls. Well, all except Elliot.

In a lot of ways, he's the most coveted Heir. Johnathon Eaton's son. Heir to the Eaton fortune. And one of Saints Cross most eligible bachelors.

Disgust ripples through me. I know the lengths the girls of All Hallows' would go to in order to secure a match with him. As if he's nothing more than a prize to be won. But it won't matter in the end what I do or don't think.

The second I enter my room, I breathe a sigh of relief.

Millie didn't follow so I don't have to worry about her watching my every move. And I don't expect the girls to show up this afternoon. Not after I told Tally early that I had plans to finish up my English coursework.

It was a lie. I have no plans to do homework.

I have no plans to do anything besides get in my pyjamas and climb into my bed and hope everyone leaves me the hell alone.

I wake with a pounding headache, hardly able to lift my head off the pillow.

My dreams were particularly dark and I spent half the night tossing and turning, imagining a dark shadow standing over me. Of course, there was no one there. Only the ghosts that haunt me.

My phone vibrates and I reach over to snatch it off the bedside table. It's the group chat I'm in with the girls.

> Tally: Good morning! Don't forget we're going to Dessert Island after classes today.

A small sigh leaves me. It's obvious she's doing this for

my benefit since she lives with Liv and Raine and could make arrangements over breakfast.

> Abigail: I'm not sure I can make it.

> Tally: You have to come, it'll do you good.

Like a slice of red velvet cake can fix a broken heart and make everything better.

> Liv: The boys have a thing, so it'll be girls only.

The insinuation stings. I know it shouldn't, but I hate that they have to point out things are awkward between me and Elliot.

I don't reply. It's too early and I really didn't sleep well.

Today is going to be hard work. But at least I didn't do anything stupid last night.

The relief I should feel isn't there though.

With a heavy heart, I sit up and run a hand through my matted hair. It's strange to know that if I did suddenly disappear, no one would mourn. Sure, the girls would be upset... for a while. But their lives would go on, their worlds would keep turning.

Mr Porter would probably force everyone to attend a cringeworthy memorial assembly and talk about what a quiet and focused student I was. But there would be nobody to organise my funeral service. Nobody to visit my grave and weep.

I'll be as alone in death as I am in life.

What a depressing thought.

It's that knowledge that makes me lie back down and pull the cover over my head.

That knowledge that has my fingers flying across the

screen to send Mr Porter an email to let him know I won't be attending my classes today.

And that knowledge makes the tears come so hard and fast I can hardly breathe.

But maybe that's a saving grace.

Because right now, it feels like that would be the easy way out.

20

ELLIOT

"Whoa, looks like someone has a hot date tonight," Reese shouts loudly when I march through the Chapel. Successfully turning all eyes on me, making me wince.

I don't want to be going out tonight.

I want to kick back on the sofa and hang out with my boys. It's not very often we get the chance now. There's always a girl or two hanging around.

The girls are great. Honestly, I couldn't think of anyone more suited to either of them. But that doesn't stop me from missing my idea of what this year was meant to be like.

The four of us against the world.

Ruling this school from the top with no thoughts about the future or anything serious.

I needed that.

I still fucking need that.

But with them planning lives with their girls and my father breathing down my neck about being prepared for uni, it seems that my dreams about what our lives were going to be this year were just that.

Dreams.

We might have the key to the Chapel but everything else is different.

Hell, I'm different.

I scoff, not wanting to respond to his stupid comment with an actual response.

"Does Abi know?" Oak asks.

The teasing over her might have lessened since her father passed, but it's still there lingering just beneath the surface.

I might be the master of keeping everything locked down from most people, but my boys... they see it.

They know I want her.

They also know that I'm not allowing myself to have her.

Sure, they all have some kind of understanding as to why, but no one really knows the full truth.

"Fuck off," I grunt.

"Have you seen her today?" Reese inquires.

Of course I've fucking seen her today.

"Uh... briefly between classes earlier, yeah," I lie. "Why?"

"No reason. I just saw her talking to Ethan Smith, is all," Reese explains, watching me closely.

"If you're trying to say something, do us all a favour and just spit it out, yeah," I snarl.

I don't react to his words, but on the inside, I'm fucking feral.

They don't need to know that though.

"I just thought you'd have something to say about her hanging out with another lad."

"I don't own her. She can hang out with whoever she

wants. We should probably all be happy that she's actually in school and talking to anyone."

"Didn't Ethan lose both his parents when we were in year ten or something?" Theo asks.

"See," I say through gritted teeth, "they have common ground. It'll probably do her good to talk to someone who understands."

I take off toward the front door, more than ready to get tonight over with.

"So where are you going if it's not a date?" Oak asks.

"Been ordered home for dinner," I confess, halting any more questioning.

"Well, I would say have fun but…" Reese trails off.

They all know that my dad is a cunt. They don't need all the truth to come to that conclusion.

"I'll see you all later."

"The girls are doing something, a yoga thing with Liv. They'll probably be back before you," Oak explains.

"Okay," I mutter as I pull my coat on.

So much for spending what little will be left of my night with them. If the girls are here, then I'll be forced to spend the evening watching them dry humping over the sofas. Either that or I'll be alone while they all lock themselves in their rooms.

Living the fucking dream…

Scrubbing my hand down my face, I step out in the miserable drizzle. It might have been a nice sunny spring day earlier, but the weather has taken a turn that matches my mood.

The drive to my parent's house seems to be faster than ever, and in no time at all, I'm pulling through the massive gates and pulling into the space that was allocated to me when I started driving—the farthest one from the house.

Killing the engine, I pull my phone from my pocket and unlock it. Without even thinking, I open up my message thread with Abigail.

We've only exchanged a handful of bullshit messages over the past few months but that doesn't mean I haven't done this exact thing a million times over.

Many times, I've even tapped out a message. Something—anything—to let her know that she's not alone. That I'm thinking of her, that I hope she's okay and not doing something stupid.

But I promised myself I wouldn't after she ran from the Chapel, silently letting me know how she felt about my reaction the day Theo stormed in and found us together in my bed.

She doesn't want my help, my support, then that's fine. It's for the best anyway.

I was getting too close. Too attached.

Her life is already hard enough to deal with right now, the last thing she needs is the pressure of everything I have to endure adding to her issues.

No one deserves that.

This...

I look up at the house. All of the curtains are open, showcasing the showhome-like home inside.

It's pointless and pretentious as fuck. The driveway is so long that no one walking past can gaze in and be impressed. The only people who'll see it are being invited in any way.

With a sigh, I take one more look at the small thumbnail picture of Abigail. She's got her hair down, hiding the scarring on her face as she peers around it at the camera. She's got a lightness in her hazel eyes that I haven't seen for far too long.

There was a stupid, naïve part of me that thought I'd be able to bring it back. That I could make her smile and laugh in a way that she'd be able to push aside the grief and pain for just a few minutes.

I couldn't.

I wasn't good enough at that either.

Movement in the drawing room catches my eye, and when I look over, my stomach knots as I find my father staring back at me impatiently.

Steeling myself, I pocket my phone again and push the door open.

The sooner I get in there, the sooner this will be over… I guess.

I have no idea what I'm being invited for, but that's not unusual. Dad hardly ever explains himself. He just dishes out the orders and I'm expected to follow, no questions asked.

But I was expecting—hoping—there would be more people here than just me.

As unbearable as his business dinners are, I prefer that than to having to spend time with just him. I'd do anything not to have to spend one-on-one time with my father. Even if it means enduring my brother at the same time.

By the time I get to the front door, the shadow of his body has vanished from the window making my stomach knot.

He's waiting for me.

Rolling my shoulders back, I twist the handle and push the door open.

"You're late." His voice rumbles around the cold, silent house making my blood turn to ice.

I bite back any kind of response. It's not worth it.

His top lip peels back as he assesses me. I'm wearing

Johnathon Eaton approved black dress trousers, a white shirt, and a black wool coat. I've no idea what he could be offended by, but from the look on his face, he seems to have found something.

But whatever it is, he doesn't feel the need to share. Instead, he spins on his heels and marches toward his office.

By the time I catch up to him, he's finishing a glass of bourbon and setting the glass back down. He doesn't offer me one. But then, he never does.

Probably too worried that it'll loosen my tongue and allow me to say what I really think.

Although... something tells me that he'd enjoy that. Or more so the punishment that I would bring on myself.

Stalking around his desk, he lowers himself to his ostentatious chair, rests his elbows on his mahogany desk and steeples his fingers.

A unique type of hatred seeps through my veins as I stare at him.

I'm pretty sure I'm meant to be impressed by him. In awe of him and his position in his town. I know almost everyone else is.

But all I feel for him is loathing and resentment.

He isn't a father. Not the kind that any child needs.

"I spoke with Mr Porter earlier today, and got an update on your progress as exam season approaches."

"I already told you how it was going," I quietly seethe, unable to keep my mouth shut.

"Yes. Well, forgive me. I wanted it from the horse's mouth. I need assurances that you're achieving as you should. I don't trust that you wouldn't try and flower it up for me. You're just like your mother."

My stomach knots as he mentions her.

She's the only bit of good in this house. How she's still here, fuck only knows.

Well, no. I know exactly why she's still here.

She's under his control.

She has no choice.

None of us have any choice.

It's Johnathon Eaton's way or no way.

"He assured me that you're making good progress. However, feedback from your teachers is that you could be a little more prepared for your exams. They have reported that your focus has been lacking in the past few weeks. Care to explain why that might be." He raises a brow, impatiently waiting for me to fill in his blanks.

"I'm fully focused," I lie.

"Your teachers don't lie, Elliot," he warns darkly.

The tone of his voice makes my skin prickle.

Thankfully, the slamming of the front door stops him from saying anything more. And not thirty seconds later, footsteps outside his office door get louder before Scott lets himself in.

It doesn't escape my attention that he doesn't knock, and that he's not scalded for it. If I were to invite myself into Johnathon Eaton's office, I would get a very different reaction.

He walks in, bold as brass, and drops into the empty chair in front of our father's desk that I've avoided.

I ignore any opportunity to be lesser than my father in any way, and that includes any kind of height disadvantage.

"I know you said to be here for eight, but we were running a little late," he explains after our father fails to chastise him on his punctuality like he did me the second I stepped into the house.

I just about manage to contain my frustration.

SAVAGE VICIOUS HEIR: PART ONE

This is how it always is.

Scott is the golden child who can do no wrong. And I... Well, I've apparently been nothing but a disappointment since the moment I was born.

You'd think I'd be used to it by now.

"No problem," Dad says. "How's uni been this week, Son?"

The two of them chat away about Scott's life while I zone out, wondering why the fuck I was summoned here. Well, any other reason for him to nitpick about everything I do.

"Right," Dad eventually says, banging his palms on his desk and standing. "We've probably kept them waiting long enough."

My brows pinch but I don't ask the burning question. I wasn't aware anyone else was here. I mean, I guess Mum is somewhere. Probably hiding out in the sunroom where she can usually be found tending to her plants.

When Dad gets to the door, he pulls it open and gestures for Scott to go ahead. I take a step forward, expecting him to let me go, but just as I step up to him, Dad follows Scott out, leaving me to either catch the door or have it hit me in the ass.

My teeth grind as rage unfurls within me. But it's not until soft female voices float from the kitchen that my hackles really rise.

Zoey appears the second Scott steps into the room and he pulls her into his side.

She smiles up at him like he's just hung the moon. I've no idea what kind of bullshit he fills her with, but they've been together for years now and it's never changed. Clearly, she sees an entirely different person to the one I've known all my life.

"Zoey, you look as stunning as ever," Dad greets

politely before turning to someone else. "And this must be Lauren."

The second he says another girl's name. My heart sinks into my feet.

I glance to the right, staring at the front door with longing.

How far could I get before they give chase...

"Elliot," Dad snaps when I don't follow them into the room fast enough.

Not very far.

The second I step into the room, my eyes land on a pretty blonde girl standing boldly in the kitchen.

"Elliot, this is Lauren. She's a friend of Zoey's. She's starting at Saints Cross U later in the year as well. Her father is an associate of mine and thought it would be fantastic if you met and spent some time together."

"Lauren has applied for the same course as you," Zoey adds.

I wonder if she had any choice over that...

Forcing a smile onto my face, I step forward and hold my hand out. I might have been blindsided by this, but I won't be rude. It's not her fault she's been dragged into the middle of this shitshow.

"Fantastic. There is a table booked for the four of you at The Manor. The car will be here any moment."

Lauren slips her hand into mine. It's warm. Soft. But I don't feel anything. Not a fucking thing.

"I've no doubt that Elliot will show you a good time tonight. Won't you, Son."

My head is spinning so hard that I miss movement to my left and before I know what's happening, his hand lands on my shoulder. My muscles instantly lock up, and before my brain has registered the move, my arm has lifted and I'm shoving him away.

The second I make contact with him, I realise my mistake.

My eyes meet his, and I take a step back when all I find is the promise of a whole world of pain if—*when*—I fuck this up.

21

ABIGAIL

"Abi, wait up," Ethan calls after me as I try to get into the building without drawing attention to myself.

"How was your weekend?" He pulls open the door for me and I gawk up at him.

"What are you doing?"

"I thought I was being friendly but let me guess, chivalry really is dead." The corner of his mouth quirks with amusement and despite knowing better, I find myself returning his smile.

"You weren't in class Friday," he says, not giving me a chance to tell him goodbye. Or tell him anything really.

"I wasn't feeling well."

"Yeah, I remember those days." He motions for me to go on in, so I do. Grateful to get out of the elements.

It feels as if the weather mimics my mood today. Thick grey clouds hanging overhead blocking out the early spring sun; the damp, cold air making it a little hard to breathe.

It's miserable out.

And misery loves company.

"Have you talked to the doc—" I cut him with a withering look and he falters. "Shit, sorry." He holds up his hands. "None of my business."

"No, I'm sorry." I heave a sigh. "It's just... hard. And we're not exactly friends."

"We could be."

"Why?" I stare up at him, aware that people are watching.

"Because we all need a friend sometimes. Besides, I know what it's like. To lose your parents."

If he thinks I want to bond over our loss, he's wrong. But I can't deny something deep inside me yearns for a friend. Someone who truly gets it.

It feels strangely wrong to be talking to him though. Like a betrayal. Which is silly. I don't owe Elliot anything. He isn't mine and despite once wishing I was his, I'm not.

Still, even though I know better, I can't stop myself from imagining how I'd feel if I found out Elliot had a new friend. Some pretty girl to share all his secrets with.

Pain locks around my heart like a vice.

"Abi?" Concern shines in Ethan's blue eyes. "Are you okay?"

"I'm fine. We should get to class," I say. Because it's the easy way out.

A distraction.

One I greatly need.

Ethan prattles on about his weekend, talking to me like we're old friends but I barely register his words.

Despite spending almost three days in bed, I feel more exhausted than ever. I look it too, the dark circles under my eyes testament to how weary I feel.

I clutch my folder to my chest like armour. I find it helps to keep my hands busy. Occupied.

Ethan moves ahead of me when we reach our classroom and opens the door again.

"Thanks," I murmur, slipping inside.

There's no sign of the teacher yet, so I hurry to my seat and try to block out all of the white noise.

But Elliot's name rings in my ears and I can't resist the urge to eavesdrop. Because it's Elliot, the object of all my desires. And even though he elicits all kinds of confusing and tainted feelings in me now, my heart is still desperate to be close to him.

To *know* him.

"Apparently he went on a date with Lauren Winrow."

My heart stopped as my fingers curled into my skirt.

A date.

He was on a date.

"Elliot Eaton doesn't date," someone else says.

It was true, he didn't.

At least, he hadn't … until now it would seem.

"My cousin Clara is at SCU with Scott Eaton's girlfriend, and she said that Mr Eaton orchestrated the entire thing. But they hit it off big time."

"Well, duh. Lauren is gorgeous and her father owns half of High Wycombe. They would be the perfect power couple."

"Abi."

I startle when Ethan lays his hand on my arm. He quickly withdraws it, guilt washing over his expression. "Sorry, I didn't mean—"

"It's fine." My smile is as weak as my resolve.

Because hearing Elliot went on a date, with his perfect match apparently, sends me spiralling into the black hole I'd worked so hard to drag myself out of this morning.

A date.

It sounds so incredulous.

But nothing is the same anymore.
Why should this be any different?

The girls insist we eat lunch together.

I wanted to retreat to my room. To hide away and not have to face them, especially not after hearing about Elliot's date.

But Tally met me outside of my two-hour class with Ethan, glared at him when he started to ask what my plans were, and promptly marched me down the hall like a child.

I love her dearly—love them all. But their overprotective babysitter routine is starting to grate on me.

"Since when are you friends with Ethan Smith?" she asks.

"We're not friends."

"He invited you to lunch."

"Actually, he didn't because you dragged me off before he could."

"I did not drag you and anyway, it's not like you would have said yes. Right?" She casts me a confused look.

"Of course not," I murmur, a little annoyed that she clearly has issues with a boy like Ethan trying to befriend a girl like me.

"Abi, I didn't mean—"

"It's fine. I know what you meant."

A frustrated sigh rolls off her making me bristle. "Look, you can be friends with whoever you want. I'm just saying be careful."

That has me on high alert.

"Is there something I should know about Ethan?"

"What? No. I just mean, you're vulnerable right now. I would hate to see someone take advantage of you."

"It was lunch, not a marriage proposal," I sneer.

"I've upset you." Guilt coats her voice and I hate that it's like this now. Me constantly second-guessing their motivations. Them constantly looking at me like they don't know what to do with me.

"Can we just not do this? It's hard enough being here without arguing with you." I go to move past her, but she grabs my arm, drawing my gaze.

"I'm sorry, okay. I'm a fixer. Something goes wrong, I fix it. But I can't fix this, and it bothers me because I just want to help. I want to make it hurt a little less, Abs."

The fight leaves me. Tally is a good person. An even better friend.

"Come on," she says, taking my hand and tugging me toward the cafeteria.

She finds us an empty table near the back of the room and orders me to sit. "What do you fancy?" she asks.

"Something plain. A ham sandwich or some chips."

"You need something substantial."

"I'm not that hungry."

"Abi." Her eyes plead with me, but I don't relent. Because if she gets me more it'll only go to waste.

"Hey." Liv appears and slides into a chair beside me.

"I'm just about to order. What do you want?"

"Chicken Caesar salad please." Liv flings her payment card at Tally.

She takes off toward the rack of trays before joining the queue.

"It's good to see you up and about." Liv lets her unspoken meaning hang between us. "How was your weekend?"

"Fine."

"Abi, you refused to see anyone or leave your room."

"I didn't feel up to it." I shrug, glancing away from her

to watch the rest of the student population go about their lunch break.

"Hey." Her hand covers mine. "I didn't mean to upset you. We're worried."

Sliding my hand away, I meet her gaze and let out a frustrated sigh. "I'm doing my best."

"Yeah, I know."

"I heard Elliot went on a date Friday."

Crap. The words are out before I can stop them.

One of Liv's brows lifts as she studies me. "Where did you hear that?"

"It doesn't matter."

I regret asking.

Regret giving her any indication that I care.

"What's going on between the two of you? He's extra grumpy than usual and you barely look in his direction anymore."

"It doesn't matter," I whisper, relieved when Tally arrives back with our lunch.

Not that I can eat.

I pick at my chips, remaining quiet as they discuss their weekend. The one they spent together, with their boyfriends.

I shouldn't feel as bitter and jealous as I do but I can't help it. The wave of noxious emotions crashing over me with such intensity I have to force myself to take a deep breath.

Before I realise what I'm doing, I bolt out of my seat, causing my test to clatter everywhere.

"Abi, what's—"

"I... I just remembered I have a thing."

"A thing?"

"Y-yeah. I'll see you later." Spinning on my heel, I

hurry away from them. But not before I hear Liv say, "Let her go."

That's all I want. To be given space. Time and distance. But her words still sting. They still drive another nail in our friendship.

I burst out of the cafeteria and scan the hall for my escape route. I need to get out of here. It feels as if the walls are closing in around me. Trapping me.

Suffocating me.

Breath, Abi. Breathe.

It doesn't work though. I'm in fight-or-flight response. Panic surging through my bloodstream, screaming and screaming at me to run, run, run.

A couple of girls stare at me as I stumble down the hall, my heart racing in my chest so fast it feels ready to explode.

They don't try to help me.

Why would they?

Finally, I reach the door and spill into the murky air. It wasn't raining this morning, but it is now.

Still, I stand there, sucking in big greedy mouthfuls of air as the rain pelts down on me saturating my hair and my uniform. But there's something grounding about it.

Something soothing.

"Abi?" A voice calls, and I blink against the downpour. For a second, I picture Elliot storming toward me. Strong, silent Elliot Eaton.

The boy I wanted to give myself to.

But it's Ethan who cuts through the sheet of rain, frowning down at me.

"What the fuck are you doing?" he grabs my shoulders, concern etched onto every line or his face.

"I... I needed to get out of there."

"You're wet through," he says. "Here, take my jacket."

"No, that's not—" But he's already shucked out of it to wrap it around my shoulders.

"Come on, let's get you somewhere dry."

"I... yeah, okay."

He hooks his arm around my shoulder and pulls me toward the boys' dorm building.

And despite the warning bells in my head—despite Tally's warning—I don't protest. Because if I go back to my dorm room alone, I'm not sure I can fight it.

This time, I'm not sure I want to.

22

ELLIOT

I stare in disbelief as Abigail allows Ethan fucking Smith to lead her into the boys' dorms in the middle of the day.

There are kids everywhere, not that any of them—aside from me—are paying any attention.

They're all too busy focusing on their own bullshit lives to care about what two of the quietest members of the cohort are doing. Even if it is unheard of for a girl like Abigail to willingly step inside that building.

Just like with the girls' dorms, members of the opposite sex aren't allowed. And yet she's following him without a second thought.

My fists curl so tightly that my fingers begin to cramp as they both disappear inside the building. All the air in my lungs rushes past my lips as the rain continues to drench me.

I shouldn't have followed her when I saw her fleeing from the cafeteria, but like with most things that involve Abigail, I couldn't stop myself.

If I were just a few seconds earlier, I'd have gotten to her first.

I could be the one leading her into my bedroom to comfort her.

Instead, I'm standing here like a loser, watching her disappear into someone else's room.

Images of what they could get up to in there, all the ways he could distract her from her grief flicker through my mind, only fuelling the already out-of-control inferno of anger and jealousy erupting inside me.

Rain trickles down my face as students continue to run back and forth, hurrying to congregate under the canopies around us, sheltering from the downpour.

I have no idea how long I stand there staring at the building, hoping that she might leave as fast as she entered.

It's for the best though. She needs to find a nice guy who can treat her right, who can understand what she's going through, and help her find a way through it.

That guy isn't me.

You held a pair of scissors to her thigh.

You are not the guy to help her through this darkness.

Not when you struggle to deal with your own on most days.

A pained sigh spills from my lips as I finally talk myself into moving but I barely take five steps when someone calls my name.

Looking up, I find Theo marching toward me. "Mate, you're fucking soaked. Secret rendezvous in the woods with your secret date?"

A whole fresh wave of irritation rolls through me.

"It wasn't a secret," I mutter.

"Well, no. We all know it happened. You're just holding out on giving us the details. I found her on Insta.

She's a fucking stunner, mate. You banged her, right? That why you're being all cagey and shit?"

I bite on the inside of my cheeks, hoping the pain will be enough to help talk me down from laying him out right here in the middle of campus.

"No, I didn't bang her," I hiss.

"Ah, she not the first date fuck kind of girl? That sucks, mate. You could really use a good shag."

"Why the fuck are you still talking?" I growl.

"Well, how about you start and I'll willingly shut up. I want to know all about Miss Winrow," he smirks.

"There's nothing to tell."

"You're such a shitty liar," he teases, making my teeth grind.

Despite wanting to argue with him, I keep my mouth shut and yank the door open, leaving Abigail and her new friend to it.

"What the fuck happened to you?" Oak asks when we get to our usual lunch table.

"Fuck off," I scoff, dropping into a free chair.

"He needs to get laid," Theo says, still not getting the hint that I don't want to fucking talk about this shit.

"Well, yeah. That's not fucking new, mate," Reese agree, making me wonder what I didn't just fuck off home.

Because Mr Porter will report to your father that you're not in class. That's fucking why.

"Did you see who Abi was talking to earlier?" Oak asks, really rubbing salt in the wound.

"She was talking?" Theo asks in surprise. "Is she doing better? Raine hasn't said anything."

"I'm not sure, but her and Ethan Smith looked pretty cosy earlier." Theo shoves me in the arm. "You listening to this, mate?"

"Abigail is free to talk to whoever she wants. I'm not her fucking keeper."

"No, but you want to be. Don't you?"

"There is nothing between me and Abigail so cut it the fuck out," I snap before pushing to my feet, ready to walk away from this bullshit.

"Sit down, Eaton," Oak demands before I manage to get away. "Theo, put a fucking can in it."

"But—"

"No fucking buts. Can we just hang out without having an argument for once?"

"Where's the fun in that?" Oak asks with a smirk. "Fighting with you is my favourite thing to do."

"No, it's not," Theo offers. "It's fighting with Reese over the fact he's fucking your sister's tight pus— Ow. Motherfucker," he complains when Oak's full bottle of water bounces off the side of his head. "The fuck, mate?"

"Don't talk about my sister's..." Oak shakes his head. "Just don't talk about my sister like that."

"He's right," Reese says, making me think he's jumping to his girlfriend's defence. That is until he says, "It would be all too easy for us to bring up Millie and her budding new friendship with Marcus Jones."

"Is that little fucker still breathing?" Theo seethes, thinking of his little sister's new friend.

"Fucking hypocrite," Oak mutters.

"He seems like a sweet kid," I say, happy to help push the knife in deeper after the way Theo's tormented me in the past twenty minutes. "She could do worse than losing her virginity to him."

The roar that rips from Theo's lips is inhumane, but I'm one step ahead of him and jump out of my chair a beat before he can grab me.

"I'm out, motherfucker," I say, tugging my wet bag up higher on my equally wet shoulder.

I should go home and change. But that would require me to walk past the Orwell Building, and I can't guarantee that I won't divert, and do whatever it takes to find out which room is that motherfuckers and drag her out. Screaming, if necessary.

Keeping my head down, I make a beeline to the bathroom instead.

Thankfully, it's empty when I walk in. And to ensure it stays that way, I flip the lock on the main door. Dropping my bag to the floor, I come to a stop in front of the row of basins and wrap my fingers around one of the bowls.

I keep my head bowed, not yet ready to look myself in the eyes. Instead, I allow myself to continue to be tortured by the images playing out in my head.

I've spent enough time in those dorm rooms over the years that I can picture one almost as clearly as if I was there.

I see him leading her into a non-descript room and her staring at him like he has the answers to all her problems.

He walks straight toward his bed and straightens the sheets before he pulls her down on it and immediately follows her, caging her in with his arms and ducking his head to—

"FUCK," I bellow, my first curling and before I can stop myself, I throw it into the mirror before it.

It shatters on impact, my knuckles ripping open along with it, but it's not enough to stop me.

"Fuck. Fuck. Fuck," I chant, punching it over and over as shards of glass rain down on the countertop, other smaller bits, impaling my skin, causing blood to drip from my hand.

"Fuck," I breathe, the adrenaline draining out of me.

Blood runs down my fingers when I grip the basin as pain shoots up my arm, feeding the beast within me that's always begging to be released.

Ripping my eyes open, I lift my hand, inspecting the damage. Pinching my thumb and forefinger together, I pull one of the larger shards out. The pain that shoots up my arm as I do so instantly helps settle me.

My heart races as temptation makes itself known in a whole new way.

Before Abigail crashed into my life, things were... okay.

I was... coping. I'd found some—probably toxic—habits that were making life easier. But then there she was, and she threw everything into a tailspin.

My coping mechanisms with other girls were no longer appealing. But without it, it left me craving something I shouldn't give into. A darkness that no one but me understands.

No one until her...

She gets it.

But I can't burden her with the knowledge of my weaknesses. I can't weigh her down more than she already is.

Nothing good can come from the two of us exploring anything together.

It would be toxic, and unhealthy, an obsession I allowed myself to indulge in. It would never end well because, despite our connection, we can't have a future.

She's not a Lauren Winrow of the world.

She's not the kind of girl my father wants me to spend my life with.

Yes, she might be Judge Bancroft's daughter, but that isn't enough for him.

It's better this way.

It's better that she's in a dorm room with another guy right now and I'm being forced to date girls I have zero interest in.

The rest of the day passes as a blur of nothingness. I might be present in class, but it's only in body. My head is firmly elsewhere as I hide my fucked-up fist under the table.

With no rugby training tonight, and no energy to call the team in despite Coach's absence for them to run drills and generally be the evil and twisted kind of cunt they expect me to be, I sulk off home to lick my wounds and torture myself more with what could be happening in the boy's dorms.

I make a beeline to the kitchen for supplies before locking myself in my room before the others appear. The last thing I need is the fucking Spanish Inquisition about my hand.

No sooner have I cleaned and wrapped it in the hope I can forget about the relief the pain gave me, do I pull my laptop from my bag and flip it open.

It takes me less than two minutes to hack into the school's CCTV system. It's something I've done so many times in the past few years, I could probably do it in my sleep at this point.

I go back to the time when I saw Abigail walk into the building and fast forward the footage of the front door, waiting to see her leave.

But she doesn't.

Hours of footage pass and she's still fucking in there.

My stomach knots painfully and my heart races as realisation settles within me.

She's done.

I fucked it up.

I let her think I was ashamed of spending time with her, and she stuck to her words and latched onto Ethan instead.

An unfamiliar pain shoots through my chest and I lift my hand to cover it as the footage catches up with real-time and slows down.

She's spent all afternoon in his room...

I want to look away. I don't want to see what time she eventually leaves and disappears back to her own room. But I can't.

All I can do is stare at the screen and wait.

And wait.

And wait.

Eventually, long after it's dark, I finally get what I've been waiting for.

A grainy yet familiar figure comes into view, and I finally get to watch as he leads her out of the building and walks her home.

She doesn't invite him inside the girl's dorms, instead, they loiter awkwardly outside before she gives him a quick hug and darts into the building.

My eyes remain locked on him as he combs his fingers through his hair and briefly looks up at the sky.

Is that the look of a guy who's just had the best afternoon of his life?

Or is it the look of a man frustrated to hell because he's had a girl in his room all afternoon and got nothing out of it?

It's going to fucking kill me not to know.

I wait another two hours before I make my move. I wanted to wait longer, but my patience is only so good when it comes to Abigail Bancroft.

I manage to slip out of the Chapel unnoticed and use

the shadows around campus to my advantage, making my way to the Bronte Building.

All day I've stayed away.

But I'm done now.

I need my fix.

23

ABIGAIL

By the time I get back to my room, I'm exhausted.
I shut the world away and go through the motions.

Shower. Change. Brush my teeth.

At least I can remember how to perform basic hygiene rituals.

Ethan offered to let me shower in his room, but I declined. The same way I'd told him no when he offered to take me out for dinner.

I have no interest in bonding with him. But something had broken inside me earlier. Another piece of my heart shattered.

I knew if I didn't go with him, I'd do something I would regret. So I went.

He didn't push me to talk or do anything really. He simply offered me some water, a dry hoodie, and space. I curled up on his bed while he studied quietly at his desk. Then when I finally felt back in control of my emotions, he walked me back to my building.

I don't know how to feel about his sudden interest in

being my friend but there was something comforting about being in his room. Alone but not alone.

My phone vibrates and I check the incoming texts. One from Tally and two from Raine.

I ignore them all and climb into bed instead.

It's still early, too early to be even thinking of going to sleep. But every day the claws of grief, of utter hopelessness pull me a little bit closer to that black, bottomless abyss.

I'm trying. Putting on a brave face and attending most of my classes. But I'm barely present. Even if I smile here and there, nod, and offer the occasional answer when called upon in class, I'm not really there.

Tears burn the backs of my eyes as pain rocks through me, bartering my insides. It's been weeks but I'm not getting better.

Time is proving not to be the great healer everyone talks about.

I'm different. Inherently changed.

Inherently broken.

And I can't seem to piece myself back together.

Maybe it's because I lost more than just my father that night.

I lost the future I craved. The boy I think I might love.

Love.

Ha.

What do I know about a word as fickle and fantastical as love.

All I know is heartbreak and loss and loneliness. They're my old friends. The place where I belong.

At least, that's what it feels like.

I wake with a start, that same strange feeling seeping over me. The crawling, lingering sensation of being watched.

My eyes scan the darkness, and something catches my attention. The click of a door.

My door.

But no, I must be dreaming because when the fear clogging my throat dissipates and I blink, trying to clear my weary eyes, there's nothing there.

Silly girl. You're dreaming.

I can't shake the hazy sensation of something being here though. The heavy weight of a stare as I abruptly wake from a dreamless sleep.

But it's my imagination.

It must be.

Unless...

No.

He wouldn't.

Would he?

I've heard the stories of Theo sneaking into Raine's dorm room. Whispers of the boys holding the master key to the building.

But it makes no sense.

Elliot wouldn't do that.

Not for me.

It was nothing more than a dream.

That's all.

No matter how much I wish it was real.

Ethan is waiting for me when I walk into class the next day. His smile does little to ease my mood though.

"Hey, I thought you weren't coming." He shuffles over to give me room to lower into my seat.

"I slept through my alarm."

The lie comes so easily, I don't like it. But I don't know how else to protect myself. If I tell him the truth, that I sat on the edge of my bed, staring at my bathroom, thinking... things, he'd probably report me to Mr Porter and Miss Linley.

I didn't do anything though. I didn't hurt myself.

That has to count for something.

"Abi?"

"Sorry, what?" I try to focus on Ethan, but my thoughts are too jumbled.

My gaze drifts past him to the door, the small window there, and my breath catches because I'm seeing things.

I must be seeing things.

"Abi, what's wrong?"

"I... I have to go." I shoot out of my chair and grab my bag.

"Miss Bancroft," my name rings out. But I'm already at the door, my lungs tightening, blood roaring in my ears.

Crashing through the door, I scan the hall for Elliot. But he's nowhere to be seen.

Because he isn't out here.

My eyes must be playing tricks on me, conjuring him from the recesses of my mind.

Of course he wasn't out in the hall, watching me through the window. Just like he wasn't in my room last night. Or any of the other nights I've felt someone there.

I'm losing my grip on reality.

Before I can stop myself, I hurry down the hall and burst out of the emergency exit, spilling into the murky morning.

It feels familiar. To be standing out here with rain pelting down on me.

Only this time, no one comes to save me.

I lift my face to the sky and close my eyes, letting it wash over me like a river. I wish it could cleanse me. Purify me and rid me of this dark stain on my soul.

"Red," a voice says, and I turn slowly to find Elliot standing there, watching me.

"You." The word leaves me on a sharp inhale. "It was you..."

He has been watching me.

"Abi, I—" He takes a step forward but I step back, the word 'no' forming on my lips.

"No. No, no, no, no..."

Everything comes crashing down around me. The fragile sense of survival I have left. The walls I've built around myself—my heart.

The pennies drop faster than I can process, and I practically stumble over my own feet to get away from him. Because I'm not ready to deal with the truth.

Not after everything that's transpired between us.

I take off toward the Student Welfare Centre but veer off down a less trodden path toward the old shed on the edge of the grounds.

The second I slip inside, I'm met with the smell of soil and dust. Discarded pots and planters line the shelves, a collection of rusty gardening tools hanging on a rack along the wall.

All Hallows' is old but this place looks like it's ready to crumble.

My uniform is a wet sodden mess again. But I don't care because feeling something is better than feeling nothing. And for those few seconds, standing under the rain, I felt... alive.

Not this permanent state of stasis I've found myself in.

I brace my hands on the worktop and inhale a deep

breath, trying to steady my racing heartbeat. But it doesn't work.

Instead, it builds.

Heart pumping faster.

Harder.

Blood pounding between my ears until I'm a trembling mess, my vision blurring at the edges.

Breathe, I order myself. "Just. Breathe."

But the panic comes in waves. Crashing over me. Building higher and higher until I'm drowning.

My hands slip under my skirt, finding the almost-healed scabs there. The first scratch stings but it isn't enough. I dig my nails harder, gouging them into the tender skin. I hiss, gritting my teeth as relief seeps into me.

"Abi?" Elliot's voice startles me.

He isn't supposed to be out here.

Yet, he strides into the shed and this time, there's no mistaking he's real and not some figment of my imagination.

"What the fuck?" he grits out, taking in my dishevelled appearance, my fingers at my thigh, the trickle of blood there.

His nostrils flare as he glowers... and glowers. A silent storm ready to strike.

I don't cower though. Not this time.

"Why?" I ask, and he frowns.

But I know the truth now.

Maybe I knew all along and just didn't want to admit it to myself. Because the truth doesn't change anything.

Still, I repeat my question.

"Why, Elliot?"

"I don't know what you're talk—"

"Don't do that. Don't pretend like I'm losing my mind.

I thought I was, you know. I thought I was imagining it. But it's you, isn't it? Watching me."

He stares through me, giving nothing away. And I hate him for it.

Because even now, he won't give me the truth.

"You should go," I sigh.

"You're hurt." His eyes darken.

"I'll live."

The air crackles almost violently between us. He's angry at me. For my lack of self-preservation, for breaking my promise. But I don't owe him anything.

I don't answer to him.

"Why?" He flips the question on me.

"Why?" Maniacal laughter spills from my lips as I clamber to my feet. "Because it's the only thing that helps. It's the only thing that gives me any semblance of relief."

"What, lover boy not doing it for you?" The sneer on his face makes me see red.

"Oh, you'd like that wouldn't you." I push into his space. "You'd like to hear all about how Ethan made me forget all my problems. How he fucked them right out of me. Would that make you feel better?" I shriek. "Would that appease your guilt? To know that I've moved on? That I don't want you anymore? Because I wish it was that simple, Elliot.

"I wish I could just forget all about you. But how the hell am I supposed to do that if you're watching me from the shadows? How am I—"

"Enough," he commands, and I submit.

The air is so thick around us now, I can hardly breathe.

Elliot's eyes burn into me, his presence taking up every inch of space. He's larger than life. A cold mask of fury as she glared down at me. But he's beautiful too.

Those dark intense eyes, his sharp angled jaw, and prominent nose. It isn't any wonder every girl in All Hallows' wants a piece of him.

The last Heir standing.

He slowly reaches for me, but I counter his touch, knocking his hand away.

"Don't."

"Abi..."

"No, Elliot. You don't get to do that. You don't get to care. Not after you went on a date with Lauren Winrow."

His brows bunch, confusion flitting across his expression. "You know about that?"

"Everyone knows!"

"It's not what it looks like," he says quietly.

"I don't care. But I can't do this. I don't know why you're watching me, sneaking into my room at night, checking up on me in class... but it has to stop. It's confusing and it isn't fair. You made your choice."

And it wasn't me. I swallow the words, refusing to give them life.

"You think I chose—" He stops himself, reaching for me again. "Lauren isn't important. You are. And I need you to stop hurting yourself, Red."

"Why?" My voice cracks, my entire body trembling.

There's something about the way he watches me. Something different.

"Because despite what you think, I care, Abi. I fucking care, okay. But it doesn't change anything. It doesn't..." He trails off, not giving me the rest of his words.

A fresh wave of frustration bubbles inside of me. Because I don't understand. Not really.

All I know is I feel so hopeless, so lost and alone. And Elliot is standing here looking at me like I'm precious. Like he cares. Like he wants to fix this.

Fix me.

If I didn't know better, I'd go as far as to say he's looking at me like I'm his.

24

ELLIOT

My heart races as I stare at her.

My body begs for me to do something. To take what I've been craving for weeks.

Months.

But I can't.

You've just confessed that you care...

Make the move.

Every single muscle in my body is pulled tight as I battle with myself.

All the while, Abigail stares at me with her broken, shadowed eyes. But there's more than just a girl who's lost in her grief staring back at me right now.

There's a girl who's desperate to get out of her own head. To forget about reality and let go, if only for a few minutes.

No words are said between us, my confession hangs in the air, taunting me. Reminding me of all the reasons why I shouldn't have said the words out loud.

But they're true.

So painfully fucking true.

"It doesn't what?" she finally asks, curious about where I was going.

Raking my bottom lip through my teeth, I give her the truth.

"It doesn't matter."

Her eyes narrow a beat before her lips thin. The second she stands taller, her shoulders squaring, I know I'm in trouble.

"Do you know what I think?" she asks, although she doesn't actually give me time to respond. "Everyone around school thinks you're this larger than life, scared of nothing Heir. But that's not true, is it?

"Red, I—" I start in the hope of calming her down.

With every word she says, I can practically see the anger bubbling up in her green eyes.

The shadows from before are beginning to disappear as the blaze of fury swallows them.

"You're nothing but a coward, Elliot Eaton."

My lips part, but she's not done.

She's far from fucking done.

"You're a coward who can't admit what he feels, what he really wants.

"Instead you hide in the darkness, in the shadows, telling yourself that it's enough. Letting it satisfy your guilt, or whatever the hell you're feeling.

"But if you really were the person they all think you are," she sneers, waving her hand in the direction of the school campus behind me. "Then you wouldn't be sneaking around, slipping into my room in the middle of the night, watching me through windows, following me down to this shed.

"What is it you really want here, Elliot, because I'm struggling to—"

I surge forward, cutting off whatever she was about to say as I get in her space.

Her breasts brush my chest and her warm breath rushes over my face as she stares up at me. That soft pink mouth of hers parts in shock before her tongue sneaks out, licking across her full, tempting bottom lip.

The movement of her chest becomes more and more erratic as my eyes jump back up their hers.

The air crackles between us as my fists clench at my sides.

Her sweet scent fills my nose and I find myself leaning closer still, my eyes dropping to her lips again.

She's right there. Merely a centimetre away from me. I could take exactly what I've been imagining all these months. Get another taste of the girl who's been driving me crazy with her less than discreet glances in my direction.

You're not good enough for her...

The pull I feel toward her steals the space between us until the heat of her lips burns mine.

She's too good to be pulled into your bullshit life.

"Fuck," I breathe, closing my eyes and taking a step back.

I expect her to shout at me, hit me, anything to punish me for what I just did.

But that's not what happens.

Instead, she laughs.

The sound drips through my veins like acid making my teeth grind as I find her eyes again.

"See," she says through her laughter. "Coward. You make out like you—"

The red haze descends and she gasps as I reach out, wrapping my hand around her throat and pin her back against the rough wall behind her.

Her throat ripples as she tries to swallow, shocked by my sudden move as I get right in her face. "Are these the actions of a coward, Red?" I sneer, my nose a hairsbreadth from touching hers.

She whimpers, fucking whimpers and it turns my blood to lava.

Holy shit.

She likes it.

I flex my fingers, cutting off her air supply.

Her eyes widen. But not in fear, in interest, as another needy whimper spills from her lips.

"Fuck," I breathe, pulling back enough so that I can look at her.

"Please," she whispers.

"Red," I warn but it doesn't have the effect I need it to.

Instead, she pushes the bottom half of her body from the wall.

My gaze drops to the single trail of blood that's tracking down her thigh from where she's hurt herself again.

Before I know what I'm doing, I have her skirt lifting and I'm staring at the wound she's opened up. "You hurt yourself again," I muse, my eyes locked on the red and angry skin around the wound.

Tucking her skirt up, I lower my hand to the trail of blood and swipe it up with my pointer fingers.

"Oh my God," she gasps as I lift it between us.

"You shouldn't be making yourself bleed, Red. Your skin is too fucking beautiful."

Her eyes widen as I move my finger toward my lip.

My grip on her throat relaxes as I push the digit past my lips and suck.

"Holy crap," she whispers, her hips jolting forward again.

I stare at her, wondering how a girl who's so sweet and innocent on the surface but is so dark and depraved under the surface.

A girl who might just understand me.

"More," she breathes, making something unfurl within me.

"You cut for release." It's not a question.

It's a statement.

One I understand all too well.

She nods once, regret and shame glittering in her eyes.

"What are you doing?" she asks when I move closer, pressing my thigh between hers, putting pressure on her pussy. "Oh God."

Just as I thought.

I press harder against her, earning a moan to spill from her lips before I press my thumb into the freshly opened wound.

"Feel that?"

She nods eagerly, her pupils dilating as the pain and pleasure mix.

"You want more?"

She nods again. Her hips grinding against my thigh.

Desire like I've never experienced before shoots straight to my dick, making it ache with need.

"Shit, Red. Do you have any idea how fucking hot you look right now?" I groan, letting her take what she needs from me.

Her head falls back against the rough wall as she finds her rhythm. Her eyelids lower, threatening to sever our connection.

"Eyes, Red. They need to be on me. I want you to know who's giving you this release."

I have no idea if she's willingly following orders, or if my demand shocks her so much that her eyes widen.

"That's it. Use me, Red. Be a good girl and find the release you need."

The heat of her pussy burns through her knickers and my trousers.

The need to replace my thigh with my fingers is so fucking strong. But I know that if I do that. If I feel how wet she is right now then I won't be able to stop.

"Oh God," she whimpers, the blush on her cheeks spreading down her throat and disappearing beneath her school shirt.

"That's it. I bet you're so beautiful when you come, Red."

I press my thumb into her wound harder as my hand on her hip drags her closer, upping the friction on her clit.

"Oh God. Oh God," she whimpers as her release approaches.

The greenish-brown flecks of her eyes are almost completely black.

"Did he make you feel this good?" The words slip free, and I hate myself for asking the second they roll off my tongue.

She doesn't react, and I pray that she's already too far gone to have heard them.

The last thing I need is her to know just how fucking jealous of that motherfucker I really am.

She spent hours in his dorm room yesterday.

But right now, she's mine.

Fuck. I want to sing it from the rooftops.

But I can't.

This stolen moment is purely for us.

For her.

No one can know.

It would be too dangerous if the outside world discovered this... Whatever this is.

"Elliot," she whimpers, her breathing erratic as she makes the final climb to the edge.

"That's it. Let go for me, Red. Let go of everything and just feel."

"Yes. Yes. Elliot," she whimpers as her body locks up, pleasure saturating her limbs.

Her movements against my thigh jerks as she falls.

And I was right.

It is fucking beautiful.

So fucking beautiful and everything I hoped it would be.

Finally, she loses her fight with keeping her eyes open and her lids lower.

The second they do, coldness washes through me.

Once I'm confident she's ridden out her high, I take a step back, letting her skirt fall back into place.

Lifting my hand between us, I stare at the blood coating my thumb.

And that's how she finds me when her eyes open again.

"Elliot," she warns. But I can't help myself. My need to taste her is too strong.

She reacts as viscerally to me cleaning the blood from my thumb as she did the first time.

"Next time you feel the need to hurt yourself," I warn. "I want you to call me. I don't care what time it is. Where you are. I want to be the one to give you the release you crave."

She shakes her head, refusing my demand.

"It wasn't a suggestion, Red. You're not hurting yourself again. And if I catch you—"

"What?" She snaps, pushing from the wall, the after-effects from her release clearly long gone. "If I hurt myself again then you'll what?"

My teeth grind and my jaw pops as the image of her in my bathroom with a pair of scissors in her hand not so long ago fills my head.

"How about we don't find out the answer to that," I suggest, reaching down to rearrange myself.

Her eyes follow as I adjust my hard on.

I have no idea what it is about that move that pushes her over the edge after what we've just done but she stumbles forward toward the door, her eyes wide with... fear? Regret?

Shame?

I don't know what it is, but I don't fucking like it.

"Red, wait," I say, spinning around but I'm too late, she's already got the door open, ready to escape.

"No, Elliot. This was a mistake. Whatever this was... It shouldn't have happened. Whatever you're doing with me... It's over.

"I'm nothing to you, remember. Just a girl you're ashamed to have in your bed. A girl you've been stuck with due to our friends."

"That's bullshit and you know it," I argue.

She's already turned around, cutting off any kind of connection we've shared in here.

"It's over, Elliot," she whispers. "We're done. You're not responsible for me, you never have been."

And with those ominous words hanging in the air between us, she takes off.

"Fuck," I breathe. "Fuck. Fuck. FUCK."

My fist collides with the rough wooden wall, the cuts from the mirror opening back up.

Pain shoots up my arm, but I embrace it. Embrace the release. Just like Abigail did not so long again.

Leaning forward, I rest my forehead against the wall

and close my eyes, remembering how she looked when she fell.

"This isn't over, Red," I breathe. "This is far from fucking over."

25

ABIGAIL

I don't know how it happened, but as the week went on, Ethan became a constant in my day.

He walked me to class. Insisted on joining me for lunch. He even asked me to hang out with him after class.

I said no, repeatedly. But it didn't deter him from asking.

I spent less and less time with the girls, avoiding their texts and calls and attempts at inviting me to sit with them at lunch. It was easier that way. Easier to staunch the pain.

Easier to avoid Elliot.

Not that he hasn't done an excellent job of that all on his own.

I've barely seen him around college, and if I have, I quickly walked in the other direction.

I'm not ready to deal with him—what happened between us.

Even if I can't get it out of my head.

He touched me. He tasted my blood. Pinned me against the dirty wall of the abandoned… And I liked it.

I more than liked it, it made me feel something.

But it was wrong. Sordid and depraved.

I've heard the stories. Whispers of the dungeon below the Chapel, the things that go on there. Or at least, did before Reese, Oakley, and Theo all fell in love.

Girls at All Hallows' wear their illicit night with an Heir like a badge of honour.

But the noise surrounding Elliot is quieter. Girls want their pound of Elliot Eaton's flesh, but the jury is out on how many have been successful.

A streak of jealousy runs hot through my veins. The idea of him with anyone else makes my stomach curdle.

I have to constantly remind myself he isn't mine.

Even if he touched me like I was.

I shake my head, forcing the thoughts out as I cut through the post-lunch crush to get to class.

It's Friday, and I'll be glad when I can retreat to my room and lock the world away.

"Abi, wait up," Tally calls after me.

Reluctantly, I slow, waiting for her to catch up. "What's up?" I ask, hoping she won't start quizzing me again.

"I've barely seen you all week." Sadness washes over her. "If I didn't know better, I'd say you are avoiding me."

"I'm not."

"So where have you been? You won't sit with us at lunch. You've always got a reason you can't come out with us." She takes her hand in mine and gives me a soft smile. "I know things are hard, but we're worried. I'm worried."

"I'm fine. Just trying to keep myself busy."

"But I miss you."

Guilt strikes hard and fast, making me flinch a little. "I miss you too. But things are different now." My eyes shutter as I try to fight the surge of sadness that crashes into me.

"What do you mean?"

"We only have a few weeks of college left. Then it'll be the summer."

"So?" Her eyes crinkle in confusion.

"You all have so much to look forward to, Tally. And I'm happy for you, I am. But I can't—" The words get stuck so I swallow them down.

I don't want to have this conversation. Not when I'm barely clinging on by a thread as it is.

Tally is the closest thing I've ever had to a best friend. But the secrets between us make her feel like a stranger again. It isn't her fault, that blame lies with me. I know that. Still, I don't know how to let her in. Not when she has everything she's ever wanted. Oakley will give her the world and more and I'm happy for her, I am.

But I'm not that girl.

I'm not the girl who will inspire rich entitled spoiled boys to renovate old buildings into a fancy new student welfare centre or change his manwhorish, drug-taking ways.

I'm not that girl.

And my place isn't among Tally and her boyfriend and his best friends.

I realise now, it was a fool's wish to ever think it was.

A small part of Elliot might want me. But he'll never want me the way I want him.

A sinking feeling spreads through me. I don't know what Tally sees written all over my face, but it makes her wrap me into a hug.

"Oh, Abs. I wish you could see yourself the way I see you. You're so strong, babe. And I don't care what you think, you are one of us."

Tears well in my eyes but I tamp down the emotion.

Because I can't fall apart again. Not here. Not in front of her.

If I'm going to survive the rest of the year at All Hallows' with my secrets intact, I have to do better.

Because if she ever found out.

It doesn't bear thinking about.

It's bad enough that Elliot knows. That he—

No.

I will not keep thinking about him. About how it felt to let him do those things to me.

A shudder goes through me and Tally frowns again.

"Abs?"

"I'm fine." I muster the best smile I can.

"I know you'll probably say no, but I wondered if you want to come over later and hang out?"

"Come over? Where—"

"The Chapel."

"I don't think so."

"But the boys will be at some dinner thing with their dads. We'll have the place to ourselves, and we've promised Millie a pyjama party. It won't be the same without you." She pouts and I almost feel myself relenting. Because it's Tally and she's my friend, and I want so desperately to cling to the fragile threads of our friendship.

"Please." She gives my hand a little tug. "Don't make me cause a scene because I will." Her eyes twinkle but I don't share her amusement.

Still, I find myself saying, "Okay."

"Really? You'll come?" Tally's face lights up.

"Yeah. For a little while."

At least if I'm with them, I'll be distracted.

Saying yes has everything to do with making Tally and the girls happy.

And absolutely nothing, *nothing* to do with the fact I

might catch a glimpse of a certain boy I know I need to stay away from.

"You came." Tally pulls me into a big hug as she ushers me into the Chapel.

I shuck out of my coat and let her hang it on the rack. "Sorry I'm late."

"Don't be. We're still arguing over what to order. Raine and Liv want pizza. Mills and me fancy Chinese. We figured we'd wait for you to decide." She stares at me with gentle anticipation.

"Pizza sounds good." It doesn't, but I don't have the heart to tell her I barely have an appetite these days. It would only worry her, and I don't want to deal with their mothering.

Not tonight when it took everything inside me to force myself to come.

"Look who's here." Tally calls as she leads me into the living area.

The Chapel is an open-plan in style but despite its haunting eerie vibes, I've always found it to be a beautiful space.

The girls all stop mid-conversation and smile over at me.

"You came." Millie jumps up and bounds over to us. "Are you okay?" She studies for me and for a second, it feels like she's looking for the cracks.

"I'm fine."

I can do this.

I just have to smile and pretend.

Smile and pretend.

Easy.

But Millie's brow furrows and she moves closer as Tally leaves us to join the girls. "Abi?"

"I'm fine," I reiterate. "How are you?"

"I'm good. Fine." There's a hint of sarcasm in her voice. "Theo is being a total pain in my arse about Marcus."

"He's your big brother. It's his job."

"Yeah, well my big brother needs to back the hell off. I like Marcus. I like him a lot. If Theo ruins—"

"He won't ruin it." Raine joins us, slinging her arm around Millie's shoulder. "I won't let him. It's good to see you." She turns her attention on me.

"You too." I move past them and make myself comfortable in one of the huge leather armchairs.

Every time a new cohort of Heirs move into the Chapel, they get to decorate the place to their tastes. But Elliot and the boys really did a great job. The place is a storm of black, dark grey, and silver. It's creepy and gothic, yes, but there's something alluring about it.

I've always liked it here. Despite feeling completely out of my depth.

"So did we decide? Pizza or Chinese?" Raine asks.

"Pizza," Tally pulls out her phone as she sinks into the plush leather sofa. "Usual?"

The girls all nod. Because this is just another normal Friday night for them. They live here now. They have routines and traditions.

They have a life together.

A found family.

"So Abs," Liv says. "Ready to spill the beans about Ethan?"

"There's nothing to spill."

"But you've been hanging out a lot." She glances at Tally who subtly shakes her head.

"More like he follows me around and won't take no for an answer."

"He hasn't tried anything, has he?"

"No, I didn't mean… It's not like that."

"Babe," Raine tsks. "It's always like that. He likes you."

"I don't think so. I mean, why would he?"

They all look at me like I've lost my mind.

"What do you mean?" Tally asks softly.

"Well, I'm… I'm me. And he's gorgeous."

"Oh, Abs." She slides to the edge of the sofa and reaches across for my hand. "You have to know how beautiful you are."

"I really don't want to talk about it."

I want the ground to open up and swallow me whole.

Why can't they understand that I'm not like them—that I never will be?

Sure, for a little while there, I began to believe I could be different. More confident and self-assured like the three of them.

That maybe one day, someone would look at me and see past my crippling shyness and hideous scars.

"Okay, okay." Tally sighs. "We didn't invite you to interrogate you, I promise." She levels Liv and Raine with a scathing look.

"Hey, I'm just saying, I think Ethan could be good for her," Raine says, giving me a knowing look.

I glance away, trying not to let my emotions run away with me.

Ethan pities me. He doesn't like me.

Grief does funny things to people. Bonds and tethers them. But it doesn't mean he has actual feelings for me. I barely know him.

Thankfully, Liv's phone bleeps loudly and she laughs as she reads the incoming message.

"I knew he wouldn't be able to hold out." She holds up the screen to reveal a selfie of Reese, Theo, and Oakley.

"Where's Elliot?" Millie asks, and my entire body locks up as I brace myself for her answer.

"He's right there, look, in the background. Talking to his Dad and—" She stops herself and I suddenly find my nails interesting.

"Who is that?" Millie doesn't pick up on the undercurrent.

Her words are invisible daggers as I brace myself for the two little words I know will follow.

"That's Lauren Winrow."

But it's her next words that really cut deep.

"Oh, she's beautiful."

26

ELLIOT

"Where are you going?" Scott shouts as I make my way through the hotel's entrance.

The charity gala tonight has been about as exciting as all the other events we've been forced to attend over the years.

Sure, it's for a good cause. They always are.

What better way to make the corrupt citizens of Saints Cross than to organise lavish events and raise a shit ton of money for those in need.

Dad, as always, was one of the biggest donors to tonight's children's charity.

I almost laughed out loud when he raised his paddle, playing a stupidly high winning big on some fancy weekend away in the Alps. If he wanted to support young people and give them the possibility of making their own choices for the future, then he really should look a little closer to fucking home.

"Home," I shoot over my shoulder.

As far as I'm concerned, my obligations for the night are over.

"But Dad booked you a room," Scott argues, making my hackles rise.

Yeah. A fucking double with Lauren.

My father is all kinds of fucked-up, but for some reason, having him attempt to pimp me out for a night of fucking with Mr and Mrs Winrow's daughter is just a whole new level of fucking weird.

Maybe if things were different, if this happened before Abigail became a part of my life, I'd go for it.

Take what he's offering, enjoy it and then walk away once I got what I wanted.

Maybe I'd even entertain the idea of dating her for a bit, if she was worthy of my time.

But right now, there is only one girl taking up time in my head, and it isn't Lauren Winrow.

"Yeah, and I've already told him that I won't be making use of it."

"But Lauren was looking forward to getting to know you better."

"Really?" I deadpan.

We haven't talked about the fact we've been pushed together by our fathers, but something tells me that she's about as happy about the whole thing as I am.

She's got a life of her own just like I have. She's also a beautiful, intelligent girl. I'm sure that if she wanted a boyfriend, she wouldn't need her father's help to get one.

"Yes, she—"

"I'm leaving," I say, standing up to him.

It's probably a bad decision, one that I'll regret once this gets back to our father, but right now, I really don't fucking care.

I've spent all night smiling and making small talk with people I've no interest in talking to. I've barely even seen the guys, they've also been too busy schmoozing with their father's acquaintances.

In fact, they're still in there flashing fake smiles and talking bollocks with anyone who cares to listen.

Well, they're more than welcome to it.

I, however, am done.

"He's not going to like this," Scott warns.

"Yeah? Well that makes fucking two of us," I snarl.

Before he has a chance to argue, I take off, pushing through the ginormous doors of the hotel and out into the night before Scott, our father, or anyone else can stop me.

The valet takes one look at me and smiles, and for the first time tonight, I give him a genuine one in return as he moves to open the door to my pride and joy. My Aston Martin.

Scott's attention burns into my back, making my shirt and tie feel two sizes too small, but I don't turn around or let him know that I'm aware of his stare. Of his disappointment, his anger.

Fuck him.

Fuck both of them.

The second my arse hits the seat, I reach up and loosen my tie, sucking in a deep lungful of fresh air and willing myself to calm down.

Anxious energy thrums through my veins. My need to go and do something to burn it off, making my muscles ache. But with the guys still inside working the room, I don't have anyone to spar with.

Not that it's getting sweaty with the guys really sparks my interest right now.

Someone else though...

Bringing my car to life, I press my foot to the accelerator and spin away from the front of the hotel.

"FUCK," I roar in the safety of my car before I slam

my palm against the wheel, one, two, three times in the hope of squashing my desire.

It doesn't work.

Nothing fucking works.

Slowing at a set of traffic lights, I close my eyes for a beat and focus on my breathing. But the second darkness comes, all I see is her.

Her eyes are wide with fear, confusion, and desire as I wrapped my fingers around her throat and squeezed. Her flushed cheeks that only got redder before she came. Her dark hazel eyes that I swear darkened with every second that passed during our time in that shed until they were almost black.

Fuck. She was enthralling. Mesmerising.

Incredible. Beautiful.

Everything.

I startle when a horn sounds behind me and when I look up, I find the lights changed back to amber and then red again.

With a sigh, I wring the wheel, forcing myself to stay focused and trying to convince myself that I should just go home. As much as I might crave the feeling I get every time I slip into her room covered by darkness, I know I need to stop.

She's found me out. She knows what I'm doing.

That should be more than enough to force my hand.

It takes every ounce of my self-restraint I possess to walk toward the Chapel after parking my car in my usual spot.

It might be dark on campus, but the lights that surround the Bronte Building taunt me from the second I pulled to a stop.

With my fists curled tight and my heart racing, I force myself to walk through the front door.

Everything is quiet, although there is mess everywhere. The scent of pizza and something sweet lingers in the air, and as I pass the kitchen, I find half-eaten bowls of popcorn and empty bottles of premixed cocktails littering the countertops.

"Fucking girls," I mutter under my breath, my muscles twitching with my need to clean up after them.

I hate mess. Fucking hate it.

I need order and cleanliness. The rest of my life is a mess, I need my home to be serene.

I almost bark out a laugh.

I can't remember when this place resembled anything anywhere near serene. Not since the girls joined us, that's for sure. The guys were bad enough but add them and there is always shit everywhere.

Ignoring it and telling myself that I'll demand they clean it up in the morning, I hit the stairs, pulling my tie off as I go and unbuttoning my shirt.

The place is in darkness, I can barely see my hand in front of my face, but I know it well enough by now not to need a light.

I hit the top of the stairs, still trying to convince myself not to turn around and go to her instead when a floorboard in front of me creaks before I collide with a body.

A small, sweet-smelling, familiar body.

Abi's shriek of shock rips through the air, the sound confirming what I already knew. Even if my brain hadn't caught up. My body knew. It always does when she's close.

Acting on instinct, I reach out and wrap my arm around her waist as she stumbles back.

I might not have been expecting her, but I'm probably double her body weight and could take her down with very little effort.

She gasps as I pull her into my body, and the second

the curves align with my hard planes, something inside me settles. "It looks to me like you're trying to do the walk of shame, Red," I whisper in her ear as she fights to get away from me.

"Let go, Elliot," she demands, but I do no such thing.

I can't. Not when she feels so fucking good against me.

"But the question is, what are you running away from?" I ask, ensuring my breath rushes down her neck.

She shudders against me, and I smirk.

Oh yeah, she remembers what happened the last time we were this close as viscerally as I do.

"I-I need to leave," she whispers.

Begs.

"You can, but you know I'll only follow you," I warn. "I almost went to your room tonight," I confess. "I was trying to do the right thing and come back here. To go to bed. But it seems you're here waiting for me instead."

"N-no, that's not—" As she struggles to come up with an argument, I take a step forward, forcing her to take one back. To move closer to my room.

"Why are you here then, Red? Why are you in my house in the middle of the night wearing..." I run my hands down her sides trying to picture what she's covered in. "Pyjamas? Were you planning on having a sleepover?"

"I was hanging out with—" Her words are cut off as her back presses against my bedroom door. "The girls. They had a pyjama party with Millie and I—"

"Waited for them to fall asleep so you could sneak out in the hope of avoiding me?" I ask, cutting off her explanation.

She swallows thickly. I might not be able to see it very well, but I hear the gulp, feel the anticipation, the excitement rippling off her in waves.

I lean closer, pinning her in place as one of my hands

grips her waist and the other reaches for the door handle. "You're still thinking about it, aren't you?" I ask.

She doesn't answer straight away leaving only the sound of her heavy breathing filling the silence around us.

I wait.

I want her answer before I make my next move.

"Yes," she finally whispers. "I shouldn't be but I can't—"

"Elliot," she cries when I swing the door open and the two of us stumble inside.

"Shush," I chastise, covering her mouth with my hand. "I thought you were trying to be discreet," I say as the door closes softly behind us and I continue walking her backward until her legs hit my bed.

The LED lights I left on give the room a soft glow, and for the first time since we collided, I get to see her.

Her nostrils flare as she tries to suck in the air she needs, but I don't let up. Not yet. Instead, I drop my eyes down her body, taking in her thin shirt and red tartan lounge trousers.

"You know, I think I'd prefer you in silk and lace," I muse.

Her chest heaves as my eyes roll back up her body, her warm breath tickling over the back of my hand.

I stop when I get to her breasts and find her nipples hard and desperate behind the white fabric.

I bet they're so fucking pretty.

My mouth waters as I imagine dragging it off her and sucking her into my mouth.

She'll be so sweet.

My cock aches as my imagination runs away with itself.

Reaching out with my free hand, I brush my fingers up the soft fabric hiding her thighs. "Have you been a good girl, Red?" I ask, stopping where I know her cuts are.

Her entire body trembles as I wait for her answer.

Long painful seconds pass where I start to believe that the only answer can possibly be no before she finally nods.

"Is that why you're really here?" I ask, remembering the demand I made while we were in that shed.

"Next time you feel the need to hurt yourself. I want you to call me. I don't care what time it is. Where you are. I want to be the one to give you the release you crave."

"Do you need me?" I ask, my head spinning with the possibility that she does.

Need me, Red.
I beg you, fucking need me.

27

ABIGAIL

"Do you need me?"

Elliot's words circle my mind, blood roaring between my ears as the room closes in around us.

Such a loaded question that I refuse to answer.

My eyelids flutter closed but Elliot's fingers wrap around my throat and make them fly open again, fear sliding down my spine.

"Look at me, Red," he demands. "Do. You. Need. Me?"

His thumb brushes over my thigh, right where my healing cuts are, and I can't fight the shiver that rips through me.

It's so wrong.

Depraved and disgusting.

I shouldn't feel so... so turned on by the way Elliot manhandles me. But there's something so freeing in handing myself over to him. Letting him give me what I need.

Even if he'll never cross that line and give me what I really want.

No.

I won't allow my emotions to get the better of me, not here. Not while he's staring at me with such heavy expectation.

He wants me to succumb. A realisation that only fuels the fire raging inside me. That deep dark part of me he's unlocked.

"Do you trust me?" he asks, his eyes so dark he looks soulless.

And it occurs to me, maybe he is.

Maybe Elliot Eaton is exactly the boy the halls of All Hallows' whisper about.

But I don't believe it, I can't. Because no matter how much this version of him terrifies me, no matter how much it hurts to remember, I've seen his softer side. The side dead set on protecting me, on giving me a safe space to step out of my comfort zone.

Now he's pushing me in entirely new ways and as much as I want to stop, I'm not sure I can.

Or even want to.

"I... yes." I nod because despite part of me wanting to get up and run, another deeper part of me wants what he's offering.

Elliot moves away and goes to his chest of drawers, pulling open the bottom drawer. When he comes back over to the bed, I begin to tremble.

"Hands above your head," he orders, and I lift my arms. His knees hit the mattress and then he's there, looming over me.

"Elliot?" My voice cracks, trepidation swimming in my veins.

This is crazy.

I'm crazy.

But then, I haven't quite felt on solid ground since the

night Elliot rejected me and I found out my father had died.

"Cross your wrists," he adds, leaning over to grab my hands and bind them with the tie in his hand. He secures the tail to the bedpost and tests its restraint. "If you need to tap out say Red."

"What are— Ah," I cry out, wrists straining against the silk tie, as he lowers his mouth to my thin material covering my breasts and blows a stream of hot air right over my nipple.

"Fuck, I've imagined this so many times."

His words make my head spin but it's his teeth grazing my hard peak that makes me shudder.

"You like the pain, don't you, Red."

"Yes. Ye— Yeah." Air rushes from my lungs as he bites down harder, making me hiss. But the pain grounds me. Smothers all the grief and heartache writhing inside me.

Reduces my existence to Elliot. The feel of his warm, wet mouth closed over my pyjama-covered breast.

He turns his attention to the other, repeating his actions. Making me shiver and squirm.

"Oh God," I breathe, trying to force air into my lungs as I unravel.

But for as good as it feels, I need more.

So much more.

"Elliot." I strain against my restraints once more, desperate to touch him. To run my fingers over his body.

"Patience," he chuckles, the sound vibrating through me as he moves down my body, taking my pyjama bottoms with him.

His fingers dance along the inside of my knees, gliding up thighs, lingering on the cuts there.

The wet slide of his tongue across my marred skin sends a whimper through me. It feels so good. But the pleasure is only intensified by the fact I'm bound at the wrists.

He licks and sucks at thighs, grazing his teeth along the cuts and healing skin. My head knows it shouldn't feel so good, so erotic, but my body doesn't care. Every inch of me trembling with anticipation.

"More," I murmur. "Please."

"Like this?" He breathes the words onto my most intimate place. "Or how about like this?" Tugging my underwear to the side, he slides two fingers along my seam, baring me to him.

And then he strikes.

Biting down on my clit so hard that pleasure shatters through me until I see stars.

"Oh God, *God*," I cry out. Over and over. As Elliot soothes the sting with his tongue, drawing out the pleasure wreaking havoc on my insides.

I'm vaguely aware of him rising over me to unbind my wrists.

It's only when I finally come down to Earth, I realise that I'm wrecked and ruined, laying half-naked on his bed.

And Elliot is still fully clothed. He didn't let me touch him. He didn't let me kiss him.

He gave me something I needed but he took nothing from me in return.

"You can sleep here if you want to," his voice is steady when my thoughts are a jumbled mess.

"Will you stay?" The words are out before I can stop them.

"I don't think that's a good idea." A ripple of something passes over his face but it's gone before I can decipher it. And I'm too tired to try and work it out.

"Fine," I murmur, trying to sound indifferent. "Shut the door on the way out."

Rolling away from him, I pull the sheets over my body and close my eyes.

Refusing to let the tears fall.

"Good morning," I say quietly as I join the girls at the kitchen island.

"And where did you get to last night? Millie said she woke up and you weren't there?" Suspicion coats Liv's words but I shrug it off.

"I couldn't sleep so I came down here for a bit. Elliot found me on the sofa and let me take his bed."

"And where did Elliot—"

"I took the sofa." His voice ripples through me, tugging at my heartstrings.

But I lock it down.

Whatever happened between us last night was another lapse in judgement. But I'm like an addict craving their next hit, and only Elliot can give me the intense high I need.

Tension descends over us as the girls watch me. But thankfully, the arrival of the rest of the boys cut through the strain.

"Hmm, something smells good," Oakley grins, making a beeline for Tally. He grabs her arse and pulls her in close for a kiss that makes me blush.

"Knock it off, dickhead," Theo murmurs, rubbing his head.

"What's up, Theodore? Head a little sore."

"Ugh, don't." Raine scowls. "I spent half the night cleaning up puke."

"Mate!" Oak and Reese fall about laughing.

"Fuck off, it was those shots you insisted we do." Theo

drops into one of the chairs. "Somebody get me some water and paracetamol."

"Abs," Oakley smiles, "Almost didn't notice you there. It's good to see you."

"Hi." I give him a small wave, feeling completely and utterly exposed.

Can they see the marks on my skin? The ones put there by my own hand and Elliot's teeth.

Can they see my secrets? The ones I hide underneath my weak smile and quiet words.

"How was it last night?" Raine asks. "I didn't get much out of Theo."

"Oh, we had a whale of a time." Reese chuckles. "Didn't we, Elliot?"

My heart stutters as I finally look at him. He glares at Reese, a silent conversation unfolding between them.

"What's going on?" Liv's brows knit as she glances between them.

"Daddy dearest made sure he and Lauren had a chance to get to know each other a bit better, didn't he?"

Oh God.

I smother the whimper crawling up my throat.

"It wasn't like that, and you know it," he grits out, his dark gaze finding mine.

Why?

Why would he do that?

Go on another date with her and then come back and touch me like that?

It doesn't make any sense.

Except, it does, if I finally accept that he's not the boy I believed him to be.

God, I'm so tired.

So wrung out and dejected.

"I think I'm going to go," I declare to no one in particular.

Out of the corner of my eye, I notice Elliot flinch. But he doesn't try to stop me unlike the girls who all voice their protests.

"Breakfast is almost ready, you can't leave yet," Tally says.

"I'm tired and I have a bunch of homework to finish."

She comes over to me and takes my hand. "You know, you don't need to put so much pressure on yourself."

"It keeps my mind busy." I force a smile. "Thanks for last night, I'm glad you persuaded me to come," I say. And I mean it.

But I can't help but replay what Elliot said to me.

Maybe he's right.

Maybe I did only agree because deep down, I can't let go of my silly notion that there's something between us.

Something real.

God, I'm such a mess. The way I let him touch me. Tease me. And make me break apart.

But for those few stolen moments in the dark, I was free. I wasn't plagued by the paralysing loneliness I feel day in and day out. The constant ball of grief lodged in my throat.

Elliot's touch—no matter how toxic—is like a balm to my broken, weary soul. It makes sense that I would crave that. Gravitate toward it.

It isn't healthy. It isn't right. But it isn't entirely wrong either.

Is it?

"If you give me a minute, I'll walk you back."

"You don't have to do that, I'll be fine." I wrap an arm around my waist, holding myself together.

It's too much being here, with Tally and my friends. Their boyfriends.

Elliot.

I was a fool to think I could pretend. That things could go back to even a shred of what we all had before.

"I'll walk you," Elliot says gruffly. "I'm going for a run anyway."

"I don't need a babysitter."

"Abs, that's not... no one thinks you do, right, boys?" Tally glares at each of them but no one answers her, the truth etched on to each of their faces.

That's always been the difference between me and the girls. The boys don't have to coddle them or babysit them. Because they're strong enough to walk in the Heirs' world.

The same can't be said for me.

I'll always be the outsider. The girl they took pity on and invited to skirt the edge of their tightly knit circle.

But I can't do it anymore.

I can't pretend I'm something I'm not.

Hurting myself, reducing myself to... to this, only cements that.

"I'll see you on Monday," I say, moving to the door.

I walk out without looking back.

And really, it's no big surprise when no one comes after me.

28

ELLIOT

"Mate, wait up," Reese calls as I take off on a run.

I want to get away. No, I need to get away.

The way they all look at me when Abigail is with us.

I hate it.

It's a mix of amusement and pity.

They know how I feel about her. I haven't been able to hide my interest. But they don't understand why I'm holding back. Not that I expect them to. It's not like they really know the truth. And I have no intention of explaining either.

"I'm fine," I shout over my shoulder, picking up speed in the hope of outrunning him. "I don't need company."

"Well, tough, you've got it."

I groan as he catches up with me.

"What the fuck was all that this morning?" he asks after a few seconds of tense silence.

"Nothing," I grunt, hoping my tone will be enough to stop him. I should be so fucking lucky.

None of us are that easily dissuaded.

He laughs, but there is no amusement in it. "We've let this go. But you're fucking miserable. She is too. When are you just going to—"

I spin on him, fist his hoodie and slam him back against a thick tree trunk. "None of your fucking business," I bellow in his face.

He doesn't react. There isn't so much as a flicker of fear or hesitation on his face as I glare at him, our noses almost touching.

My heart races and my chest heaves as anger surges through my veins. But it's not just that. There's more. So much more that I struggle to even decipher them all.

I'm pretty sure most of it is self-hatred though.

Self-hatred for my inability to stand up against my father, to take what I really want, to live the life I'm desperate for instead of the one I'm forced to endure.

"Go on," Reese finally taunts. "Hit me if you think it'll fix anything."

My free hand curls into a fist as I think about the surge of pain and relief that'll come with it.

Fuck. I want it.

My nostrils flare as I think about the rush.

The same exact one I gave Abigail last night.

She was beautiful.

And her taste...

Fuck. My mouth waters as I remember the moment her sweetness flooded my mouth all too vividly.

I knew from the moment we collided that whatever was going to happen next was going to be a mistake. But I couldn't stop myself.

After the night I'd already endured, I needed her as much as she needed me. If only I could have taken more...

"Didn't have you pegged as a pussy, Eaton." He tilts his

head and stares at me with nothing but pity in his eyes. Fury erupts within me, fire shooting down my veins but it's nothing compared to my reaction to his next statement. "Just like you're too much of a pussy to admit you want Abi."

Before he's even finished talking, I've pulled my arm back and I'm throwing all my weight into the punch that lands on his cheekbone. He roars as pain blooms from the hit, but he doesn't shy away, not that I expected him to, instead, he rushes me. But while I might predict the move, I'm not ready and he sends me flying backward.

I land with a thud and a grunt of pain.

"Come on, Eaton," he says, bouncing on his feet like we're in the ring. "Let's fucking go. You need to work off some of that tension. And seeing as you're not fucking it out of your system you need to fight it out."

I roar with determination as I jump to my feet, and we collide in a fury of fists.

He gets two hits in before I take the upper hand again. The mud beneath our feet squelches as we churn it up, and in only a few minutes, we're both covered.

"More, Eaton. I said fucking bring it," Reese taunts. "Hit me like you want to fuck her," he demands.

"I don't," I seethe.

"Fucking admit it. There's nothing wrong with it. With you. With her. Fucking own it, mate."

"I can't," I roar, diving toward him with a fresh rush of adrenaline.

Before long, we both hit the ground, rolling around in the mud like a pair of stupid boys—which of course is exactly what we are—while he continues to taunt me, and I refuse to budge.

"Fuck," I groan, finally giving in and falling back into a puddle.

It's cold and wet, but it's not something we're unfamiliar with after spending most of our lives on the rugby pitch.

"Gonna admit you want her yet?" he asks breathlessly.

"Reese," I groan.

"It's okay to want her. She's hot."

My teeth grind.

"And you make a good couple despite your differences," he continues.

"Our differences?" I ask, getting sucked into this conversation.

"Yeah, you're all... I dunno, scary to some people I guess and she's all sweet and innocent. On the surface of it, anyone would think you'd eat her alive but there's more to her than meets the eye, isn't there?"

I don't respond, I don't need to.

"What are you so scared of? Haven't the six of us proved to you by now that coupling up isn't that terrifying really."

"I'm not scared of coupling up," I argue.

"Then why aren't you together? She wants you and you know it. She doesn't exactly hide it. And neither do you, by the way."

"I'm not right for her."

"Says fucking who?" he snaps, clearly unimpressed by my excuse. "That's bullshit."

"Is it?" I hiss, pressing my hands into the sloppy ground beneath me and pushing myself up. "Abigail is too good for me. I know it. You know it. Everyone fucking knows it. I'll ruin her, and she's already doing a good enough job of doing that herself. And even if I don't, can you even imagine what my dad and Scott would do?"

"Accept her because she's important to you?"

I scoff. "Don't be so fucking naïve, Reese. Just because

your parents are cool that you're fucking your stepsister, it doesn't mean everyone else is so accepting of their kid's choices."

"So your dad might not like her, what's the big deal?"

"The big deal is that I don't have a choice," I hiss, climbing to my feet.

My hoodie and sweats are sodden and cold, my muscles still aching for a release.

"You'll be at Saints Cross U soon, far enough away from Daddy Eaton that you can—"

"But I can't, Reese. He has it all planned for me and—"

"Lauren," he sighs, standing to his full height.

"Yeah, no. Fuck. I don't know," I say, throwing my arms up. "I don't know what the fuck I'm doing. Is that what you want to hear?"

"No, not really," he mutters.

"I know what I want, but I also know what I can't have. It doesn't fucking work. It never has."

"What is that supposed to mean?"

My lips part really to say more that'll open up too much of my past, but I manage to catch the words before they spill free.

"If you don't want to talk to me about it, that's fine. I get it. How about you go and talk to her instead?" he suggests.

"I can't."

"You seem to be saying that a lot for someone who has a rep for getting whatever the fuck he wants."

"Yeah well, maybe I'm nothing more than a fucking fraud." I take a step back, ready to walk away from one of my best friends in the hope of forgetting this conversation ever happened.

"Bullshit. You're one of the most honest and reliable people I know."

I shake my head, unable to accept his words.

A bitter laugh falls from my lips as I put even more space between us.

"Whatever the fuck is going on in your head, you need to figure it out. You deserve better than this. You both do."

With those words ringing in my ears, I take off, cutting back through the trees to the Chapel. I don't bother trying to run, everything I'm wearing is too wet and caked in mud for that.

Instead, I strip off at the front door and storm through my house in my sopping-wet boxers.

"What the fuck happened to you?" Oak and Theo ask as I pass them.

"Fuck off," I grunt viciously enough to stop them from following me.

The second I slam my bedroom door behind me, I realise my mistake. I shouldn't have come back here. All I can smell, all I can see, and taste is her.

She's on my bed, her limbs twisted up in my sheets. Her thighs pinning my head as I—

"FUCK," I roar, focusing on my bathroom.

The second I'm inside, I turn the shower on as hot as it'll go, shed my soaked underwear and step under the stream of near-boiling water.

My skin instantly prickles but despite the burn, I don't move. Instead, I embrace the pain.

Sucking in a deep breath, I hold it for a beat before releasing it. I repeat over and over in the hope of talking myself down.

By the time I turn the scalding water off, I've successfully washed the mud down the drain but that's about all I've achieved.

Reese's words float around in my head as I drop into the chair in front of my desk and attempt to get some studying done. But every time I try to work, my mind drifts back to the few moments I stole with Abigail last night.

Just for those ten minutes, everything was so perfect.

Everything felt so right.

The chaos inside me settled.

For ten minutes, I felt... I felt like I was where I was meant to be.

"How about you go and talk to her."

My eyes drift to the window and I gaze out in the direction of the Bronte Building.

Is she there in her room alone? Or is she with him?

Is he giving her everything I want to give her?

I squeeze my eyes closed as the image of them doing exactly what we did last night. His blond hair instead of mine between her thighs as he—

The crash of my chair hitting the floor startles me as I surge to my feet.

I've pulled a hoodie on and shoved my feet into my trainers before I know what I'm doing.

It's not until I pull the door open, and the bright lights of the hallway burn my eyes that I realise I was sitting in the dark.

Voices float up to me as I descend the stairs, but I ignore all of them as I rush toward the front door.

"Elliot, where the fuck are you going?" Oakley shouts, but I don't bother responding.

"Leave him," Reese says just before the front door swings closed behind me.

Stars twinkle in the inky night sky as I make my way toward the girls' dorm building.

All I want to do is see if she's there. See if she's alone.

But by the time I get to her door room and pull the master key from my pocket, I know that there's no way I'm going to be able to slip in and out unnoticed like I have so many times before.

I've spent one too many nights sitting in the shadows in the chair in the corner of the room watching her over the past few weeks. It was fine when she was unaware.

But she's figured me out.

She knows I can't put her behind me.

And last night proved she can't move forward either.

Not without me.

Pushing her door open, I slip into the darkness and breathe in a deep lungful of air that's laced with her scent.

I breathe a sigh of relief, but I don't get to fully relax because when I look at the bed I find a wide pair of eyes staring back at me.

"Red, I—"

29

ABIGAIL

"Elliot." His name leaves my lips on a surprised whisper. "What's wrong?"

Because I see it.

The tension on his face, the haunted look in his eyes.

"I... I needed to see you."

"What happened to your face?" I sit up, pushing the sheet off my body. "You're hurt."

I should be mad at him—part of me is. But he's here and he's hurt, and my head loses the war to my heart because before I can stop myself, I'm up out of bed, crossing the room to him.

"Elliot, what happened?" My fingers trace the wicked looking bruise along his cheekbone, the dried blood on his lip.

"It's nothing." He tries to move my hand away, but I swat at him.

"It's not nothing. You were fighting."

"I was burning off some steam. I'm fine, I promise."

"You're a terrible liar, Elliot Eaton." I smile as he

flinches at my touch. "I have a first aid kit in the bathroom. Sit."

He lets me tug him over to the bed without any resistance. When he drops down onto the edge and stares up at me, my heart flutters wildly in my chest.

Something has changed between us, and I can't deny that I'm finding it harder and harder to resist the tug I feel toward him.

Especially now that I know how addictive his touch can be.

But I'm still not sure he feels the same. He feels something, I know that. I know it deep down in my soul.

I just don't know if it's enough.

Not when he's been dating Lauren Winrow.

"I'll be right back," I say, hurrying to fetch the first aid kit. But when I return, Elliot tugs the small green pouch from my hands and drops it behind him on the bed.

"What are you—" He slides his hand up the back of my thighs and draws me between his legs.

"Just give me a minute." Dropping his head to my stomach, he inhales a deep breath.

I can't resist stroking my fingers through his hair, wondering what is running through his mind. "What's going on, Elliot?" I whisper, louder than intended because he looks up at me, his eyes sparking in the darkness.

"I... Fuck, Red. I can't keep doing this."

"Doing what?" I swallow, my heart crashing against my rib cage. A living breathing thing in my chest, desperate to escape. To declare my feelings for him.

But I don't. I can't.

Because the last time I put myself on the line, Elliot rejected me. He broke something inside me that I'm not sure he'll ever fix.

"Fighting this. Keeping you at arm's length."

So don't, I want to scream. *Pick me. Choose me. Love me.*

But I trap the words. Because Elliot has demons all of his own.

Instead, I ask, "What about Lauren?"

His expression darkens. "What?"

"Lauren. Surely you haven't forgotten her already. The girl you were with last night before..." I trail off, unable to say the words.

Silence stretches out between us, fraying the invisible tethers that bind us.

"This is a mistake." I go to pull away, my heart shattering in my chest. But Elliot bands his arm around my back, anchoring me in place.

"Lauren is no one."

"And I am?" I scoff.

"You know you are." A shudder rolls through him. "But it isn't that simple." He drops his face and I instantly feel the loss of his searing gaze.

"Elliot." I slide my fingers under his jaw and bring his face back to mine. "What do you want?"

"You."

That one word rocks me to my core.

It's all I've wanted to hear. That big bad Elliot Eaton wants me. That he feels the same as I do. But it isn't the declaration I was hoping for. Because despite not wanting to believe, he's right, things aren't simple between us.

"What?" he says, reaching for me to press his hand along the curve of my throat. "Tell me what you're thinking."

"Tell me why you were fighting."

"You really want to know, Red?" I nod and his lips twitch. "Because you drive me in-fucking-sane. Because I saw the look of devastation on your face when Reese mentioned Lauren. Because I wanted to claim you right then in front of everyone and I knew I couldn't.

"My life… My life is a fucking shitshow, Red. I don't want to pull you into that, I won't."

"Because I'm weak? Because I'm not as pretty or popular or—"

"Stop. Just stop." He grabs my hands and pulls them to his mouth, kissing my knuckles.

"You're one of the strongest people I know, Abi. Strong." He turns over my hand and kisses my palm. "Beautiful." A feather-light kiss across my wrist. "Resilient." His lips trace a path up my arm to my shoulder until he pulls me down on his lap. "Kind. Brave. Loyal."

His hand finds its way to the back of my neck and his fingers dive into the hair there, pulling my face down to his. "Wanting you isn't the problem, Red." He stares at me for the longest time, and I feel like I'm soaring. My stupid foolish heart falling headfirst into his words.

Until he says, "But we don't always get what we want, Abi. My life isn't a fairy tale and I'm certainly not a prince."

My stomach sinks.

"Don't look at me like that." Elliot's stone-cold mask slides back over his face. "You know the kind of person I am."

"So that's it then." I pull away slightly, trying to build back up my defences.

"Fuck, Abi, I don't know, okay. I've never…" He lets out a steady breath, but I can feel the tension radiating off him.

"You think I've ever done this? That I've ever let someone—" My eyelids flutter as I remember how it felt to surrender to him.

"Fuck, Red. You're thinking about it, aren't you?"

My eyes open and I stare right at him. "I'm always thinking about it."

"I didn't... scare you?"

"I think more than anything, I scared myself."

"You were perfect. You are perfect, Abi. And in another life, I'd make you mine in a heartbeat."

God, I hate this.

I hate that we're both so broken. So shackled by our demons.

"So what do we do? Because I can't keep doing... this, Elliot. Having you but not having you."

"Lie down with me," he says, surprising me.

"You want to—"

"Lie with you, yeah. I'm in fucking agony over here."

I suck in a breath and hit his chest gently. "I knew that had to hurt. Let me clean you up first."

"In the bed, now."

His commanding tone shoots a thrill through me, and I scramble off his lap to get into bed.

Elliot yanks off his hoodie and kicks off his jeans and climbs in beside me. "Need you closer," he murmurs, wrapping his arm around me to drag me closer.

The way we fit together shouldn't feel so right but it does. I feel safe. Protected and cherished.

This cold guarded boy makes my heart soar and my body burn. And I know I should demand answers, keep pushing for some clarity on what we are. On what he wants from me. But I guess I'm a coward too, because I don't want to ruin the moment.

So I lie there, waiting. Tracing my fingers over his sculpted chest and down his arm while his fingers toy with the hem of my pyjama shorts.

It doesn't feel sexual though. There's something softer about it. Almost innocent.

"Elliot?" I whisper, trying to move to look at him.

He drops a kiss on my head and tucks me closer. His body sinks into mine as he relaxes, the rise and fall of his chest evening out.

Elliot Eaton is in my bed, wrapped around me like a koala and he's asleep.

I don't move. Darednt' even breathe for fear of waking him.

But he's here.

And for now, it's enough.

Pleasure stirs deep inside me, dragging me from a dreamless sleep.

My eyes flutter open as I try to get my bearings.

"What— Ah!" I cry out as Elliot's tongue swipes at my centre.

Oh God.

He's going down on me... after spending the night in my bed.

My mind reels as the weight of what is happening. But another swipe of his tongue has every thought evaporating out of my head.

"Good morning," I breathe, sliding my fingers into his hair.

"I love the sounds you make in your sleep while my fingers are deep inside you."

Jesus. Is he trying to drive me wild?

He lifts his head and smirks at me while sliding two fingers inside me. "Just. Like. This." He curls them deep and the sound that works its way up my throat is positively wanton.

"Oh God," I pant, hardly able to breathe.

It's too much, too good.

"Good?" he asks, and I nod. "Want more?" One of his hands slides along my thigh until his fingers graze my cuts.

A new, different kind of pleasure sparks off inside me. Darker and more depraved.

When he withdraws his hand, I whimper.

"Thought so." He chuckles, still working me with his fingers, sliding them back and forth inside me. "Such a good girl for me." Tracing his tongue down my hip to my thigh, he grazes his teeth over an unmarred piece of skin, causing a full body shiver to roll through me.

"I want to watch you break apart for me."

I'm so close.

So, so close.

But something is missing.

His thumb circles my clit faster, making my writhe and thrash beneath him but it still isn't enough. And he knows it.

Elliot knows exactly what I need as he sinks his teeth into my thigh, shattering the mental block on my pleasure.

My fingers twist into the bedsheets as the wave obliterates through me, sending me spiralling into white-hot bliss.

"Ohmygod, ohmygod, ohmygod," I cry over and over.

As I slowly come down, Elliot looms over me, his expression almost feral. "You good?"

I manage a small nod, wrung dry from his wake-up call.

"You're still here," I say, reaching for his face. He catches my hand and nips my fingers and then kisses the sting away.

"You thought I wouldn't be?"

"It's new."

"A lot of things are new where you're concerned, Red."

"Are you staying for a little bit? Or do you have to leave?"

His eyes narrow with suspicion. "Do you want me to leave?"

"No. That's not what I was thinking at all, actually."

"So what were you thinking?"

My heart crashes violently in my chest as I gaze up at him, sleepy and completely sated. "I... I want to touch you, Elliot. I want to make you feel good."

"Abi, come on." He starts to pull away. "You don't need to—"

"Please." I grab his arm. "I want this, Elliott. I want you to teach me how to make you feel good."

"Pretty sure anything you do to me will feel like heaven, Red."

"Lie down on the bed." I barely manage to disguise the quiver in my voice. But I'm so bloody nervous.

Elliot blinks at me as if he can't believe what's happening but then he surprises me by sliding his arm under my waist and flipping us in one smooth movement, so I'm straddling his hips.

"This better?" he smirks up at me, a mask of utter arrogance. But I'm no fool. I heard the hitch in his voice. I see the flicker of vulnerability in his eyes.

For once, he's giving me the upper hand.

Handing me the power.

And despite my nerves, despite the fact I don't have the first clue what I'm doing, I don't intend on wasting it.

30

ELLIOT

I stare up at Abigail with my heart in my throat and desire coursing through my veins.

Her taste still coats my tongue. I want more.

I want so much more.

But that doesn't mean I should be allowed it.

Usually, I take. And the girls I occasionally hook up with are more than happy for me to do so just so they can brag to their friends. Not that they're allowed to say much. I have a way of making sure they keep most of what happens in the dark with me to themselves. And thankfully, they're all too scared about their reputation to risk breaking my rules.

Abigail though... Right now, there are no rules.

This thing between us is different and it makes me want to experience all of this in an entirely different way.

I don't just want to take...

And that in itself is a massive head fuck.

Testing the water, she rolls her hips over me. The burning heat of her pussy burning my aching dick through the thin fabric of my boxers.

She's so close. Right fucking there.

I could just...

I grit my teeth and force myself to swallow.

Waking her up, after dragging her knickers down her thighs and spreading her legs, was a risk. But the second I woke up, tasting her again, feeling her body trembling, and watching her fall—not that I could see much of it in the dark—was the only thing I could think about.

And fuck, was it worth it.

She rocks forward again, and I just about lose my fucking mind.

She stares down at me with wide, hungry eyes. She's hesitant and scared but there is so much more burning in those depths, and for once, it's not all-consuming guilt and pain.

Sucking her bottom lip into her mouth, she bites down, and the move sends a rush of arousal straight to my dick, making it leak for her.

I want those lips. I want them on mine. I want them wrapped around—

My brain short-circuits as she reaches out and places a finger right in the middle of my chest.

It's innocent. So fucking innocent, but she might as well be holding a match against for me the way it burns.

Slowly, painfully fucking slowly, she drags it down.

My breaths come out in short sharp bursts as we both watch her finger descend toward where my dick is trying to escape out of my boxers. My stomach muscles tighten, my dick aching beneath her pussy as she takes her time exploring my body.

I hate it almost as much as I love it.

"Red," I breathe, starting to think that she's changed her mind.

She should. Taking this any further—allowing her to feed my obsession is wrong.

But at the same time, nothing about her touch feels wrong.

"E-Elliot," she whispers, her fingers hesitantly tucking beneath the waistband of my boxers. "I-I've never—"

"Shush," I soothe, reaching out to cup her cheek, letting my thumb brush over the scar there.

Her eyes shutter. She hates it, we all know that. But I don't.

Her breath catches as the intimacy levels reach all new heights between us.

"You don't have to do anything you're not ready for. I'm happy just to—"

Without warning, she scoots lower and suddenly drags my boxers down, letting my cock spring free.

Her eyes hold mine for a beat before they finally drop.

Squeezing my eyes closed tight, I remember that it's dark. That while she might be staring, she can only see the basics. And there's a little bit—okay, a lot—of me hoping that she'll be impressed enough not to look closer.

"Shit," she whispers. "It's—"

Abi swallows her words leaving me to guess what her thoughts are and instead, she reaches out and continues her trail down my body. She traces the indent of my V before her finger brushes against my cock.

It takes everything in me not to blow right there and then with her innocent touch and eyes on me.

It doesn't matter who has come before, right now I might as well be a virgin again experiencing all this for the first time.

"Red," I groan when she drags her finger over the head of my cock, smearing precum over me.

"Tell me what to—"

"Wrap your hand around me," I answer before she's even finished asking the question. "Holy shit," I gasp as she instantly follows orders.

Her grip is light, her touch gentle but it does crazy things to me.

Reaching out, I wrap my own hand around hers, tightening her grip and then slowly start to move, showing her just how I like it. "Fuck, Red," I groan, my hips jumping from the bed, fucking into her hand. "Fuck."

"That feel good?" she asks nervously as I let my own hand fall away and allow her to take over.

"So good," I assure her.

She strokes me a few more times, making both my head and body want to explode.

"You're perfect," I blurt, watching her sitting there in her oversized nightshirt, her hair messed up from sleeping and desire darkening her eyes.

"Elliot," she warns, hating the compliment.

"I don't say things I don't mean, Red. The only thing that would make it better would be you wearing an All Hallow's shirt with my name across your back."

Her breath catches at my words.

"No one wears your number," she whispers.

Of course they do. But she doesn't mean just anyone. She means girls.

And no, they fucking well don't.

"It would look so fucking good on you," I tell her.

I have no idea if it's my words or being able to feel how much I'm enjoying what she's doing, but it gives her a new surge of confidence.

"Where are you going?" I ask in a panic when she releases my cock and climbs from the bed.

She doesn't answer, but I soon discover her intentions.

"Red, what are you—" I swallow my words as she drags

my boxers farther down my legs and drops them to the floor.

My heart races for a whole new reason as she nudges my legs apart so she can settle between them.

"What's wrong?" she asks when I don't immediately move. "Don't you want me to..."

Forcing my hesitation back down, I stare up at her. Her eyes are locked on me and before I know what I'm doing, I'm making space for her.

She has no idea. No fucking idea how much of a head fuck for me this is.

But it's her.

It was always meant to be her.

She doesn't know it yet, but she gets it. She understands me.

We're the fucking same.

Her fingers wrap around me again and I lose all sense of thought as her grip tightens and she works me just like I showed her to.

"Oh fuck, Abi. So good. So. Fucking. Good."

"Yeah?" she asks, pride obvious in her expression.

"Yeah, baby. Keep doing that I'm gonna cu— Red," I hiss when she drops lower and brushes her lips against my thigh.

It's a move similar to what I did to her, and it makes my brain short-circuit.

The wet heat of her tongue collides with my skin, and she drags it up.

Reaching out, I thread my fingers through her hair, holding tight enough that it'll send a shot of pain down her spine.

Surprise has her eyes flying up to meet mine. I smirk, I can't help it.

"That got you wet for me, didn't it?" I ask, my voice raspy with desire and the need to watch her finish me.

She licks her lips as she sits up slightly. Her mouth hovers right over my dick, all I'd have to do is lift and—

"Got me wet?" she asks, holding my eyes. "Think it's a bit late for that."

My mouth waters as the memory of bringing her to ruin with my tongue hit me, but only a second later it's all forgotten.

Sticking her tongue out, she licks up the length of my dick before swirling around the tip like I'm her personal lollipop.

"Holy fuck, Red... Abi, Shit."

I can't hold it. The sight of her with her mouth on me sends me crashing over the edge. My dick jerks violently in her hand before I cum all over my stomach.

She watches the entire thing in amazement, her eyes wide and curious.

"I did that," she says proudly.

I can't help but laugh. I'm fucking delirious as the high from my release continues to rush through me.

"Yeah, baby. You did."

She sits there between my thighs alternating between looking at my softening dick, the mess I've made, and my eyes.

I've no idea what she's thinking, but I'm fucking desperate to know.

"I'll go get some tissue," she finally says, climbing from the bed and disappearing into the bathroom briefly.

I'm still half comatose when she returns, my eyes locked on hers, watching her every move. It shouldn't come as a shock as she leans toward her bedside light and illuminate the place so we can see better, but it fucking does.

I'm on my feet and ripping the tissue out of her hands in a heartbeat.

I shouldn't do it.

I should trust her in the same way that she's trusted me. But habits die hard, I guess.

"Elliot, what—"

"We should go out," I say, cutting her off as I wipe the cum from my stomach and drop the tissue in the bed.

"Go out?" she repeats like it's the craziest idea she's ever heard.

"Yeah," I breathe, stepping up to her and cupping her face in my hand. "Go out."

I search her eyes as my other hand slides up her leg. I hitch it up around my hip before slipping under her shirt, finding her bare ass.

Leaning forward, I let my lips brush her ear. "If we don't, I'm not sure I'm going to be able to do the right thing, Red," I confess.

Her gasp of shock fills the room when I roll my hips, letting her feel how hard I am.

"Again?" she whispers before a moan spills free when I grind harder against her.

"Yeah, Red. Again. You're standing here in nothing but a thin shirt with your pussy bare and ready for me. What else do you expect?"

"You..." She swallows not wanting to continue.

"Red," I groan, demanding she finish her thought.

"You really want me? Even after everything you've seen me do."

Pulling back, I look into her eyes. They're full of unshed tears, but again, they're not sadness, more... disbelief, I guess.

"Yeah, like you wouldn't believe," I confess before

doing the right thing and releasing her in favour of pulling my boxers back on.

"Get dressed," I demand. "I'm taking you out. It's time to get out of this place for a bit."

"Where are we going?" she asks, watching me a little too closely.

"Somewhere we can just be us. Elliot and Abigail. A place where no one knows who we are."

Her face lights up at the thought.

"Get dressed, Red," I say reluctantly as I drop my eyes down her body.

I desperately want to reach out and peel it from her. I want to see what she's hiding beneath. I can't right now. I know it'll be a step too far. But one day.

One day soon I'm going to strip her naked and have her laid out waiting for me.

But until then, I'm going to give her a day she'll never forget.

31

ABIGAIL

I've been in Elliot's Aston Martin before, but this feels different.

He's taking me out.

Me.

After letting me touch him in a way I've only dreamed about.

Watching him come undone like that, knowing that it was all because of me, was one of the sexiest things I've ever seen.

"Where are we going?" I ask, breaking the thick silence.

I'd be worried that he regrets asking me to spend the day with him except he hasn't let my hand go since we got in the car.

"Somewhere off the grid."

"Sounds ominous."

"Scared, Red?" He flashes me a playful grin. And I love it.

I love that I get to see this side of him.

"With you, never."

Elliot focuses back on the quiet country lane, but I catch the flicker of doubt in his eyes.

A weary sigh escapes me. Even after everything we shared last night and this morning, he's still guarded. But maybe getting away from Saints Cross for a little bit will give me a chance to uncover the mystery that is Elliot Eaton.

Like why he hesitated when I tried to go down on him this morning. Or the flash of panic in his eyes when I returned with some tissue to clean him up.

He thinks I didn't notice, but I did.

I've always noticed the little things where Elliot is concerned.

Like the mask he wears, the front he projects to protect himself—his secrets.

We drive in comfortable silence, the smell of the pastries Elliot grabbed from the local bakers on the way out of town wafting through his car.

The fact he thought to grab us something to eat warms my heart and has my mind running away with itself again.

We pass a sign for Thame, and I frown over at him.

"Thame?"

"Yeah, it's a small village along the River Thame. Me and Oak found it once. The town is nothing special, but we found this cool abandoned church overlooking the river."

"You're taking me to an abandoned church?" A shiver runs down my spine.

"Don't you trust me?" He squeezes my hand.

"I do."

"You shouldn't," he whispers so quietly I barely hear him.

"Elliot, I—"

"Don't. Not yet. Can we just have today? Then we can deal with everything else."

"Of course."

"Have you ever brought anyone else out here?"

I'm fishing, I can't help it.

I want to be strong and confident and sure of myself, but it doesn't come easy. Especially not after his blatant rejection of me all those weeks ago at the party.

I'm not like the rest of the girls at All Hallows' vying for the Heirs' attention.

I never have been, and I never will be.

And the truth is, I don't want to be.

I'm me.

Abigail Bancroft.

I have scars and trauma and insecurities. And I want someone to love and accept me in spite of that.

"Like who?" Elliot casts me a dark look.

"You know what I mean."

"Yeah, but I don't understand why you're asking. You know I haven't."

"I didn't mean..." I stop myself and take a deep breath. "This is all new to me too, Elliot. I'm way out of my depth here."

"Stop overthinking it," he says as if it's that easy. "I want you, Red. I thought I made that pretty clear. And yeah, things are complicated but right now, I'm here with you because I want to be here."

"Okay." I offer him a small nod.

Elliot turns off the main road and takes a dirt track through the woods.

"Should we be out here?"

"It's part of the country park, I think."

Despite the thick clouds rolling overhead, it's still beautiful. Bursts of green and yellow, gold and pink hint at the arrival of summer.

It feels significant somehow. To be in a place of such beauty as it moves from one season into another.

Like a rebirth.

If only I could find that within myself. If only I could figure out how to put my grief and pain behind me and move forward.

When I'm with Elliott, I feel hopeful. But it's a dangerous thing to pin my healing on one boy.

A boy who has made it clear that things between us will never be straight forward.

The trees began to clear, and I gasp. The abandoned church sits on the edge of the river, a small quaint building with a private cemetery still intact.

"It's beautiful."

"Yeah." Elliot says in wonder. But he isn't looking at the sight before us, he's staring at me.

I turn to look at him and something crackles between us.

"Come on, let's go explore."

He climbs out of the car and comes around to get my door. My heart skips a beat as he offers me his hand and gently tugs me to my feet.

"Thank you."

His mouth twitches as he leads me toward the building.

At first glance, it looks to be in pristine condition but on closer inspection, I notice the fissures in the bricks, the trail of ivy growing out holes and cracks. When we step inside, it also becomes apparent that half the roof is missing.

But there's still something so serene about the place.

It's quiet except for the gentle rustle of the breeze and trickle of the river.

I drop Elliot's hand and move between the pews, standing before the altar.

"Do you believe in God?" Elliot asks me.

"I don't but sometimes, I wish I did." I glance over my shoulder at him with a sombre expression. "Do you?"

"Religion has no place in my world," he says cryptically. "Hungry?"

The change of subject is a little jarring but my stomach grumbles giving him my answer.

"Come on, I want to show you something else."

Elliot grabs the bag from his car and leads me around the side of the church.

"Wow, this is... Wow."

From this viewpoint, there's nothing but rolling green and gold fields. For as far as the eye can see.

"It's like something out of a painting."

"I thought you'd like it." He tugs me toward a rickety old bench nestled under a giant oak tree, and we sit.

I take it upon myself to dish out the breakfast pastries, choosing an apricot tartlet for myself while Elliot demolishes two sausage rolls and an almond croissant.

"Hungry?" I chuckle as brushes flakes of pastry off his hoodie.

"Always. You have a little pastry"—his thumb glides over the corner of my mouth—"right here."

His thumb lingers and without thinking, I dart my tongue out to flick the pad.

"Fuck," he breathes, eyes flaring with lust.

"Sorry, I—"

Elliot's hand curves around my neck as his mouth comes down on mine.

The kiss isn't soft or gentle, it's full of heat and yearning, and I can't help but climb into his lap to get closer.

"Easy, Red," he murmurs as I press closer.

"Sorry." I pull back, shame staining my cheeks.

"Don't apologise. I love you like this. But I didn't bring you out here for this. Okay? We have time." He touches his head to mine, inhaling a ragged breath.

"Yeah, okay." I go to slide off his lap, but Elliot wraps his arm around me, pulling me into his side.

"I haven't been out here in a long time."

"You used to come here a lot?"

"Sometimes, when I needed to get away."

"Because of your dad." I test the waters, not wanting to push him to give me any more than he wants to.

"My brother Scott is the golden child. A chip off the old block. Me, not so much."

"I find that hard to believe." I peek up at him.

"Believe it, Red. Johnathon Eaton is a hard man to impress, and I've always been his biggest disappointment."

He tenses beside me, anger rippling off him in palpable waves.

"What about your mum?" I ask, because everyone talks about the formidable Johnathon Eaton but Julia Eaton rarely comes up in conversation.

"I'd rather not talk about it."

"Oh, okay."

Silence turns to awkwardness, and I feel the icy wall start to build between us again.

"Fuck, Abi. I don't... I'm not..." Anguish coats his voice, tugging at my heartstrings. "I don't do this."

"Hey, hey." I twist around to him and take his face in my hands. "You don't have to tell me anything, Elliot. But I want you to know that you can trust me with your secrets. And when, if you ever want to tell me, I'm here."

He stares at me with utter disbelief and then mutters four little words that crush me.

"I don't deserve you."

"But I'm here, and I'm not going anywhere."

"It won't be easy," he says. "Being with someone like me."

"Because of your dad?"

"Among other things." He glances away. "I'll need time to figure some stuff out."

"What do you mean?"

Elliot looks at me again and his broken expression sends dread streaking through me. "I want to be with you, Abi. I want you to be mine. But he won't accept it. He won't accept—"

"Me." My heart sinks.

I always knew I wasn't the kind of girl good enough to stand at Elliot's side but to hear him admit it... Well, it reinforces every negative thought I've ever had about myself.

"I wish it were different. But that's the kind of man my father is. And I refuse to let you become a pawn in his fucked-up games."

"So what are you saying?" I stare at him, confused how I can feel so happy whilst feeling such a sense of dread at the same time.

"We can be together... but we have to keep it a secret."

"I see."

"I know it's a lot to ask and it isn't forever... It's just until I figure things out."

A secret.

He wants me to be his dirty little secret.

"You'll have to keep dating Lauren?"

"No, fuck no." Elliot clutches the back of my neck and draws me to him. "I want you. Only you." His lips ghost over mine. "I just need some time. Can you give me that?"

"I..."

I shouldn't agree.

If I was a smart girl, if I knew to think with my head and not my heart like my father tried to teach me, I would say no.

But it's Elliot.

I can't deny him.

Not now—not after everything.

So I nod.

I wrap my arms around his neck and kiss him back, silently hoping that I'm not making a big mistake handing my heart and my trust to a boy who holds the power to completely ruin me.

32

ELLIOT

"What is this place? Abigail asks as I pull into the busy car park.

It's just a field. A field that's been churned up with endless traffic over the past few days. It's muddy as fuck, and I can only imagine the state of my car after this.

But one glance over at her with her wide, excited eyes locked on what lies before us, I know it's worth it.

"It's a funfair, Red," I tease.

I swear, she bounces in her seat.

"Really? And we're going?"

"Yeah," I say, shaking my head in disbelief.

"I've never been before," she confesses quietly. "My father always—" she swallows her words as a wave of grief washes over her.

Tightening my grip on her hand, I lift it to my mouth and kiss her knuckles.

She sucks in a shaky breath that makes my chest ache. "I'm sorry," she whispers, keeping her eyes locked on the window.

"Red," I breathe, pushing my seat back as fast as it will go and lifting her from hers, so she has no choice but to straddle my lap.

"What are you doing?" she gasps before realisation sets in. "No," she argues, pressing against my shoulders and trying to move back. "We can't do this here, there are kids everywhere."

"Stop," I demand, reaching up and wrapping my hand around her throat, instantly stopping every single one of her movements.

Just like I expected, her eyes darken with need and her chin drops in surprise.

"Never apologise for being sad, Red. For missing him."

She nods as I slip my hand around the back of her neck and draw her in for a kiss.

The second our lips collide, everything in me relaxes.

I've never felt anything like it. I may not have kissed the majority of girls that I've been with in the past, but I know that if I did, it wouldn't have been like this.

The moment she feels my tongue sneak out, her lips part, more than ready to let me in.

A deep groan rumbles around the car as our kiss gets hotter. With one hand on her hip, holding her against me, encouraging her to roll her hips against me.

I know she wants it. The heat of her pussy is burning through my trousers, making my dick impossibly hard for her.

"Elliot," she gasps, finally ripping her lips from mine in favour of air.

"It's okay, Red," I say, slipping my hand inside her hoodie.

"Oh God," she moans when I squeeze her breasts, her hips now moving of their own accord as she chases the release. "More. Elliot, more."

Fuck. Hearing her beg is like music to my ears.

I tuck my fingers into the cup of her bra, more than ready to give her anything she desires when someone begins hammering on the window.

My heart jumps into my throat and I react on instinct, wrapping my arms around Abigail and tugging her into my body so I can protect her, hide her from whoever is outside watching.

"Oh my God, Elliot," she gasps in my ear.

But when I look over, I don't find a pissed off parking steward, or anyone, in fact.

"There's no one there, Red. It was just someone messing around and trying to ruin our fun."

"You make me do crazy things," she confesses, her lips brushing against my throat.

"I didn't make you do anything," I argue.

"No, I know. I don't mean like that," she says, sitting back up and looking me in the eyes. "I just mean, you make me feel..." She pauses as she thinks of the right word. "Wild. Confident."

A smile pulls at my lips. "Oh yeah?" I ask, my heart racing inside my chest. I fucking love that I'm able to give her that.

"I've never... I've never done anything like this before. When I'm with you, I forget all the rules." Her cheeks blaze red with her confession, and I can't help but lift my hand and cup her jaw, my thumb grazing across her soft skin.

"Rules are meant to be broken, Red. That's where the fun lies."

"Is that why you do it?"

"Do what?"

"Sneak into my room. Watch me sleep."

I shake my head. "No, I don't do that just because I've

been told not to. I do it because I have to. Being close to you, Red. It's an obsession."

The air turns thick around us as we stare at each other.

"We should go," I say. "It's time you experienced a funfair."

Lifting her back into her seat, I quickly rearrange myself before pushing the door open and stepping out. I suck in a deep breath of fresh air in the hope that it'll squash my need to back her up against the side of my car and take her for anyone who cares to watch.

I count to five, praying that it's enough before I walk around to her side and open her door.

As I reach for her hand and help her out, my eyes run over every inch of her. She looks so much more put together than I feel right now.

"You're beautiful," I whisper, as I drag her into my body.

"Elliot," she breathes.

"I know you hate it but I'm going to keep telling you what I think until you get used to taking a compliment, Red."

She shakes her head, but I ignore her, taking her hand and tugging her toward the entrance.

Her eyes are wide as she looks around at all the rides and stalls.

"Where to first?" I ask, half expecting her to choose all the tame rides. So when her eyes move to the tallest ride here, I couldn't be more surprised.

"That one," she says, her eyes crawling up the mega drop to the people currently hanging at the top.

"Yeah?" I ask.

"You wanted to give me a thrill, right?"

I laugh, pulling her into my body and pressing my lips

to the top of her head. "You've no idea, Red. No fucking idea."

She shrieks when I suddenly release her and all but run toward the ride.

Over the next two hours, we hit up every single ride. Watching her scream with delight as she flies through the air is one of my new favourite things. There is so much life in her eyes, so much excitement. It's addictive. It's all I can do to rip my eyes off her and experience all of this for myself.

"Come on," I say, tugging her toward the Haunted House where we turn the corner and find no queue.

"Uh... I'm not sure—"

"Red," I tease. "You're not scared, are you?"

She hesitates. "N-no.'

"Aw, baby. I'll look after you. No scary ghosts or ghouls are going to get my girl."

Her breath catches at my words and my heart jumps into my throat as I realise what I said.

I remember all too well the things I said to her on that bench by the church.

I want this.

I want this so fucking badly, but I know I can't have it. Asking her to keep it secret is too much. She shouldn't have agreed. Hell, I never should have asked but I can't help myself. Having her, being close to her. It's everything.

And I never want it to end.

"Go peek inside and see how bad it is," I tell her before walking up to the young guy manning the ride and slipping him significantly more than it costs to enter.

With a nod of appreciation, I step up behind Abigail. "Boo," I breathe in her ear, laughing as she startles.

"You really are scared, huh?"

"I just... I don't like things that make me jump."

Taking both her hands in mine, I walk backward into the darkness. "Let's see if I can find a way of taking your mind off it."

She laughs lightly as if I'm joking, and I play along… for now.

She clings to me as we pass through the sections, each clown or zombie making her flinch.

"Can you stop laughing at me?" She sulks as she edges around yet another clown with an admittedly terrifying grin.

"Sorry, I can't. You're just too cute."

"I'm anything but cute right now," she huffs as we step into a room full of mirrors.

Everywhere I look, all I can see is the two of us hand in hand.

"Yeah, you're right. You're not cute."

She screams as I back her up against one of the mirrors.

"You're hot. So fucking hot I can hardly think straight."

Hitching one of her legs around my waist, I lean into her, letting her feel exactly what she does to me.

"I-I think… I think that's because all your blood has rushed south," she teases, her cheeks burning red hot.

"Like this every time I'm near you," I confess, trailing wet kisses down the side of her throat. "You get me so hot, baby. All I can think about is making you scream again."

"Elliot," she warns, her hands pressing against my chest to push me back.

"Be wild with me, Red," I say, lifting her arms so they rest over my shoulders instead.

"We can't. There are kids and—"

I cut her argument off with a kiss. An all-consuming, dirty kiss that leaves her panting and desperate for more.

And fuck, do I want to give it to her.

Sliding my hand under her hoodie, I find the waistband of her leggings and shove my hand beneath.

"Oh my God, you can't— Elliot," she cries when I find her swollen clit.

"I can and I will," I tell her, my voice rough with need as I push lower, finding her soaked and ready for me. "Argue all you like, but your pussy tells a different story. You're dripping for me, Red."

I push my fingers inside her, letting the heel of my hand put pressure on her clit. "Just think, if we weren't interrupted in the car, they could have watched you fall for me. They'd have seen just how beautiful you are when you lose control."

Liquid heat floods my fingers.

"Oh, little innocent Abigail Bancroft isn't so sweet really, is she?" I taunt, curling my fingers in a way that makes her gasp and cling to my shoulders.

"Oh God. Elliot."

"You're so wet for me, Red. You're running down my hand."

Her head falls back against the wall and her eyes close, severing our connection.

I'm not down for that.

"Eyes, Abi," I demand harshly as my hand darts out to collar her throat. "I want you to watch me as I make you shatter. I want you to know who's doing this to you."

"You," she breathes. "Only ever you."

"Is this mine?" I ask fucking her harder. "Does this tight little pussy belong to me, Red?"

She nods.

"Then prove it," I demand, tightening my grip on her throat, cutting off her air. "Come for me."

The second I say the words, her body quakes and she

shatters, right there in the middle of the Haunted House, surrounded by nothing but our own reflections.

Leaning forward, I rest my brow against hers as her breath races over my face. Seconds turn into minutes as we just stare at each other, the air crackling around us.

I'm desperate for her. It would be so easy to take more. I know she'd allow it. And fuck, watching myself take her surrounded by all these mirrors would be so fucking hot.

But I can't.

I've already asked too much of her. Taken too much from her.

"I-I—" She swallows thickly as I finally pull my hand from her leggings. "I can't believe we just did that, anyone could have walk— Oh God," she moans when I lift the two fingers that were just inside me to my mouth and push them past my lips.

Her taste floods my mouth as I suck on them. "Delicious," I murmur, making her pupils dilate.

A scream rips through the air, and we jump apart.

I guess that our time's up.

"Come on," I say, grabbing her hand and pulling her away from the mirrors. "Fancy some candy floss?" I ask, unable to stop the filthy images that erupt in my head of eating it from her body.

"Sure," she agrees, making me look over, and the second I catch sight of the wicked glint in her eye, I can't help but wonder if she's having similar thoughts.

33

ABIGAIL

I haven't stopped smiling.

Today has been incredible.

We've talked and kissed and shared things with each other. Elliot even won me a cute teddy on the strong man game.

I haven't stopped cuddling the slightly imperfect bear, clutching it to my chest like it's a sack of gold.

But when Elliot pulls up outside my building in the cover of darkness, my heart tumbles.

"What's wrong?" he asks me, cutting the engine.

"I guess all good things come to an end." I offer him a sad smile.

I want to be brave and strong and pretend that it doesn't matter that he's asked me to keep things between us a secret, but the truth is, it does.

"It's not forever, I promise. I just need some time to figure out—"

"I know."

We stare at each other in the darkness. And I wonder if this is the life we're destined for. To always remain concealed in shadows and half-light. Never truly able to step into the light.

I've always felt safer there, more at ease. Something tells me Elliot has too.

Maybe it is where we belong, after all.

But how will that work if we can never let our relationship be public? If we can never tell our friends or his family?

What kind of life is that?

Dread churns in my stomach as every doubt and insecurity I've ever had starts to rise inside me like a tidal wave.

"I want this," he says roughly, leaning over to palm my cheek. I turn into his touch, both loving and hating the way his fingers brush my scars. "I want you."

I nod, not trusting myself to talk.

"Words, Red. I need you to use your words. Tell me you're in this with me."

"I... I'm in."

As if I ever had a choice.

Before she died, my mum always told me that one day I'd meet a boy who would steal my heart.

I just didn't expect him to be an Heir.

But maybe that's always been my fate. Betrothed to one Heir, falling for another.

I smile to myself.

"What?" Elliot frowns in that super serious way of his.

"Nothing. Do you"—I hesitate—"have to go or can you come in for a little bit?"

"No, I can come in for a—" The blare of his phone cuts through the tension swirling around us. "Shit," he says, checking the screen. "It's my brother."

"You should answer it." I slouch back in my seat, my chest tightening.

"Scott, yeah." Elliot drags a hand over his jaw. "What? Now? Yeah... No, okay. Fine. I said fine didn't I." He hangs up and exhales out a frustrated breath.

"Is there a problem?"

"I have to go."

"Oh, okay."

"I'm sorry—"

"No, it's fine. You should go. I have some homework to do anyway."

"I'll see you tomorrow, okay?"

"At school. Where we'll pretend we're not... You know?"

"Abi, I don't—"

"It's fine." I smile tightly while my hand scrambles for the door handle. "I'm fine."

"You're sure? I can call the girls or Millie or—"

"No, no!" Forcing myself to inhale a deep breath, I lift my eyes to his. "We knew today would come to an end eventually."

"I'll find a way to come over tonight."

"You will?" My heart soars.

"Yeah." He leans over and steals a kiss. "You're my girl now, Red. Nothing will keep me away."

Elliot didn't come over.

I woke to an empty room and a sense of dread. But for the first time since my father's death, I don't allow myself to stay in bed and wallow. Instead, I force myself into the shower and get ready for a day of classes.

I'm sure Elliot has a good reason for being a no show, and I'm sure he'll tell me when he's ready.

At least I hope—

My phone vibrates and I hurry to snatch it up, failing to withhold my nervous laugh when I see Elliot's name.

> Elliot: Sorry I didn't show last night. Family stuff.

My brows furrow. It's not quite the explanation I hoped for, but I can't expect him to share everything with me straight away. Revealing the deepest, darkest parts of yourself to another person takes time and trust.

> Abigail: That's alright. I hope everything's okay?

> Elliot: It will be.

My teeth worry my bottom lip as I consider my reply. Clearly, he doesn't want to talk about it. And I don't want to come across as pushy or needy. But I also don't know the rules here.

Before I can reply though, there's a knock at my door.

I hurry over and check the peephole before opening it.

"Ethan." I frown. "What are you doing here?"

"I thought I'd see if you want to get breakfast."

"How did you get in here? Bronte is a girls' only dorm."

"Relax. No one is going to say anything on a Monday morning. So what do you say?"

"Sorry, what?"

"To breakfast? No strings, I promise." He lifts up his hands in surrender.

"Don't you have other people you could eat breakfast with?"

"Of course I do. But I'm asking you."

"I... I'm not sure that's a good idea." I might not know

the rules around keeping things a secret with Elliot, but it doesn't feel right having breakfast with another boy.

"What? Why?" Hurt flashes in his expression. "It's just breakfast, Abi. We've got to walk right past the cafeteria to get to our first class anyway, so what's the big deal?"

"I... Fine."

I'll just tell Elliot, and then he can't get weird about it.

"I'll wait out here," he replies as if I was ever going to invite him in.

I quickly text Elliot and grab my bag.

> Abigail: Ethan asked me if I want to get breakfast on the way to class. I can tell him no but he's being pretty insistent about it.

> Elliot: It's fine. Ethan is a good guy. You should go

> Abigail: You're sure? I don't have to if you don't want me to.

> Elliot: It's just breakfast, Abi. Make sure you eat something.

Disappointment wells in my chest. I guess deep down, I hoped for a different reply.

"Abi, let's go. I'm starving," Ethan calls.

I pocket my phone and head for the door, joining him in the hallway.

"So how was your weekend?"

"My weekend?"

"Why do you always do that?" he chuckles, and I frown.

"Do what?"

"Answer with a question."

"I... I'm sorry."

"Don't be sorry," he says. "It's cute. But you also sound so unsure of yourself, Abi. Like you can't actually believe I'd want to be your friend."

"Why do you want to be my friend? It doesn't make any sense."

"Like I said before, I know what it's like to lose your family. I didn't really have anyone to help me when... Well, you know?"

"You've got tons of friends Ethan."

"You can be surrounded by people but still be lonely, Abi."

"I'm sorry."

"Again with the sorrys, Bancroft." He grins down at me as we leave my dorm building and cut across the lawn toward sixth form. "You seem a bit better," he remarks. "Lighter somehow. That's good. I was worried there for a second."

"Really?"

I still find it odd that he cares. But I guess that's what years of being the odd girl out will do to you.

"Really." He rolls his eyes as he pulls open the door for me to enter the building.

There are a few students milling around but the morning rush hasn't arrived yet, which I'm grateful for.

"Something smells good," Ethan says as we reach the cafeteria.

I still don't feel entirely comfortable being here with him but that empty, lonely part of me is grateful for a friend. Especially when so many students cast their sympathetic, pitiful gazes towards me.

But it isn't really Ethan I want to be here with. It's Elliot. And that can't happen. Not today. Not tomorrow.

Maybe not ever.

"What do you fancy?" he asks me, nudging me toward a table.

"I can get my own—"

"Relax, I've got it."

"Fine. I'll have a cup of tea and a toasted bagel, please."

"Butter? Cream cheese? Jam?"

"Just butter, thank you."

"Sit. I'll be right back."

Ethan strolls off like the two of us having breakfast is the most normal thing in the world, and I can't help but think maybe I had him all wrong in the beginning. Because he has been a good friend to me, when I've let him be, at least.

And in a strange way, it's nice to have a friend outside of the Heirs and their inner circle.

A few minutes later, he returns with what looks to be more than a toasted bagel and tea.

I arch a brow and he chuckles. "Okay, so here me out. I know you said to get a bagel, but the egg and spinach muffin looked so good, and it's blueberry muffin Monday so I grabbed one of those too."

"Ethan, I'll never eat all of this." I barely have my appetite back as it is.

Although he's right, it does look good.

"It's all good. Whatever you don't eat, I will."

"This is really nice of you," I say as he sits down.

"What can I say, I'm a nice guy?"

Familiar laughter draws my attention and I watch as the girls enter the cafeteria.

"Abs, you're—" Tally draws up short, flicking her gaze to my table mate. "Having a breakfast date with Ethan Smith."

"Oh no, it isn't a date. That's not... I mean, we're not—"

"Relax, Bancroft. Tallulah is just messing with you."

"I knew the two of you were hanging out, but this is weird. It's weird, right?" She glances to Liv and Raine for back up.

"It's just breakfast." Liv shrugs. "I'm just happy she's eating something." Shame burns my cheeks, and she lets out a soft sigh. "Abs, I didn't mean—"

"It's fine."

"Can we join you?" Raine asks.

"Sure, have at it. I actually need to go anyway."

"What? Why?" I gawk at Ethan.

We literally just got here, and he wants to leave already?

"Your friends are here now." He winks and gets up, grabbing his egg muffin and the blueberry muffin. "See you in class."

He walks out without so much as a backward glance and I stare after him.

"What was all that about?" Tally nudges my arm.

"Honestly," I murmur, staring at the door. "I have no idea."

34

ABIGAIL

I didn't see Elliot all day at school yesterday and he didn't come by last night.

If I didn't trust him not to hurt me again, I'd wonder if yesterday was a dream.

Some vivid fantasy my weary mind created to help me escape the grief-filled void.

There's been nothing except a couple of vague texts to say he's dealing with family stuff.

I hope he's okay. There's something sinister about the Eaton family. Something he's reluctant to tell me. But I'm not so naïve that I don't have my suspicions. I just hope I'm wrong.

Because I can't imagine anyone hurting Elliot. He's so big and strong and formidable.

A force to reckoned with.

"Abi?" Tally approaches and I blink up at her.

"Hi." I give her a weak smile.

"What are you doing?"

"Just... sitting."

"I can see that. Are you waiting for someone?"

"Just enjoying some fresh air," I lie.

From the bench outside sixth form, I can see the rugby field and the Chapel in the distance.

It seems silly now to be sitting here. But I guess part of me was hoping to catch a glimpse of Elliot. To know that, even if he hasn't been in touch much, he's okay.

"What's going on with you?" She sits beside me.

"Nothing, I'm just—"

"Abigail, you are many things. But a good liar you are not. Is this about Ethan?"

"Ethan? God, no. Why would you even say that."

"Oh, I don't know." Her lips twist with amusement. "You two seemed pretty cosy yesterday morning."

"It really isn't like that."

"Because you're still hung up on Elliot?" I press my lips together and she releases a weary sigh. "What happened between the two of you, Abs? Really?"

I could lie or I could tell her the truth.

Now that Elliot has admitted he does feel the same, it doesn't seem so important anymore to keep the kiss to myself.

"I kissed him. At the party, the night I found out my father died."

"Oh, babe. I'm so sorry. I knew something had happened, I just didn't think... You kissed him?" I nod and she grimaces. "Oh, Abs. I didn't ever think you'd actually go for it. I take it he didn't respond the way you hoped?"

"No, he didn't."

"Well, it's probably for the best. Elliot is—"

"Out of my league."

"You know that isn't what I mean. But he is a complicated boy with a complicated life. I'm not sure you're ready to walk in his world. Ethan, however, now there's a boy I can see you being happy with."

Her lack of faith in me and Elliot hurts but I can't really blame her. It's only what everyone else thinks, even Elliot.

"I sensed some tension between the two of you," she adds. "I can't believe you kissed him. What was it like?"

"I'd rather not talk about it."

"God, sorry. Of course."

I stand, needing this conversation to be over. "I'm going to head back to my room."

"Abs, come on, don't go. We can hang out. I miss you. The boys don't mind you coming to the Chapel, and Elliot is still at his parents' house so you don't have to worry about seeing him if you don't want to."

"Maybe another time." I offer her an apologetic smile and take off toward my building.

I know if I keep pushing her and the girls away, eventually they'll stop trying. But I can't go to the Chapel now. Not when things are so up in the air with Elliot.

I check my phone again, wondering if I have poor signal or something. But it's in full working order which can only mean Elliot hasn't found time to text me... or wanted to.

God, I hate this.

I hate that I'm so insecure my thoughts instantly go to a negative place.

Elliot said he wants me and only me, I have to believe that.

I have to hold onto that.

I just wish he felt able to share things with me more easily, instead of keeping me at arm's length.

I almost leap off my bed later that afternoon when my phone finally vibrates.

The sight of Elliot's name eases the giant knot in my stomach.

> Elliot: Can you meet me?

> Abigail: What? Now?

> Elliot: Yeah. I can't come back to All Hallows' yet, but I want to see you.

> Abigail: Where do you want to meet?

> Elliot: There's a bar just outside town. The Black Swan.

A date.

He wants to take me on a date, in public. I don't know whether to laugh or cry.

> Abigail: Are you sure? Isn't it too soon?

I inhale a shaky breath.

> Elliot: It's fine, I promise. Meet me at seven? Wear something pretty. Just for me.

> Abigail: I'll be there.

> Elliot: Such a good girl for me. See you at seven. E

Panic overtakes me as I realise I have less than an hour to get ready and nothing to wear.

God, I wish I could call Tally and ask for her advice. But there's no time and I don't know if they all know yet.

I'm guessing they don't if Elliot is still at his parents' house.

Still, I feel giddy as I sift through my wardrobe trying to find something to wear. There isn't much to work with, but I do find a pretty dark green sweater dress that contrasts my hair and complements my pale skin. I wouldn't exactly call it sexy, but it hugs my slim figure and looks nice with my black ankle boots and black jacket.

After dusting my eyes with a bit of smoky eyeshadow and glossing my lips, I don't give myself any time to overthink things and head out to my car.

Thankfully, no one is around to question where I'm going at this hour all dressed up. Not that anyone apart from a Millie talks to me in the building.

The drive through Saints Cross takes me less than fifteen minutes and another five to find somewhere to park near the pub.

I've never done this before. Gone into town to go to a pub. But unsurprisingly, I'm more nervous about seeing Elliot than I am at the thought of walking into a busy pub.

I half-expect the entire place to turn my way when I step inside, but no one pays me any attention as I scan the room, immediately spotting Elliot in one of the booths lining the wall.

I smile, the knot in my chest unravelling with every step as I move in his direction, desperate to see him. Nervous but excited to be taking the next step in our fledgling relationship.

But I ground to a halt when I realise he isn't alone.

A beautiful blonde leans into him, laughing at whatever he just said, and the ground goes from under me.

No.

No.

I don't understand.

He invited me here.

I stand in the middle of the pub surrounded by laughter and chatter but all I hear is the roar of blood between my ears as I watch them.

They look perfect together. Beautiful and wealthy. Elliot's arm rests along the back of the booth, toying with her hair.

Vomit churns in my stomach, rushing up my throat and I have to clasp a hand over my mouth.

I need to go.

God, I need to get out of here before—

"Ah, there you are. We've been expecting you." A hand clamps on my arm and starts dragging me toward the booth. "Elliot is going to be so happy to see you. Look who I found," the man says before I can figure out what the hell is going on.

"Scott, what— Abi." Elliot's expression falters for a split second before his stone-cold mask slides into place.

"Abi?" the blonde asks. "Who the fuck is Abi?"

"This is Elliot's friend from All Hallows' isn't that right, little brother?"

"What are you doing here?" Elliot asks coldly, and I barely recognise this boy in front of me.

This isn't my Elliot.

It isn't him at all.

"I—"

"Abi?" another voice says, and I turn to find Ethan approaching us, wearing a deep frown.

"Ethan."

"What's going on, Scott?" Elliot asks.

Scott.

His brother.

I should have realised but I feel completely blindsided.

Scott sits back in the booth, grinning like a criminal mastermind watching his master plan in action. "I told Ethan to stop by so you could settle up with him."

"Scott," Elliot says in a low warning, and I glance between them, trying to work out what I'm missing. Because something is going on, something I don't understand.

"Look, mate," Ethan holds up his hands. "I'm not sure what's going on, but Scott said if I stopped by tonight you would settle up what you owe me because you no longer need me to—"

"Don't." Elliot growls and I finally snap out of it.

"Settle up?" I ask, looking to Ethan. Guilt flashes in his eyes and my stomach tumbles. "Ethan? What's going on? What do you mean, settle up what Elliot owes you? What does he owe you?"

"Fuck, Abi, I didn't... I don't. Shit." He glances to Elliot, but I force myself not to look at him yet. I need Ethan to tell me the truth.

"Do you want to tell her or should I?" he asks Elliot.

"Scott," the girl beside him hisses. "What have you done—"

"Relax, babe." He smirks right at me. "It seems my soft-hearted brother here paid Ethan to befriend Miss Bancroft after she developed an unhealthy little crush on Elliot and he rejected her."

I flinch at his cruel words. The truth behind them. But more than that, I wince at the betrayal shattering through me.

He paid Ethan.

Elliot paid Ethan to be my friend.

Oh my God.

I clutch my throat feeling utterly exposed.

"So pathetic," the blonde rolls her eyes at me before sipping on her expensive looking cocktail, like I'm not worth her time or the interruption of what is clearly a double date. "For God's sake, Elliot, just pay him so we can move on from this little soap drama."

"Yes, Brother. Why don't you pay up? What was it you agreed on? A meagre two hundred quid?"

"Uh, it was five actually," Ethan pipes up, and I stare at him incredulously. "No hard feelings, yeah. You're an all right girl and everything but I needed the money and well, nobody says no to an Eaton."

I look at Elliot for some kind of explanation, anything to undo this nightmare.

But he just stares through me, saying nothing.

What is even happening right now?

"I-I should go," I rush out, the walls of the upmarket pub closing in around me.

I can't breathe.

Oh, God, I can't breathe.

"Don't leave on our account," Scott calls after me, his laughter twisting the knife in my heart a little deeper as I all but run toward the door, desperate to get out of here.

To get as far far away from Elliot Eaton and his web of deception and lies as I can.

I burst out of the pub into a sheet of rain. But I welcome the deluge. At least it will hide the fat ugly tears rolling down my cheeks.

At least it will conceal my absolute devastation.

For a second, I glance back at the entrance, sucking in a ragged, broken breath, hoping and praying that Elliot will appear at any second to come after me.

To explain.

But he doesn't.

And yet again I'm left lost and alone at the hands of Elliot Eaton.

Only this time, my heart isn't just wounded.

It's completely and utterly destroyed.

SAVAGE VICIOUS HEIR: PART TWO

1

ELLIOT

"*It seems my soft-hearted brother here paid Ethan to befriend Miss Bancroft after she developed an unhealthy little crush on Elliot and he rejected her.*"

Scott's words repeat over and over in my head as blood roars past my ears, stopping me from hearing the laughter that rings out around me.

Ethan still stands at the end of our table looking both embarrassed and terrified, but it isn't him I care about.

Did I do what Scott just explained to Abigail? Yes, in a way, I did. But my intentions were never so cruel, so vicious.

I was trying to protect her.

I shake my head and pain slices through my chest.

"Here," Scott snaps before throwing a wodge of notes down on the table and shoving them towards Ethan. "Now fuck off, yeah?"

Ethan's eyes drop to the cash before moving to mine.

"Take it. We're done," I confirm, my voice barely sounding like my own.

I learned the art of cutting myself off from reality and

pulling on a mask, armour, long ago but Abigail always manages to penetrate it.

Usually, I can appear unaffected by anything, but right now, I fear that I'm not hiding my true feelings.

"Just for the record," Ethan says as he swipes up the notes and pushes them into his pocket. "I think you're an arsehole for what you've done to her, Eaton."

My chin drops in surprise. No one usually dares to say those kinds of things to our faces. Especially someone with the social standing of Ethan Smith. But I quickly find that I don't have any words to come back with.

For the first time, I truly care about the pain I've caused.

Scott, on the other hand, scoffs before a sinister smile pulls at his lips. "We're Eatons, kid. Arsehole is our middle name. Now, we've got shit to discuss that doesn't include you so fuck off, yeah."

Scott shoos him away as if Ethan is nothing more than an irritating fly.

The second he steps away from our table, my head twists around without instruction from my brain as I search the tinted windows that hide the busy street housing the pub for Abigail.

"Don't even think about it," Scott sneers, predicting exactly what I want to do.

What I *need* to do.

A warm hand slides up my thigh and I jerk away from Lauren. Her hand is like being touched with a branding iron. It burns, and not in a fucking good way.

I need to get out of here.

I need—

Sliding from the bench, I push to my feet but the second I stand to full height, Scott's demanding voice rings through my ears.

"Walk out and the first thing I'll do is call Dad," he warns. "And I won't just tell him you refused this date, I'll tell him all about your little *girlfriend* too."

My blood runs cold, the walls of the pub closing in around me.

Having Scott know about my feelings for Abigail is bad enough. But my father can't know.

He'll ruin her and he'll force me to watch.

With acid burning up my throat at the thought of the pain Johnathon Eaton could cause a sweet girl like Abigail, I retake my seat, gritting my teeth when Lauren's hand returns to my thigh, squeezing in what I assume she thinks is a supportive gesture.

It's not.

There is nothing supportive about the vapid bitch my father thinks is a good match for me.

He's got it all planned, I know he has.

A handful of dates, a public engagement announcement followed by a bullshit show of a wedding.

It's exactly how Scott's life will go, and exactly how mine isn't.

I might toe the line, keep my head down, and avoid the pain our father is capable of delivering, but I will not accept that.

I just need to find a way out. And more importantly, a way out that won't leave those I love behind and in the firing line.

With gritted teeth and my muscles pulled tight, I force myself to sit through the rest of the unbearable double date I was forced to partake in.

By the time we leave and head towards our cars, I'm barely holding on by a thread.

I need to go and find Abigail. I need to somehow try to

explain, I need to apologise, I need… Fuck… I don't even know what I need to do at this point.

She'd have every right to refuse to listen to anything I have to say. Every right never to talk to me again.

The thought of that happening makes me sick to my stomach.

I've fought my attraction to her for so long. Longer than I should have. I've caused us both more pain than necessary by holding back. And despite warning her that being with me wasn't going to be easy, I never expected for it to blow up in our faces quite this quickly.

I want her dammit.

I need her.

I've also probably royally fucked it up before it's even started.

The all-powerful Elliot Eaton, fucking everything up he touches.

Dad would have a field day with this.

The only girl I've ever truly liked, and I've barely made it a few days before shattering what we've found together.

"You need to take Lauren home," Scott points as he rips the passenger door open.

I'm already strapped in with the engine on ready to gun it back to campus to find her.

"You take her. I'm not interested," I mutter under my breath so she can't hear. Not that I really give a shit.

Lauren might be pretty, but that's about all she's got going for her. That and her father's money, I guess. But I'm about as interested in that as I am in her looks.

"Do you really want that getting back to Dad?"

I narrow my eyes at him. There is no point calling his bluff, he'll snitch on me for anything he possibly can. I'm pretty sure I learned that fact about my big brother before I was even walking.

Trust him with nothing. Keep him away from anything you deem precious. He will destroy it all in a heartbeat and with a smile on his face.

Just like he did tonight.

I sit with my fingers wrapped around my wheel in an iron grip as Lauren drops into my passenger seat, ensuring her skirt is short enough that I know what colour her knickers are before she straps herself in and begins adjusting her top to show off her assets. Assets I'm not interested in.

"You really should start taking this more seriously," she says as I floor it from the car park.

"I have no interest in this, and that won't change no matter how much you expose yourself to me," I snap.

"My father won't like to hear that."

"Lauren," I sigh, hating that I'm losing control. I usually have a better grasp on myself than this.

But you don't usually have a girl you care about with a broken heart waiting for you to find her…

"I'm sorry, okay?" I lie. "You're a great girl, Lauren. Beautiful, smart." Another lie. There's a reason her father wants to sell her off to someone who should be successful. "But you're not what I'm looking for."

"And there is your problem," she points out. "You seem to be forgetting that we don't have a choice in this."

I just about manage to catch the bitter laugh that tumbles from my lips at her words.

"You think I want to be stuck with you?" she scoffs.

"I'm an Eaton," I say arrogantly. "I thought that was every girl's dream."

Unlike me, she's unable to contain her bitterness at my comment. "Sure. If you need your ego stroking. This is a business transaction between our fathers, you know that as well as I do."

"Yet you seem to want it," I point out.

"Why wouldn't I? Stick with you and I'll be set for life. I can think of worse ways to live. Mansion, fancy holidays, everything I could possibly want."

"What about love?" I blurt taking a left at the lights that will lead us towards SCU and her house.

She lets out a bitter laugh. "What about it? It's bullshit. Surely you of all people know that."

My mouth opens and closes a couple of times as I try to come up with a response.

A few months ago, I would probably have agreed with her.

Until watching my boys fall for their girls, every relationship I'd experienced were just like the one my father is trying to set up here. A business deal. It's the reason why him and Mum are together, my grandparents before them. Scott and Zoey are no different.

The joining of power-hungry families so they can claim even more of the things they love most. Money, power, and respect.

It's all bullshit.

I knew it before embarking on this thing with Abigail, but now, after falling for her, it couldn't be more obvious. And I don't want to live a life that has been planned out for me with a girl who's been chosen because of her social status. Just like I don't want to attend a university because it's expected of me, or study for a degree that will help the family and the business I'm expected to work for.

My grip on the wheel tightens until my fingers begin to cramp.

I want to argue with her. But what's the point?

She's fully on board with this.

"I'll let you fuck other women if that's what you want,"

she offers. "I'm not precious. Of course, I'll be doing the same. No offence, but you're not actually my type."

My brows lift. I'm not sure I've ever heard that before. Not that I give a shit.

She's not fucking mine either.

My teeth grind before I force out. "How generous of you."

"We just need to make the best of it. We could have a good life together."

"Yeah," I muse. In another fucking universe.

Thankfully, the bright lights of SCU come into view up ahead, and I turn into the street where Lauren lives.

Few words are said between us as I pull the car to a stop and she climbs out. She doesn't even offer for me to come up.

Maybe she's not as dumb as I first thought.

Lauren is about to close the door and allow me to finally go and find Abigail when she thinks better of it and leans in. "You need to be careful, Elliot," she says and I'm sure I catch a hint of concern in her eyes. "You're playing a dangerous game here."

"Oh yeah?" I taunt. "Why's that?"

"Your father won't accept her no matter which way you spin it. The best thing you can do is forget about the girl and do as you're told."

Irritation drips through my veins.

I've been doing that my whole fucking life and look where it's got me.

"Thanks for the advice," I say, putting the car into drive and pulling away, giving her little choice but to close the door before I take off with it still open.

The journey back to All Hallows' is longer than I've ever known. The second I pull to a stop in my usual space,

I all but fly from the driver's seat as I race towards the Bronte Building.

It's still early and there are girls loitering around. All of them turn to look at me as I let myself in. A couple move forward as if they're going to attempt to intercept me, but I'm gone before they get anywhere close.

I take the stairs three at a time before marching down the hallway towards her room.

In seconds, I'm standing before Abi's door trying to decide what to do. Should I do the right thing and knock, warn her that I'm here, and ultimately allow her to ignore me? Or do I just storm my way inside and force her to face me?

I almost laugh to myself that I'm even considering the former as an option.

Pulling the keycard from my pocket, I hold it to the panel beside the door. The second it beeps and the locks disengage, I storm inside.

"Red, we need—"

But my announcement is cut short at what I find.

2

ABIGAIL

Tears stream down my face as I drive.

I don't know where exactly I'm going. All I know is I can't go back to All Hallows'.

Not yet.

Not after...

God, I'm such an idiot.

A lovesick fool blinded by my own desperation to feel something other than the crippling loneliness I've felt every day since my mum died.

I should have known.

I should have realised that someone like Ethan Smith would never really want to be my friend. Just as I should have known that a boy like Elliot Eaton couldn't be trusted not to hurt me.

He paid Ethan. Paid him to be my friend.

He betrayed me.

Elliot paid Ethan to befriend me, to take pity on me.

I don't know what hurts more—that Elliot initiated the whole thing or that Ethan accepted.

And to think I finally believed I was more to him than an obligation.

A burden.

When I'm nothing more than a foolish girl tricked by her heart.

His brother was there. The girl he's been dating.

The girl he told me meant nothing to him.

God, the way she'd looked at me. With utter disdain and disgust. How could I ever hope to compete with her?

Beautiful, confident, poised. Everything I'll never be.

I've been nothing more than a pawn in their savage, vicious games and now everything is ruined again.

I'm ruined.

Another sob claws its way up my throat. So desperate and ragged, it echoes around the car as I physically try and hold myself together.

Why did he do it?

Why pay Ethan to befriend me? To humiliate and hurt me?

The second I arrived at the pub and Scott intercepted me, guiding me over to their table it was obvious Elliot didn't invite me to be there. That I'd been set up by his evil big brother. But it doesn't change anything because deep down, I know if tonight had never happened, Elliot wouldn't have told me about Ethan, about their arrangement, or the fact he's still dating Lauren.

What was it she called me?

Pathetic.

I sure feel it.

The signs were there—the rumours. The whispers. But I didn't listen because Elliot is a master of deception. Of navigating his way around a world I'll never quite belong in.

Who does that?

Who pays somebody to become someone's friend?

The jaws of humiliation tighten around my heart and I let out another choked sob as I picture their faces.

Scott Eaton and his gorgeous girlfriend.

Ethan.

Elliot.

His date.

His beautiful, perfect date that looked at me like I was nothing more than a speck of dirt.

Completely and utterly beneath her.

Beneath them all.

I felt it too. Felt so insignificant and pathetic as they all looked at me with a mix of pity and amusement.

He warned me.

Elliot warned me.

Time and time again he tried to warn me but I ignored him. I willingly handed him my heart and my body. All because it felt real. I thought he felt it too.

Every second with him, every stolen kiss and desperate touch... It had all felt too real to be a farce.

Another wave of pain splinters through me as the houses and shops begin to give way to the gloomy, dark countryside.

Rain pelts off the car, drowning out the sound of my heart breaking. Shattering in my chest and bleeding out all over my car.

I have no one to call. Nowhere to go.

I have—

A thought occurs to me and I feel a flicker of relief.

Why didn't I think of it sooner?

Probably because when I left home and moved into the dorms, I thought I'd never look back.

But I don't have anywhere else to go.

And regardless of how much it hurts to be there,

nothing hurts more than knowing the boy I love betrayed me.

When I finally pull up to my childhood home, I don't get out of the car.

Instead, I torture myself by reading my last text thread with Elliot. The messages that led to this point.

This utter despair and devastation.

> Elliot: Can you meet me?
>
> Abigail: What? Now?
>
> Elliot: Yeah. I can't come back to All Hallows' yet, but I want to see you.
>
> Abigail: Where do you want to meet?
>
> Elliot: There's a bar just outside town. The Black Swan.
>
> Abigail: Are you sure? Isn't it too soon?
>
> Elliot: It's fine, I promise. Meet me at seven? Wear something pretty. Just for me.
>
> Abigail: I'll be there.
>
> Elliot: Such a good girl for me. See you at seven. E

God, I'd been so giddy at the thought that he wanted to be seen with me in public—that he wanted to go on a date.

I was so eager to soak up his attention, the thrill of being his girl, I didn't question it.

I didn't even consider that—

I swallow over the lump in my throat.

Why would I have assumed anything was wrong?

It's Elliot.

I trusted him.

I trusted him not to hurt me.

Even if he wasn't the one to send those messages, to set me up, he still showed his true colours tonight when he stood by and did nothing while his brother tore me to shreds in front of their dates and an entire pub full of people.

Frustrated at myself, I shove my phone in my bag and climb out of my car, trudging towards the house.

It looms over me, dark and foreboding, as if to say, 'We knew you'd be back, we knew you wouldn't survive out there.'

And I hate it.

I hate that there's even an ounce of truth to it.

But I can't go back to All Hallows' tonight.

I can't call Tally or the girls or Mr Porter or the dorm aunt.

I just can't.

So I dig my key out of my purse and slide it into the lock, opening the door.

A film of fusty air greets me as I step inside.

The house feels strange.

Unfamiliar.

Vast and empty.

The silence is deafening, not even the gentle muffle of my sobs drowning out the hollow loneliness I feel.

All because I was tricked by a dangerous boy dressed up in an expensive, pretty package.

Nausea washes through me and I sway on my feet, before darting down the hall and running into the downstairs bathroom.

I drop to my knees and wrench the toilet lid up just in time for my meagre stomach contents to make an appearance.

I purge my soul into the bowl. Wishing I could erase every memory, every touch and kiss.

Wishing I could erase the moment I willingly handed Elliot my fragile heart.

Trusting him not to break it.

After cleaning myself up, I manage to find a lonely glass discarded at the back of one of the kitchen cabinets and pour myself some water.

It's late and I'm exhausted, so I drag myself upstairs into my old bedroom.

It's an empty shell now, most of my belongings tucked safely away in my dorm room. But it still holds a sense of familiarity that eases the storm raging inside me a little.

Kicking off my boots, I undress down to my underwear and climb into my bed and pull the covers up high, relieved that Maureen thought to keep the beds dressed for the listing photos.

I never wanted to come back here, but now, in the dead of night, it feels fitting.

My life was irrevocably changed here. First losing my mother, then my father.

And now losing the last shred of hope that I have a place here in Saints Cross, a home.

I thought Elliot could be that for me.

I thought he was the missing piece to my tragic life story.

But he was nothing more than a fantasy.

A beautiful nightmare, and my greatest fears all rolled into one.

The girls warned me.

They told me Elliot was a complicated boy.

But I didn't listen.

I didn't want to hear it because I thought I knew him. I thought there was shred of decency inside him.

It was all a lie.

One I'll never fall for again.

3

ELLIOT

She's not here.

Her bed is a mess, but despite the lump, I know she's not here.

I can't feel her.

"Red," I call again, hoping that I'm wrong.

Praying that I'm wrong.

I blow around her room like a tornado before throwing her bathroom door open.

There's a part of me that expects to find her in a heap on the tiled floor with a knife in one hand as she bleeds out, and I'm so fucking relieved when I find the room empty.

My heart thunders in my chest as I spin around feeling totally out of my depth.

I hurt her tonight. I hurt her bad.

You warned her...

I shake my head trying to banish the unhelpful thoughts. I told her this was going to be hard, that I was going to have to keep us a secret to protect her.

I knew my family would be the ones to fuck all this up.

I just never expected it would happen so fast or in such an explosive fashion.

Doing what I did with Ethan was a risk.

When I first asked him to step in and be her friend, I hoped that it would help with my obsession with her, and in turn, hers with me. But the first time I saw them together, the first time I saw her smile at him like he was someone special, I knew I'd fucked up.

It didn't sate the desire I had for her, it only made it burn hotter. And the jealousy... That was something I hadn't banked on.

Fuck. I've never experienced anything like it.

And I did it to myself.

Self-sabotage at its finest. But I didn't—I don't—know what else to do.

The pain she's suffering right now was inevitable.

It could have happened now or in three months' time.

It didn't matter when, it was always going to happen.

It's why I've kept her at arm's length all this time.

A sweet girl like Abigail doesn't belong in my dark and twisted life.

Swiping the All Hallows' hoodie from the end of her bed, I shamelessly lift it to my nose as I fall back into her chair.

"I'm so fucking sorry, Red," I whisper into the silence as regret after regret slams into me.

Resting my elbows on my knees, I drop my head into the soft fabric and breathe her scent in.

Where is she likely to go?

Before her dad died, I'd have said she would go straight to the girls. But since she lost him, she's been pulling farther and farther away from them.

She's pulled away from everyone... *apart from you.*

I grit my teeth as I try and come up with options.

Where would she go to hide?

With a sigh, I push from the chair, throw her hoodie back on the bed, and storm out of her dorm room. I'm probably—no definitely—the last person she wants to see right now, but that isn't going to stop me from finding her.

I need to know that she's okay.

If she does something stupid and it's all my fault, I'll never forgive myself.

My hands tremble with fear as I start my car and take off again, leaving the Bronte Building and the Chapel behind me.

I drive around town, checking out all the places I've ever heard her talk about. I figure my best bet is Dessert Island, but when I get there I find that the closed sign is swinging on the door and all the lights are out.

There's only one other place I can think to check. A place she hasn't been since she moved into dorms.

She confessed to me while she was safely locked up in my bedroom that as soon as her father died, it no longer felt like home.

Tightening my grip on the wheel, I head across town and towards Judge Bancroft's house. Dread drips through my veins as I close in on the property.

It's one of the oldest houses in Saints Cross and it sits on a vast amount of land. I wouldn't even want to guess how much it's worth. The fortune Abigail is sitting on.

It's enough to set her up for her entire life.

She'll never want for anything—*anyone*.

The thought guts me as I drive up the road that leads to the house. It's dark and deserted, and as I pull up to the impressive driveway, I find that the home is the same.

I pull up next to the double garage and kill the engine, plunging me and my surroundings into darkness.

I sit there staring at the house, waiting to see any sign of life.

But there is nothing.

Sinking lower in my seat, I tip my head back and close my eyes. I deserve this punishment. I deserve not to know if she's dead or alive.

I should call the girls. Get them to try and contact her but that would mean telling them what I've done.

All this time, I've kept everything I've felt for Abigail under wraps—kind of. They might have suspected I had feelings for her, but they never knew the truth.

And they certainly don't know about everything that's happened between us in the past few weeks.

The shared pain.

The anguish.

The tears, the blood... the release.

My nails dig into my palms as the need to feel just a hint of that right now begins to get the better of me.

Not knowing what else to do, I get out of the car and march towards the front door.

I stand there with my finger hovering over the bell. Just because there isn't any sign of life, it doesn't mean that she's not here.

Abigail is hiding. And quite honestly, this is the best place for her to do it.

It might not be the biggest of houses but it's certainly big enough.

My need to see her, to protect her from herself battles with my need to do the right thing.

I guess it all comes down to one question…

Do I trust her?

Do I trust her not to hurt herself? And if she does, do I trust her not to take it too far?

I pull my phone from my pocket and stare down at the notifications piled up on the lock screen.

But none of them are from her.

Not one.

The most recent one makes my blood run cold.

> Scott: I hope you're not chasing that sad pathetic mouse around town like a loser.

As if he's waiting for me to read that first message, he begins typing.

> Scott: Lauren is your girl. Do the right thing by both of them.
>
> Scott: You won't like the consequences if you fuck this up for us, little brother.

Anger courses through my veins. I'm mad. Mostly at myself.

This is why you tried to put a barrier up.

You knew this would happen.

You knew you'd hurt her whether you wanted to or not.

Closing down his messages, I find my conversation with Abigail.

My heart drops into my throat when I find messages I didn't send. My hand trembles as I read *my* request for her to meet me tonight.

That fucker. I didn't even know he'd taken my phone.

Feeling totally hopeless, and completely fucking worthless, I tap out a simple message.

> Elliot: I'm sorry, Red.

I hang my head in regret. My heart feels like a lead

weight in my chest, but there is nothing I can do to make any of it better.

There is no coming back from this.

I can shout, scream, beg, plead. It won't change the fact that I knew something like tonight would happen eventually, yet I allowed for us to become something.

I may not have put tonight's events into action. But I'm still guilty.

> Elliot: I'm so fucking sorry.
>
> Elliot: Please, I'm begging you, call the girls. They'll take care of you. They'll understand.

I don't know what else to do.

I want to storm inside this house, turn it upside down searching for her and then pull her into my arms and tell her that everything is going to be okay.

But it's fucking not.

If we continue down this road—assuming she could ever forgive me—then we'll just be waiting for the next hit. And when it comes, it'll be harder, and even more painful than this one.

Pushing my phone back into my pocket, I trudge back to my car, turn the engine on and regretfully leave the house—and possibly Abigail—behind.

I park in my usual space outside the Chapel and just sit.

It's late. Hopefully, late enough that the others will have already gone to bed to stop me from having to answer their questions about where I've been.

They probably already know that I was out with Lauren. There is no way that Scott and Zoey haven't already posted our entire night on Instagram.

I cringe at the thought of how they've portrayed it. It'll look nothing like reality, I know that much.

It takes me the longest time to convince myself to get out of the car, and when I do, I quickly find that my legs don't take me in the direction of my bedroom, instead, I find myself approaching the girl's dorm again.

I can't help myself.

I know she's not there, but after the night I've had, I need to feel close to her.

I wake to a cold and empty bedroom with nothing but a heavy heart and a shit load of regrets.

Without thinking, I swing my legs off the side of the bed, pull my clothes on, and embark on the walk of shame out of the Bronte Building.

If only spending a night in Abigail's bed was the most shameful thing about the past twenty-four hours.

There was a part of me that hoped she might return in the middle of the night. It's the reason I didn't force myself to go back to my room, but I can't say that I'm surprised she didn't.

The sun is quickly rising in the sky as I make the short trek to the Chapel. They should all still be asleep. I should be able to slip in unnoticed.

Hell knows I would have been able to before the girls gatecrashed our bachelor pad. Things are a little less predictable now. Hell, I've woken up to find Liv and Tally with their arses in the air as they do some kind of sunrise worshipping yoga a few times now.

All I can hope is that this morning isn't one of those days.

I slip into the building with bated breath, but as soon as

I step into the quiet open space living area, I breathe a sigh of relief that it's in silence.

I'm not going to be able to hide from all of this for very long. The girls will soon notice that something is wrong with Abigail, but I'll take a few more hours before I have to start lying to my best friends, if I can.

I make it to the top of the stairs and I'm about to reach for my bedroom door, already dreaming about stripping down and stepping into a scorching hot shower when Oak's door suddenly opens, and a little blonde appears.

My heart sinks as I pray that I can vanish on the spot.

Tally quietly closes the door and is about to creep away when she notices me.

Her gasp of shock rips through the silence before her eyes narrow in suspicion. "What's going on?" she asks, her eyes dropping and then widening when she discovers I'm wearing the same clothes I went out in last night.

"Nothing," I grunt, twisting my door handle ready to escape.

"Where have you been?" she asks curiously.

"Out. Obviously."

"With her?" she sneers.

I know what Tally thinks about me spending time with Lauren Winrow. Hell, all the girls have the same opinion, but no one voices it quite as loudly as Tally does.

"It's none of your business who I do or don't spend time with."

Her expression hardens and she takes a step closer. "When you're hurting one of my best friends it does," she hisses. "I know, Elliot. Abi told me what happened between you."

Shock rocks through me and I bite my lips shut to stop from saying anything I shouldn't.

"You're a…" Her cheeks redden with anger and her eyes blaze. "You're a… You're an idiot."

I want to laugh at her inability to curse me out, but I'm too fucking broken. Too exhausted and emotionally wrecked to react.

"Tally," I sigh.

"No," she spits. "Don't fucking Tally me when you've been out all night with that… With that…"

"Can you do me a favour?" I ask cutting off whatever pathetic insult was about to come out of her mouth.

"You? Do *you* a favour? Who do you think you're—"

"Can you check in on Abigail this morning?"

I fucking hate to ask. It's going to open up a massive can of worms. But I need someone to check that she's okay.

I need to know she hasn't spent the entire night bleeding out on her fucking bathroom floor.

My stomach knots painfully as Tally assesses me.

I know what she's going to say before she even opens her mouth, and she doesn't disappoint.

"What have you done, Elliot Eaton?"

I shake my head and finally push my door open. "Just check on her, yeah?" I struggle to meet her heavy stare. "She needs her friends around her right now."

"You think I don't know—"

I cut her off as my door slams shut.

I want to say I leave her cursing up a storm on the other side of the door, but we all know she's not.

4
―――

ABIGAIL

The next morning, I wake to eight text messages—three from Elliot which I ignore—two missed calls, and a scathing voicemail from Tally informing me that if I don't call her back, she's going to report me missing.

She's bluffing but I don't risk it.

> Abi: I'm okay. x

> Tally: Abi, where the hell are you? I stopped by your dorm this morning and you weren't there. Classes started an hour ago and you're nowhere to be found. What did that idiot do?

My heart stutters.

Did Elliot tell her what happened?

No, I don't believe that. He wouldn't. Unless she found out another way?

Oh God. Do they all know what he did?

How will I ever face them again?

Panic floods me, my fingers trembling as I text her back.

> Abi: What are you talking about? Elliot didn't do anything. Things just got a bit much and I needed some space. I'll see you soon, okay. x

> Tally: Space is fine, Abi, but WHERE are you? Tell me and I'll come and be with you. Elliot asked me to check on you. He seemed worried. I know something happened. x

I don't know how to feel about that, so I shove it down and text her back.

> Abi: Really, it's fine. I'm fine. x

> Tally: You're a terrible liar. But you're also one of my best friends so please just tell me where you are. x

> Abi: I'm sorry but I can't. Just know that I'm safe and I'll be okay. I need some time. x

> Tally: Abs, come on. You're stronger than this. x

I'm not though.

I can fool myself into thinking I'm fine but I'm not. The urge to hurt myself, to allow myself the one thing I know will give me some measure of relief burns inside me. Calling to me.

Whispering like a siren in the night.

I ignore her, for now. Trying to focus on my pain. My heartache. Trying to acknowledge and sit with it until I can breathe through it.

It's in this moment that the conclusion I come to is that I am completely and utterly alone in this world.

Sure, Tally is pissed at Elliot now. But that won't last

forever. She's an Heir's girlfriend. Her loyalty will always be to *them*. The same goes for Liv and Raine.

No matter how much they want to stand up for me, they'll always be a part of the inner circle, and I'll always be on the outside looking in.

I knew that before, and I know it even more now.

I let my feelings for Elliot cloud my judgement.

I let myself believe that he truly wanted me.

But wanting someone and treating them with respect and dignity and... love are two very different things.

Maybe Elliot Eaton really is incapable of feeling anything beyond surface level emotion.

Because I refuse to believe that if he cared about me at all—

"Stop, you have got to stop this," I whisper to myself.

These thoughts—the ones replaying over and over in my head—agonising over every little detail is going to get my nowhere.

What's done is done.

And no matter how much it hurts, how devastated I am, I can either sink or swim.

I just need some time.

My phone vibrates again.

Tally: Abi, please...

I start to text her back, but my battery dies, and I don't have a charger.

I don't have anything I need here really. But the solace is better than going back to All Hallows', better than facing the aftermath of last night.

A fresh wave of pain hits me, but I swallow it down, forcing myself to inhale a deep, steady breath.

I can do this.

I can.

But I can't do it without supplies. And with no way to contact—

A thought hits me.

The landline phone, of course.

Pushing back the covers, I climb gingerly out of bed and head downstairs.

Maureen has done her job, making sure the house is stripped bare of my father's belongings. Ready for when I decide to put it up for sale.

A decision I haven't wanted to think about yet.

But the electricity and water are still connected. So hopefully the phone line is too.

With trembling fingers, I breathe a sigh of relief at the sound of a dialling tone. I dial her number, a number I know almost as well as my own, and wait.

"Hello," her familiar voice comes over the line.

"Maureen, it's Abigail."

"Oh, sweetheart, how wonderful to hear from you, how are you?"

"I... I need your help."

"Abi, what's wrong? What happened?" Panic clings to her every word.

"Nothing, I... I'm fine." The words get stuck over the lump in my throat. "But I'm at the house and I have nothing."

"I don't understand. Did something happen? Why aren't you at school, sweetheart?"

"Please, Maureen, I'll explain everything once you get here. I just need some basics. Milk, tea, some biscuits. Some toiletries."

"Of course, I can do that. But sweetheart, tell me what's happening, you're worrying me."

"I'm fine, I promise." The lie tastes like ash on my

tongue, but I swallow it down. "I just needed to come home for a little while."

"Give me half an hour and I'll be there."

"Thank you." I hang up and breathe a deep sigh of relief.

Maureen is the only person I can count on now. But even she has her own life, other responsibilities.

While I'm waiting for her, I wander around the big lofty house, trying to muster even a single good memory. But everything good is tainted by the loss. The pain and heartache and grief.

Once Mum was gone, life became bleak. The weight of my father's illness looming over us like a dark cloud blotting out the remaining shreds of lights.

It hardened his heart, and it shattered mine. And as the years went on, we drifted apart. Both of us, too scared about what the future held.

I run my fingers over the dusty sideboard, a gnawing ache inside me that this could be my future.

Dark bleak loneliness.

The doorbell echoes through the house, startling me. I hurry and open it, relieved to see Maureen standing there.

"Oh, Abigail." She drops the bags and pulls me into her arms. "Whatever is the matter?"

"I'm fine," I whisper, trembling in her hold, losing the fight against the tears burning the backs of my eyes.

"You're not fine, you're shaking. Come on, love. Let's get you inside and I'll put the kettle on." She presses a kiss to my hair and steps back to pick up the bags. "I brought you a few extra things in case you need them."

"You didn't have to do that."

"Hush now. I promised your father I would always take care of you. Now why don't you sit down and tell me what happened?"

She ushers me down the hall and pulls out a chair for me.

"I'm—"

"Abigail, sweetheart, if you tell me you're fine one more time, I'll be forced to call Mr Porter and find out what the hell is going on up at that school."

"I met a boy."

"A boy, how wonder— Oh, I see." Her expression drops. "He didn't hurt you, did he? Force you to do things you're not—"

"No, no. Nothing like that." Heat stains my cheeks. "He turned out to be someone else."

"Ah." She makes the tea and joins me at the table, pushing a mug towards me. "Boys are complicated creatures, Abigail. They often say one thing and do another."

"Yes, they do."

"But you're still young, sweetheart. There's plenty of time for boys. You're in a vulnerable place right now." Her expression hardens a little. "It will make it easier for people to take advantage of you."

Too late for that, I trap the words behind my lips. Refusing to let myself remember.

I gave Elliot control of my body, my pain. I submitted to him.

And I liked it.

I don't know if that's because of everything I've been through or because deep down, it's in my nature.

I guess it doesn't matter now.

I'll never trust him with my body again, let alone my heart.

I smother the sob caught in my throat, wondering how things could change so quickly.

How I went from thinking Elliot had chosen me, that

he wanted me—to standing in that pub being utterly humiliated.

But I guess I know the answer.

It was staring me in the face all along.

Elliot Eaton is out of my league.

And I'm just the lost, lonely girl he thought to take advantage of.

Maureen stayed with me a little while, helping me unpack the groceries. She even made me breakfast. But she had to get to her new job, and I didn't want to burden her anymore than I already had.

Before leaving though, she insisted I take her spare phone charger.

I almost declined.

I'm not sure I want to be tethered to the outside world yet.

The girls will no doubt keep texting me. Tally might even keep her word and report me missing to Mr Porter.

I hope she trusts me enough not to do that.

I just need some time to process everything and figure out what I'm going to do.

At least the house is still functional so I can have a hot shower and keep myself distracted watching on the old television in Dad's study.

But no matter what I do to take my mind off it, I can't forget about last night.

A new kind of pain has taken root inside me.

Was it all a lie?

Was Elliot just toying with me all along?

Even now, my heart doesn't believe it. The things he said, the things we shared...

But deep down, I know the truth.

I know that no matter what I let him do to me in the dark, it never meant I'd get to walk with him in the light.

Tears streak down my face as I pull the blanket higher, trying to focus on the blurry images on the screen.

My phone bleeps but I ignore it.

I'm not ready to talk to anyone yet.

I'll have to go back to All Hallows' eventually, or Tally really will inform Mr Porter, or the worse, the police.

I can't return until I have a better hold on my emotions though.

I can't return until I know that I can be around Elliot and not fall apart.

5

ELLIOT

"Fuck," I groan, rolling over and opening my eyes, wishing that it was all a bad dream.

But it wasn't.

Abigail didn't return to school yesterday like I hoped she would.

The girls are worried. Hell, even the guys are worried.

Tally watched me with accusatory eyes. She might not have the details, but she knows I did something.

Something bad.

Something to send Abigail into hiding.

I shouldn't be here, in her dorm room. In her bed. It's probably the worst possible place for me to be for a number of reasons, but I can't stand going back to my room at the Chapel.

I know where she is.

Every night I've sat out the front of her house and watched. Waiting.

There's been no movement, no evidence of life inside, but I know she's there hiding.

Locking herself away from the world. From me.

It's only what I deserve, I know that. But it doesn't make it any easier to swallow.

It's that knowledge that makes me stop me from walking up to the front door and knocking until she has no choice but to let me in, to talk to me.

I'm trying to do the right thing. To give her space. Time.

But I fear no amount will ever be enough.

And it shouldn't be.

She shouldn't forgive me for this.

I told her I would hurt her.

And I have.

I warned her that my family would destroy us.

And they have.

Pushing myself so I'm sitting in the middle of the bed, I stare around the generously sized dorm room around me.

I've cleaned it within an inch of its life in the past twenty-four hours. The scent of bleach is thick in the air, and everything that Abigail owns now has a home. Her desk is meticulously organised. Everything is placed just so. The photos on the shelf above are all aligned at the correct angles. But while it might make me feel a little more settled, it doesn't help.

Not really.

I'd take her forgiveness a million times over this tidy room.

It's bullshit.

I knew it was before. My need for cleanliness and order is just a way to try and keep some kind of semblance of control over my life. But it's a pretence, a mask, just like the one I'm forced to walk around wearing every day of my goddamn life.

Lifting the duvet to my face, I inhale a hit of Abigail's scent.

I'm being a pussy. I know I am. But it's like I fell into a black pit on Wednesday night and now it's impossible to pull myself out of it.

I'll give myself the weekend. Two more days before I pull my head out of my arse and sort my shit out.

I don't have time to be mourning the loss of a girl who could never be mine.

I've got exams. Family commitments. A fucked-up future laid out before me.

I don't have time for a girl.

I don't need a girl.

Maybe not, but... *you fucking want her though, don't you?*

Throwing the duvet from my body, I swing my legs off the edge and pad through to her bathroom. The second I step inside, all I can see is her curled up on the floor with blood running down her thigh.

My heart begins to race as I think about what she might be doing inside that big house all alone.

Has she done it again?

Is she cutting herself because of me?

Or worse... Is that why I never see any movement?

My hands tremble as I reach for the toothbrush I found in the cupboard and made mine. If she's done something stupid because of me, I'll never forgive myself.

My skin prickles with self-hatred.

Elliot Eaton, never quite good enough.

A failure at being a son. A best friend. A... boyfriend.

Reaching into the shower, I turn it as hot as it'll go, shove my boxers from my legs, and step inside, letting the burn feed the darkness that is beginning to consume me.

It's been a long time since I let it control me, and I have every intention of fighting it. But every now and then, it's comforting to let the old friend come and play.

It's like scratching a rash. For those few seconds, it's fucking bliss. But then, when it's over, it only leaves more pain in its wake.

I stand there until my skin glows red from the heat and the worst of my demons have been washed away.

For now, at least.

Wrapping Abigail's towel around my waist, I walk back into her bedroom to find my phone vibrating across her bedside table. Hope erupts within me that it might be her, that she might want to talk about what happened.

It's wishful thinking, but I can't help it.

Sadly, though, when I get there, I find that it's Reese.

Knowing he won't let it drop until I answer, I swipe the screen. "Where the fuck are you?" he barks.

I look around the room I'm in the middle of. "Uh... Out," I mutter, unwilling to explain where I really am and how pathetic I've become.

"I fucking know that. You've been *out* since Wednesday night."

"I've got shit going on," I say quietly, naïvely hoping it'll be enough to put an end to his questions.

"Yeah, like meeting me in the gym twenty minutes ago. I swear to God, man. Her pussy better be fucking gold-plated or some shit."

"Because you've never forgotten our plans because of Liv," I counter.

"So there is a girl." He's smug as fuck and I can picture his accomplished smirk from here.

"No there isn't a fucking girl."

"Making the most of Lauren, then. She's hot. I wouldn't blame you if—"

"I'm not fucking Lauren. I'm not fucking anyone."

"That's your problem, right there. All work and no play makes Elliot Eaton a real miserable fucker."

"Did you actually want something?" I ask, getting bored of his teasing.

"Yeah, to work out with my mate like we'd planned. It's Saturday fucking morning. You can't have any better offers if you're not fucking anyone."

I sigh. "Fine. Fine. I'll be there in ten."

I hang up before he can say anything else and look at my rucksack sitting by Abigail's desk chair.

As if it's not pathetic enough that I'm here, I even packed for a few days.

Maybe Dad is right. Maybe I'm not good enough for the life I was born into.

I'm not like him and Scott. I'm not cold and ruthless.

I care.

I care too fucking much.

I always have.

With my heart aching, I pull on a pair of sweats, a t-shirt and then a zip-up hoodie.

Making sure everything is clean and tidy, I leave Abigail's dorm with my hood up, attempting to hide from the world.

The second I step outside, the sound of the birds singing hits my ears, and the warmth of the spring warms my skin, but it does little to lighten the darkness festering within me.

Keeping my head down in the hope it makes people second-guess attempting to talk to me, I make a beeline for the gym.

Reese is right. This is our time. The four of us have exclusive access every Saturday morning. It's a tradition that's gone back through the generations, just like us being allowed to shower first, and alone, after practice.

If any of the other sports teams at All Hallows' want to come and train, they have to wait.

I can't lie. It's pretty sweet. Although, I'm not sure it's worth it.

I'd happily hand it over to lose the other bullshit and pressure that comes with being an Eaton heir.

Pulling the heavy door open, I march through towards the gym. The sound of heavy footsteps pounding the treadmill fill the air. I find Reese there, his AirPods in, as he runs as if he's trying to escape the devil, totally oblivious to my arrival.

Letting the door close behind me, I look around for something to greet him with.

An empty water bottle sits on the floor beside the bin, it makes my eye twitch, but it serves a purpose. Picking it up, I launch it across the room. It hits its mark and bounces off the side of Reese's head.

"Ow, what the fuck?" he barks before he loses his footing and shoots off the end of the belt.

Watching him flail around like a baby giraffe is exactly what I need, and I double over laughing as he battles to right himself.

"You're a fucking cunt," he bellows as he finally gets his feet on the floor and pushes to stand.

Twisting his arm around at a funny angle, he stares down at his grazed elbow.

"Aw, poor baby. Have you got a boo-boo?" I tease.

"The fuck, bro?" he barks, finally looking up at me.

I shrug. "Sorry, couldn't resist."

"That's not what I mean. Your face."

I turn towards the wall of mirrors. "What's wrong with my face?"

"I've never seen you look so...

"So?" I prompt when he can't find the word.

"Miserable."

"Gee, thanks. I'm really fucking glad I came."

"Shit. I didn't mean it like that," he says scrubbing his hand down his face, regret flickering through his eyes. "It's just... Shit, Elliot."

Grabbing his drink bottle, he lowers his arse to his now stationary treadmill and takes a drink. "Sit," he demands, jerking his head towards the machine next to him.

"I thought we were working out," I counter, nerves beginning to assault me.

I shouldn't have come here. I should have known that he'd take one look at me and immediately know I was drowning.

"Yeah, we will. After you've talked."

"I don't want to talk, Reese."

"No, I don't either really, if I'm being honest. But I'm pushing that aside in favour of being a good mate. I don't care what it is, what you've done, or haven't done. It's fucking eating you from the inside out. Spill it."

Falling down onto the treadmill, I drop my head into my hands and close my eyes. The sight of Abigail standing at the end of our table utterly devastated appears as clear as fucking day in my head and it takes everything I have not to claw my own eyes out in an attempt to make it go away.

"I've fucked it all up," I confess quietly.

"Well, yeah. I kinda figured as much."

He falls silent, refusing to fill the void and forcing me to do it.

"Abigail and I... We..." I don't need to look over to know he's smirking. "We kinda started something. But then Scott found out and—" I scrub my hands down my face. "Fuck. I hurt her so bad, Reese. I don't know what to do to make it better."

"Have you tried... I don't know, apologising?"

"Smart-arse," I mutter. "She won't see me even if I tried."

"You haven't tried?"

"She's locked herself away in her house. She doesn't want to see me."

"Are you sure about that? She might be waiting for you to fight for her?"

"I can't, Reese. Fuck," I bark, jumping to my feet so I can start pacing.

I'm too fucking restless to sit still and have a heart-to-heart.

"We didn't even make a week before my family steamrolled in and fucked it up. It'll only happen again. They won't accept her."

"And you care more about their opinions than you do her?"

"No. Fuck, not a chance. She's—" I cut myself off and look at him.

His expression is sympathetic and hopeful. I want to wipe both clean off.

"She's what, Elliot?"

Everything. Incredible.

The one...

The words taunt me but I shove them out as I rasp, "Too good for me and my bullshit."

"You're too good for this bullshit, Elliot. Don't you see that? You're letting them pull your puppet strings and you're fucking miserable. You can't continue like this. It wasn't until I saw you smile at her that I realised how fucking miserable you've been these past few years."

"What the fuck am I meant to do about it, Reese?" My expression crumples. "My old man has a plan. There is no wavering. He'll disown me if I go against him."

He raises a brow and says five little words that punch me in the gut.

"Maybe you should let him."

6

ABIGAIL

A loud knock on the door startles me and I bolt upright.

It's Saturday and I've been hiding out for two days.

Another knock has me shoving off my blanket and padding down the hall.

Maybe it's Maureen bringing me more supplies.

Oh, who am I kidding? I know it isn't Maureen. She called to check on me yesterday and I told her I was fine. Which means my options are either Tally or Elliot.

I resent the stab of disappointment I feel when I see a feminine silhouette beyond the stained-glass panels in the top half of the front door.

"Abi, it's me," Tally calls. "I know you're in there and I'm not leaving until you speak to me."

God, she's relentless.

She's also a really good friend.

Reluctantly, I unlatch the chain and crack open the door.

"Thank God." Relief flits across her expression. "I've been going out of my mind with worry. How are you?"

"I'm fine." My lips purse and she narrows her eyes at me.

"Aren't you going to invite me in?" She peeks over my shoulder trying to get a better view of the house.

"I... Okay." I step to the side and let her pass.

"What the hell is going on? You just up and disappear and—"

"I told you, I needed some time."

"You also keep telling me you're fine, which is clearly a lie." She gives me a pointed look.

"I don't know what you want me to say." I hurry down the hall towards the kitchen with shame nipping at my heels.

Tally got her happy ending. She got the boy and the huge grand gesture.

"How about you start with the truth," she says, following me. "I know there's more to the story than you're telling me."

"I..."

"Abi, come on. This is me. You can trust me."

"It's not that simple," I whisper.

I want to tell her, I do.

She's my friend.

But things are different now—an invisible line drawn between us. She's my friend but she's Oak's girlfriend.

She belongs to an Heir now. And they'll always side with Elliot, no matter how messed up things are.

"Fine," she huffs when I don't offer her further explanation. "Maybe a cup of tea will get you to open up a little."

I'm hardly surprised when she moves past me into the kitchen and heads straight over to the kettle.

"I thought the house was almost ready to be sold?" she asks.

"It was. I mean, it is." Her questioning gaze finds mine and I shrug. "I didn't plan on coming back here."

"You ran."

Tally knows. She always does. I don't know how she does it, but she can sniff out a lie like a hound scenting blood.

"Sit." She makes the tea and I take a seat at the table. "Do you have milk?"

I nod, flicking my eyes to the fridge.

"Someone brought you supplies?"

"Maureen."

"She was your father's carer?"

Another nod.

"Here." Tally slides the cup of tea towards me and takes the seat opposite. "The girls miss you. We all do. But I think Elliot—"

"Don't." I flinch at his name.

"What happened, Abi? I know how the Heirs can be. They're intense and determined and honestly, scary when they decide when they want something. But I didn't think..." She trails off, giving me a sad smile.

"You didn't think it was like that between me and Elliot."

"I know there's always been a strange connection between you. We've all seen it. But it's Elliot, Abs. He's different to the others. And you're..."

"Weak."

"No, God no. You're one of the strongest people I know. But you're good and pure and... innocent. You're like night and day. Sunshine and darkness."

"We're more alike than you think," I murmur, running my thumbs around the mug.

"Whatever happened, Abs, you can tell me." Tally looks at me with nothing but gentle understanding.

"We... He and I, we've been..."

"Oh my God." She gasps, startling me. "You had sex with him. You had sex with El—"

"No. No. We didn't... We didn't do *that*."

Her brows furrow and I shrink into myself.

"You didn't... Oh. Oh."

I nod again. "We've been seeing each other. Kind of."

"You and Elliot..."

"Can you please stop saying it like that?" I sigh. "I know you think he's too good for me but—"

"Abi, God no. It isn't that at all. It's just we've all heard the rumours about Elliot. He likes to be in control..."

"I know." Shame burns my cheeks as I glance away, trying so hard not to remember how good it felt to be with him. To have his hands on my skin.

"Wow, okay. So the two of you... Wow."

"Forget it," I rush out, standing. "I shouldn't have said anything."

"No, it's me, I'm sorry." Tally smiles. "Please, don't go. I want you to talk to me about this. It's just a lot. But I guess people might have said the same about me and Oak at first."

"Oakley loves you," I point out. "He would never hurt you."

Her expression darkens as she considers my words. "What did he do, Abs? And don't try and tell me Elliot isn't the reason you're hiding out here."

Inhaling a shuddering breath, I try and figure out how much I want to reveal. How much I can trust her with.

But it's too late to go back. Tally knows something is going on, and she won't quit until I tell her.

"Ethan..."

"Yeah." Her brows furrow. "What about Ethan?"

Panic rises inside me. I don't want to repeat what he did, what they all did. It feels too embarrassing, too unbelievable. But not telling her will only drive the wedge deeper between us. And the truth is, I need to talk to somebody about this.

I need... I need a friend right now.

"If I tell you all this, you can't tell anyone, Tally. Swear it."

Concern masks her expression. "You can trust me."

"Ethan never wanted to be my friend." The words hurt more than they should. "He didn't feel sorry for me, and he wasn't interested in me."

"I don't understand. What are you saying?"

"Elliot paid him."

"He... *what*?"

I nod slowly, fighting back the tears. "Elliot paid Ethan to befriend me. He's been dating Lauren this whole time while we were..." A sob lodges in my throat as I remember the last time we were together, the lies that he whispered to me.

Tally rushes over to me and wraps me in her arms. "I don't understand. Why would he do that?"

"Elliot texted me the other night to meet him, so I went into town." The words pour out. "I was so nervous, I thought... I thought he wanted to take me out. Like on a date." A small, self-deprecating laugh tumbles out of me. "But when I got to the pub he was there with Lauren."

Tally frowns, holding me at arm's length. "That doesn't make any sense."

"It was Scott. Scott must have texted me from Elliot's phone and lured me there. Ethan showed up too. I've never felt so stupid as I did standing there, realising that everything that happened between us was a lie."

"Wait a minute, Scott orchestrated it all?"

"I guess so. You should have seen the smug look on his face, Tally."

"And what did Elliot do?"

"Nothing."

"Nothing?" she hisses.

"He was obviously annoyed at Scott for making a scene. But he acted like..." God, I can't even say it.

I think that's the worst thing.

Realising that the boy I've fallen for doesn't exist.

"Like what?"

"Like I meant nothing to him." I close my eyes, trying to blink away the tears.

"Abs, Abi, look at me." Tally soothes. "It doesn't make any sense. Elliot cares about you."

"I thought he did too. But you didn't see how cold he was to me. He just sat there while Scott embarrassed me in front of his girlfriend and Lauren."

"Something doesn't add up. Elliot—"

"It doesn't matter," I rush out.

I don't want to hear her try to defend him.

I can't.

Elliot Eaton is the villain in my story now and I need him to stay that way if I'm going to survive whatever comes next.

"I just need a few more days and then I'll be okay."

"But—"

"No, Tally. I'm done," I say firmly. "Promise me you won't say anything."

She stares at me with a mix of pity and surprise. But to my relief she concedes. "I promise."

"Thank you. I just want to get through the last few weeks of college and then move on with my life."

Not that I know what moving on looks like. I've missed

so much college since my father died there's no way I'll be able to sit my final exams and pass.

"You will come back to All Hallows' though, right?" she asks.

"I don't see that I have much choice. I need to talk to Mr Porter and figure out a plan."

"I know it's complicated because I'm with Oak, Abs, but you're one of my best friends. That will never change." She hugs me tight and for a second, I want to believe her.

But as she pulls away, I know confessing doesn't change anything.

Tally will probably want to knee Elliot in the balls for a little while but eventually, it will all blow over.

It's just how it is with the Heirs.

"Do you need anything?" she asks. "I can bring you some things."

"No, I'm fine. Truly."

"Abi—"

"I promise. I just... I need some more time."

Tension builds inside of me like a pressure cooker.

I need her to leave.

I need to be alone.

I shouldn't have told her.

I hate that she knows—that she's looking at me with so much pity and sympathy. It reminds me too much of life before I knew her and Liv, and Raine. When I was no one. Just the weird shy girl with scars on her face. The girl people laughed and stared and pointed at.

The girl who preferred to stay in the shadows.

I'm not her anymore.

But right now, I wish I was.

I want to hide. To let the darkness swallow me whole so I don't have to face reality.

"Abi?" Concern shines in her eyes as she reaches for me.

"I'm fine." I flinch. "I'll walk you out."

I need her to go.

"Oh, I don't have to leave yet. I can stay. We can—"

"I just want to be alone."

Her expression crumples. "Oh, okay." Tally gets up and I walk her to the front door. "If you need anything, you have my number."

"Thank you."

She opens the door and relief trickles through me. But then she pauses at the last second, looking back at me.

"I know you don't want to hear it, Abs," she says. "But none of this makes sense. Elliot cares about you, I know he does. In his own twisted way, he cares."

"Maybe so," I say, hating that she can't just let it go.

Hating that her words will burrow their way into my heart and embed themselves there.

I give her a sad smile and whisper, "But he obviously doesn't care enough."

7

ELLIOT

Despite my resistance, after our little heart-to-heart, Reese drags my arse up and insists I hit the gym harder than I ever have in my life in an attempt to banish the demons.

I'm not sure any kind of workout has the power to eradicate my father and Scott from my life, but I was willing to give it a good go.

I can't lie. It feels good—the pain, the exertion, the trembling muscles. Focusing on something other than the pain in my chest and the colossal mistakes I've made is what I need.

By the time we walk out of the gym, I can barely hold myself up. But for the first time since Wednesday night, I can think about something other than Abigail.

At least for a few minutes.

"You need to go and talk to her," Reese says as we make our way across campus, officially ending my 'do not think about Abigail' mantra.

"She's not here," I reason.

He laughs, although there is no humour behind it.

"Like you don't know where she is," he mutters. "There are only a handful of places she'd go. And even if there weren't, you're Elliot Eaton, you'll find her."

"Maybe you overestimate my skills," I mutter, not entirely sure I like the picture he just painted of me. It sounds a little like two other men I'd rather have nothing in common with.

"Okay, so where have you been every night then?" He smirks. "And do try and bullshit me into saying you came back late. I know you didn't."

"It doesn't matter," I say under my breath, wishing he'd change the topic of conversation.

"Of course it fucking matters. You're gone for her, bro. You need to man up and do something about it. You fucked up. Newsflash, we all fucking do that. It's the grovelling and how you apologise that counts now."

"It won't be enough." I shake my head, not wanting to believe. Not wanting to hope.

"Says who? You?" he scoffs. "Not being funny, mate, but your dark aurora right now isn't going to let you believe anything positive."

"My dark aurora?" I repeat. "Fucking hell, you need to spend more time out on the rugby pitch and less time on a yoga mat. It's aura, smart-arse."

"Whatever it is. Laugh all you like. I'm right and you fucking know it."

I fall silent, unable to argue with him.

The Chapel is quiet as we let ourselves inside. "Where are the others?" I ask, marching towards the fridge to grab a fresh bottle of water.

"Fuck knows. I'm going for a shower. You want to hit the books after?" he offers.

Combing my fingers through my sweat-soaked hair, I

tug it back until it burns. Pain shoots down my neck, giving me a hit of what I really need.

"Sure," I finally concede.

It's the right thing to do. Focus on my future. A future that's been mapped out for me since I was a twinkle in my father's cold cruel eyes.

Sure, Saints Cross is a great university. It doesn't have a choice to be anything but based on the donations it receives from the elite families who expect it to be the best.

I'll do well there, assuming I survive Scott and the Scions. But do I want it?

I shake my head as I trudge up the stairs.

No, is the simple answer.

I don't want it.

Being an Heir was one thing. I wanted this. I wanted to step up with my boys and rule All Hallows' as we saw fit.

But being a Scion is a whole other ballgame.

The expectations, the games, the depravity of searching out the weak and pushing the strong... I don't have the time or the energy for it.

But just like defying my father with Lauren, refusing Saints Cross would be akin to suicide.

He'd never accept it.

Instead, he'd wear me down, break me in any way he could until I had no choice but to agree. And then, only then, would the real pain start.

Wrapping my hand around the back of my neck, I pull down. I don't fucking need this shit.

My skin is itching by the time I crash into my room. Shedding my damp clothes as I move, I'm naked before I step into the bathroom and turn the shower on as hot as it'll go, just as I need it.

But at the last minute, I pause.

It isn't going to be enough.

I can already feel the burn and it won't be e-fucking-nough.

Doubling back, I pull my wardrobe open and reach for the box I keep on the top shelf.

Out of sight, out of mind...

Well, right now, it's front and fucking centre; the only thing I can think about.

Knocking the lid off, I stare down at the contents. Scissors, razor blades, a flip-knife. All the things I promised myself years ago that I'd get rid of.

I knew that if I kept them that one day temptation would become too much.

I've held strong. Not once have I even considered reaching for it since moving in here. But that's all gone to shit, and it's all my fucking fault.

Searching through the contents, I find what I need.

It's not what I want. That's the flip knife. That would sate the desire I have coursing through my veins right now.

But I can't.

With a sigh, I pull a scalpel blade free. The steel glints under the bright lights from above and my mouth waters.

I should be trying to talk myself out of it, I know I should. But I'm too far gone.

With it pinched between my forefinger and thumb, I march back into the bathroom. I place it on the small shelf in my shower before finally stepping inside. My skin prickles as the burning water rushes over me, and I grit my teeth when the need to lower the temperature becomes unignorable.

But I don't.

Stepping away won't help.

I need this.

I need it so fucking badly.

As the seconds tick on, my muscles begin to relax, my need for pain sated for a few minutes.

But I know it's only a short reprieve. I've played this game many, many times over the years.

A few things help stave off the need. Rugby. Going hard in the gym. Fighting. Sex. Sometimes, it's enough to distract me. But often, it's not.

Sometimes nothing comes anywhere close to touching it.

Squeezing my eyes closed, the image of Abigail curled up on her bathroom floor from a few weeks ago appears in my mind. The sight of her with those scissors in her hand and blood trickling down her thigh hit me so fucking hard.

It took every ounce of my strength to focus on her and not crumble to my own dark vices.

The sight of her doing the exact same thing that I've done to myself more times than I want to count cut me deeper than any blade could.

It was like watching my own worst nightmare come to life. Only it wasn't me bleeding. It was the girl I couldn't get out of my head hurting herself.

The roar that rips from my throat doesn't sound anything like me as I bounce around the room, echoing, tormenting me.

My palms slam against the tiles, sending pain shooting up my arms. But it's not enough.

It should be but it's not.

Resting my head against the cool wall, I focus on my breathing.

In. Out.

In. Out.

In— "FUUUCK," I bellow.

In a rush, I turn the shower off and grab the blade.

My hand trembles as I rest my back against the wall and expose my inner thigh.

Scarred, damaged skin stares back up at me.

It's better than it used to be.

There came a point—when girls started paying attention to me—that I realised I needed to get a better handle on things.

That opened up a whole new level of distraction, as long as they didn't get too close, of course.

That's where my need for control came in.

If their hands were bound behind their backs and I had their hair in my fist, the only inches of my body they'd be exploring was the appendage in their mouths.

It worked.

It was fucking great.

Until her...

She's the reason I'm standing here now about to fall back into toxic habits I thought I'd banished.

With gritted teeth, I bring the sharp point of the blade to an unscarred patch of skin.

I'm not going to do it.

I'm not. I just—

I twitch with it almost touching my skin and it cuts through me like butter.

The rush is like nothing I've ever experienced as blood pools at the surface.

I stare at it for a beat before reality seeps back in and I throw the blade across the room in a fit of anger and frustration.

I should have been better than that.

Dropping my foot back to the floor, I snatch a towel from the rack before storming back into my room, self-hatred poisoning every ounce of my blood.

I quickly dry off and I'm about to find a clean pair of

boxers to hide the evidence of what I've just done when my bedroom door flies open and an angry little blonde flies into the room.

"Tally, what the fuck?" I bark quickly cupping my junk.

One look at the fury on her face and I know what's coming.

She's seen Abigail.

She knows...

She knows what I did.

"What have you done?" she shrieks. Her voice is so high-pitched, I'm pretty sure that only dogs can hear it.

"You need to stay out of my business, Darlington," I snarl, my nostrils flaring in frustration. "Get the fuck out."

"No chance," she snarls right back. "We are talking. Right here, right now. Wait... you're bleeding," she says, cutting off her rant and staring down at my thigh.

My stomach knots, acid burning up my throat as I consider the chances of her figuring out what I've done.

"It's nothing. All of this is fucking nothing."

Turning my back on her, I finally pull my draw open and drag a pair of boxers out before pulling them on.

"Nothing? *Nothing*?" she shrieks. "Do you have any idea how much you've hurt her?"

I'm pretty sure a knife through my chest couldn't hurt worse than hearing those words.

Turning back around, I stare Tally dead in the eyes. I need her to see how serious I am with my next words. "It's for the best," I lie. "Abigail doesn't belong in my world. I did her a favour."

Crack.

I really should have seen it coming. But this is Tally, not Raine, or even Olivia. The second her palm connects with my cheek, my head whips to the side and pain shoots down my neck.

A growl of fury rips from my throat and I take a warning step towards her.

Most girls—hell, most guys—would immediately step back and cower. But, oh no, not prim and proper Tallulah Darlington. I have no fucking idea what Oak has done to her, but she's not scared of anything these days.

"The fuck, Tallulah?" I snarl.

"She loves you," Tally cries.

I stumble back as her words hit me like a truck.

"She loves you and all you do is hurt her. She doesn't deserve it."

"Finally, something we agree on." I lock down every emotion swirling inside of me. "She deserves more than this. More than me."

Tally's eyes widen at my confession, my moment of vulnerability.

"She needs to forget about me and move on. It's better for everyone."

"Everyone?" she asks, lifting a brow. "Better for you, you mean?"

"It doesn't matter about me. None of this is about me."

"Exactly, it's about her. So what are you going to do about it?"

"Nothing. I'm giving her time and space to figure out what we already know."

"And what is that exactly?" Her eyes narrow in suspicion.

"That Abigail Bancroft is too good for the likes of me."

A bitter laugh spills from Tally's lips. "Wow. The high and mighty Elliot Eaton has finally figured out that he's not all that."

My chest heaves, my breaths coming hard and fast as I glare at her.

"While I might agree," she adds, letting her eyes drop down my practically naked body with her top lip curled in disgust. "Abigail sees something in you. And"—she moves towards me, poking me hard in the chest—"you are going to make this right. You are going to fix it in whatever way you can. Get her out of hiding. Convince her to come back to school. To life. I'd do it myself if I could, but I don't have the power. Only you have that."

I snatch her finger, stopping her from poking me before gently shoving her away from me.

She goes easily enough, although her angry stare never leaves me.

"Do we have a deal?"

I shake my head before raking my hair back. "I... I can't, Tally."

"Tough. You have to. You did this, Elliot. It's on you to fix it."

8

ABIGAIL

I've never minded being alone.
There's something oddly comforting about being at one with yourself.

But being alone here, in the house where I grew up, the house where I lost my parents and my life fell apart, haunts me.

I barely slept last night. Pacing the big, empty house like a cat on the prowl.

Maybe it was Tally's visit—her parting words. Or maybe it's the fact that I know I can't stay here, that I can't hide forever.

Either way, sleep didn't come easy.

Not until I found a small paring knife in one of the kitchen drawers and sliced it across my thigh.

Shame sits heavy in my chest as my fingers dance over the fresh dressing there. But the small measure of relief I felt was worth it.

I don't want to die.

I don't particularly want to live right now either. But I know deep down, I don't want to die.

I just need... I need—

A knock at the door echoes through the house, startling me.

I should have known Tally wouldn't stay away. But I'm not sure I'm ready to go back to All Hallows' yet either.

The fresh cut on my thigh stings as I hurry down the hall to the door and yank it open expecting to see—

"You."

"Can we talk?" Elliot runs a hand down the back of his neck, barely meeting my gaze.

It shouldn't hurt, but it does.

"No, go away." I go to slam the door in his face, but he presses his palm against it.

"Please, Abi. I... I'm worried about you."

A bitter laugh leaves my lips. "I find that hard to believe. I'm fine. You've seen me. You can leave now."

His stormy eyes narrow, dropping down my body, his nostrils flaring as his gaze lands on my thighs.

Lust and shame swirls inside me as I yank down my t-shirt over my pyjama shorts.

"You cut yourself again." There's a quiver in his voice that I'm sure I must be imagining.

"I'm fine," I snap.

"Abi, you can't—"

"No, Elliot," a weary sigh rolls through me, "You don't get to do this. You don't get to turn up here pretending you care when we both know it's a lie. That I'm nothing more than a game—"

His hand shoots out and he grabs me around the throat. My hand goes to his and we stand there, his fingers curled tenderly around my skin, locked in a stalemate.

"Why are you doing this?" I whisper, my heart ratcheting. "Why can't you just let me go?"

"I... Fuck. *Fuck*." He snatches his hand away and jams his fingers into his hair, pacing like a caged animal.

"Elliot, calm down. Just—"

The crack of his fist driving into the wall stuns me and I clap a hand over my mouth, watching as blood trickles down his hand.

Pain contorts his features as he stares at me, pleads with me for something I don't understand. "I shouldn't have come," he says with a defeated sigh.

"So why did you?"

"Because..."

The invisible thread between us twists and tightens.

There's no escaping him. I realise that now.

So long as we're both still in Saints Cross, attending All Hallows', I'll never be able to escape him.

But there's only a few weeks left until exams. Then college is over, and they'll all be moving on to university.

"Come on." I tip my head. "I'll clean you up."

Elliot hesitates but I take his good hand and tug him further into the house.

"You should have slammed the door in my face," he murmurs.

"Yeah, well, I'm not as cold and heartless as some people."

He flinches behind me, but I ignore him.

If I don't, I'll crumble. And I can't afford to let Elliot in again.

No matter how much my heart yearns for him.

Silence greets us as we enter the kitchen.

"Sit," I say, motioning to one of the stools at the breakfast island.

It isn't lost on me that this isn't the first time I've cleaned him up. We have a habit of patching each other up —of attempting to fix each other.

But it's only ever temporary.

Elliot drops onto the stool, blood still dripping down his wrist and arm.

"That was silly," I state as I gather the first aid kit and a clean towel.

"Yeah, well, we can't all be as perfect as you," he bites back but there's no venom in his words.

Another bitter laugh crawls up my throat as I meet his icy gaze. "I think we both know that's not true," I whisper.

"Abi, I—"

"Don't. What's done is done." My heart twists. "Nothing you say can undo that night, Elliot. Nothing you say will change the fact that I'm me and you're... you."

He drops his head, peeking up at me through his dark lashes. "For what it's worth, I'm sorry. I'm so fucking sorry, Red."

I ignore him, arranging the first aid supplies on the marble countertop and take his bleeding hand in mine. "You might have broken something," I point out.

Elliot flexes his fingers, letting out a small huff. "I haven't."

"Very well."

Methodically, I clean his hand, taking extra care over his busted knuckles. The air is thick and heavy between us, full of regrets and shame and hurt.

I hate him.

But I hate that I still want him more.

"Tell me what you're thinking," he says, breaking the tension, the awkward silence threatening to suffocate me.

"This probably requires medical attention."

"I'm a quick healer."

My eyes flick to his and I instantly regret it. He's looking at me with such reverence. It confuses me.

It makes my heart beat faster.

Despite everything, it makes me wish things were different.

Makes me want things.

Things I know I can never have.

"Will you at least let me explain?" he asks quietly. Softly.

Too soft for a boy like Elliot Eaton.

"Will it change anything?" My brow arches and his expression drops.

I let out a small, defeated laugh.

Of course it won't.

"I need you to do something for me," I say.

"Anything."

He means it. I know he does.

But those days are over.

"I need you to stop."

"Stop?" He frowns.

"Acting like you care."

"Abi, I do—"

"Not enough." I shake my head, digging deep to find the courage to say the words without falling apart.

"You don't understand," he grits out as I begin to bandage his hand. "My family—"

"I get it. I do. But it doesn't excuse what you did. How humiliated you made me feel."

A shudder goes through me, but I force myself to look at him.

To really look at him.

"I trusted you, Elliot. I…" I stop myself.

Nothing good can come from confessing the depth of my feelings towards him.

Not now.

"I never wanted to hurt you."

"But you did." A sad smile tugs at my lips as tears burn

the backs of my eyes. "There." I tie off the bandage and lower his hand. "All better."

"Thanks."

A beat passes.

And another as neither of us speak.

Blood roars in my ears, the silence between us deafening.

Elliot reaches for me, tucking my hair behind my ear. "You need to come back to school."

"I will. I mean, I am. Tomorrow."

I'd already decided that before he showed up.

"Good. That's... good." He swallows hard, his thumb brushing my cheek.

It's such a small, innocent touch. But it still makes my breath catch and my heart race.

"We're not okay, Elliot. I need you to know that." Something flashes in his eyes, but I ignore it. "There are only a few weeks left of school. I'm sure we can manage to stay out of each other's way."

"Is that what you really want?" He studies me, his expression so intense it makes it hard to breathe.

"Yes." No.

Elliot drops his hand and stands. I back up, giving him space all while a sinking sensation spreads through me.

"Okay then. I'll do my best to stay out of your way."

"Good."

My stomach churns at how awkward things have become.

Somewhere along the way, Elliot had become my safe haven. My sanctuary. The one place I didn't have to hide.

But he ruined it.

He did that.

And now, I can't trust him anymore.

This is what I want.

I want him to leave me alone. I want him to back off and give me space to get over him.

So why does the idea of him walking out of my house—out of my life—hurt so much?

Elliot doesn't leave though.

He stands there, staring at me.

"Elliot, what—"

He stalks towards me and slides his hand along the side of my neck. I gaze up at him, my heart crashing in my chest.

His lips brush my forehead, sending shivers zipping down my spine. "See you around, Red."

Elliot walks away from me without a backward glance, and I realise that I was right all along.

I'm not the kind of girl worth fighting for.

"You can do this," I chant to myself as I stare at my reflection in the mirror.

It's early but if I want to make it to class on time, I need to leave soon since I didn't go back to my dorm room last night.

I almost did.

I packed my things and everything. But something stopped me.

My phone vibrates and I grab it off the worktop.

>Tally: How are you feeling?

>Abigail: I'm okay.

>Tally: Good. I'll see you soon. xx

I might not have made it back to campus, but I did text Tally letting her know I'd be in this morning.

Something clicked into place last night after Elliot left. I might be shy little orphan girl Abigail Bancroft. But I'm also so much more than that.

I can do this.

I can.

I inhale a shaky breath.

It's only a few weeks, and they'll be gone. I know Mr Porter is probably going to suggest I resit my second year. But that's okay.

It will give me more time to figure out what I want to do after.

I grab my bag and keys and head out to my car. The sun is shining, and I can't help but think it's a sign.

The universe's way of letting me know that everything will be okay.

But as I get nearer to All Hallows' my false bravado begins to crumble.

What if they all know?

What if Ethan told everyone? Or even worse, Scott did?

Anguish twists inside of me as I grip the steering wheel tighter. But I refuse to turn around.

I need to do this.

I have to.

All Hallows' looms in the distance and I force myself to take a deep breath.

I have survived so much already.

I can survive losing my heart to Elliot Eaton.

9
———
ELLIOT

My entire body was heavy as I walked away from Abigail's house.

I didn't really expect her to welcome me with open arms and forget about everything that happened.

I prayed for that, but I'm not that stupid.

Still, I was hoping she'd at least let me explain. Instead, I barely managed to get a decent apology in before she sent me away telling me that I was to avoid her at all costs.

Not the outcome I wanted but ultimately one I should have been more prepared for.

Tally was right, I needed to go. I needed to face her. I just didn't anticipate how much it would hurt to look into her dark, pain-filled eyes.

And the sight of that dressing on her thigh though, that cut me deeper than any blade could.

Movement at the front of the classroom catches my attention and I glance up just as she walks inside. This is the only class we share. For a few months now, it's been my favourite class. Five hours of my week where I've been able to sit and watch her without anyone ribbing me for it.

I've learned a lot about Abi here. From the fact that she underlines all her work with a purple gel pen to how she prefers to sit with her right leg crossed over her left. How she never, ever puts her hand up to answer a question despite the fact I know she knows the answer. Her worst nightmare is having to speak up, to attract the attention of our classmates. The second our teacher looks around to pick on someone, she physically shrinks in her chair.

Once this year our teacher has chosen her. But despite her anxiety, she stood up and gave a perfect answer. She was confident and direct, and explained her point easily and clearly. She'd never agree that she did, but I saw it with my own eyes.

Abigail Bancroft might be shy. She might want to hide in the shadows and try to ignore the pain she's suffered and avoid the curious looks of others. But there is so much more to her than that.

I just wish I could get the chance to discover it all.

It was stupid of me to think we could have anything.

We were never going to work, and our parting ways now is for the best.

Even though it feels like the absolute worst.

Abi makes it no more than five steps into the room before she senses my attention.

I'm the only one here, choosing to arrive early in the hopes of getting these few precious seconds with her.

She should have seen it coming. I did it on Tuesday as well. She looked as shocked then as she does now.

Doesn't she know me at all?

Of course I was going to be here first. I just expected her to wait until the last second so that she could try to blend into the crowd as they walked in.

My lips part, my nickname for her teetering on the tip of my tongue, but I manage to keep it inside.

She asked me to keep my distance, and I fully intend to keep that promise… for now.

She's been in school every day so far this week. I want to be relieved that she has returned to normal life. Shit, I am relieved. But with her back in her dorm, I've lost my connection to her.

Every single night I've laid in my bed, staring up at the ceiling and wondering if she is doing the same thing.

I have the key, I could go and find out.

Hell, a couple of nights I even left the Chapel with the intention of doing so, but I stopped myself before walking into the Bronte Building. Instead, I chose to walk around the corner and look up at her window. Each time, her light was out, but something told me that she wasn't sleeping.

Abigail hesitates, and my heart jumps into my throat that she's going to say something to me. We haven't spoken since I left her house on Sunday and I'm desperate to hear her voice, but it seems that today isn't the day.

No sooner have our eyes connected does she rip hers away, preferring to look at her feet as she finds her desk and gets her books and pencil case out.

The air between us is thick, charged with everything we still feel for each other and all the words we're not saying.

It only takes about thirty seconds before it all becomes too much.

Her entire body tenses as the sound of my chair slides back. I hate it. I hate that she dreads having to talk to me so much she has such a visceral reaction.

I get to my feet, ready to march over to her when voices from the hallway fill the room. Before I've taken my first step, a group of students spill into the room, stopping me from going to her.

Every single set of eyes turns to me as I lower myself back into my chair. In contrast, not one person turns to look at Abigail. It's like she's invisible.

Just like she's always tried to be.

As much as I love that I've seen snippets of the real girl behind the scars, it kills me that no one else knows how incredible she is.

Only a few minutes later, the room is full of students. We might still have a whole day and a half left of the week, and our exams might be approaching faster than most of us are ready for but that doesn't stop everyone around me from forgetting about reality and focusing on their weekend plans.

We're having a party tomorrow night. It's been a few weeks and apparently, there's been talk about the Heirs losing their edge. Total fucking bullshit. So in order to quash any rumours and assert our authority before we're forced to hand the key over to the next generation, we've got to give the people what they want.

A kick-arse fucking party.

Not so long ago, I'd have been all over it. Now though... Honestly, I can't think of anything worse. The only thing that could make the night bearable would be if Abigail was there. But I already know that's a long shot.

The girls might try and convince her, but I'm not sure anything they could say would make her agree.

"What do you mean you're not coming?" Reese barks at Olivia as I lower my tray to the table we all usually sit at.

It hasn't been the case this week.

It's like someone has turned back the clock. The boys and I have been sitting here, holding court in the dinner hall while the girls sit elsewhere with Abigail.

Don't get me wrong, I'm glad they're putting her needs over those of their demanding boyfriends. I just fucking wish they'd all come and sit here with us. The second the Heir chasers got a whiff of something being off with their blossoming relationships, they descended like a swarm of gnats.

We used to love that shit. Every single day we used to lap up their attention, and demand more even. Now, their behaviour and desperation are just a turn-off. Not a single one of them sparks any kind of interest in me.

It got so bad yesterday, I actually broached the subject of us eating in the private room we have access to, should we want it just to get away with it all. But predictably, like the pussy-whipped motherfuckers they are, the guys refused to leave their girls.

I got it. I didn't want to walk away from Abigail either. But something told me she'd probably relax better and eat properly if I did.

It's a bitter fucking pill to swallow.

"I mean," Olivia says, placing her hand on her waist and popping her hip. "We aren't coming to your party."

"B-but you have to come," Reese stutters in utter shock.

"Umm... No actually, I don't think we do."

"You do," Oak pipes up. "You're our girls. It's your job to be there."

Olivia's eyes almost hit the ceiling. "*Our job?*"

"You're a part of us now, babe," Reese explains as if she doesn't know exactly what he's referring to. "Your presence will be expected."

She rolls her eyes. "Your loyal subjects will get over it," she teases.

"What are you doing instead?" I ask, already suspecting where this is going.

She turns to me looking somewhat relieved I asked a serious question. "Girls' night. Abi deserves it, don't you think?"

My heart aches getting the confirmation I was expecting. Abigail won't be at the Chapel tomorrow night.

It was wrong of me to hope that she might have come, had a few drinks, and let go a little. But I couldn't help it. I need something to fucking latch onto here or I'm going to completely fucking drown.

"You can do that Saturday night," Reese points out.

"No, we're doing it tomorrow night."

Without waiting for another word from her boyfriend she marches off through the dining room with her head held high and her school skirt swishing back and forth.

"The fuck?" Reese barks, sinking down in his chair.

"Right?" Oak agrees, looking utterly mortified.

"Nah, man," Theo says, focusing on Oak. "You're looking at this all wrong. If the girls aren't there, you won't have to watch Reese touch up your sister all night."

"Fuck you," Reese grunts. "You can't tell me that you're happy about partying without Raine."

"Of fucking course I'm not, but they've got a point."

Both Reese and Oak sigh. They're friends with Abigail too. They know that the girls need this time with her, even if it comes at their expense.

Together the four of us finish eating, but it doesn't take long for Oak and Theo to slink off in search of their girls. I expect Reese to go with them to teach Olivia a lesson for her little announcement earlier, but he doesn't. He stays put and locks his attention on me.

"What?" I snap, not in the mood for another Reese Whitfield-Brown heart-to-heart.

"You look rough, man. Have you slept at all this week?"

I don't respond. What's the point? The fact he's bringing it up means he knows the answer.

Between obsessing over Abigail and studying, I'm pretty much running on empty.

"Say whatever you want to say then fuck off," I mutter.

"Just worried about you, bro."

Shaking my head, I scrub my hand down my face. "No need. I've got everything under control."

"Bullshit," he scoffs. "Why don't you try and talk to her again?"

"And say what? I can't fix this, Reese. Why can't you understand that?"

"Okay fine." He sighs, clearly frustrated with me. "Talk to your father instead."

"Oh yeah, because that will fix all my fucking problems."

"Well, you've got to do something. You can't keep up like this."

No. He's right. I fucking can't. But I've been left with two impossible options.

Forget about Abigail and get on with my bullshit life.

Or...

Defy the orders of the man who has control over every aspect of my life and effectively sign my own death certificate.

There really is no right answer here.

10

ABIGAIL

"I'm not sure about this." I run my hands down the black bodycon dress hugging my figure.

"Abs, we are doing this." Tally flashes me a reassuring smile.

"She's right," Liv adds. "You look amazing, and it'll do you good to get out and let your hair down."

I don't share their optimism but when these girls put their mind to something there's no arguing with them.

Besides, maybe they have a point.

I've managed a whole week of attending classes. Of going through the motions.

They've been there every step of the way, meeting me first thing and walking me to class, sitting with me at lunch. They even dropped the boys so I didn't have to sit with Elliot.

I'm grateful, even if I know it won't last forever.

"Here, drink this." Liv hands me a glass of something.

"What is it?"

"A little Dutch courage. Don't worry, we won't let you get drunk."

I take it from her, sniffing the contents. It smells fruity and a little bit bitter, but it doesn't stop me from downing it in one.

"Holy crap, Abi." Raine grins. "Atta girl."

"You want another?" Liv asks and I shake my head.

"I think one is enough for now."

I'll never admit it to them, but what I really want is to lock myself away in my room and—

No.

Not tonight.

Not while I'm with them.

I've managed to resist the urge to cut myself all week. Kept myself busy with revision and mindless TV. But it's always there. A nagging little voice at the back of my mind whispering that it will make it all feel better.

"You know, you didn't have to do this," I say.

"Do what?" Tally frowns.

"Take me out. I know there's a party at the Chapel tonight."

It's all everyone at school has talked about all week.

I'm surprised my sudden disappearance wasn't the talk of the school, but I guess I have the girls and their boyfriends to thank for that.

"The boys can manage one little party without us." She scoffs. "Besides, I'm so over watching the Heir chasers and their pathetic acts of desperation."

"You're not worried one of them might try something?" I ask.

I know how vicious those girls can be. How sneaky and manipulative.

"Oakley knows better."

I glance at Liv and Raine and they both smirk.

"The boys know if they so much as look at another girl they'll regret it," Liv adds.

God, I envy them.

Their confidence and unwavering belief in their relationships.

"Okay, I think I'm done." Tally smacks her lips together, blotting the corners of her mouth with a tissue. "What do you think?"

"You look gorgeous," Liv says. "We should totally snap some photos to send to the boys. Show them what they're missing out on."

"Good idea." A devious smile graces her lips as the three of them huddle together. "Come on, Abs, you need to get in here."

"Oh, I don't think so." I wave them off, pretending to fix my hair in the mirror.

They don't push it and I'm relieved even if a little disappointed.

But then someone thrusts another drink at me, and Tally declares a toast, "To girls' night."

We down our drinks and a shudder rolls through me.

"Ready?" Raine asks me quietly, and I nod.

As I'll ever be.

The bar we go to is a weird mix of students and locals. The music vibrates through my chest making me feel a little light-headed, but I soak it up, enjoying the distraction from my own thoughts.

"Shots?" Tally calls and the girls nod as we make our way to the bar.

Liv leads the way, cutting a path through the sea of bodies as if she owns the place.

I guess when your surname is Beckworth, your brother

is an Heir, and your father is one of the county's most revered lawyers she kind of does.

"Abs, you good?" Tally squeezes my hand, startling me. But I cover my momentary panic with a smile.

"Yeah, fine."

"I'm really glad you came," she goes on. "I know it's been a horrible few weeks but you have to try and move forward."

"Yeah." My smile is tight.

"Do you want a soft drink?" she asks as we finally reach the sleek black and chrome bar. I shake my head.

"No, I'll have a drink but nothing too strong. And no shots."

"Are you sure? A shot might help."

"Fine." I concede. "Maybe one."

She turns to Liv to order our drinks and two minutes later, I have a shot glass in one hand and a sugary cocktail in the other.

"On three," Raine announces, holding up her shot. "One. Two. Three."

They all knock back their shots and I hesitate. This isn't me, not really. But I don't want to be sad little Abigail Bancroft. Not tonight.

I want to forget.

To forget my grief and heartache and the constant pit in my stomach.

Without overthinking it, I drink my shot, chasing it down with the sugary sweet cocktail.

"You good?" Raine studies me a little too closely.

"Fine." I stare out at the dance floor, jealousy burning through me as I watch all the people dancing without a care in the world.

I've never had that.

I've never been able to truly let go and be free.

"Can we dance?" I blurt, expecting the three of them to gawk at me like I've grown a second head.

I should have known better.

Tally grabs my hand and grins. "Let's go," she says, tugging me through the crowd.

The alcohol courses through my veins, making me all warm and a little fuzzy headed. But I like it. Besides, the girls will look out for me, I know they will.

They all start moving to the music, sexy and seductive. The way I've seen them do before. It isn't me though, it never has been.

But I wish it was.

I wish I didn't care what people thought about me or the scars marring my skin.

I wish I had whatever it is that makes them so desirable.

Confidence. Beauty. The determination to go after what they want.

The power to keep it.

I'm not that girl though.

I'm not the girl worth fighting for.

But maybe for tonight, I can pretend.

I can be somebody else.

Maybe tonight, I can be just like Tally or Liv or Raine.

Maybe.

"Maybe you should slow down," Liv suggests as I sip drink number... Crap, I lost count about an hour ago.

But I feel good, so good.

Everything feels warm and fuzzy and great.

"I love you, Olivia. You're a good friend." I fall against her, hugging her tight.

"And you make a cute lush, but I think you should switch to water," she admonishes.

But I'm too happy to care.

Or listen.

"Let her have this," Raine says. "It's one night. She can sleep off her hangover tomorrow and go back to moping."

"Moping? You think I've been— Ooh, shots." I grab the arm of the waitress passing by with a tray of Jäger bombs.

"Oh no, you've definitely had enough of the hard stuff," Tally adds. "We're good thanks."

"Meanie." I pout right as the DJ changes up the music.

Some eighties pop rock song blasts out of the speakers and I'm hit with a memory of me and my parents in the kitchen. The two of them dancing to this very song. So happy and healthy and... alive.

"I love this one," I shriek excitedly, darting towards the dance floor.

"We should take her home," someone murmurs behind me but I'm too lost in the music to care.

I weave my hands in the air like the other girls around me, closing my eyes and giving over to the beat while the raspy voice sings about six strings and diners and dreaming of running away.

And I'm smiling.

Not because I'm drunk or I'm dancing or because for once in my life I don't feel like the scarred, damaged girl afraid of her own shadow.

I'm smiling because this song reminds me what life was like before the accident. Before Mum died and Dad got sick.

It reminds me of a better time.

A time when my house was filled with love and hope and happiness.

"Well aren't you a cute little thing." A heavy arm

wraps around my waist and yanks me back into a hard chest. Panic slams into me and I freeze for a second, until my fight instinct takes over.

"Get off me," I shriek. "Get off—"

"Relax, we're only dancing. We're—"

"I think she said get off, dickhead." Raine glares at the boy—*the man*—holding me.

"Jealous, babe? I'm down for a threesome if you're—"

My elbow connects with his stomach, and he lets out a pained groan. "Fucking bitch."

Raine reaches for me, pulling me into her side as Tally and Liv call for security.

Two burly doormen fight their way through the crowd and Liv whispers something to one of them. He gives her a small nod before grabbing the man by the scruff of his neck and shoving him towards the door.

"Are you okay?" Raine asks.

"I-I..." I choke on a sob.

"Come on, let's get out of here." She grabs my hand, and we follow the girls out of the bar.

The cool spring air hits me and the world tilts. "S-stop," I inhale a sharp breath, trying to stave off the crippling wave of nausea.

"What's wrong?" All three of them stare at me with concern.

My eyelids flutter as I try to stay focused. "I don't feel so good. I—" I vomit all over the path.

"Shit, okay. I'm calling Oak," Tally says.

"No, no," I murmur, bent double as the nights worth of shots and cocktails burns my oesophagus and splatters all over the ground.

"Just call a taxi," Raine suggests as she rubs my back.

"Sorry," I murmur. "I'm so—" Another wave of nausea rocks through me.

"Abi?" someone yells but I'm falling.

Down. Down. Down.

"Oh God, Abi."

"Fine, I'm fine."

Except, I don't feel fine. My head feels too big for my shoulders and everything is spinning.

"He's going to kill us," Tally says.

"W-who?" I ask but the words are quiet and slurred.

"Oak is on his way," someone else says.

But I feel too sick to focus. Too tired and disoriented.

Maybe if I close my eyes for a little while, I can sleep it off.

Shadows dance across my vision as darkness floods in.

But I welcome it.

After all, it's where I've always belonged.

11

ELLIOT

The party rages around me, but I might as well be sitting alone in the Chapel for how much it excites me.

I've always known that I'm broken. Dad and Scott have made sure to always point out my flaws and how I'll never stand up to them. But since looking up to find Abi's heart shattering before my very eyes in that pub last week, it's worse than ever. And I fear it could be irreparable.

I should be enjoying myself with my boys. I have them all to myself. It's what I've craved since they all started falling in love and losing themselves to their girls. I just wanted another night of just us. A night like all those we planned in the lead-up to our final year at All Hallows'. But I can't find it within me to enjoy it.

I haven't touched a sip of alcohol. I'm not interested. Yeah, it might numb everything. But I don't want that. I want to suffer. I want the pain.

I watch everyone as they chat with their friends, laugh, dance. That should be me. I should be out there living up my last few weeks of this.

I'm going to blink and all of this will be over. The next Heirs will be ripping out any evidence of our reign from this building and making it theirs.

Our time here will be nothing but a memory. One that is going to end with pain and regret for me.

Fuck. It wasn't meant to be like this.

One girl wasn't meant to have the power to finally sever the thin threads that were holding me together.

But here we are.

My eyes land on my boys. They're in the kitchen with a few other members of the team. Each of them has beers in their hands and even from here, I can see that their eyes are alight with happiness.

That should be me.

I should be up there with them.

My fists curl, my short nails pressing into my skin.

It's not enough.

Nothing ever is.

I haven't relapsed since that day in the shower.

I told myself that I'll be stronger. That I'll fight it. If I can do it, then maybe Abigail can too.

The thought of her being in her dorm room taking a blade to her beautiful porcelain skin rips me apart inside.

All I can do is trust that she's being strong, that she's fighting the darkness more effectively than I am.

I keep my eyes on Oak, Reese, and Theo, wishing my life was as easy as theirs are right now. They've overcome everything that was thrown at them this year and come out the other side with their girls standing firmly beside them.

I guess it should give me hope. Especially when I remember how hopeless some of their situations seemed at certain points this year. But it's not helping.

Nothing is.

My brows pinch as Oak lifts his phone up to look at the

screen before he swipes and puts it to his ear. There's only one person who would call him tonight. Everyone else is here.

My heart begins to race as I think about what the girls are doing.

What Abigail is doing.

Oak and Reese told me earlier that they were going out.

The thought of my sweet Abigail in a club surrounded by drunken arseholes without us there to protect her has acid sloshing in my stomach.

I want to be there. To make sure that every motherfucker within a ten-mile radius knows that she's mine.

She's not yours though. You fucked it up, remember?

Oak pushes a finger into his other ear so he can hear what's being said on the other end, and I sit up straighter as he turns his back on the others, his shoulders widening.

What's happening?

Is Abi okay?

I can't see his face so I don't stand a chance of reading his lips, but I clearly see the moment he nods before hanging up.

He just agreed to something.

What?

He steps up to Reese before saying something in his ear and then marching towards the front door.

"Fuck," I grunt, jumping to my feet and forcing my way through the crowd between us to find out what's happening.

Something is wrong. I can feel it in the very depths of my soul.

He's out of the front door by the time I catch up to him. The second he's in touching distance, I grip his shoulder and spin him around to face me. "What's going on?"

He studies me for a beat. I want to say that it's because he's surprised to have been stopped and not because he's drunk.

Sure, he's had a few beers but not enough to be wasted. Unless he's had something I haven't seen.

Oakley isn't stupid enough to put his girl in danger, a little voice says in the back of my mind.

If that's even where he's going…

"Nothing," he finally says. "Go back inside."

I move closer. "Not until you tell me where you're going."

"Elliot."

"It was Tally, wasn't it?" I ask. "You're going to the girls. Are they okay? Is Ab—" I cut myself off, but it's pointless. Oak knows. They all fucking do.

They always have.

Tally is the only one who has railed me for what I did, but I'm not stupid. There's no way she hasn't told her boyfriend every second of it. I wouldn't be surprised if all the others know by now too.

"They're drunk, okay." He exhales a weary breath. "I'm just going to pick them up so they don't have to get a taxi."

"Sounds good, let's go."

"Elliot," he warns, his expression hard.

"What?" I spit, unwilling to have a fucking discussion about this. If he thinks Tally's call was important enough to leave mid-party, then I'm fucking going too. "You've been drinking."

"I've had two, maybe three, beers max. I had a feeling she'd call."

"Then let's go and get them."

He hesitates as I move towards where we park our cars.

"What?" I snap. "What are you hiding?"

His teeth clench and his shoulders tense. "Go back inside, Elliot. I've got this."

My heart begins to race. "It's Abi, isn't it? What's happened?"

"For fuck's sake, man," he complains rubbing the back of his neck.

I glare at him, refusing to back down until he gives me the truth.

We don't lie to each other. Ever.

"Fuck. She's wasted, okay. Tally called for a lift because she was vomiting on the pavement."

"She's what?" I hiss as I take off running towards my car.

"They took her out to let her hair down," he calls after me.

"It sounds like it might have backfired," I retort as I pull the driver's door open and drop into the seat.

I have the engine running a second later and I floor the gas as soon as Oak drops in beside me.

"Tally is going to kill me for this," he complains. "She specifically said to come alone."

"I don't give a shit. Get down on your knees and grovel. Do whatever it is you do that makes her swear."

"Fuck, yeah," he growls. I don't need to look over to know he's got a shit-eating grin on his face. There is nothing he loves more than driving Tally to the brink of insanity and forcing dirty talk out of her mouth.

"Where are they?" I ask as I head into the middle of town.

Pulling his tracking app, he syncs it to my car's Bluetooth so I can see their location on the screen.

"Bingo," I hiss, zeroing in on Tally's pin.

It takes us less than ten minutes thanks to my slight breaking of the speed limit. It's worth it, not that something as small as speeding would stick. I don't need my father's power to get something like that swept under the rug, Oak's dad could make it disappear in a heartbeat as well.

I slow my speed as the club appears in the distance before the shadow of a group of girls huddling together a little down from the entrance becomes clear.

"There," Oak says, pointing out of the window as if I'm fucking blind.

Jerking the wheel to the left, I bump up on the curb and bring the car to an abrupt stop. I throw the door open and jump out. I have no idea if I close it behind me, my only concern is the girl slumped on the pavement.

Tally, Raine and Liv all jump up the second they see me coming.

"I called Oak," Tally spits, her anger more than obvious.

"I don't care. If anyone should be looking after Abi, it's me."

"Bullshit," Tally replies, her eyes widening in shock as she hears her own curse.

She must be drunk.

"Get out of my way," I demand, pushing past them to get to my girl.

My girl.

Knowing that it's pointless to put up a fight, they move aside, and I drop to my knees before her.

She's pale but when I reach out and cup her face, her skin is clammy. Sliding one arm under her knees and another behind her back, I effortlessly lift her into my arms.

"What the hell are you doing?" Tally screeches.

"Getting her off the fucking street, what does it look like?" I grunt. Isn't it fucking obvious? "Open the door," I demand when I get closer to my car.

Oak pulls it open, and I lower Abigail into it.

"If you all want a ride back, I suggest you get the fuck in before I drive off and leave you all here."

"What the hell?" Tally asks again before the sound of her slapping Oak's shoulder fills the air.

"Babe," he complains. "I tried, okay. He saw me leaving and guessed. What was I meant to do?" he asks as I jog around the front of my car.

"Lie, anything," she seethes.

"Two seconds or I'm leaving without you," I warn before dropping into the driver's seat.

"It's okay, Red," I say, double-checking I strapped her in. "Everything is going to be okay."

I study her for a beat while the others pile in behind us. Tally sitting on Oak's lap while the girls all squish in next to them. It's a tight squeeze but they manage.

Abi is totally out of it. Her eyes are firmly closed and her chest is rising and falling steadily.

"How much did she drink?" I demand.

"Too much," Liv offers unhelpfully.

"She was just enjoying herself. Getting a little drunk after everything she's been through isn't a crime, you know," Raine spits. "She is allowed to be an eighteen-year-old."

"I fucking know that," I fume. I just wish she could have done it where I was so I could keep an eye on her. "Oak, call the guys, clear the Chapel out. The party is over," I say, staring him dead in the eye in the rearview mirror so he knows how serious I am.

What would have happened tonight if she'd wandered off? If the girls got separated?

My heart pounds harder against my chest.

She's vulnerable. Too fucking vulnerable and it's all my fault.

If anything happened to her... I'd never forgive myself.

She doesn't so much as stir all the way back to the Chapel, and thankfully, she doesn't vomit in my car.

There are a few lingering drunk students who are still attempting to figure out how to get home, but I don't pay them any attention as I lift Abigail into my arms and march towards the Chapel with her.

"Put her on the sofa," Tally demands from behind me. "I'll get her pillows and sheets."

"Fuck that, Darlington. The only place she's sleeping tonight is in my bed," I shoot back over my shoulder.

"Elliot, you can't, she—"

"I don't give a fuck what you think. She's sleeping in my bed. She can hate me for it tomorrow all she likes."

With Tally still shouting at me, I march through the Chapel, ignoring Reese and Theo as I head for the stairs. No one on this Earth could stop me from taking care of my girl right now.

No one.

12

ABIGAIL

My eyes flutter open as I try to get my bearings.
Something feels wrong.
I feel wrong.

Oh my God. What happened to me?

I blink, scanning the familiar room. Certain, I must be seeing things. Because there's no way...

Except, I feel him. Hard and hot behind me. His hand curled possessively over my hip like I belong here.

In Elliot's bed.

My stomach roils and I inhale a thin breath, trying not to wake him. Trying desperately to remember how I ended up here.

The last thing I remember is drinking shots. Lots and lots of shots. The rest is blurry. Some man trying to dance with me. The girls shouting. Vomiting all over myself.

Oh God.

I gingerly lift the soft sheets and glance down, relieved that I'm wearing what appears to be a clean t-shirt and not the vomit covered dress I must have come back in.

Did Elliot shower me? Clean me up and dress me in one of his Saints rugby shirts?

Why does the idea of him taking care of me make my heart flutter?

Foolish little thing.

It doesn't mean anything beyond his need to look out for me. The girls probably called him to pick us up.

To rescue me.

How embarrassing.

I start to slide his arm off my hip, but Elliot's grip tightens on me and he pulls me closer until there's only a sliver of space left between us.

My breath catches at his proximity.

I've imagined this scenario so many times. Imagined what it would be like to fall asleep in his arms every night and wake up beside him every morning.

And although this isn't the first time I've ended up in his bed, it feels different.

Bittersweet.

Bile rushes up my throat as his betrayal replays in my mind.

How could he be so cold and vicious that night? How could he let his brother humiliate me like that and do nothing?

I know there's probably more to it than meets the eye—Elliot told me as much when he said we needed to keep our relationship a secret. But something broke in me that night and I'm terrified that if I give him a chance to explain, I'll relent. And if I relent, when he hurts me again, I won't survive it.

Because I realise now that there's no happy ending for us.

There never was.

"I've missed you." His raspy voice sends a shiver racing down my spine.

"What am I doing here, Elliot?"

"You don't remember?"

"I remember bits. Not how I ended up in your bed wearing your rugby shirt."

"You were sick again. I had to clean us both up before we got into bed."

Probably explains why I can taste the lingering hint of mint from the mouthwash.

He did take care of me.

But instead of leaving me to sleep it off, he got into bed with me.

I'm not sure how to feel about that.

"You're angry," he whispers.

"I'm confused. I thought we agreed—"

Elliot rolls me onto my back and hovers above me, his eyes a glacial storm that burns right through me. "Let's get one thing clear, Red. You might have walked away from me but I'll never walk away from you."

The air crackles between us, so charged I want to run. But I can't move. Elliot has me pinned and not just in a physical sense.

His words, the weight to them—the *truth* in them—almost makes me want to take it all back.

But how can I trust him after what he did?

The answer is, I can't.

Even if I want to choose him and ignore everything else that's happened.

"Fuck, Abi. Don't look at me like that."

"Like what?" My voice cracks.

"Like I won't ever change your mind."

"You won't."

"You sure about that, Red." He leans down, brushing

his nose along the curve of my jaw. My heart stutters. Once. Twice. Before taking off at warp speed.

"Elliot." I press my hands against his chest, trying to gain the upper hand. But a low groan rumbles in his chest, vibrating through me.

He doesn't stop, ghosting his lips over the corner of my mouth and back over my jaw and along the curve of my throat.

A whimper slips free as my body stirs to life.

This.

This is what he can give me.

A temporary reprieve from the dark thoughts circling my mind.

But I shouldn't take it, shouldn't be that girl.

I only let him touch me before because I care about him, because I thought—

No.

I refuse to go there.

This doesn't have to be anything more than a simple transaction.

I trust Elliot enough to make me feel good, even if I don't trust him with my heart.

"Your body still wants me," he whispers against my heated skin, "even if you hate me now."

Making the decision, I clutch his shoulder and arch my neck.

"Thank fuck," he murmurs, licking a path along my collarbone before sucking the sensitive skin underneath my ear, dragging another whimper from deep inside me.

"You like that?" he asks.

But I refuse to answer.

We don't need to talk to do this.

Elliot doesn't push but he does let his hand dip underneath his shirt. His fingers splay on my stomach, brushing upwards, mapping every dip and curve along the way.

My skin vibrates at his touch, comes alive in a way that scares me. But right now, I'd rather burn than hide in the dark, cold abyss alone.

I arch into his touch, silently seeking more. Elliot smirks against my cheek, slowly sliding his mouth to mine. I duck my head, not ready to be kissed by him. To give him the satisfaction of thinking he's won.

He hasn't.

But I can't deny that his touch soothes me. Settles and calms me.

"Look at me, Red." His hand comes to my jaw, guiding my face back to his. "There she is."

Something softens in his gaze as he rests his forehead against mine. "I'm sorry I hurt you. I'm so fucking sorry."

"Elliot, I—"

He kisses me and I realise my error as soon as he lips brush mine.

Kissing Elliot is like waking up from a lonely, dreamless sleep. He invades every crack and fissure in my heart, stitching them together and making them whole.

His hand is in my hair, his body a comforting weight above me. He rolls over me fully and my legs fall open to accommodate him.

This is dangerous territory. For my heart.

And my sanity.

But I can't seem to stop myself.

I can't seem to tell him no.

Maybe we can pretend for a little while longer.

"I want you, Abi, I want you so fucking much," he whispers so quietly I can't be one percent certain I heard him right. Because I'm me… and he's Elliot Eaton.

He can have any girl he wants.

Girls like Lauren Winrow.

Beautiful. Strong. Rich.

His kiss turns harder. Possessive and desperate in a way that makes my toes curl. I'm lost in him, the thrill of having him so close.

He rolls his hips into me, letting me feel exactly how much he wants me and I suppress another whimper.

"Use me," he urges, tangling his fingers in my hair. "Get off on me. Take whatever you need."

"T-touch me," I say. "I want you to touch me."

Something flares in his eyes and for a second, I think he might deny me.

"You sure?" He searches my face and I nod, too scared to give him my words.

Elliot exhales a soft sigh as he pushes his hand between us, finding my centre wet and wanting.

"Fuck, Red, you're soaked," he croons, hooking my underwear to the side to slide a finger into me. And another.

"Okay?" he asks, and I nod, letting my head drop back as I give over to him.

There's no hesitation, no second-guessing myself, no cynical dark thoughts.

Everything just melts away, my awareness narrowed onto only one thing—Elliot touching me. His fingers curling deep inside me as his thumb rubs circles over my clit, making me shiver and moan.

I'm soaring. Climbing higher and higher, chasing that moment of sheer bliss that I know will follow.

Nothing else feels this good. Not the sharp edge of a blade slicing into my skin. Not the poison running through my veins as I danced wild and free last night.

Nothing—*nothing* feels this good.

My body trembles beneath him as I race towards the edge.

"That's it, Red. Come for me. Come all over my hand."

Elliot kisses me through it, stroking his tongue into my mouth as I shatter.

"Oh God," I cry, clutching his bedsheets.

It's too much.

Too intense and consuming.

I could lose myself in this.

In him.

"S-stop." I push him away, panic saturating every inch of me.

What have I done?

"Abi, what the fuck?" Elliot leaps out of bed at the same time I do, staring at me as I wrap my arms around myself and sway on my feet.

"Fuck." He rushes over to me and catches me just before I fall.

"I... I-I don't know what happened." I blink up at him, confused and light-headed.

Disappointment clouds his expression, but it's gone in an instant. "Come on," he says. "Sit down and I'll get you some water."

Elliot helps me back to bed and fluffs up his pillows so I can sit up.

"I'll be back," he says, hesitating.

"Elliot, I—"

"Don't, yeah." Defeat coats his voice and in that second, I hate myself.

I crossed a line this morning.

I gave him hope that things could go back to how they were.

I took something for myself and in turn, I hurt him.

I'm a mess.

And the worst part is, I want him to fix it.

I want Elliot to fix me.

He finally leaves me alone, and the silence has never felt more deafening.

I thought I could hide from him.

I thought I could ignore him and pretend he didn't exist.

But one thing is clearer than ever, so long as we're both still at All Hallows' I'll never be able to escape Elliot Eaton.

Or my feelings for him.

13

ELLIOT

I thought my father made me feel like a failure, a fraud, but he has nothing on how fucking useless I feel as I walk away from my room.

But she asked for it, a little voice pipes up.

I shake my head.

It doesn't mean I should have done it.

I pushed her into it, I know I did.

I used every move I've learned to make her bend to my will, and I got what I wanted.

Mostly.

I am no different to him. To them.

If I were a better person, I'd have taken Abi back to her dorm last night and let the girls look after her.

But I didn't.

I couldn't.

The Chapel is silent as I make my way to the kitchen, the place is fucking wrecked though, with evidence of the suddenly abandoned party the night before everywhere.

I groan. I'm usually the one up first to embark on the tidying up, even before the paid help gets here. But today, all I want to do is go back upstairs, to attempt to make up for what I did this morning.

I grab two bottles of water and some painkillers because despite what Abigail's body craved this morning, there's no way she's not suffering from the hangover right now.

She was wasted last night. Thoughts of what could have happened if Tally hadn't called Oak make my blood run cold.

In seconds, I'm climbing the stairs once more, closing the space between us.

She might not forgive me, or ever be able to forget about what I did, but that doesn't mean that I'm not going to steal every second of time I can get with her.

When I'm with her, she makes me feel different. Not worthy, because this morning alone has proved that I'm not that. But I want to be. I want to figure out a way to be good enough for her, to be what she needs.

But you can't...

I sigh as I head towards my room.

No matter what happened between us from here on out, there can't be an us.

Scott has already tried to ruin it once, what is going to come next?

It'll be from my father, I know that as much as I know I'm going to take my next breath, and he won't mess around.

I can't put her through that, I know I can't but also... I don't know how to let her go.

My room is still in darkness and completely silent as I slip inside. For a second, I think she's gone, run into the night to escape me. She should, but then Abi hasn't ever done any of the things she should.

As my vision adjusts to the darkness, I find that she's

curled back up in my bed, probably praying that I didn't return.

Walking over, I drop to my haunches before her and pass her a bottle of water and two pills.

She hesitates but eventually takes them.

"Good girl," I whisper into the darkness.

My heart is in my throat, my stomach a tight knot of anxiety as I watch her, waiting to see what's going to happen next.

But when nothing does, I push to my feet, stalk around to the other side of the bed, and slip in behind her. The warmth of her body instantly heats mine as I press my front against her back, tucking my crotch tightly against her ass.

I shouldn't do it but... fuck. I can't not.

"Elliot," she whispers brokenly as I slide my hand across her stomach, my arm locking around her.

"Sleep, Red. Everything will feel better in the light."

It's a lie. We both know it. But right now, it's all I've got.

Just like the rest of the night, I lie there listening to her as she drifts back off to sleep.

It never comes for me though. Instead, my head spins with a million and one thoughts, most of them completely useless. Almost all of them are about her and the life I know we can't have together.

Every time she moves, I hold her tighter. This could very well be the last time I get this.

I'm fucking well going to make the most of it.

By some miracle, I must eventually drift off because I startle when Abi attempts to slip from my hold.

"No," I grunt, my grip tightening.

"I need the bathroom," she whispers, her fingers dancing over my arm before peeling my hand from her.

I groan in frustration, irritated at myself. Our time is over, and I fell asleep and missed some of it.

Knowing I can't keep her here forever, I finally relent and allow her out of bed. With the sun streaming through the window, I watch her pad through my room wearing only my Saints rugby shirt, my dick aching painfully beneath the sheets.

My body burns up and I throw the covers off as the sounds of the Chapel waking up around us fill the air.

The start of a new day should bring the promise of hope, of new beginnings, and all that. But all I feel is dread.

Dread and desire.

Reaching out, I squeeze my dick through my boxers, praying it'll be enough to squash the ache but already knowing it's not.

But it's hopeless.

I smother a moan as it jerks hopefully, desperately.

I'm so lost in my own head that I don't hear the bathroom door open, or her step out. I damn sure feel the second she turns her gaze on me though.

The fire that was burning through me turns into an uncontrolled inferno the second our eyes lock.

"Red," I breathe, pushing myself up so I'm resting against the headboard, not bothering to cover up how my body reacts to her.

I want her to see. I want her to understand how badly I need her.

Her eyes drop down my body. They get darker with every inch she takes in until her breath catches.

Precum spills from my tip as I let my mind run away with me, imagining her crawling on the bed between my feet, curling her fingers around my boxers and dragging them down my legs and—

"You were the best head of my life," I blurt like an imbecile.

Her cheeks blaze as red as her hair. I fucking love it.

"Elliot, y-you can't say—"

"It's true," I assure her, cutting off her argument.

"Well..." She fidgets on the spot, clearly not knowing what to do.

She still wants me, I felt it in her touch, in her kiss, in the way her body responded to me.

It's her head that's the problem.

I get it. I really fucking do. But I want her more.

Throwing my legs over the edge of the bed, I stalk towards her. She takes a step back, but quickly discovers that an escape is futile because all she achieves is bumping into the wall behind her.

Abi gasps, but I don't make the most of the opportunity like I should, instead, I slide my hand to her throat, holding gently as her pulse flutters against my fingertips.

"W-what are you doing?" she asks, her wide eyes bouncing between mine.

"I'm not going to kiss you again," I confess, hating every single syllable in that sentence.

Kissing her is all I want to do. But this isn't about me. It's about her.

"The next time I kiss you, you'll have to beg me for it."

She swallows, the tendons in her neck pulling tight against my palm before I lean closer letting my lips brush her ear and my cock rub against her hip.

"The next time you want me to touch you, you'll have to beg too."

I smirk at the quiet whimper that spills from her lips.

It drives me fucking crazy with need.

Reaching for her hand, I wrap my fingers around her wrist and press her palm against my length.

"Elliot," she whimpers, attempting to pull her hand away, but I hold it steady.

"This barely scratches the surface of how I feel about you, Red," I confess with my face tucked into the crook of her neck.

We're in a little bubble. A place where it is only us. Somewhere no one can hurt us.

"I'm obsessed with everything about you, every single inch of you. I'm so fucking sorry for what happened, I was —" I cut myself off, swallowing and attempting to force down the lump clogging my throat. "I was trying to protect you… from me. From my fucked-up life.

"When I want something, I usually get it no matter the consequences. But you're different. The consequences matter with you, everything matters with you.

"Elliot, I—'

"No," I say, releasing her hand in favour of pressing two fingers to her lips to cut her off.

I stare her dead in the eyes, unable to notice that she hasn't pulled her hand from my body as quick, and she'd probably like to.

She's as addicted to me as I am to her.

It's a fucking heady feeling. But also one I know she isn't going to give into easily.

"I want you, Red. Never ever forget that. Everything I've ever done, will ever do has been for you."

She shakes her head refusing to believe me.

I shouldn't be surprised or disappointed, but I am.

"Have breakfast with me," I demand.

"I can't, I need to go—"

"It's just breakfast, Red. It's not a date." It's totally a date. "Just two friends eating and spending time together."

She stares up at me as silence stretches between us.

She wants to say no, but she can't.

It's the sign I need that I should step back and let her go. But I can't do that either.

"Come on," I say, grabbing her hand and pulling her from the wall. "We need coffee. Everything will seem better then," I lie.

I pause to grab a pair of sweats. While I might be willing to allow her full, unrestricted access to my body knowing that she'll understand the pain it shows, I'm not willing to share it with anyone else.

The second I'm covered, I retake her hand and tug her out of the room.

She doesn't say a word as we descend the stairs. My heart is in my throat thinking that she'll bolt the second she discovers that we're no longer alone, but we can't hide forever.

All eyes turn on us the second we emerge, and she stills behind me.

They want to ask all the questions under the sun, I can see it in their eyes, but being the kick-arse friends that they are, they hold it back... for now.

"Abs, do you want coffee?" Tally asks, jumping to her feet.

Pulling her into my side, I wrap my arm around her shoulders and press a kiss on her temple.

The weight of their stares presses heavily down on my shoulders, but while she's in my arms, I don't give a fuck.

"Reese and Theo want to go out for breakfast," Olivia says, attempting to shatter the tension. "You guys want to come with?"

Abigail freezes but then her stomach growls loudly, answering for her.

"Looks like I'm going to have to share you," I whisper in her ear.

"I... I'm not sure—"

"We're your friends, Red. You deserve it."

Dropping my arm from her shoulder, I tap her on the arse, gently pushing her towards the girls. It's the last thing I want to do, but it's also what she needs.

I stalk towards my boys, keeping my eyes on her the whole time, and not just so I don't have to see their gleeful smirks.

"So..." Oak starts.

"Nothing happened," I warn. "Don't get excited."

"Fucking hell, man," Theo groans, scrubbing his hand down his face. "You do know that you're at risk of losing it if you don't use it."

"Give him a break," Oak barks, slapping Theo across the head. "He's already finding it *hard* enough. He doesn't need you making it worse."

"Trust me," I mutter. "Nothing about Theo makes anything hard here."

As they laugh, Raine says something to Abigail that makes her do the same and I swear, the sight of her happiness, of her smile, lights something up inside me.

Fucking hell, I'm in real trouble here.

14

ABIGAIL

Elliot's arm brushes mine as he reaches for the salt.
"Here." He passes it to me.
"Thanks."

"You need to eat," he adds, staring at me as I stare at my untouched plate.

I'm not hungry.

Not even a little bit.

But if I don't eat, he'll cause a scene. And there's been enough of that this morning already.

Stabbing a piece of bacon with my fork, I shove it in my mouth and glare at him. His gruff laughter makes my stomach flip.

"So Abs, are we going to talk about the fact you—"

"Theo," Elliot barks, and his friend holds up in his hands in surrender.

"Before you leap across the table and hurt me, I wasn't being a dick. We were worried. Especially the girls."

"Yeah, well, she's back now." Elliot gives me another meaningful look.

I don't know how this happened, but I can't deny that part of me is glad it did.

I miss the girls. I miss being a part of their inner circle.

The truth is, I'm tired.

Tired of being alone. Tired of questioning everything. I'm not sure I can trust Elliot or even trust myself where he's concerned, but maybe we can find a way to move forward after all.

So long as I don't get drunk again, or end up in his bed, begging him to touch me.

Heat burns through me as I remember how good it had felt. How addictive.

God, I'm a mess.

I drop my fork and Elliot stares down at me.

Like a moth drawn to a flame, I lift my weary gaze to his and his eyes darken. "What's wrong?" he asks quietly.

"Nothing." I smooth my hair over my shoulder.

"Don't do that," he whispers, reaching out to tuck my hair behind my ear. "Don't hide from me."

I swallow over the lump in my throat and realise our little corner of the café has fallen quiet.

Everyone is watching us.

My gaze finds Tally and she gives me a sad, sympathetic smile that makes my stomach roil.

"I'm fine," I say weakly, and to my relief, they go back to their conversations.

It's surreal to be sitting here with them. Eating breakfast in a small café just outside of Saints Cross.

But nothing is more surreal than the way Elliot keeps watching me or how some part of him keeps brushing against some part of me. As if he needs to touch me. To reassure himself that I'm still here.

I know I jumped to conclusions that night at the pub with Scott but I'm not sure it changed anything.

I was still humiliated. Elliot still did nothing.

And I'm still Abigail Bancroft—a girl nowhere near strong enough to walk in his savage, vicious world.

After last night though, after the way he held me this morning, I'm not sure he'll accept that.

"Abi?"

I blink at Tally who smiles when I realise she's been talking to me.

"I asked how you're finding it back being in class?"

"It's okay, I guess. But I think I'm going to have to defer my exams. Maybe even the year."

Elliot goes rigid beside me, his hand white knuckling his fork. I peek up at him, hardly surprised by the tension in his jaw.

"You won't be finishing with us?" Oakley asks, and I shake my head.

"It's unlikely. There might be the option to resit my exams in the summer but that's only if I've caught up."

"We can help," Liv suggests. "We can have revision sessions and—"

"Oh no, I wouldn't expect you to do that. To be honest," I say, shrinking under their rapt attention. "After everything that's happened, I'm not sure I'm ready for university in a few months."

"But what will you do?"

I shrug, turning my attention to the food on my plate. "I'm not sure."

I thought not having a plan would scare me. But there's something oddly liberating in it.

Maybe I'll take a year out and do some voluntary work. Maybe I'll travel and see the world. Or maybe I'll stay in Saints Cross and work on myself. On healing.

"There's time," she says, as if I'll change my mind.

But if this year has taught me anything, it's that plans can change in an instant.

"Well, I'll still be here next year. So if you decide to retake any classes you won't be alone." Raine gives me a reassuring smile.

"And Millie will be around," Theo adds, slinging his arm around her. "My girls will look out for you."

"I..." It's on the tip of my tongue to argue. To tell them all they don't need to coddle me. But Elliot's hand squeezes my knee gently and my gaze flashes to his.

'*They care,*' he mouths, and those two words crack something inside me.

"Thanks," I murmur, forcing myself to look away from him and at Theo and Raine. They give me a knowing smile that does little to settle the nerves coursing through me.

I was so certain that I couldn't be here, that I couldn't be a part of their tight knit circle if things didn't work out with Elliot.

Maybe I can.

Elliot though, he's a different entity all together, and I'm not sure where we stand.

Or what I even want from him anymore.

But one thing's for certain...

I'm not sure I'll ever be able to escape him.

"How are you feeling?" Raine asks me as we watch the boys deep in an Xbox tournament.

"I'm okay, I guess."

"It's okay if you're not, too. You know that, right?"

I shrug. Because telling her—or any of the girls for that matter—the truth about just how not okay things are isn't on the cards.

"He cares about you a lot," she adds, tipping her head towards where Elliot sits on a black bean bag, his expression a mask, predatory and hyper-focused.

"It's not that simple."

"No, I guess it never is with these Heir boys."

"Theo doesn't talk much about Elliot's family, but it's obvious he's under a lot of pressure."

"Yeah," I murmur. "His older brother Scott is... not a nice person."

"So I've heard." Her lips twist with disgust. "You know, Theo's dad didn't approve of me either."

"Theo's dad murdered his mom." I deadpan.

"These families aren't normal. And honestly, sometimes I wonder if I should have run and never looked back..." She looks over at Theo and something softens in her gaze. "But he's worth it, Abi. It's all worth it."

"I'm happy for you," I reply, unsure if it's the answer she's looking for but unwilling to give her anything else. "I'm going to get a drink."

I excuse myself and head for the sleek kitchen in the corner of the open-plan room.

I've been here enough times now that I know my way around even if I never truly feel at ease here.

"I would have gotten that for you," Elliot says from behind me as I root around in the fridge for a can of pop.

"I'm capable of getting myself a drink," I retort, unable to keep the exasperation out of my voice.

"You're angry at me." He moves closer, coming right up behind me and resting his hands on my hips. My heart flutters wildly in my chest, my skin vibrating at his touch.

"I'm not, I just... I don't know what you want from me."

He drops his head to my shoulder, his lips brushing my neck. Once. Twice. Sending a wave of shivers through me.

He isn't playing fair. Elliot knows exactly what he's doing and I both hate and love him for it.

"I think you're lying to yourself, Red," he murmurs against my skin. "You know exactly what I want from you. You're just too scared to give it to me."

"I'm not scared." I twist in his arms. "I just don't know if I can trust you anymore."

His eyes flare with irritation but he doesn't argue. "I know I fucked up. But I want to fix it... Just give me a chance to fix it. Please."

Elliot drops his head to mine, not caring one bit that our friends can see us.

I shouldn't cave, I know that.

I know it with every fibre of my being. But I'm so tired of hurting. And being with Elliot, it makes all the pain and grief go away.

It shouldn't. But it does.

Without overthinking it, I wrap my arms around his neck and hold him closer.

We don't kiss.

We don't do anything except stand there, holding each other.

Wishing it can be as simple as me forgiving him.

We spend the day at the Chapel. Hanging out, taking it in turns to play the boys on the Xbox.

I don't join in at first, letting Raine and Liv tag team Theo and Oakley. But the third time Reese asks if I want to join in, Elliot plucks me off my position on the end of the sofa and pulls me down between his legs and thrusts the controller at me.

"You can take over for me," he says, wrapping an arm around my waist and easing me back against his chest.

It's intimate, too intimate given we're with our friends and we still haven't defined what we are to them—or each other.

But I don't argue, trying desperately to focus on the television screen and not Elliot's hand as it slips beneath the t-shirt I borrowed from Tally to caress my skin.

"Is this okay?" he whispers, his warm breath brushing the back of my neck.

"That is very distracting," I admit.

"Let the girl breathe, Eaton," Theo teases. "Or she'll stand no chance at kicking Oak's arse."

I blush at his insinuation, but Elliot doesn't seem to mind.

In fact, he seems completely at ease.

It's confusing. Even if I do get a small thrill at being with him like this.

Still, it's tainted by everything that's happened.

The seed of doubt from that night has taken root, growing inside me and coiling around my heart.

I can't trust him.

And yet...

"Stop overthinking it," he says, kissing my shoulder. "You're safe here, I promise."

Safe.

He's right, I do feel safe with him.

But he still has the power to hurt me. To wreck and ruin me.

Then he says six little words that make me melt.

"I want you, Abi. Only you."

15

ELLIOT

"What are you doing?" Abigail groans, her voice rough with sleep as I slide into her bed behind her.

"Missed you," I confess quietly.

Her breath catches.

"My bed was cold and empty last night. I didn't like it."

Saying these things to a girl feels alien, but they're true.

I did miss her last night.

I'd offered for her to stay, but she insisted that she had revision to do, something I also offered to do with her, but she wouldn't have it. Raine walked her back to the dorms not long after the sun went down, and she's stayed locked in here ever since.

"Elliot," she chastises, finding the words hard to believe.

I get it. I really fucking do.

Wrapping my arm around her stomach, I pull her back tighter against me before peppering kisses across her shoulder and working up to her neck.

She shudders against me, a little whimper spilling from her tempting lips.

"Admit it, you missed me too, didn't you, Red?"

"Elliot," she warns again.

"You don't have to forgive me, Abi. Hell, you don't even have to like me, but you've got to admit that there's something here. You want me, I know you do."

Shifting my hand higher, I cup her breast, brushing my thumb over her peaked nipple.

"Elliot." This time my name is nothing more than a moan.

"Fucking love the way that sounds, Red."

She's silent for a few moments as I continue kissing and nipping the soft, sweet skin beneath her ear.

"We can't do this."

Those four words float around in the air between us.

Taunting me. Fucking haunting me.

She's right. I know she is.

But it's not good enough.

We have to do this.

I have to do this.

I can't fucking focus without her.

Unless we're like this, our bodies pinned together, her wrapped in my arms, nothing feels right anymore.

"I can't think about anything else," I admit.

Like this, in the dark, just the two of us, it's easy to say all the things I keep locked up inside.

"You're everything, Red. The only thing I want. The only thing I care about."

"But—"

"Shh. Not now," I beg.

I just want this moment together where we can forget reality and just be us.

She sighs and I tighten my grip on her expecting her to try and escape. But she never does.

"Tell me something," she finally says.

"Uh…"

"Something no one else knows. Something you keep hidden from everyone else. Trust me with something."

My heart is racing long before she's finished talking.

I might keep many secrets from those around me, but there is only one that Abigail will understand.

But the thought of saying the words. Confessing to the dark places I've visited more often than I'd like to admit makes me feel physically sick.

I've hidden it from everyone.

But my time is up.

If I want to keep her, if we stand any fucking chance of figuring out a way to make this work together, then I need to allow her to see my worst, just like I have her.

But how do I tell her?

The right words just don't exist.

"Elliot?" she whispers, letting me know that I've been silent for too long.

"Red," I sigh, pressing my forehead to her shoulder. "You already know that my life isn't what it looks like from the outside.

"I'm privileged, sure. But that has come at a cost."

"Your father?" she whispers.

"Yeah. I've done things. I-I—" The lump in my throat stops me from forcing another word out.

I try and swallow it down, but it only grows larger and larger.

I shake my head, trying to summon up the courage for what I need to do.

With one more kiss on her shoulder, I push away from her and climb from the bed.

"Where are you going?" she asks, panicked as she sits up.

With the lights off and only the silvery glow of the moonlight illuminating the room through the cracks in the curtains, I can only make out her profile, but it's enough to know that she's tense.

She thinks I'm going to refuse her request and run.

It's just another reason to do the opposite.

She doesn't think I'll open up. She doesn't think I trust her enough.

But my trust in her has never been the problem.

It's my own issues, my own shame, that stops me from revealing the truth to those closest to me.

"Red," I whisper as I tuck my thumbs into my boxers and shove them down. "I'm not going anywhere."

Her breath catches as my underwear drops to my ankles. She might not be able to make out the details, but she can see enough.

"I asked for a secret, Elliot. Not for—"

"Give me your hand," I demand, holding mine out for her.

"This isn't—"

"Trust me," I urge, my heart beating even faster with fear that she won't.

"I... uh..."

I breathe a sigh of relief when her warm fingers brush mine as she shifts so she's fully sitting up in bed.

Lifting my foot from the floor, I place it on the edge of the mattress and guide her hand towards the hidden scarred skin.

The second her soft fingertips touch me, I stop breathing.

The darkness I'm all too familiar with threatens to engulf me. The memory of creating the newest scar only a few days ago fills my mind as self-hatred and shame flood through my veins.

"Elliot, what is this?"

"You know," I whisper, my voice so quiet I'm not sure she even hears me. "You know, Red."

I know the moment she understands, the gentle stroke of her fingertips over my marred skin pauses. "No," she breathes. "No, Elliot. You can't—"

"I've never judged you, Abi. Never. Not once. I couldn't... I can't because I know." Silence fills the room, the weight of my confession sitting heavy on both of our shoulders. "I know the pain. The darkness. The feeling of being utterly useless and not knowing how to make it—"

"Stop," she finishes for me.

Reaching for the bedside lamp, I close my eyes as I flick it on, flooding the room with light and allowing her to see what no one else ever has.

"Oh my God, Elliot," she whispers.

I hear her scoot closer before her warm breath dances over my skin.

But I don't look. I can't.

Her fingers move, gently tracing over every scar, every inch of ugly marred skin.

Once she's finished on one thigh, she moves to the other, finding exactly the same thing.

"How long?"

I bite down on my cheeks, hating every single second of this.

"Started when I was eight. Dad... He... I... I fucked up and..."

Suddenly, she's moving and before I know what's happening, her arms are around my shoulders and her face is tucked into my neck.

It takes a moment to register anything, but the second I

do it's the wetness against my skin that steals my attention, a second later comes a sob.

"Oh shit, Red. No. Don't cry. Please, I'm not worthy of your tears."

"No," she argues, holding me tighter as I attempt to push her back so I can look at her. "No, that's not fair. You were just a child."

"So were you," I counter.

She shakes her head but finally, she pulls her face from the crook of my neck.

"Red," I breathe, staring into her watery eyes. Reaching out, I wipe the tears from her cheeks. "Don't cry for me, baby."

Her eyes search mine. A million and one questions are floating around within them, but none pass her lips. Instead, she leans forward and brushes those lips against mine instead.

"Abi," I breathe.

"I've found a better way to help me forget," she murmurs.

"Oh yeah?"

"Yeah."

She wraps her hand around the nape of my neck and leans back. We both crash onto the bed. I just manage to catch myself before I crush her tiny frame. Her tongue sneaks out and the second it collides with mine, I forget about everything but her.

Slipping my hand inside her tank, she wraps her legs around my waist, holding me close as we lose ourselves in each other.

She's right. There is something so much better than a sharp blade.

Her.

Sure the girls that have come before were a good

distraction when I needed it. But they were nothing compared to her.

Needing more, I pull my lips from hers and drag her top from her body, exposing her chest.

"Fuck, you're so beautiful," I groan before dropping my lips to her neck and working my way down until I can suck her nipple into my mouth.

"Elliot," she cries when I suck hard, nipping hard enough to send a little pain shooting through her.

"Can't get enough of you, Red," I confess.

I move lower before flattening my tongue on the scar that cuts across her stomach.

"No, don't," she half begs half moans, her fingers sinking into my hair in an attempt to push me away. "It's ugly."

"Abigail," I chastise. "There isn't an inch of you that comes anywhere close to that. Your scars are beautiful. They show your strength. I wouldn't have you any other way."

"No." She thrashes her head from side to side, refusing to believe me.

"Yes. I want you like I've never wanted anyone before."

"I'm broken."

A bitter laugh spills from my lips. "So am I, Red. So am I."

I've barely finished talking before I've tucked my fingers beneath the waistband of her sleep shorts and knickers, dragging them down her legs.

The second they're free of her feet, I throw them behind me and press her thighs wide.

I let my eyes linger on her glistening pussy before taking my time in taking the rest of her in.

Finally, my gaze locks on hers. Emotions war in her green eyes. Desire, fear, excitement and anticipation.

"Tell me you don't want this—want me—and I'll get dressed and walk out right now." I'm not sure it's true, but I offer nonetheless.

"I-I want you," she whispers.

"Fuuuck," I groan, my dick jerking between us.

The temptation to sink into her right here and now is almost too much to ignore. But she deserves more than that. She deserves the world, not just a release from all our pain and darkness. Okay, well, not just that.

"I want to hear you scream my name, Red," I tell her before dropping to my front and licking her arse to clit.

She squeals, her hips rolling as her fingers sink into my hair, holding me in place.

Her taste floods my mouth, spurring me on, and I eat her like a man possessed before I slide two fingers inside her, upping the ante.

"Elliot," she moans, grinding herself against my mouth.

"Come for me, Red," I demand, curling my fingers against her G-spot. "Show me how tightly you'll squeeze my dick when I push inside you."

"Oh my God," she cries as she races towards the end.

"My name, Abigail. Let everyone know who's doing this to you."

"God, Elliot. Ah... Ah, shit," she screams as she crashes. Her body sucks my fingers deeper as I suck on her clit, letting her ride out every second of pleasure.

Once I'm happy she's finished, I sit up and take myself in my hand.

I'm already riding on a knife's edge, and embarrassingly it only takes a handful of strokes before I groan out her name and come over her chest and stomach.

Our chests heave as we come down from our highs, the

reality of what we just did, of what I confessed floating around us.

Reaching out, I push my finger into a blob of my cum before writing my name across her stomach, right over her scar.

"You're mine, Red. Mine," I tell her, sounding much more confident than I feel about what the future holds for us.

16

ABIGAIL

"You might want to tone it down," Reese says quietly to Elliot. "You're so fucking obvious."

Heat rushes into my cheeks as I look away, fighting a smile.

We're back to hiding our relationship from the world—if you can call what we're doing a relationship.

Every night Elliot sneaks into my dorm room and climbs in bed beside me, finding new ways to make me fall apart. But every morning I wake alone, only the rumpled bedsheets and the lingering ache between my legs a reminder he was ever there.

Part of me wonders if I gave in too easily, but Elliot makes it too difficult to hate him.

And he showed me his scars.

That has to mean something, doesn't it?

"Stop teasing them," Liv warns, shooting me an apologetic look.

"It's fine," I say. "I need to go anyway. I have a meeting with Mr Porter about my plans." I stifle a groan.

I don't want to discuss the future. Not with Mr Porter or anyone else. Getting through each day still feels like wading through quicksand. But the girls make it easier. And I hate to say it, but so do the boys.

In their own strange way, Oakley, Reese, and Theo have all proved that they care too.

Then there's Elliot...

My feelings about him—about us—are still complicated, and I'm not wholly convinced that sneaking around is the right thing to do but I'm tired of fighting it.

"I'll walk you," he says, going to stand. But I pin him with a questioning look.

"Is that a good idea?"

"Let the boy walk you," Theo mumbles. "He'll only send one of us if you don't."

It's true.

All week one of them has been glued to my side at all times. It's overwhelming to say the least, but I don't hate it.

In fact, I kind of like knowing that I still have them in my corner.

On Monday, Ethan tried to talk to me but couldn't get past Oakley and Tally. For a second, I thought Oak was going to do something stupid and hit him.

Thankfully, he didn't. Ethan got the message, and from the lack of stares or whispers as I move from class to class, I'm assuming that word quickly spread that I'm off-limits.

"Fine." I concede, turning my attention to the girls. "I'll see you later."

"If you need anything..." Tally adds, and I nod.

"I know."

"Come on." Elliot presses his hand to the small of my back and follows me out of the dinner hall.

"You didn't have to come with me," I say.

"Actually, I did." He scans the hallway, grabs my hand and pulls me inside an empty classroom.

"Elliot, what are you—"

Caging me against the wall, he pulls down the window blind and rests his forehead against mine. "Do you have any idea how much it kills me not being able to touch you in public."

"We're at school," I remind him. "Anyone could see and run off to tell your brother."

A low growl rumbles in his chest as he looks up to the ceiling, trying to contain his anger.

"Elliot," I sigh. "You know I'm right." I curl my fingers into his school shirt and give a little tug. He lowers his face to mine and his expression softens.

"I want the world to know you're mine."

The intensity in his words melts something inside me.

"Your family—"

"Fuck them." His mouth crashes down on mine, and he kisses all the doubts right out of my head. "You matter, Abi. You and my boys."

"And the girls, don't forget about the girls."

"Yeah." He smiles against my lips. "I'm done playing by their rules. I just need some time to figure out how to make sure none of this blows back on you, okay?"

I nod. Because what else can I do?

I still don't truly understand the inner workings of Johnathon Eaton and his family.

All I know is he hurt Elliot when he was nothing more than a child.

He hurt his own son and has still managed to maintain an iron grip on his life.

"Maybe we should be more careful," I suggest, trying to wriggle out of his hold.

But Elliot moves closer, pressing his big strong body up against me. "Don't do that." His voice wavers as if he's barely in control. "Don't pull away from me."

"I don't want you to get hurt," I whisper.

Not because of me, I swallow the words.

"I can handle my father." His fingers trace the scar on my face. I try to pull away, but he doesn't let me. "You're beautiful, Red."

"I wish I could believe that." I offer him a sad smile.

"You will by the time I'm through with you."

The dark promise in his words make me shiver.

"Let me take you somewhere this weekend," he blurts.

"Where?" I tilt my head at him.

"I don't know yet. But I want to be alone with you."

"Oh."

"We don't have to."

"No, I want to. I just thought you meant..."

"We can invite the others," he says. "But it might get a little awkward for what I have planned."

For what he has...

Oh my.

My stomach clenches.

"So, is that a yes?" he asks, moving to brush his lips over the shell of my ear.

"Yes," I breathe, knowing that if we cross this line, there will be no going back.

"I'll make the arrangements." He steals another kiss, and I hold on tight.

Hoping to God that I'm strong enough to survive whatever is coming our way.

"I hear you and Elliot have a hot date tomorrow night," Tally slides into the seat next to me.

The entire sixth form is crammed into the hall to go over the revision timetable for the looming exams. Since I've deferred all mine until the next year, it doesn't apply to me, but I came anyway. Not wanting to be alone any longer than necessary.

"Shh," I hiss.

"What? No one is paying us any attention. Do you know where he's taking you? I asked Oak but he won't tell me."

"It's a surprise." I glance down at our row, grateful to be seated on the end.

The row behind us begins to fill up and I'm hardly surprised when Elliot and the boys file in.

His eyes lock on mine, sending a blast of desire through me so potent my breath catches.

"Oh my God, you've got it bad."

"Tally, please stop."

Oakley hooks his arm around her neck from behind and pulls her back for a wholly inappropriate kiss.

"Mr Beckworth," one of the teachers warns. "This is neither the time nor place."

"Sorry, sir. It's just that my girl is looking sexy as fu—" Reese elbows him in the ribs and everyone around us starts snickering.

"Oakley!" Tally shoots him a death stare.

"I'll make it up to you later." He winks, and she silently fumes beside me.

But I catch the heat in her gaze. The longing.

Mr Porter commands everyone's attention and begins outlining the plans for the next few weeks. I barely follow, too aware of Elliot behind me, his eyes burning holes in the back of my head.

He shifts behind me, stretching his long legs out beneath my chair, the tips of his shoes hitting the backs of my legs.

Tally smothers a laugh beside me, grinning like the cat who got the cream.

'*Stop,*' I mouth, not brave enough to glance back at Elliot.

But I feel him. Watching me. Toying with my hair.

My heart flutters wildly as I will myself to pay attention.

"Psst, Abs," Oak whispers. "Want to swap seats?"

"Oakley, you're going to get us all into trouble," Tally chides.

"Relax, babe. Porter isn't—"

"Mr Beckworth," he booms across the room. "Something you care to share with the rest of us?"

"Just eager to start revising, sir."

"I'm sure you are." Mr Porter's lip twitch with disapproval. "Now as I was saying, we expect all second years to attend their respective revision classes at least twice a week. No exceptions."

"Bullshit," someone coughs along our row causing another round of snickers.

"Okay, okay." He loosens his tie. "I can see that some of you are unable to sit quietly for more than ten minutes. Please exit the hall in an orderly fashion and don't forget to take a revision timetable from the table."

"Thank fuck," Reese murmurs as we stand and wait for our rows to file out.

Oakley moves one of the chairs and pulls Tally through the gap. "Come on, Abs," he adds.

"I..."

Elliot gives me a reassuring nod and I slip into their row, standing awkwardly at his side.

"Hi," he whispers.

"Hi."

"I missed you last night."

He didn't stop by because of some rugby team thing. The girls had showed up instead to keep me company.

"I missed you too."

"I missed you three." Oakley shoves his head between us and grins.

"Fuck off, idiot." Elliot pushes him away and apologises.

"It's fine. I'm used to his antics by now."

"See, she's used to me." He winks, slinging his arm around Tally's shoulder as we begin to move down the row.

"Can we go somewhere?" Elliot asks over my shoulder. "I need to talk to you about something."

"Now?"

"Yeah."

"Okay." Dread churns in my stomach.

"Follow me when we get out of here, okay?" He slips around me, and I nod, my mind going to a hundred places I don't want to think about.

Students hurry to their first lessons of the morning as Elliot cuts a path through them and down the hall. I say goodbye to Tally and take off after him, keeping a safe distance between us.

He seems agitated, and I can't help but wonder if he's going to cancel our date tomorrow.

I follow him all the way to the end of the hall and out of the back door leading to the gym. Elliot waits under one of the few shelters dotted around the campus.

"What's wrong?" I ask.

"I want to be honest with you, okay?"

"Okay." My brows furrow.

"I need to go out tonight… with Lauren."

"What?" My heart tumbles, the ground going from under me. "But I thought…"

I stop myself because I don't know what I thought.

All I know is, I didn't expect this.

I stare at my feet, trying to get my emotions under control.

"Abi, look at me." Elliot reaches for me, fisting my blazer and pulling me into his chest. "She means nothing to me. Nothing. But until I figure some things out, I need to play the game."

"I… I don't know what you want me to say."

"I need you to say you're okay with this," he pleads.

"If it was the other way around, would you be okay with me pretending to be with another boy?" A stone mask falls over his expression, and I let out a bitter laugh. "Then it isn't fair of you to expect me to be okay with it."

"I know. Fuck, I know. But she's on our side."

"You've talked to her about me?"

I don't know how to feel about that.

"Not in so many words," he replies. "But she doesn't exactly like our arrangement either. If I don't show, it will raise suspicions and I can't give Scott any more reasons to go after you, I won't."

"I'm not scared of your brother, Elliot."

"You should be." He drops his head to mine, inhaling a shaky breath. "I won't kiss her. I won't even touch her, I swear. But I have to go."

Anguish lines his face, and I can see how difficult this is for him. But it's not exactly easy for me.

"I saw you with her, Elliot. She's beautiful," I admit, shrinking into myself. "You looked good together."

"But she's not you," he says. "She doesn't know me, Abi. Not like you do."

"Fine. Go. Do what you need to do. But if you cross that line with her—"

"I won't, I swear. I'm yours and only yours."

"Elliot, I—"

"Don't say anything." His thumb drifts across my bottom lip. "Just let me have this."

Elliot seals his mouth over mine, sealing his promise with a kiss.

17

ELLIOT

Nerves assault me as I move closer to Abigail's dorm room to pick her up for our date.

Tonight is a big deal, and I want it to be perfect.

I want to prove to her that what I feel for her is real, that despite the obstacles surrounding us, I want her. That she is the single most important person in my life.

That I want her to be mine.

Voices from the other end of the corridor float through the air, but I ignore them. I don't give a shit if they see me picking my girl up for a date. If I had my way, I'd be screaming it from the rooftops.

Abigail Bancroft belongs to me, and any motherfucker stupid enough to go anywhere near her will feel every ounce of my wrath.

Shaking those thoughts from my head, I lift my hand to knock.

I told her to meet me at my car so that we could slip away unnoticed. But sitting down there behind the wheel felt wrong.

She shouldn't have to walk to me alone, I should pick her up like a real gentleman. Like a man she can be proud to call hers.

Knock. Knock. Knock.

There is nothing but silence that follows, but I can't say I'm surprised. She might have agreed to come out with me tonight, and things between us might have been incredible this week, but that doesn't mean she's ready to open up to the rest of the world just yet.

Our friends know that we're busy tonight, so she knows it won't be them knocking, and she's not expecting me.

She's hiding.

Pulling the key from my pocket, I unlock the door, hopefully clueing her in to who's here.

I push the door open and I'm immediately hit with the sweet scent of her perfume. My body reacts instantly, my cock hardening and my mouth watering.

Later, I promise myself. *You can have everything you want later.*

My heart sinks when I discover that her room is empty, but then the bathroom door opens, and *holy shit...*

"Red," I breathe, totally lost for fucking words at the vision before me.

Abigail stands before me in an emerald green cocktail dress. Her hair has been braided and rests over one shoulder and her make-up is light but flawless.

She'd told me that the girls were coming to help her get ready, but wow...

"Do... Do I look okay?"

"Are you kidding," I ask, moving closer to her. "You look fucking incredible."

She lifts her hand, smoothing down the hair that covers the scarred side of her face. No sooner do I come to a stop in front of her, do I wrap my fingers around her wrist and pull her hand away. Instead of using it to hide, I tuck the lock of hair behind her ear, showing off her beautiful face.

"Elliot," she whispers, her eyes glistening with emotion as I lean closer and press my lips to the centre of her scar.

"Never hide your beauty, Red. You're perfect just the way you are," I say, my lips brushing against the soft skin of her cheek. "Are you ready for our date?"

"I thought I was meeting you at the car."

"I couldn't wait any longer, and I'm so glad I didn't."

"But the others," she says in a panic.

"Fuck the others. Tonight, you're mine. All mine."

She's smiling when I pull back.

Holding my hand out, I make a show of letting my eyes drop down the length of her. "Are you ready for the best night of your life?"

Her brows lift. "Very sure of yourself, Mr Eaton."

"Girls like a guy with confidence, don't they?"

"I guess you might find out tonight."

Her eyes search mine. I know what she's hunting for, but I told her everything about my date with Lauren last night.

There is nothing between me and Lauren Winrow. Not one single ounce of chemistry or interest.

Abigail doesn't want to believe me. She's struggling to accept that she's the one I want, that she's everything to me that Lauren isn't. Sure, Lauren is beautiful, I'm not blind. But she isn't Abi. Not by a long shot.

"Come on," I say, tugging her towards the door.

I can tell her over and over again about last night, about how I feel but something tells me that actions will speak louder.

"This your bag?" I ask as we pass the holdall sitting on her bed.

"Yep," she agrees, sounding nervous about the night to come.

Picking it up, I throw it over my shoulder. "You trust me, right?" I ask before opening her door and stepping into the outside world.

"Yes, Elliot. I do."

With those words ringing in my ear, I pull the door open and tug her out.

Hand in hand, we make our way down to the car. It's a risk, but there is no way I'm hiding her tonight. She looks way too good to be banished to shadows.

"Where are we going?" she asks when we've been driving for a little over thirty minutes.

"You're not very good with surprises, are you?" I muse.

"Can't say that I've had a lot of good ones," she confesses sadly.

Reaching over, I squeeze her thigh. "From here on out, that's going to change," I promise her.

It's another forty-five minutes before we pull off the main road. There is only one place on the map, so it's no longer much of a surprise as to where we're going.

"Oh wow," Abi breathes as we pull into the luxury country club.

The sun has set leaving the sky a beautiful pink hue and the lights that are strung up around the old farmhouse and surrounding cabins are twinkling in the dimming light.

It's really quite something.

"You approve?" I ask.

"I do. It's incredible," she says with a wide smile playing on her lips.

"I've managed to snag us the best suite in the place," I announce as I kill the engine, ready to get out and get our night started.

"How have you done that at such late notice?"

I wink. "It's always good to have friends in high places."

The excitement on her face vanishes in a flash, replaced by fear. "Someone here knows us?" she whispers, nervously looking out the window.

"You said you trusted me, remember? I promise nothing bad is going to happen here. Someone owed me a favour."

She sucks in a deep breath before looking me in the eyes. "Okay."

Pushing the driver's door open, I climb out before racing around to open hers. I want to make all of her sweet daydreams and dirty fantasies come true tonight, starting with helping her from the car and carrying her bag.

With her hand in mine, I lead her away from the main building and towards one of the smaller cabins looking out over the lake.

"Shouldn't we be going over there?" she asks, looking at the lavish entrance.

"Nope. We don't need to check-in like normal guests. Tonight we're VIPs."

She doesn't say another word as I lead her towards our cabin, but she does slow down the second a figure comes into view.

"Elliot," she whispers.

"Trust me, remember," I remind her as we move closer to the woman waiting for us.

"Abigail," I say as we come to a stop. "This is Lauren."

Abi gasps, her grip on my hand tightening.

"It's so lovely to meet you. I've heard so much about you," Lauren says softly.

Abi looks between the two of us with her brows pinched together.

"You talk about me?" she asks quietly as if she's hoping Lauren won't hear her.

"Are you kidding?" Lauren laughs, making me instantly regret allowing her to do this for us. "Last night, you were all he talked about."

Abigail's cheeks redden.

"He's smitten, girl. You don't need to look so worried."

"B-but... I don't understand."

"Trust me, I'm not going to be stealing your man, Abigail. I mean, he's pretty and all, but not quite..." She thinks for a moment before gesturing to my body. "Hot enough for me."

"Not hot enough. Are you blind?" Abigail blurts, making me smile like a lunatic.

Lauren chuckles before spinning around and opening the double doors to our cabin. "Come on, love birds," she shoots over her shoulder.

"Oh my God," Abi gasps as she steps inside ahead of me.

The cabin Lauren secured for us is self-contained. It has a small kitchen, a large living area that leads out to a deck that overlooks the lake. Then there is a massive master bedroom at the rear, again with a deck that showcases the lake. Huge beams run through the ceilings and there is exposed brickwork everywhere with heavy oak furniture and soft cream accents. It's stunning and homely. The perfect place for us to take our relationship to the next level.

"Beautiful, isn't it," Lauren says. "Let me show you the bedroom, you're going to love it."

Her eyes lock on mine, silently demanding that I stay put and give her a minute with my girl.

I told her that she didn't need to be here tonight, but

she insisted that talking to Abi would help reassure her about our relationship.

All I can do now is hope that she's right.

I watch them both disappear before spinning around and walking out to the deck. The heaters are already on and the small table has been set up for a romantic meal.

Making my way over to the railing, I rest my forearms on the chunky wood and look out over the glistening lake before us.

The moon and stars are reflected in the vast blackness making the place even more serene.

We're totally secluded from the rest of the club and accommodation. We could hide out here for the longest time without anyone knowing about it. It's exactly what we both need tonight.

We need to be just us, forgetting that the rest of the world exists.

My watch vibrates and I pull my sleeve up. I find a message in our guy's group chat staring back at me.

> Reese: Enjoy your night fucker. Please, try not to break Abs, my girl quite likes her.

It buzzes again.

> Theo: We know it's been a while, maybe go rub one out in the bathroom so you don't embarrass yourself.

I smirk. My friends are fucking idiots.

> Oak: If she can walk tomorrow, you haven't done your job properly.

Shaking my head, I pull my phone from my pocket and open up our chat.

> Elliot: Thanks for the invaluable advice. I'll make sure to ignore all of it.
>
> Elliot: See you on the other side.

Nervous energy courses through me as I power off my phone and slide it back into my pocket as footsteps move closer.

Spinning around, I find my girl walking towards me with a smile on her face.

"Where's Lauren?" I ask, watching her approach.

"Gone. She said to let you know that dinner will arrive in thirty minutes and that there is champagne in the fridge."

She doesn't stop until she's right in front of me. But it's not close enough. Sliding hands over her waist, I grab her ass and tug her body up against mine.

"Hi," she breathes, staring up into my eyes.

"Hey. Everything okay?"

Her smile grows and it totally settles me. "This is incredible, Elliot."

I shake my head, ducking my head, my lips meet hers in a sweet yet all-consuming kiss.

"The only incredible thing here," I breathe onto her lips, "is you."

18

ABIGAIL

This place is like something out of a fairy tale.

I know Elliot and the Heirs are filthy rich. I know they'll never have to want for anything in life. And I guess I can include myself in that, but this... This is more than I could ever dream of.

"Is everything okay?" he asks, watching me from across the table.

Dinner arrived forty minutes ago. A mouth-watering three course meal of fillet mignon steak, crushed potatoes, and garlic broccoli. The server wanted to stay and wait on us, but Elliot was quick to usher him away, insisting that he could do it.

"It's amazing, thank you," I reply. "But I don't think I can eat another thing."

"There's still dessert." Hunger simmers in his eyes, sending a violent shiver through me.

Part of me still can't believe we're here, at Lauren's family's country club.

When I first saw her here, my heart sank.

For a second, I wondered if this was all another

elaborate plan to humiliate me. But after our brief conversation, I realise now that I was wrong.

It seems I've been wrong about a lot of things.

As if he can hear my thoughts, Elliot says, "What did you and Lauren talk about?"

"She wanted to reassure me that she has no intentions of stealing you away from me," I reply honestly despite the blush staining my cheeks.

"You know that would never happen, right? She's not the girl I want, Abi. She never will be."

"I'm beginning to get that."

"Maybe I should show you." His eyes darken, making my tummy clench.

"Maybe you should."

The air crackles around us, charged with anticipation.

"Later," he says, and a pang of disappointment goes through me.

Everything has been so romantic but I'm restless. My skin feels too tight and the butterflies in my stomach haven't stopped fluttering.

The truth is, I want... more.

But aside from the toe-curling kiss when Lauren left us, he's barely touched me.

I guess part of me thought—*hoped*—Elliot would get me alone and be unable to keep his hands off me.

Maybe I should have worn something sexier. Something a little more risqué.

Maybe I should have tried harder to be like Lauren.

Old insecurities rise inside me, and I shrink into my chair, suddenly finding the last few florets of broccoli on my plate far more interesting than they are.

"Abi, what's wrong?" Elliot's commanding voice coaxes me to lift my eyes and I give him a small listless smile.

"Nothing."

"Don't do that," he says. "Don't lie to me."

"I'm not."

"You think I don't know when you're freaking out about something." His eyes turn stormy, their intensity sucking the air right out of my lungs.

"Fine." I let out a small, resigned sigh and place down my cutlery. "I was disappointed just now."

"Disappointed, what are you— Oh." Something flickers in his hard gaze, but he doesn't acknowledge it.

"See, now I've made it awkward."

"I want you to be honest with me, Abi," he says. "If this is going to work, we have to trust each other. If something isn't working for you, you need to tell me."

I tilt my head slightly. "And you'll do the same?"

Elliot gives me an imperceptible nod. "But I should warn you, I'm not used to this," he admits.

Before I can ask what he means, he adds, "I don't want to fuck things up again and I don't want to rush you into something you're not ready for."

"You won't." The words spill out before I can stop them.

He gives me a self-deprecating smile. "We both know it's not that simple. Part of me still wants to tell you to run and never look back."

"And the other part?" My breath catches.

The way he looks at me does things to me.

Dark depraved things that I still don't quite understand.

But I'm way past thinking rationally when it comes to this boy.

Still, his silence does little to ease the knot in my stomach.

"You don't have to treat me like some shy, innocent girl, you know," I hedge.

"That's not what I'm doing." He scrubs his jaw and I see a flicker of exasperation in his eyes. "I'm trying to be a gentleman."

"And if I don't want Elliot the gentleman? What then?"

"Abi..." he groans.

"Sorry." I drop my gaze. "This is all new to me."

The awkward silence returns and I wish I never brought it up. But now the words are out, lingering between us.

Haunting us.

"Excuse me," I murmur, standing abruptly. "I'm going to the bathroom."

"Abi..." He calls after me, but I hurry through the cabin and down the hall, locking myself in the small luxurious bathroom.

I don't want to be like this.

Always second-guessing myself.

Always doubting Elliot and his intentions.

But years of being the odd girl out has left scars so deep that sometimes I can't help it.

"Abigail, open the door." Elliot knocks softly.

"I'm fine. Just give me a minute."

"I'm not leaving until you open the door."

Damn him.

I just need a second.

But then my reflection catches in the mirror, and I freeze. The girl staring back at me doesn't look like me.

She looks beautiful.

Poised and perfect.

I guess that's what enough make-up and styling will do.

My heart sinks.

"Abi, open the—"

"Just a minute," I rush out, my heart in my throat. "I'll be out in a minute."

The lock jangles and then the door swings open.

"Elliot, what are you doing?"

He pins me with a dark look, his eyes searching my body for—

"Oh. You thought…" I trail off.

"No," he says but I see the guilt in his expression. "You ran off and I thought… Fuck."

"I just needed a second."

I glance away from him, giving myself a moment to catch my breath.

But Elliot doesn't wait.

He stalks towards me, his stormy gaze holding mine in the mirror. His big strong hands find their way to my waist as he steps up behind me. "Tell me what really happened just now."

I stare at him in the immaculately polished glass, forcing myself to take a deep breath. "I guess I'm finding it hard to understand why you want me when you know girls like… like Lauren."

There, I said it.

I watch him in the mirror, gauging his expression.

But Elliot's face remains an impenetrable mask as he brushes the hair off my shoulder and strokes the skin there.

"How many times do I have to say it? It's you, Abi. You."

He drops his head to my neck, pressing a soft kiss there. My breath catches again, my stomach swimming with nervous anticipation as I tilt to the side a little to give him better access and he begins a slow, torturous path with his tongue. Dragging it over my pulse point.

"Elliot," I whimper, clutching onto his arm. The one moving south, towards the hem of my dress.

He shoves his hand underneath, his fingers dancing over my thighs. I tremble, his touch like wildfire across my skin.

"Relax," he breathes as I tense against him. "Let me show you just how beautiful you are when you come for me."

My head drops back against his shoulder as his fingers find the waistband of my underwear and slip inside.

The first pass of his fingers makes me shiver. The second glide makes me cry out. And the moment he presses two inside me makes me melt.

"Elliot," I cry softly.

"Shh, I got you, Red." His eyes lock on mine in the mirror.

It's so obscene, so dirty, I want to look away. But I'm a prisoner to his hungry gaze. Slave to the intense feelings he evokes in me.

He presses another kiss to the side of my throat, keeping his eyes right on me.

My eyelids flutter as his thumb circles my clit and desire and lust and red-hot pleasure pool low in my stomach.

"God, it's... Oh God,"

"Do you believe me yet?" he whispers, pressing in closer behind me so that I feel the hard bulge in his jeans. "It's you, Abigail. Only you."

"I..." I inhale a shuddering breath as my control slips.

"The things I want to do to you... with you," he murmurs the words onto my skin, chasing them with his tongue, his lips. "You're all I see, all I think about. The only girl I want to bury myself deep inside. The only girl I want to bare myself to.

"You, Abigail. Only ever you."

Oh God.

I can't handle it.

His honest words, his searing touch.

I'm burning from the inside out and I'm terrified I might not survive the fire.

"Elliot..." I pant, arching into his touch.

"Tell me what you want, Red?"

"I... I..." My legs tremble, my heart pounding in my chest as the wave builds inside me.

"Words, Abigail. Use your words." His free hand coasts up my chest and settles around my throat.

Another shudder goes through me.

"You like this, don't you? Submitting to me? Handing me control?"

I nod, barely able to focus as his fingers curl deep, rubbing that magical spot inside me.

"I will always give you what you need, Red. You just have to ask."

My heart stutters.

Is it really that simple?

"I... I want—" The words die on my lips and Elliot rubs his nose along my cheek, his eyes still on the mirror.

"Words..." he demands. "Use. Your. Words."

"You." It lands like a bombshell between us, but I feel a new sense of confidence sweeping through me.

Elliot isn't here with Lauren or an Heir chaser or any of the girls who stare at him around school.

He's here with me.

He wants me.

He cares about... *me*.

I bring my hand up and lay my palm on his cheek, revelling in the stark portrait we paint in the mirror. Small and big. Soft and hard. Light and dark.

But we're more alike than I ever realised. And he knows it.

Elliot knows.

"I want you, Elliot Eaton. All of you."

The words shatter something and the wave crests, pleasure crashing over me as I cry out his name.

"Fuck," he hisses, his fingers flexing around my throat as he twists my head to the side and crashes his mouth down on mine.

Elliot doesn't kiss me, he devours me. His tongue strokes mine as he lays waste to every doubt, every insecurity and worry I have.

His kiss isn't just a kiss, it's a claiming.

I'm his and he's mine.

The revelation—the truth—slams into me, settling deep in my soul.

Elliot wants me.

Me.

And I'm done waiting for him to show me who he really is.

19

ELLIOT

Needing more, I spin her in my arms and press the front of her body against mine. Her soft curves line up perfectly with the hard planes of my body.

Our kiss goes on and on. It's everything I need yet nowhere near enough all at the same time.

With my hands on her arse, I take a step back towards the door without severing our connection.

After untucking my shirt, her hands slide up my back, the heat of her palms searing through my skin, the sparks from her innocent touch shooting straight to my already painfully hard dick.

She quietly whimpers with need, and it does things to me.

"Fuck, Red. Do you know how many times I've imagined having you to myself like this," I confess against her lips.

Her eyes flicker open and the dark green stares up at me with so much desire, so much emotion it makes a lump crawl up my throat.

I've never felt this before.

Sure, I've been with countless girls. But they never meant anything.

They were nameless, faceless bodies that I used as a coping mechanism in the hope of forgetting my pain, of banishing my ghosts.

It worked momentarily, but everything came rushing back all too quickly once we were done.

None of them offered me the relief that Abi does.

Just being with her brings a light to my life I used to crave. But doing more, getting close to her, being intimate, it's like nothing I've ever experienced before.

With my eyes locked on hers and my heart trying to beat out of my chest, I walk backward, blindly navigating our way towards the bedroom.

I want this to be everything she's ever dreamed of, but while I've tried my best to make it romantic and memorable, I know my efforts will never be worthy of a girl like Abigail Bancroft.

She's an angel and deserves the world.

And I'm...

I lock that thought down as I reach out and shove the door closed, locking us inside the bedroom and shutting the rest of the world out.

My insecurities and fears don't belong here.

It's us.

Only us.

Just the way it should be.

There's soft romantic music playing through the hidden speakers, and the air glows with the flickering of all the candles I placed around the room.

But despite how pretty I think it all is, she doesn't once look at anything but me.

"Is it okay?" I ask, unable to keep my mouth shut.

"Elliot," she whispers, sliding her palms up my chest before cupping my jaw.

"It's perfect. You are perfect."

My breath catches at the sincerity in my voice. No one has ever told me that before.

"You didn't need to do all this. Just being with you is enough. We could be in a tent for all I care."

I baulk. "I'm not going camping, Red."

She smirks. "Bet you would if I asked."

My lips twitch up into a smile as I press my forehead against hers. "I'm pretty sure there isn't anything I wouldn't do if you asked it of me," I confess.

Her smile grows. "That's good to know. But right now, all I want is you."

"Are you sure?"

She stares up at me with wide eyes full of innocence and hope. "Yeah, Elliot. I want this. I want you." Stretching on her toes, her lips brush against the shell of my ear. "I want you to be my first."

"Fuck," I breathe, suddenly feeling the pressure like never before.

"Just remember," she whispers. "I've no idea what I'm doing."

With each word she speaks, she undoes a button of my shirt before pushing the fabric from my shoulders and letting it fall to the floor at my feet.

I swallow thickly, my dick pressing painfully against the fabric of my trousers, desperate to be unleashed.

Fuck. I'm going to blow the second I'm inside her, I know I am.

"Are you—" She cuts herself off in favour of leaning forward and pressing a kiss to the side of my throat. There's no way she doesn't feel just how fast my pulse is racing.

She presses one kiss there before moving lower to my

collarbone. "You're nervous," she finally says, deciding against forming it as a question now she's felt the answer.

"Of course I am. It's you, Red."

She sucks in a sharp breath before releasing a giggle. "How do you think I feel? I'm with *the* Elliot Eaton."

"No," I say a little more harshly than I intended. She startles and I mentally kick myself for not being what she needs right now. "Red," I say, cupping her jaw with my hand and grazing her scar with my thumb. "You're not with the Elliot Eaton. He's a wanker. You're with me. Your Elliot."

Her throat ripples against my palm before she leans into my touch.

"You're right." I freeze, unsure of what she's about to say. "That Elliot can be a wanker."

Amusement bubbles up inside me until it spills from my lips. Her laugh follows.

"Fuck, Red. I love you."

I swear to God, the second those words fall from my lips, all the air is sucked from the room.

"Elliot," she whispers, her eyes filling with tears.

"Shit, no. Don't cry. Please. Fuck… I'm trying really hard not to fuck this up, Red. You're gonna have to help me out he—"

Her hands find my face again and she crashes her lips against mine, effectively shutting me up.

Without second-guessing what I just confessed, I lose myself in her kiss. My fingers sink into the soft hair at the nape of her neck and I position her exactly as I want her.

Feeling impatient, her hands slide down my stomach, making my muscles jump before she begins tugging at my belt and then the button of my trousers.

The second she's released it, she tucks her hands under

the fabric and pushes them down my legs. Her trembling hands give away how she's really feeling, but fuck if I don't love this side of her. The confidence to take what she really wants.

She reaches for me and I'm powerless but to break our kiss. Even through the fabric of my boxers, it's almost too much. The anticipation is fucking killing me.

"I'm not going to last," I confess like a pussy.

She smiles at me before pressing a kiss to the centre of my chest and then working her way down my stomach. When she gets to my navel, she drops to her knees before me.

"Abi," I whisper. "Fuck."

Tucking her fingers under the waistband, she drags my boxers down my legs, letting my cock spring free.

"Jesus," I mutter as she licks her lips in preparation for what I hope is coming. "This is meant to be about you."

"It's about us," she says, gazing up at me. "Let me be what you need. We've got plenty of time."

My mouth runs dry the second she leans forward, but she doesn't do what I'm expecting and my dick jerks in protest, but then her lips press against my thigh, only an inch away from my hidden scarred skin.

"Red," I whisper.

With our eyes locked, her tongue sneaks out and drags up my inner thighs.

It's intimate, even more so than the blow job I'm still hopeful of, and it makes my chest ache in the most incredible way.

I've shown her my darkness, the worst parts of me and she's embracing them.

It's more than I ever expected to experience.

Those three little words that I said before dance on the

tip of my tongue again, but they don't get a chance to fall free because she pulls back and wraps her lips around me.

"Holy fuck, Red," I bellow as my hips involuntarily punch forward.

But she's ready for it and she relaxes her throat, taking as much of me as she can.

Wrapping one hand around the base of my shaft, the other locks on my hip for leverage, she begins bobbing up and down on me like she's been doing it all her life.

Fuck. I really hope she continues doing it for the rest of her life.

Proving my previous words right, it only takes an embarrassing few minutes before my balls are drawing up and I'm riding the fine edge of release.

She groans, the hand on my hips shifting to cup my balls and I fall, my cock jerking violently as I fill her mouth.

She takes it all, swallowing down my seed before cleaning me up and sitting back.

"You're perfect, Red. So fucking perfect."

I have her on her feet in a heartbeat and spin her around so that I can pull the zip of her dress down. The second it's undone, I push the fabric from her shoulders, revealing the sexy lingerie set she's wearing beneath.

It's like nothing I've seen her wear before and I immediately know that she bought it, especially for me.

It's black, lacy, and so fucking sexy I would have probably come on the spot if she hadn't already sucked me dry.

"You look..." I start, spinning her around before me. "Fuck." The lace is so sheer, I can see her rosy pink nipples and just a hint of what's hiding between her thighs.

She twists her fingers in front of her nervously. It's a

million miles from the confident woman who just ripped my boxers from my body to get to my dick.

"You're beautiful, Abigail. Every inch of your body is perfect," I say, reaching out and tracing one of the scars across her stomach. "I'm obsessed with you."

Her eyes lift to find me, and the second we connect, all bets are off.

Reaching forward, I grab the back of her thighs and throw her back on the bed. She's still bouncing when I crawl onto the end, spread her thighs and fall on top of her, catching myself on my palms planted on either side of her head.

"Elliot," she gasps before I claim her lips.

I kiss her until she's breathless and writhing against me.

Resting on one elbow, my other hand roams over her curves. Gently squeezing her breasts and pinching her nipples through the lace before grazing over her stomach and then over her pussy.

"So wet for me," I mumble into our kiss when I find the lace soaked with her arousal.

"Please," she whimpers, lifting her hips from the bed in invitation.

"I guess I do have a favour to return."

Pushing up, I slide one hand behind her back and almost effortlessly undo her bra before tugging it free from her body, exposing her incredible tits for me.

Leaning forward, I suck one into my mouth and then the other before kissing a trail down her stomach, tracing the lines of her scars with my tongue, worshipping them and the strength they show before curling my fingers around her knickers and dragging them down her thighs.

"Mine," I muse, reaching out and trailing a single finger through her folds. "All fucking mine."

Then I drop to my front and suck her clit into my mouth, eliciting a scream from my girl before I soothe at the sting with my tongue.

I work her hard and fast, building her higher and higher, but before she falls, I pull away and sit up.

She writhes on the bed, her eyes closed, her lips parted and her skin flushed with desire.

It's so fucking hot I can barely stand it.

Sliding my hand beneath the pillow, I find the stash of condoms I hide under here earlier and pull one free.

When I sit back, I find that she's watching me with wide, terrified eyes.

"Trust me, Red. I won't hurt you, I fucking promise."

She smirks, silently letting me know that she'd probably be okay with it if I did.

My girl gets off on a little pain just as much as I do, after all.

20

ABIGAIL

My entire body trembles as Elliot lowers himself over me, sinking between my thighs like it's the most natural thing in the world.

I'm nervous but I'm not scared.

Tonight has been perfect—so perfect, it's hard to believe it's real.

But his words are branded on my mind, his possessive touch branded on my skin.

I'm powerless to stop this.

I don't want to.

Not even a little bit.

Even though I know that things are complicated, even though I know Johnathon and Scott Eaton will never accept me, I can't walk away.

I love Elliot.

I am desperately, hopelessly in love with him.

I have been for a while.

"You're so fucking perfect," he rasps as he notches himself against my entrance. My breath catches as he pushes inside. Slowly. Torturously.

"Elliot," I breathe, staring up at him with sheer emotion.

"I love you, Abigail." His voice cracks. His strong, powerful body trembling above me.

He leans down, touching his head to mine as he thrusts into me, breaking through the final barrier of my innocence. "Mine."

The word ghosts my lips and then he kisses me; deep, drugging kisses that blur the edges of pain into something more.

Something addictive and all-consuming.

Something I never want to end.

"I'll never hurt you again," he whispers between kisses. "You're mine now, Red. Mine."

Elliot starts moving, rolling his hips with impressive restraint. It feels amazing. But I need more. I need—

"More." The word falls off my lips in a breathy plea.

"I don't want to hurt you." He gazes down at me with icy reverence.

"You won't. Don't hold back." I frame his face with my hands, brushing my lips over his.

"I'm not made of glass, Elliot. I won't shatter. I don't want you to hold back with me."

I want him.

All of him.

Every savage, vicious part.

"Fuck... Okay." One of his hands slides down my body to grab my leg and hitch it around his waist. He pulls out slowly and rocks forward without warning, stretching me.

The new fit is deeper. Closer... More.

"Okay?" he asks, and I nod, pressing my lips together, trying to focus on every sensation rushing through me.

"You... You feel perfect."

Something flashes in his expression. A rare glimpse of emotion that tightens the invisible thread between us.

Connecting us.

He grabs my hand, threading our fingers together and pressing them into the pillow beside my head as he ups the pace. Making everything inside me go tight and loose all at the same time.

It's too much and still not nearly enough.

"Elliot," I cry, lifting my hips, chasing the end of the coil deep inside of me.

Waiting for it to snap.

"I could stay buried inside you for days," he traces his lips over my jaw and down the column of my throat, licking and nipping the skin there.

I clutch the back of his head, demanding more.

Needing more.

His throaty chuckle vibrates against my pulse point, sending shivers through me.

But it's when he grazes his teeth at the juncture of my throat and bites down, hard, that I shatter, the final restraints on that coil snapping.

"Oh God... God, God," I whimper, a wave of intense pleasure crashing over me.

"My girl likes a little pain, doesn't she?" He licks at the bite mark, lifting his head enough that I catch the slight tinge of blood on his lips.

"You marked me."

"You loved it." He smirks.

"I…"

I don't deny it.

"I'm going to fuck you now."

"N-now?"

His smirks turns wicked. "I'm not nearly done with you."

Oh God.

How is it possible I already want him again?

And again.

And again.

Going back to All Hallows' and keeping this a secret is going to be impossible now I know how he feels above me.

Inside me.

"Get out of your head, Abigail." He smothers me in kisses while moving above me with slow, shallow strokes that stir something deep in my stomach again.

"It feels…"

"Good?" He chuckles and I blush.

"So good."

"Fuck. The things I want to show you. Do to you."

"Do them," I pant, barely able to catch my breath, it's too good.

He's too good.

"All of them."

"Soon, baby. We have time." He stills and something crackles between us.

A silent warning neither of us acknowledge.

Because we don't have time.

Not really.

"Hey, hey." Elliot gently collars my throat refusing to let me look away.

Because part of me wants—wants to recoil and hide.

To run.

"This means something to me, Abigail," he says with utter conviction. "You mean something. The rest, we'll figure out, okay?"

I nod.

What else can I do?

I have to trust that Elliot will protect my heart this

time. That he'll prove me wrong where his reputation is concerned.

Savage, vicious Elliot Eaton.

With everyone except those closest to him.

His best friends, their girlfriends... and now, me.

"I love you," I blurt, feeling vulnerable and overwhelmed.

"In case you had any doubts about my feelings for you." He rolls his hips, slow and deep. "Let me show you."

And he does.

More than once.

"You don't have to do that, you know," I say some time later.

It's late. Some ungodly hour. But we refuse to give into sleep. I think we're both scared to ever let tonight end.

We've talked and kissed and talked some more. Elliot has made me cry and scream his name, he's made me quiver and shake.

He's learned far too many ways to make me come undone.

And I've loved every second of it.

It's more than that though. Deeper than sex and pleasure. He gets me and I get him. And there's something so terrifyingly amazing about that.

With Elliot, I feel seen.

For the first time in my life, I feel understood.

"Hush, woman," he scoffs, tracing his fingers over the scars marring my soft pale skin. "I love every inch of you."

"Keep that up and I'll start to think your reputation as the cold, cruel Heir will be forever ruined."

He lifts his head to mine and smirks again. "If you need

a reminder of exactly how cruel I can be…" His fingers dip lower and lower, gliding over my clit.

A hiss leaves my lips as I swat his arm away. "I can't… Not again. I think you broke me."

"I could kiss it better?" Amusement twinkles in his icy gaze.

"It's late. We should probably get some sleep."

Elliot crawls up the bed and looms over me. "We can sleep… if that's what you want?"

Heat flares inside me but I'm too sore to act on it.

"What's wrong?" he asks and I realise I've failed at hiding the truth from him.

Dammit.

"Nothing." I palm his cheek, stealing a kiss.

"You're really sore?" His eyes harden.

"I… Yes. But it's fine. I'm fine."

"I hurt you." Worry casts a shadow over his expression as he tries to pull away from me.

"Elliot, I'm fine." I anchor my arms around his neck, pulling him towards me. "But it was my first time, you know that."

"And I fucked it up."

"Stop, you didn't. It was perfect. You were perfect. But this is all new to me. To my body. It's going to take a little bit of getting used to." My cheeks burn as I gaze up at him, so utterly infatuated with this complicated boy.

"Wait here." He drops a kiss on my forehead and clambers off the bed.

"Elliot, what are—"

"Stay right there."

With a small sigh, I flop back down against the soft pillows and pull the sheet up over my body.

I can hear him in the adjoining bathroom, thumping

around. Then the sound of running water fills the cabin and Elliot reappears.

"Let's go." He stalks towards me like a man on a mission.

"Go? Go where? It's almost three in the morning."

Before I can untangle myself out of the sheets, he scoops me up and carries me across the room into the bathroom. Steam billows from the claw foot tub.

"You want to take a bath, now?" I stare up at him incredulously.

"I want to take care of you. I should have done it earlier."

"Elliot." A ball of emotion lodges in my throat. "You don't need to—"

He lowers me into the water, and I let out a contented moan. Damn him, it feels good.

Really good.

And the smell from whatever he added is divine.

"Feel good?" he asks, dropping to his knees at the side of the tub.

"Very much so." I offer him an appreciative smile.

He leans over and grabs the bottle of expensive looking body wash and pours some into his hands.

"Elli— Oh." I murmur as his hands slide over my collarbone and around my shoulders. The slip and slide of his fingers, the gentle pressure he applies feels amazing and I sink into his touch, my eyelids fluttering closed.

"Just relax, baby. I got you."

He massages my shoulders and neck moving around to my arms and breasts. Heat pools in my stomach but I'm so relaxed, so sleepy and sated that it doesn't kindle an inferno. It simmers under the surface, a pleasant ember.

"You're so fucking perfect." His voice sounds distant, my limbs growing heavy as the water laps around me.

"Come on, out you come," he says and I blink dazedly up at him.

"What happened?"

"You fell asleep."

"I did?" I nuzzle into him as he wraps me into his arms and carries me into the bedroom, setting me on his lap to dry me.

Elliot Eaton is drying me with a big fluffy towel and I'm barely conscious enough to appreciate the gravity of the moment.

"I love you," I murmur, pressing a kiss to his jaw as I fight the thrall of sleep.

He slides me under the sheets and climbs in behind me, pulling me into his chest, sliding his leg between mine and wrapping his arm around my waist.

"I love you too." He presses a lingering kiss to my shoulder as I begin to sink into oblivion.

But not before I hear him whisper, "You're mine now, Red. And I won't let anyone come between us again."

21

ELLIOT

I lie there for the longest time just watching Abi sleep in my arms.

My body is still singing from our first time together, my dick in a constant semi-hard state from both remembering how hot it was and being desperate to have her again.

Being with Abi was unlike everything I'd experienced before.

It was so much more. It was everything.

But at the same time, it was nowhere near enough.

I'm not sure anything will be when it comes to the shy quiet girl who matches my darkness like for like.

She's firmly under my skin. Tattooed on my heart. Buried into my fucking soul.

Her warm breath rushes over my skin, making it erupt in goosebumps as she sleeps soundly, her arm wrapped tightly around my waist and her thigh pinned between mine.

The thought of her holding onto me, the idea of her actually still wanting me to be here in the morning—and not just for bragging rights—makes my heart race in the most terrifying yet incredible way.

Unlike everyone else in my life—my friends aside—she's the only one who truly wants me for me.

I've never felt that from my parents, my brother. Everyone has always wanted more from me.

Expected more.

Demanded more.

Unease ripples through me.

As amazing as this is... It's not real.

It can't be.

Pain lashes at my chest making it harder and harder to breathe.

Now I have her, I can't imagine my life without Abigail in it.

She's the light in all my darkness. The hope I've been living without all my life.

She's...

"Fuck," I breathe, holding her even tighter.

She moans, stirring against me, and guilt instantly poisons my veins.

The last thing I want to do is hurt her. But also... I want to hold her so tight that she can never escape.

I can't help but wonder if I'm going to be battling this war for the next—my stomach bottoms out—however long we have.

I've no idea how long I lay there holding her tight, praying it can last forever, but eventually, my exhaustion drags me under and I drift off into a fitful sleep.

I've got my girl in my arms, everything should be right in my world.

But it's not.

Not even close.

The threat of my father and Scott is always going to be looming over us.

They won't approve of us. They won't accept her.

And until I can figure out a way for that not to matter then what we have is going to have to remain in the shadows.

I hate it.

I want to walk into school with our fingers entwined.

I want to proudly push her up against the wall and kiss her in public so everyone knows that she belongs to me.

I want to shout how I feel about this quiet yet strong incredible woman from the rooftops without fearing repercussions.

I want to be her everything just like she is to me.

The second I open my eyes and confirm what I already know, my stomach bottoms out.

She's gone.

I sit up so fast the room spins around me as my heart races with fear.

"Red?" I call, my panicked voice bouncing off the walls around me.

Silence.

Launching out of bed, I snag a clean pair of boxers from my open bag and pull them up my legs. I pause as my faint silvery scars catch my eye and cringe.

I love that I've been able to share them, my darkness, with her just as much as I hate it.

I want to be the strong and indestructible person everyone believes me to be.

I want her to know that I can protect her. I want her to know that she can rely on me.

But she knows my weakness.

She won't use it against you, she understands, a little voice says.

I shake it away, refusing to sink into those kinds of thoughts as I snap the waistband of my boxers into place and head out.

The rest of the cabin is as silent as the bedroom as I pad through it but it does very little to help relax me. There's no sign of her and I'm on the verge of freaking out completely when the soft curtains that cover the floor-to-ceiling windows billow out.

I all but run towards the open door and I swear my heart stops the second I round the corner and find her sitting on the swing seat, rocking back and forth as she stares out at the lake before us.

She's wearing one of my Saints hoodies and has it pulled over her legs that are hitched up against her chest, her arms wrapped around them.

Her hair is wild, sticking up in all directions and her skin is pale. But her lips... They're still red and swollen and my cock stirs instantly at the sight of them.

Memories from last night stir before exploding in my mind like a movie.

Fuck, it was incredible.

She was incredible.

Despite my heart pounding loud enough for her to hear, she doesn't make a move to look at me. She's too lost in whatever is going on in her head.

"Red?" I whisper, stepping closer.

She startles, her entire body locking up in fear. But the second her eyes land on me, she relaxes. And so do I because there is nothing in her eyes but happiness and contentment.

As I step up to her, her feet hit the deck and she pushes

herself to full height just in time for me to wrap my arms around her waist and pin her against me.

"Hey," she whispers shyly.

"I missed you," I confess. "I thought—" I swallow, cutting myself off.

I don't want to be vulnerable.

But it doesn't matter what I want. It's too late anyway, she can see it.

"I'm not going anywhere, Elliot," she assures me before our lips meet.

Our kiss is soft and sweet, and I cringe knowing that she's probably brushed her teeth already and I haven't.

With anyone else, I wouldn't care. But I don't want her to have me at my worst…

But she doesn't pull away. Instead, she licks along my bottom lip, asking for entry.

Unable to deny her, my hands drop lower, gripping her arse and pulling her even tighter against me, letting her feel exactly what her kiss, her body, her presence do to me. Then my tongue meets hers in an all-consuming, deep, passionate kiss that makes every single one of my nerve endings tingle with need.

Time and the world around us cease to exist as we lose ourselves in each other.

Lifting her from her feet, I spin around and blindly lower us to the swing seat, giving her no choice but to straddle my lap.

"Fuck, Red," I groan into our kiss as she rocks over me.

Who knew shy little Abigail had it in her?

She moans and kisses me harder.

Her passion fuels mine and I slip my hands under my hoodie and find that she's bare beneath.

"Baby," I whimper, my hands roaming higher, exploring every inch of her body that I can reach.

As I cup her breasts in my hands, she moans louder, her movements above me becoming more and more erratic.

I rip my lips away from hers. I hate to do it, but I want to watch her use me. "You want to get off again, Red?" I ask, my voice hoarse with desire.

The second her eyes find mine, my breath catches.

The green flecks in her eyes have almost been entirely swallowed by darkness.

I swallow thickly as I take in the incredible woman who is grinding against my cock right now like it's going to go out of fashion.

I pinch her nipples and she cries out in the serenity that surrounds us, making a bird close by take off in fright.

"You have no idea how hot you look right now," I tell her, my eyes dropping to her body as if she's not covered in fabric.

Fuck, I wish I could see all of her.

"Elliot," she whimpers, sliding her fingers into my hair and gripping hard.

The pain shoots straight to my dick, making me harder than I thought possible with the heat of her pussy burning through my boxers.

"Tell me what you need," I demand.

She hesitates, her cheeks reddening. "Y-you," she stutters, making my heart slam against my ribs.

"Fuck," I groan. "I'll never get tired of hearing that. But I'm going to need more details. What about me exactly do you need?"

Her entire face glows and she considers my question before looking down at my lap.

"You won't get anything unless you can say the words," I tease, torturing both of us by prolonging this.

"I... I want..."

"Yeah," I encourage.

"I want... you inside me."

My head falls back against the swing seat and I stare up at her in awe as my cock tries to rip through my boxers to give her what she needs.

"Aren't you sore?" I ask, remembering the way she winced last night.

I took it as slow as I could knowing that it was her first time, but fuck, it was hard.

Really fucking hard.

By the end of our night, soft and gentle had almost been forgotten.

I was too rough with her.

Shame burns through me.

"Nothing I can't handle," she whispers before dropping her face to my neck and pressing a kiss to my pulse point.

"I don't want to hurt you," I argue, my hands dropping to her hips and holding her still.

Her entire body freezes and she sucks in a sharp breath before pulling back to look at me. "Then don't deny us what we both want. You don't have to try to protect me all of the time, Elliot."

Her eyes bounce between mine, waiting for me to respond while my head and my cock war for supremacy.

But then her teeth sink into her bottom lip and she looks at me with these sultry eyes and I crumble.

"Take my dick out, Red," I demand firmly, giving her little choice but to follow orders.

While she fumbles with my waistband, I begin dragging my hoodie up her body and the second she's finished, I pull it over her head and throw it to the deck.

"Oh God," she whimpers as the cool spring morning air rushes over her beautiful skin.

Her arms wrap around herself in an attempt to hide.

"No," I say, wrapping my fingers around her wrists and

placing them over my shoulders instead. "No one can see you but me. And even if they could, they'd only be jealous that you're about to sit on my dick and not theirs."

Her full lips part and I make the most of the opportunity by crashing mine to them once more in a filthy kiss.

"Lift up," I demand, barely pulling back from her.

When she does as she's told, I line myself up.

We might have used a condom to start with last night. I was trying to do the right thing, but after she convinced me that she was on the pill and it was safe, I abandoned protection in favour of feeling her skin to skin.

"Take it as slow as you need, but I want you to sink down on my dick. I want to feel every— Guck," I bark as she suddenly drops, taking me inside her.

She's like heaven. Hot, warm, smooth, every-fucking-thing.

Her pussy grips my dick in a tight hold and it takes every ounce of self-control I have not to blow right there and then.

"Love you, Red," I muse, sinking my fingers into the hair at the nape of her neck and dragging her closer. "I love you more than I ever thought possible."

I don't give her a chance to respond, instead, I let our bodies do the talking.

We've got a long—or possibly a very short—road ahead of us so we've got to make the most of every moment we have together.

Who knows when it's going to be ripped away again.

22

ABIGAIL

I stare out at the lake, trying to commit every second, every kiss and touch, to memory.

I never want to leave.

But it's already time to go back to All Hallows'.

Our incredible weekend is over and now we have to face reality.

"There you are." Elliot comes up behind me, caging me against the railing with his big, strong body. He nuzzles my shoulder, brushing his nose along the curve of my neck. I let out a contented sigh, soaking up our final moments together.

Trying to ignore the pit gnawing in my stomach.

"It's so peaceful out here," I whisper.

"We can come back. I'm sure Lauren can hook us up."

"I still can't believe she did all this for you."

Elliot gently grabs my chin and twists my face to his. "For us," he corrects. "She did it for us. Now tell me what you're thinking."

"I'm thinking I don't want to leave. I don't want to go

back to school and have to pretend that we're..." I inhale a ragged breath, refusing to say the words.

I heard him whisper the words last night.

You're mine now, Red. And I won't let anyone come between us again.

But I already feel the wall going up between us. I don't even think he realises he's doing it.

I want to ask him about it. To ask how he can do it so easily. Lock his heart away and pretend he doesn't care.

But I don't.

Because I'm not sure I want to hear the answer. Not when I know I won't be able to do it.

Not after this weekend.

Not after hearing him say those three little words that mean so much to me.

As if he senses the directions of my thoughts Elliot lets out a weary sigh and says, "I know it isn't easy." He kisses my forehead. "But I don't want you to worry about anything, okay? I'll handle my father."

"Would it really be so bad if we just tell them?"

The second the words are out of my mouth, I regret them. A quiet rage falls over Elliot, his eyes growing so dark, and a shudder goes through me.

"I don't ever want you near them," he says. "Ever, Abi. Do you understand me?"

Gone is the boy I love. The thoughtful, selfless boy who has worshipped me this weekend and made me feel like the most beautiful girl in the world.

"I... Fine." I concede.

God, I hate this. Hate that Elliot isn't free to make his own choices.

If I was stronger like Tally or Liv or Raine maybe I could stand up to Mr Eaton. Maybe I wouldn't have fled that night at the pub when Scott humiliated me.

But the truth is, no matter how much I try, I'm still the shy, meek girl I've always been.

I guess when you've lived in the shadows for so long, it's hard to walk into the light.

"So that's it then." I give him a weak smile. "Back to pretending we're nothing to each other."

The muscle in his jaw tics as he steps back and puts some distance between us.

My stomach sinks.

"I love you, Abigail. I love you so fucking much. And I know it's unfair to ask you to wait for me while I figure out some things, but I will not let them pull you into my fucked-up life and use you as leverage."

"You really think—"

"I know," he grits out. "You already got hurt at the hands of my brother. I will not take the same risk with my father."

"Okay."

"Okay?" Elliot's brows furrow and I don't know if he's surprised at how easily I'm backing down… or disappointed.

"What else do you want me to say? You said you'll handle it, so I guess I'll just have to trust you."

He gives me a small nod that does little to ease the knot in my stomach. "Thank you."

"I guess we should probably head back." The words are like ash on my tongue.

Beyond missing the girls, there's nothing back at All Hallows' for me.

Nothing but heartache and bad memories.

I move around him, annoyed that our perfect weekend is ending on such a sour note.

But what did I expect?

That Elliot would march me into his family's house and announce our relationship consequences be damned?

"Wait." He grabs me and pulls me flush against him.

"Elliot, what—"

His mouth crashes down on mine. Hard and unrelenting, his tongue plunging deep. My fingers curl around his shoulders as I hold on.

Trying desperately to stay afloat in the storm that is Elliot Eaton.

By the time Elliot drives through the ornate wrought iron gates of All Hallow' campus, the tension in the car is almost suffocating.

"Do you want to come back to the Chapel?" he asks, white-knuckling the steering wheel.

"Is that a good idea?" My eyes flick to his.

"Abi..." he warns.

"Whatever, Elliot. You know best."

He mutters something under his breath, but I roll my head away and press it against the cool glass, closing my eyes.

"You know, being with you this weekend..." He hesitates and my heart flutters wildly in my chest.

"Yes?" I ask, giving into the intense connection between us. That magnetic pull that he's always had over me.

"It was everything, Abigail. Every-fucking-thing."

There's more he wants to say. It's right there in the guilt swarming in his icy gaze.

But all too soon, All Hallows' looms up ahead stealing what little time alone together we have left.

I brace myself for Elliot to drive behind the Bronte Building. But instead, he takes the road that leads to the Chapel.

"What—"

"Not ready to give this up yet," he grumbles, reaching over to grab my hand and pull it into his lap.

A hundred thoughts race through my head, most of them bad.

What if someone sees us arrive back together?

What if word gets back to Scott or Mr Eaton?

What if—

"You're panicking," he says quietly.

"I'm not."

"Don't lie to me. I can feel your pulse racing." He brushes his thumb along my wrist and I swear my heart skips a beat.

"I don't like how we left things back at the cabin," I admit.

"You think I do?"

I give him a small shrug, and his eyes flash with irritation. "No, I don't," I whisper. "But it doesn't change anything, does it? We're going round in circles, Elliot."

"I just need some time—"

"How much time? A week? A month? Longer?"

Because I'm not sure I can do it. I'm not sure I can continue being his dirty little secret. Not when I know how amazing it feels to be his.

"Give me this week."

"One week?" I clarify and he nods.

"I'll talk to them this week. But I need to get my story straight first. Figure out what the hell I'm going to do when he cuts me off."

"You think..." I trap the words because of course that's what will happen.

Mr Eaton has plans for Elliot's future. Plans that don't include me.

All along Elliot has tried to tell me that he'll use me as leverage. Make him choose between the future awaiting him and the broken, scarred girl with no idea what she wants to do with her life.

"Shit, I shouldn't have said that. It's not your problem." Elliot lets out a ragged breath. "Forget I—"

"Of course it's my problem," I quietly seethe. "I'm yours, aren't I?"

"You know you are."

"Then that makes you mine. And I'm not going to just stand by and let your father cut you off all because of me."

Elliot chuckles and I falter.

"You think this is funny?" I ask with disbelief.

"No, but I think you're so fucking cute when you get on your high horse about something."

"Oh." Heat burns my cheeks. "Well, it isn't fair. And I don't want you—"

"Shh, Red." He leans over and cups my cheek, brushing his thumb along my jaw. "Can we shelve this discussion for a bit? I don't want to spend the rest of the day arguing."

"What do you want to do?"

His brow lifts and he smirks in a way that has my stomach twisting and tightening.

"Oh."

"Oh, she says." He chuckles again and some of the tension melts away. Sliding his fingers into my hair, Elliot pulls me closer. Close enough to ghost his lips over mine.

"Mmm," I murmur, heat curling in my stomach.

"Fuck, the things you do to me." He gazes at me with so much intensity I feel like I can't breathe. "I love you."

Three little words that feel like a blessing and a curse.

"I love—"

"Yo, lovebirds." Someone bangs on the rear windscreen, and I almost jump out of my skin.

"Fucking idiot," Elliot groans.

"Better move this show inside," Oakley laughs, pressing his face against the passenger window.

"You don't care if I kill them both, do you?"

"I think Liv and Tally might have something to say about it."

"They'll get over it." Elliot shoulders his door open and climbs out, landing a wicked looking punch to Reese's shoulder.

Oakley opens my door and grins. "Do I even need to ask how your weekend was?" Amusement glints in his eyes, and I blush.

"Fuck off," Elliot growls. "Both of you."

"Oh, come on, we're just—"

A small chuckle bubbles out of me and all three of them stare at me. I wrap my arm around my waist, shrinking under their attention.

Elliot moves first, making his way around the car. He practically shoves Oakley out of the way so that he can trap me between his body and the door.

The air crackles, my heart doing little flips. Something has changed.

I feel it now.

"What do you think they're doing?" one of the boys murmurs but I only have eyes for Elliot.

"Come on, let's give them a minute."

"But—"

"You should listen to him," Elliot growls, never once taking his eyes off me. "Do you trust me?" he asks, and I nod completely under his spell.

Without warning, he scoops me up in his arms and starts off towards the Chapel.

"Elliot, put me down," I shriek.

"I told you, Red." He smirks down at me. "You're mine now."

23

ELLIOT

I say a silent prayer as I take the last turn that will lead me into my parents' driveway.

It's the very last place on Earth that I want to be. But I also don't have any other choice.

There is no longer a choice to make.

It's Abigail.

Every single thing leads me back to her.

She deserves so much more than what I can offer her at the moment.

She should never be anyone's dirty little secret, forced to hide in the shadows. She's done enough of that in her life. She deserves to be in the limelight. She deserves for everyone else to know just how beautiful and incredible she is.

I want the world to see how she shines just like I do when we're together. But until I deal with my father, there's no way for that to happen.

If I'm being honest, there may never be a way for that to happen.

I won't lie, the thought of just packing our bags and

running has crossed my mind more than once. But I know that no matter where we went, he'd find us.

His reach is far and wide and I have no doubt that he'd find me and drag me back kicking and screaming to fulfil my duty and continue his legacy.

It's one of the most depressing facts about all of this. Even if he does agree to my wishes, he'll always be there, breathing over my shoulder.

He's always fucking there. Pointing out my failings, my bad decisions. All the ways I'm not like him and Scott. All the ways I tarnish our family's reputation.

The breath I didn't realise I was holding comes rushing out of me when I find only my mother's car sitting in the driveway. That relief is quickly followed by guilt.

I'm doing this for Abigail and I should be man enough to see it through for the chance of giving us a future, not relieved that I can put it off a little longer.

Maybe he's right. Maybe I'm not man enough...

Shaking my head, I banish my father's voice from my mind and I kill the engine and climb out of my car.

The house is in silence as I make my way down the hall towards the kitchen where someone is usually hanging out. But as I turn the corner, I find that empty as well.

"Mum?" I call as I pad back through the hallway and come to a stop at the foot of the stairs, listening for sounds of life.

A noise comes from down the hall, and I immediately take off in the direction of the snug.

"Mum?" I ask again as I get closer and the sound of what I can only describe as snuffles hit my ear.

The moment I step into the room, I discover I'm right because my mother is frantically wiping tears from her cheeks.

"Mum, what's wrong?" I ask, rushing inside and dropping to my haunches before her.

I watch as her mask falls into place and she straightens her spine.

I can't imagine what her life has been like being married to a man like Johnathon Eaton. They've been together all their adult lives. He is all she's ever known. But she's not stupid. She knows he's not a good man.

Not that she's ever said a bad word about him.

Through everything, she has stood by his side and supported him no matter what. I'm not sure if I'm impressed with her tenacity or horrified by her lack of desire for a better life.

Surely, this isn't what she always imagined for herself.

Yes, she has the money, the house, the luxury holidays, the cars and the designer labels. But all of that is bullshit when it comes in exchange for spending your life with a cold, ruthless cunt like my father.

"What has he done this time?" I ask, trying a different tack.

We've never had an open conversation about him. I've never been brave enough to even attempt it for fear of what she might be hiding.

I know how he treats me, and I can't only imagine how he's treated her behind closed doors over the years. The thought turns my blood to ice.

"Oh, Elliot," she soothes, attempting to brush over the cracks.

I study her, wondering just how many times she's done that over the years.

On the face of it, the Eaton family are everything you'd expect them to be.

United. Happy. The portrait of perfection.

But the truth is very different.

We're so far from perfect it's laughable.

"I'm just being silly."

"No," I snap, a little harsher than intended, making her rear back.

I push to my feet unable to remain still and begin pacing back and forth in front of her. "If you're crying over something then it's not nothing," I spit. "If it upsets you, no matter how little it may seem to someone else, then it is not nothing."

She stares at me with wide, glassy eyes, her mouth opening and closing like a fish as she tries to find a response. "Th-thank you," she finally settles on.

I frown, confused about what she's thanking me for.

She shakes her head, brushing the comment under the carpet. "Come and sit down. You're making me nervous."

I pause, unable to deny her before dropping down in the armchair opposite her. Resting my elbows on my knees, I drop my head into my hands.

"What's wrong, Elliot?" she asks, concern laced through her voice.

Glancing up, I hold her eyes. "Why do you stay?" I ask, making her frown.

"Stay?" she repeats.

"Here. With him?"

Her chin drops but no words spill free.

Eventually, after a second, she says, "He is my husband. This..." she says, lifting her arm from her lap and gesturing to the house. "It's my home. It's where I've built my life. Our lives."

The fact she doesn't even question me tells me a lot.

"Mum, come on," I plead, desperate for the truth. "You deserve more than this."

Sadness washes through her features. "I made my

decision, Elliot. I knew what I was signing up to all those years ago."

"Did you?" I blurt. I find it hard to believe that she could have fully known what kind of man he was back then. Hell, he possibly didn't know either.

They were young. Kids. Not that much older than me.

I squeeze my eyes closed and think of Abigail. I can't imagine there ever being a time when I'll feel differently about her.

Is that why Mum is still here? Does she truly love him?

"Things aren't always as simple as they seem," she confesses cryptically. "No marriage is perfect, sweetheart. But your father has given us so much."

A bitter laugh erupts from my throat.

Ain't that the fucking truth.

"What's on your mind?" she implores, sensing that something is wrong.

I suck in a deep breath, desperate to let the truth flow free but equally as terrified to do so.

"I... I've met someone," I say, holding her eyes. They instantly light up with excitement in the way every parent should when a child says those words.

Warmth spreads through my body at the sight of her being happy for me. But without saying another word, her excitement peters out.

She knows.

She knows that whoever it is isn't who it's meant to be.

"You're not talking about Lauren, are you?"

"No," I confirm.

Her eyes bounce between mine as she patiently waits for me to tell all.

"He's not going to accept her, Mum. He's not going to accept any of it. But I can't walk away from her because of him. I won't."

She sucks in a deep breath, considering her response. "Who is it, Elliot?"

Silence follows her question. Only the loud ticking on the great grandfather clock out in the hallway can be heard as I prepare to confess the truth.

"Abigail Bancroft."

She doesn't react for a few seconds. It makes me wonder if she already suspected. If she's overheard something, maybe from the night at the pub with Scott. Or maybe it's just some freaky kind of mother's intuition.

"Abigail is a sweet girl," she finally says. "But I must admit, she's not the kind of girl I thought you'd go for."

I can't help but laugh. "We have a lot in common actually."

"Ah, my sweet boy," she teases, probably thinking of all the things I've done over the years that were anything but sweet.

"It's her, Mum. She's the one," I admit, my heart pounding against my ribs. "I'm not giving her up. I don't care what it costs me. I'll walk away from everything if it means I get to be with her. Nothing else matters."

"Oh, Elliot. You always were my soft, sweet boy."

Yeah, and it made my father hate me.

She lays her hand on my cheek. "It's not going to be that easy, you must know that, Son."

Her warning makes my racing heart sink into my stomach.

It's what I expected to hear, but the words still strike me like a physical blow.

A sympathetic smile pulls at her lips, and the sight of it makes everything worse. She doesn't think this is going to be possible.

Seeing my own fears reflected back at me is worse than I could have expected.

"Please, Mum. You have to help me," I implore. "I love her. I'm in love with her, and I can't lose her."

I won't.

It's late by the time I let myself into Abigail's dorm room, but the lights are on and she's waiting for me in the middle of her bed.

She's wearing one of my Saints t-shirts. Her hair is hanging messily around her shoulders and her face is clear of make-up.

She's unashamedly her and I love it.

"How did it go?" she asks nervously, wringing her hands together in her lap.

"He wasn't there," I confess on a heavy breath as I lock the door behind me and pull my hoodie over my head.

"Oh," Abigail whispers, deflating as I toe my trainers off, push my jeans and boxers from my hips and stalk closer.

"My mum was there. I told her everything," I confess as I crawl onto the bed.

She shrieks as I grab her ankles and drag her beneath me. My shirt rides up letting me see the white cotton knickers she's wearing beneath.

"Told her that I was in love with you, Red."

"Oh my God," she gasps, trying to tug her hands from my grip to cover her face.

Refusing to allow her to hide, I pin her arms back against the bed. "Told her you're the one."

"Elliot," she moans when I settle between her thighs, letting my growing cock tease her.

"Told her that I'd give everything up for you."

"Y-you can't. You—" I cut off her argument with my

lips, kissing her so deeply it makes my head spin and my body ache for her.

"It's the truth, and one way or another we'll figure out a way to be together," I whisper against her jaw.

"What did she say?" Abigail gasps, writhing beneath me.

"That she'd do whatever she can to support us."

"She really said that? Oh, Elliot, that's— Oh my God," she moans when I suck on the sensitive patch of skin beneath her ear.

I don't want to talk about it—I just want her.

"But what about Scott?"

"I told you, Red. Let me deal with all that. You just focus on enjoying yourself."

Releasing her hands, I drag my shirt up her body, leaving her in nothing but her tiny pair of knickers.

"Missed you today," I say as my mouth descends for her breast.

We haven't had any classes together, and after our weekend, I need her something fierce.

The only time I've had with her was at lunch, and that was from the other side of the table.

Nowhere near fucking good enough.

I want her next to me.

I want her to be mine in every way she can.

But right now, she has to remain my secret and I hate it.

But is what I want possible, or are we on a one-way track to a collision neither of us are going to survive?

24

ABIGAIL

"He's so obvious," Tally whispers before popping another grape into her mouth.

I glance over at Elliot and flush.

She's right.

All week we've done this dance. Attended classes. Sat with our friends at lunch. Together but not really together.

Not in the way that matters.

The way that I wish were.

"Yeah," I murmur, looking away first.

Elliot asked for time. He asked me to trust him. And I do. At least, I want to. But ever since he came back from his parents' house and told me his mum wanted to help us, nothing has changed.

Every time I pluck up the courage to ask him, he brushes me off or distracts me.

There's been a lot of that behind closed doors—Elliot distracting me. With his hot wet kisses and long skilled fingers.

I'm powerless against it, against him. Because when the morning rolls around and we have to leave my room—or his

—we have to go back to pretending that we're nothing to each other.

That I'm not—

"Abi?"

"Sorry, what?" I blink at Tally, and she gives me a sympathetic smile. "You've really got it bad, huh."

"I just wish it didn't have to be like this," I whisper.

"Oak says he's going to fix it."

When? I want to scream. But I don't, trapping the words behind my pursed lips instead.

I feel him watching me. Silently begging me to look at him. But I don't.

I can't.

Not right now.

"I need to go to the bathroom," I say, excusing myself.

A couple of girls glare at me as I pass their table, but I let their judgement roll off me. It all seems so insignificant now.

The whispers and stares. The rumours and cruel comments.

I'm the girl with scars. The girl who lost her mum in a tragic accident and spent years waiting for her father to leave her too. The girl who is too afraid to trust people. To put herself out there.

But I realise now, that my scars aren't something to be ashamed of. People fear differences. They fear what they don't know or don't understand. And until Olivia, Tally, Raine, and Elliot, I've never given anyone the chance to understand me.

I make my way down the hall and into the girls' bathroom, relieved to find it empty.

Being here, spending my days pretending that I'm not madly in love with Elliot isn't easy.

Even though, every night, he's determined to remind

me what we have is real. Not being able to touch him, to kiss him, and be with him in front of our fellow students is like a gnawing pit in my stomach, growing wider and wider every day.

I feel it writhing under my skin. Picking at old wounds. Wounds I haven't completely dealt with yet.

And although I don't feel the burning need to hurt myself anymore, not since Elliot made me his, I can't deny that I feel... restless.

I'm worried sick that Johnathon Eaton will make life difficult for Elliot. So difficult that he's forced to choose.

Stop. I curl my hands into fists. Willing myself to calm down.

I have to trust him. Elliot knows his family best. He knows how to handle his father.

I'm half tempted to text him and ask him to skip our afternoon classes.

I need him.

I need to know we're okay. But I'm trying to be stronger. I'm trying to be the kind of girl everyone expects to stand at his side.

But it's so hard to keep the negative thoughts out, to drown out that little voice growing louder and louder every day that he doesn't deliver any good news.

Sucking in a ragged breath, I compose myself. Elliot said he'll take care of it, I have to trust that he will.

I just hope something changes soon because I'm not sure how long I can do this.

With shaky resolve, I throw my bag over my shoulder and head out into the corridor. My next class isn't for another forty minutes but I can't go back to Tally and the girls.

So instead, I take off for the one place on campus I have always felt at peace.

The swimming pool is empty so I decide to go inside and lie on one of the loungers.

It wasn't like this before, when I used to sneak into the abandoned building to do my homework, or read, or simply escape my thoughts.

Now, it's a state-of-the-art facility, here to help students with their mental health and well-being.

Ironic really then that I've been avoiding the place.

After my father died, I half-expected to be mandated to attend counselling sessions with Miss Linley. But everyone was all too happy to leave me to my own devices.

I don't know if that made things worse, or better.

I guess I'll never know now.

I stare up at the ceiling, lost in the way the water reflects off the tiles, swirling and shimmering.

I'm so lost in my thoughts, in the restless energy coursing through me that I don't sense Elliot enter. I don't realise he's here until he's standing over me, his brows pinched with concern.

"How did you know I was here?" I ask.

"I followed you."

"You... Of course you did."

"What's wrong?" He picks up my legs and sits down on the end of the lounger, dropping my feet in his lap.

"Just wanted some space."

"From me?" His expression darkens.

"From everything." I shrug. "It's peaceful in here."

"It smells funny."

"It's the chlorine. I don't mind it."

"You're pissed at me."

He watches me, the air stretching thin between us.

"I'm not. I just... I wish things were different."

"I'm trying, I promise." He lets out a weary sigh, running a hand over his face. "But it's going to take time."

"Okay."

I don't know what else to say.

I could scream and shout and demand answers, but it won't change anything. Time and time again, the girls warned me that Elliot was a complicated boy.

But I didn't listen.

"I missed you this morning," he says, changing the subject.

"You chose to leave at silly o'clock to go work out with the guys."

"I've got a rep to uphold, you know." He runs his hand along the curve of my knee, sending delicious shivers through me.

"Elliot," I warn.

"There's no one here but us." His eyes flash with hunger as the tips of his finger dance higher, slipping under my skirt.

My breath catches, my heart crashing against my rib cage. "We shouldn't," I breathe.

"Nobody's watching you but me, Red." His pointer finger inches closer, and I can't help but shift into his touch.

"The cameras." My gaze darts to the little black orb in the corner of the room.

"You think I'd ever let anyone see you come undone for me? You're mine, Abigail. Mine." He growls the word, right as his digit finds my underwear.

"Ah," I cry as he rubs me in just the right way.

"Let me in." My legs fall open and he smirks. "Good girl."

His praise lights up something inside me and I relax into the lounger accepting my fate.

I want this.

I want him.

Any way I can get him.

"Fuck, Red, you're soaked."

"Elliot," I gasp as he slides his finger deep, curling it the way I like.

"What do you want, Red? Tell me. Use your words."

"I... More. I want more."

"Fuck yeah, you do." He adds another finger, stretching me, gliding his thumb over my clit in perfect synchrony.

My skin flushes, my blood heating as I lose myself to the addictive sensations.

My head rolls back as my eyes shutter. Six months ago, I would never have dreamed letting anyone touch me in this way. But Elliot has unlocked a part of me I never want to cage again.

But only with him.

"I love you," I murmur, my breaths coming choppy and hard as he pushes me towards the edge.

"Come for me, Abigail." He presses his fingers deeper, so deep it hurts. But I like the sting. It spreads through me, cresting and then crashing like a giant tidal wave.

"Oh God... God," I pant, my fingers curled into the sides of the lounger.

"Fuck, that was hot." Elliot slowly withdraws his fingers bringing them to his mouth and sucking them clean.

Despite my post-orgasm bliss, my stomach clenches violently, a bolt of desire going through me.

"Maybe we can—"

"Later," he says gruffly. "If we're missing from class..."

"Of course."

There goes my happy bubble.

I smooth my skirt down and sit up, running a hand through my hair, not daring to look at him.

I need a second.

To think.

To catch my breath.

To try and calm my tired, weary heart.

"You good?" he asks, sliding his hand into the back of my hair and collaring my neck. I finally lift my eyes to his.

"Like you said we should get back."

His expression hardens and he offers me a sharp nod.

"It won't always be like this, I promise." He pulls me in, pressing a lingering kiss to my forehead. "I love you. So fucking much."

"I know you do."

Loving me isn't the issue.

Because everyone knows sometimes love isn't enough.

He kisses me again, on the lips this time but the heat from earlier has gone and when he gets up, I'm left feeling cold and more restless than ever.

"I'll see you tonight?" he asks, and I nod.

Relief washes over him, and he gives me a small smile. "I'll leave first. Give it a few minutes before—"

"I know the drill, Elliot."

"Until later then."

"Later."

I watch as he disappears out of the room, then I inhale a shuddering breath.

How can being with someone be so exhilarating and so exhausting all at the same time?

He makes me so happy. He makes me feel so beautiful and special. And then he leaves, and all those old insecurities come rushing back.

A small, defeated sigh slips out of me as I compose myself and get ready to go back to class and pretend.

The thing about pretending though, sometimes you're only fooling yourself.

"Have you spoken to Elliot yet?" Tally asks me as we file out of the building sometime later.

Classes are over for another week, which means we're another week closer to exams and the end of the year. At least, for them.

"No, why?"

"Oh, crap. I... I'm not sure I'm supposed to say anything yet."

"Tally..." I warn, not liking where this is going.

She laces her arm through mine and gives me a secretive smile. "Fine. But when he tells you later, don't tell him I told you. We're going out tonight. All of us."

"We are?"

"Yes. Group date, baby."

It's hard not to be infected by her enthusiasm and excitement bubbles up inside me.

"Where are we going?"

"It's a surprise. But don't worry, the guys know we have to be discreet. We're probably going out of town."

"And Elliot definitely knows about it? I mean, he wants us to go... together?"

"What? Of course he does." Her brows knit as she takes in my hesitant expression. "Abs? What's wrong?"

"It's just been a long week," I confess.

"I know it isn't easy right now. But Elliot is dealing with it. Everything's going to be fine, babe. You'll see."

Her words lift my spirits a little after the way me and Elliot left things earlier. And it will be nice to do something with our friends, like a real, normal couple.

"What should I wear?" I ask. "I don't want to be too underdressed or overdressed."

"Oak said we're not clubbing. So nothing too dressy."

"Okay." I can do that, I think. "Is it weird I'm nervous?"

"Oh, Abs. Elliot is crazy about you. I know I had my reservations, but anyone can see he's smitten."

But no one does know. I swallow the words. She's so excited and I want to see this as a step in the right direction.

I really do.

"Do you want to get ready with me? I can do your hair and make-up?"

"Can we do it in my dorm room?"

"Of course. I'll bring some champagne for a little Dutch courage."

"Okay." We reach the fork in the path that'll take me to the Bronte Building and her to the Chapel. "I'll see you later then."

"Can't wait. And Abs?"

"Yeah?"

"This is a good thing."

I give her a small nod and take off towards my building.

A group date.

Nervous energy bounces around my stomach. I've been out with them all before but never as Elliot's girlfriend.

Maybe Tally is right, maybe this is a good thing.

I'm smiling as I open my door, mentally considering what I might wear.

I know Tally said not to dress up too much, but I want to wear something nice for Elliot. Something that means he won't be able to take his eyes off me.

A little giggle bubbles out of me as I imagine him all intense and brooding as he watches me talking and laughing with the girls.

My phone vibrates and I dig it out of my pocket, my

smile widening when I see Elliot's name. He probably wants to tell me the plans for later.

But the second I open the text, my heart sinks and tears fill my eyes.

> Elliot: I can't come over tonight. Family thing. But I'll see you tomorrow. I love you. xx

25

ELLIOT

"Cheers," Lauren's dad says, clinking his glass of whisky against mine.

"Cheers," I mutter, trying not to sound as pissed off as I feel about this.

It's like he knew...

Tonight was all planned. The eight of us were heading out of town for a group date.

Only a few months ago the concept would have made me shudder. But now... I was so fucking excited to be able to step out together, hand in hand without constantly looking over our shoulders to see if we've been caught.

"Scott was just telling me how much he's looking forward to having you join him at university in September. Just a few more exams. Hey," he says, elbowing me in the arm. "I know Lauren is looking forward to you joining them as well."

A calculated smile spreads across his face as if he can picture his and my father's plans all falling into place.

I have no idea how long they've been scheming for me

and Lauren to get together, but something tells me that it's not a recent development.

It's not a surprise. Every single minute of my life thus far has been meticulously planned out for me. Of course the woman I should be dating and then ultimately spending my life with has been too.

Bitterness twists up my insides.

I could be with Abigail and our friends right now.

But no. I'm stuck here having to pacify my father's friends instead.

My phone burns in my pocket.

Abi hasn't responded since my message apologising that I couldn't see her tonight. I didn't realise Tally had already told her the plans. After she got done railing at me, I made her promise to try and convince her to go with them.

The last thing Abigail deserves tonight is to be left alone in her dorm room.

But I also know how stubborn she can be if she doesn't want to do something.

The thought of her sitting alone in her dorm eats me up inside.

Fuck. This isn't how it's meant to go.

"I'm looking forward to moving onto the next stage of my life," I lie through my teeth.

Honestly, the last thing I want to do in September is to be Scott's little bitch again.

He may not be the Scion leader, not yet at least, but that isn't going to stop him from attempting to rule us like the sick and twisted dictator he is.

Just like he did during his time as an Heir at All Hallows'.

As if he can sense my hate-filled stare, Scott turns from his conversation with Mum and Zoey and focuses his cold, hate-filled eyes on me. A wicked smirk curls at his lips before he kisses his girlfriend's temple and makes his way over.

He nods at Lauren's dad before talking directly to me. "Talking about me again, little brother? Anyone would think you miss me."

I force a smile that I really don't feel. "I wouldn't exactly put it that way."

Lauren's dad excuses himself, leaving both Lauren and me in Scott's firing line.

"So," he starts. "How are you two getting on then? From what I've heard, you're not nearly as close as our old men were hoping for."

"Well, not everything revolves around their schedules."

"They won't be very happy to hear that, little brother," Scott sneers. "What's holding you up? Most guys would be all over a pretty little thing like Lauren here."

"Some things can't be rushed. Not that you'd know anything about that."

Scott tsks. "Anyone would think Lauren isn't your main focus right now."

Ice rushes through my veins at his words, the dark glint in his eye sure doesn't help.

"I have exams, Scott." I try to keep the tremor out of my voice. "Those are my priorities right now. I'd hate to disappoint Dad with my grades."

He studies me closely, it's almost as if he can hear the lie in my words. "Oh no," he finally says. "You really would not want to do that."

My heart slams against my chest as our eye contact holds. His threat pressing harder on my shoulders with every second that passes.

"So how are things at school?" Scott asks. "Fully focused there, I hope."

"You don't need to worry about me. Excuse me," I say turning my back on my brother and marching in the direction of the kitchen.

It's not until I walk through the door that I realise my mistake. Our parents have hired caterers for this event and there are staff everywhere.

Thankfully, they're ones I recognise and the moment the boss looks up she smiles warmly at me. "What can you get you, sir?"

I shake my head. "I'm fine, thank you, Mona. Just needed a few minutes," I confess.

"Ah, well, I've got exactly what you need for that."

As I take a seat at the breakfast table, she fusses around filling me a plate of goodies.

"Thank you," I say when she places it down in front of me.

I don't get the first canapé to my lips before a shadow falls over me. My stomach knots that either Scott or my father have followed me, but when I glance up, I find Lauren standing there.

She looks beautiful in a rich purple dress. But it doesn't matter how good she looks, I will never want her.

"Escaping already?" she asks, quirking a brow.

"I don't want to be here," I mutter under my breath.

"You and me both," she confesses, less concerned about being overheard than me. "Come on, let's go and enjoy these elsewhere."

Picking up the plate, she gives me little choice but to follow her when she makes a beeline for the French doors leading to the garden.

She studies the patio for a beat but quickly decides it's not where we're stopping before kicking off her heels and marching across the perfectly cut grass.

She doesn't stop until she gets to the old oak tree at the

very bottom of the garden, then she slips behind and disappears.

With a smirk, I follow her knowing full well that no one will see us from the house here. Not that it matters if they do. Our fathers probably wish nothing more than for us to be sneaking around together.

My heart twists painfully. I don't want him to think that I'm following his orders. What I need to be going is marching into the house and telling him to get fucked.

My hands tremble just thinking about it.

I'll do it. I will.

I'll sever everything with my family if it means I get to be with Abigail.

They have nothing that I need.

They can take my trust fund, my car, my place at Saints Cross University. I don't need any of it.

"What's going on? You're more on edge than usual?" Lauren asks after swallowing her first canapé.

With a sigh, I lower my arse to the ground beside her.

I debate how honest to be with her for all of three seconds. I've no reason to believe that I can't trust her after what we've already been through together.

"I want out."

"Out?" she echoes, her brows pinching. "Oh... Oooh. Shit, Elliot. That's... Shit."

"Yeah," I muse, agreeing with her ineloquent response.

"You have a plan though, right?"

"Uh..."

"Elliot," she chastises. "You can't go into something like this and not have a plan. They'll all eat you alive."

"Fuck," I breathe, leaning forward and dropping my face into my hands. "I just want her, Lauren. I don't want any of this bullshit. I don't care about any of it."

"I know. I get it. But as much as they like to pretend we

have some kind of choice, you know as well as I do that it's bullshit."

"I don't care, Lauren. I'm done."

"And yet you're sitting here still doing exactly what you're told," she points out helpfully.

Sucking in a deep breath, I watch as the sun sets behind the trees in the distance praying for some kind of divine intervention that will give me all the answers I need.

"Your father will never let you walk away."

"I know," I mutter, already terrified about what he will do.

"She must be one very special girl for you to risk all of this," she muses, continuing to eat the contents of the plate without offering me one. Not that I could eat anything right now even if I wanted to.

"She's everything."

"I hope it all works out for you, Elliot, I really do."

"But?" I ask, aware that despite the fact she's stopped talking, she hasn't said everything she's thinking.

"But… it's never going to work. You're an Eaton. Your father and brother won't let you go no matter how good your plan is."

"We'll see," I say, sounding a lot more confident than I feel.

Silence falls between us and I finally pull my phone from my pocket to discover what I already knew.

Abi still hasn't responded.

She read my message but hasn't reacted at all.

My fingers itch to send another, to ask if she still went with the others but in the end, I put my phone back to sleep and shove it back into my pocket.

Deep down, I know she hasn't gone. I know she's sitting alone and miserable in her dorm room.

I also know that it's all my fault.

"We should get back," I say reluctantly.

"Why? They might get all excited that we've slipped away to fuck."

I glare at Lauren. "I want to get out, not to get in deeper."

She shrugs, getting to her feet and brushing the crumbs from her dress. "Shall we?"

Reluctantly, I follow her back to the house feeling anything but ready to spend long, painful hours listening to my father schmooze his associates and watch Scott lick his ass like the perfect dutiful son he is.

Mum catches my eye the second we walk back into the formal living room, and she offers me a soft, apologetic smile.

But it does very little to calm the riot happening inside me.

"Ah, here they are," Scott says obnoxiously, ensuring that every set of eyes in the room turn to me and Lauren. "Having a little alone time, were you?"

I shake my head, but it does nothing to deter him.

"You know, when you're finally with me at uni next year, you'll be able to have all the time together you want."

"Can't wait," I mutter.

The rest of the night is just a continuation of the same. Scott pokes at me every chance he gets and more often than not is congratulated in a way by our father who finds the whole thing amusing. I mean, who wouldn't enjoy having your golden child embarrass your failure of a son in front of everyone you spend your life trying to impress?

It makes me sick.

All of it.

By the time I manage to escape, the only thing I've

managed to achieve is to confirm in my mind that what I'm going to do is the right thing.

I can't continue my life like this.

As I drive back onto the All Hallows' campus, all I want to do is go to her dorm. But knowing that I have nothing positive about the future to tell her, I turn right and head back to the Chapel instead.

Abi wants to hear that I'm making progress. All this sneaking around and hooking up in the shadows is killing her.

I want to tell her that it's done, or at least not lie that I've got a solid plan.

But I can't.

We're not even official yet and I'm already fucking it all up.

With my head bowed, I push through the ancient front door and make my way up to my room with my skin itching with disgust for myself and my actions.

I hate the way they make me feel. The way they make me question everything about my life.

There are only two things that give me any kind of relief.

And the best one isn't here.

26

ABIGAIL

"See, wasn't this a good idea?" Tally smiles as she nods at my untouched apple crumble blondie.

"Yeah." I shove a piece round the plate with my fork, my appetite nowhere to be found.

"You should have come with us last night. It would have taken your mind off—"

"Please, don't." I sigh, pushing my plate away.

After Elliot texted me, I got into bed and watched some trashy romcom, ignoring Tally's many pleas for me to still go along.

I expected him to message again when I didn't respond. But he didn't. He didn't show his face either.

I hoped it might take my mind off him—off the fact our friends were all out on their group date while I was all alone in my dorm room. Trying desperately to ignore the dark urges simmering under my skin.

I might not be proud of the fact that I let my disappointment ruin what could have been a fun night, but I am proud of the fact that I didn't give into the little voice whispering that I could make it all go away.

I don't want to hurt myself.

I don't.

But I also don't want Elliot to keep hurting me.

"Maybe this is all pointless," I blurt, earning me a heavy frown from Tally.

"What is?" she asks warily.

"Me and Elliot," I whisper his name.

You can never be too sure who's around. And I wouldn't put it past any one of the other customers enjoying one or Dessert Island's delicious bakes to know the Eatons.

"Abs"—pity glitters in her eyes—"don't say that. He's crazy about you. Oak won't stop going on about it."

I glance away, trying to shove down all the emotion and frustration warring inside me.

"Abi." Tally lays her hand on mine, coaxing me to look at her. "Elliot will fix this."

"How can you be so sure?"

I hate the uncertainty in my voice.

Hate that the one person who makes me feel so special, so cherished and seen, can also make me feel so... so horrible.

"Because it's Elliot. He has girls literally falling at his feet." I arch a brow and she chuckles. "I've seen it happen. More than once. And he's never cared, not even a little bit. Not until you."

"But his father—"

"Is a controlling arsehole by all accounts. But look at Theo. Look at Reese and Oak. Their families are the same. He'll figure it out, I know he will. You just have to trust him."

"I want to, I do."

"Do you love him?" I press my lips together and give

her a small shy nod. "Then it's worth fighting for, Abs. He's worth fighting for."

Something about her words give me pause. I've been so fixated on being Elliot's secret that I haven't really considered how hard all of this might be on him.

But how do I fight for him?

When it's his family that holds all the power?

Tally insists we spend the day together, browsing the quaint shops of Saints Cross. I humour her attempt at distracting me because the truth is, I don't trust myself to go back to my empty dorm room and not do something stupid.

"Still nothing?" she asks, glancing at my phone in my hand.

"Nope."

"I'm sure he'll text you later."

I want to ask if Oakley knows anything. But I don't.

"Are you sure I can't tempt you into girls' night at the Chapel?"

"Can you really call it girls' night if the boys are there?" My brows lift.

"Well, no, but we have endless fun torturing them with our choice of films and pamper routines."

"I think I'm going to call it an early night. But thank you, for today."

"Of course. I'm here for you, Abs. We all are. Even the boys."

I'm not sure about that but I appreciate the sentiment.

The Bronte Building comes into view and I give her a hug. "I'll talk to you tomorrow."

"Are you sure—"

"I'll be okay," I rush out. "Enjoy girls' night."

I take off towards the building and hurry inside, hoping to avoid anyone who might be hanging around the communal areas.

I can't shake Tally's words.

Maybe she's right.

Maybe I'm not fighting hard enough for him.

For us.

As soon as I'm in my room, I'll text him. I'll text him and—

I draw up short when I reach my door.

My slightly ajar door.

I know I didn't leave it open, which can only mean one thing.

Warmth spreads through me as I push it open. "Elliot." I smile. "I— You."

My stomach tumbles and my world narrows on the man standing at my window.

"Hello, Miss Bancroft," he turns slowly and gives me a predatory smile. "I don't believe we've met. I'm Johnathon. Johnathon—"

"Eaton," I finish, a trickle of unease sliding down my spine. "How did you get in here?"

He arches a brow, studying me as if I'm a puzzle he can't quite solve.

Ignoring my question, he levels me with a bland look. "I thought it was time you and I had a little chat."

"Does Elliot know you're here?"

"I thought Judge Bancroft's daughter would have more sense than that."

Heat stains my cheeks, but I can't help but feel nervous.

He clearly isn't here to make nice.

"What do you want, Mr Eaton? I have a lot of coursework to catch up on."

"Do you?"

My room suddenly closes in around me as he paces before me, hands clasped behind his back.

He's so different to Elliot and yet, there's a familiarity I can't deny. A cold ruthlessness that I've seen his son level towards more than one student at All Hallows'.

"I have it on good authority that you won't be taking your A Levels this year. That you are, in fact, deferring."

"I don't think that's any of your business, do you?"

He stops pacing and steps towards me, looming over me like a predator. But I stand my ground, trying my best to ignore the warning bells ringing in my head.

"Elliot is my son. There are certain expectations I have about his future."

"I am well aware of the expectations you have for your son, Mr Eaton." The words tumble out before I can stop them.

He runs a hand over his cleanly shaven jaw. Everything about him is immaculate. From the perfectly tailored, expensive suit he's wearing to his coiffed salt and pepper hair. The man emanates wealth and power.

His presence should terrify a girl like me, and it does.

But it also stirs something inside me.

"So you're not denying it then? Your relationship with Elliot?"

"Is there any point?"

He wouldn't be here unless he knew about us.

The cat is out of the bag. What I don't know is if Elliot finally told him or he found out another way.

The fact I'm yet to hear from Elliot suggests the latter.

The knot in my stomach twists and turns.

"I would think a girl like you realises how much she

stands to lose, Miss Bancroft. Especially after you've lost so much already."

The threat hangs between, making me suck in a sharp breath.

"Have you talked to Elliot?" I ask quietly, my heart beating so fast I feel a little light-headed.

I'm not good at this. At talking to powerful men and trying to stand my ground.

I'm used to wilting; to shrinking into the shadows where it's safe.

But it's Elliot.

My Elliot.

"My son is none of your concern. I know money will not sway your decision to do the right thing here, your father saw to that."

"*Do not* bring my father into this," I seethe, shaking with frustration. And anger.

Because I realise now, I am angry.

Angry at a man who values money and status above all else. A man who rules his family with an iron fist.

"Scott is right. The little mouse does have some bite. Still, I'm sure you can appreciate that I cannot allow your relationship with my son to continue. Elliot needs a strong woman to stand by his side. A woman who understands the rules of our world. Someone who can weld her beauty and desirability. Someone like Lauren Winrow who can continue the legacy of the Eaton family.

"He doesn't need to be with someone with your... issues."

My issues?

What is he—

"Mental illness is a dreadful thing. And it's no surprise that you're so unstable given everything that has happened.

But I simply cannot allow my son to get pulled into your mess. It is not—"

"Stop, please... stop." I run my hand along my clavicle, the world crumbling at my feet.

He knows.

Somehow he knows.

"That is exactly what I'm here to ask of you, Miss Bancroft." He pins me with a hard look. "Break it off with my son. Stay away from him and his friends. It's a few more weeks and he'll be gone from All Hallows'. Off to start the next chapter of his life. To fulfil his duties as my son."

"And if I won't do it?" I fail to hide the tremor in my voice.

His eyes flash with venom as he folds his hands in front of him.

"Then unfortunately, I'll have no choice to ensure that everyone learns who Judge Bancroft's daughter really is."

I suck in a ragged breath as I knock on the Chapel door, waiting.

"Abi." It swings open and relief floods me. "What happened?" Oakley stares at me with concern.

"Elliot," I rush out. "Is he here?"

"He's... Yeah, come in."

I follow him inside, unsurprised to find Reese, Theo, and the girls all hanging out.

"Abs?" Tally jumps up and comes over. "What's going on?"

"Elliot, I need—"

"What happened?" he appears and stalks towards me, his eyes flaring with intensity.

"Your... Your father..."

"What did he do?"

"I... He came to my dorm. He... He threatened me."

Somebody mutters, "Shit," under their breath. But I don't break eye contact with Elliot.

I can't.

I already know my decision.

"Tell me exactly what he said."

"He said that if I don't break things off and stay away from you, he'll make sure everyone finds out about my... issues."

"Issues? What do you—" His entire face blanches, the blood draining away.

I nod, confirming what he's already figured out. "He knows, Elliot. He knows things about me. I don't know how but he sounded pretty confident about it."

His eyes shutter and I'm not at all surprised when he opens them again and I find that cold indifferent mask pulled right over his expression.

"I'll fix it. I'll go over there right now and—"

"No," I say.

"No? But he threatened you, Abi. He—"

"I don't care, Elliot." I step forward, taking his hand in mine. "I'm not going to walk away from this, from you."

"You don't know what you're saying." He tries to pull away, a rare glimpse of panic in his eyes. But I hold firm, silently pleading with him to meet me halfway.

All this time Elliot has been so caught up in wanting to protect me, to avoid this very situation, I didn't consider how losing me would impact him.

"I do," I offer him a small smile. "I know exactly what I'm saying. I choose you, Elliot. I don't care what your father does, I don't care what rumours he spreads, or stories he tells about me. I love you.

"I love you, and I'm not going anywhere."

27

ELLIOT

I sit on the sofa surrounded by my boys but I'm not paying them any attention. Instead, my focus is solely on Abigail who is in the kitchen with the girls.

My anger bubbles away inside me like a volcano that's about to erupt.

He knows.

My father knows.

Not only that, but he broke into her dorm room and ambushed her.

How dare he?

How fucking dare he?

My hands tremble in my lap as I fight with my desire to go and find him. Squeezing my eyes closed, I try to force myself to think rationally.

Being impulsive won't get me anywhere.

My father is nothing if not calculated and malicious. He'll have a plan for whichever way I react. And honestly, he's probably expecting me to turn up and attempt to have this out with him.

He wants to see me while I'm vulnerable, and if he has

any clue about how I feel about Abigail then he knows the state of mind I'll be in.

He'll be able to hurt me in a way he never has before.

He'll cut me deeper and leave me bleeding out without a care in the world.

Fucking arsehole.

I hate him.

Hate him more than I ever thought possible.

The moment I open my eyes, she's there watching me cautiously across the room while the girls try to distract her from what she's been through tonight.

Because of me.

He sought her out because of me.

I drop my head into my hands and suck in a ragged breath.

"Bro?" Reese says, his hand landing on my shoulder. "Talk to us," he begs.

I wait another second before looking up at him and then Oak.

"You look like you're about to go and do something really fucking stupid," Oak points out.

"What the fuck else am I meant to do here?" I ask helplessly, looking between the two of them as if the answer will magically appear in their eyes.

"Fuck that," Theo barks from my other side. "He deserves for you to turn up and rip him a new one for this. How fucking dare he go anywhere near your girl."

"Theo," Reese warns.

"What? I'm so fucking done with controlling cunts of fathers. It's time Elliot stood up for himself."

"It's not going to fucking get him anywhere though, is it?" Oak asks. "This is Johnathon Eaton we're talking about."

"I don't give a fuck who it is. No one fucks with one of ours and gets away with it."

Hearing Theo stand up for Abigail so fiercely makes my chest swell. I fucking love that they have so easily embraced her as one of us after hiding in the shadows for so long.

She deserves to have people standing with her, helping her discover the incredible person she's always kept hidden away from the world.

"This is all my fault," I mutter, feeling those words right to the tips of my toes. "All of this. If I never—" I swallow the words as I watch my girl.

My girl.

Fuck.

She's everything.

So strong, and resilient. Sweet and caring. Smart and funny.

Every-fucking-thing.

And I'm bringing all this shit on her already hard life.

She deserves so much more than all of this. But the truth is that being with me is always going to come with drama that she doesn't need.

"Don't go there," Reese warns, predicting what I'm about to say.

"But it's fucking true. If I never let her get close then she wouldn't have a reason to have to go toe-to-toe with my father."

"But she did," Oak reasons. "She stood up to him for you."

Dragging my hand down my face, I continue to watch her with my heart a runaway train in my chest. "She shouldn't have to. Being with me shouldn't result in—"

"Elliot," Reese snaps.

"I can't be the reason she has to do this. I can't. It's—"

"She chose you, you fucking idiot," Oak says fiercely. "She stood in front of your old man, looked him in the eyes and... She. Chose. You.

"She could have backed away. She could have run in the opposite direction. But she didn't. She's here. Right fucking there, in fact. In your home, in your life, by choice."

"Oak's right," Reese adds. "She fucking loves you and she's in this fight with you because she wants to be. Let her fight for you."

"Fuck," I mutter watching her every movement as he pushes from the kitchen counter she was leaning against and begins to move closer.

She's wearing a long flowing skirt and a plain white t-shirt. Her hair is down, one side pulled across her face in an attempt to hide her scars like it always is. She's barely wearing any make-up, she doesn't need to. Her pale skin, her freckles, her scars... Everything about her is perfect. I wouldn't change a single thing. All I want to do is take the pain away. Make everything about her life easier, not harder.

A loud, pained sigh spills from my lips as she continues to move closer, her eyes locked on mine.

"She looks pretty set on her decision," Theo muses as she closes the space between us.

"It's a good look on her," Reese adds before clapping a hand on my shoulder in support.

"Hey," Abigail says when she gets to me.

"Red," I muse, staring up at her in awe.

After everything she's been through, how is she still standing, let alone willing to fight. Fight for me.

For us.

She fucking blows me away.

"Have you got a moment?" she whispers, keeping her focus on me.

Theo elbows me in the arm and I push to my feet, stepping closer to her. Wrapping my hand around the side of her neck, I lower my mouth to her ear and whisper. "I have every single moment for you, Red."

Her breathing falters and she leans closer, her body seeking mine out. Narrowing her eyes, she studies me, trying to learn all my secrets without me saying a word.

The curious stares of our friends burn into my back as we stand there lost in our own world.

"Come on," I say, taking her hand and leading her towards the stairs.

"She chose you, you fucking idiot. She stood in front of your old man, looked him in the eyes and... She. Chose. You." Oak's words from before slam into me and before I know what I'm doing, I drag Abigail in front of me and push her up against the wall.

"Elliot," she gasps before my hand wraps around her throat, squeezing possessively. Her eyes darken, her mouth popping open in surprise as her chest begins to heave.

"You chose me," I whisper, moving closer and pinning her to the wall with my hips as well.

"Of... Of course I did," she says, a small frown pinching her brows. "Did you think I wouldn't?"

I shake my head, barely able to process all of this.

Of course I hoped she would.

But telling me she would and actually doing it are two different things.

"There are only three other people in the world who have ever done that, and they're the arseholes sitting out there," I tell her honestly.

She smirks. "Not anymore."

"Fuck. I love you," I confess before crashing my lips to hers.

Her tongue immediately sneaks out and joins mine as her hands land on my body.

I kiss her as if it's our first and last all rolled into one.

She chose me when the easiest option would be to run. She stood up for me, and is willing to fight with me.

"Elliot," she cries when I wrap my hands around the back of her thighs and lift her up the wall.

The fabric of her skirt is a challenge I could do without, but in only a few seconds, I have it up around her waist as I palm her arse.

"What are you— Oh God," she hisses as I grind my hips against her, letting her feel just how hard I am for her.

"Need you, Red," I confess, kissing up her throat before nipping her earlobe and making her cry out. "I need you. Right. Fucking. Now."

"Oh my God. We can't, Elliot. They'll hear. They're—"

"Don't give a fuck," I grunt as I shove my hand between us, ripping my jeans open and freeing my aching dick.

"Oh God," she moans as I shift her position and drag her knickers to one side.

"Are you ready for me, Red?"

Her cheeks blaze the colour of her nickname, silently giving me the answer I need.

Dragging the head of my cock through her folds, I coat myself in her juices before finding her entrance. I'm desperate to push inside her and feel her squeezing me so fucking tight I forget my own goddamn name.

"Please," she whimpers when I pause just a centimetre inside her.

Her muscles ripple, desperately trying to drag me deeper.

But I don't move. I don't do anything but stare down into her eyes.

"Me and you, Red. Nothing else matters."

I hold her eyes, waiting for her to say the words I need to hear.

The guys are right. I don't need to go racing to my father to have it out with him. I need to be right here. Here with my girl, the one who's going to stand beside me and fight this.

"You and me, Elliot," she repeats. "Nothing else matters."

I thrust forward, making her cry out and leaving very little question about what's happening up here right now.

"I don't care what he threatens me with," Abigail forces out as I set a frantic pace. "He can do his worst. I'm not ashamed."

"Fuck, Red. You're incredible."

In only minutes, my balls are drawing up.

I want it to go on forever. I want to lose myself in her and never come up for air.

"Never going to get enough of this. Never."

Pulling her arse from the wall, I fuck her deeper, harder, giving her everything I have despite knowing that it'll never be enough.

"Yes. Yes. Elliot," she cries, making my chest puff out with pride.

My girl.

My fucking girl.

With her hands gripping my upper arms and her nails sinking deliciously into my skin, she comes all over my dick, squeezing me impossibly tight and giving me little choice but to fall over the edge with her.

"Abigail," I roar as my cock jerks deep inside her, filling her with my seed. "Fuck."

Before my limbs give out from the intensity of the release, I pull her from the wall and lower her to the stairs.

It's not the most comfortable place to lay her, but I need a minute before even considering carrying her up to my bed where she belongs.

I've barely come back to myself when noise from downstairs hits my ears.

"Oh my God," Abigail gasps, quickly covering her face with her hands as the round of applause from downstairs gets louder.

"Fucking morons," I mutter into the crook of Abigail's neck.

She laughs deliriously, her arms wrapping around me. She holds me so tight, I can't help but wonder if she thinks I'm going to try to escape.

"We're going to figure this out, Red. One way or another, I'm going to break free. The only person I belong to is you."

28

ABIGAIL

"Hmm, this is nice," I murmur as I trail my fingertips across Elliot's chest.

"Want to wake up with you every morning," he replies sleepily, tightening his arm around my hip.

Heat flares inside me but I don't act on it.

I'm too content lying here in his bed, tangled up in his arms.

For a second, I thought he might do something stupid like confront his father. But whatever the boys said to him seems to have worked.

"Elliot, I need to pee," I whisper, aware that he still hasn't opened his eyes.

He releases me and I slip out of bed, hurrying to the bathroom. Every inch of me aches but in the best possible way.

Something changed last night. It's always intense between us but there's been a shift.

I want to believe it's because he's finally accepted that I'm his. That I'm not going anywhere regardless of his father's threats.

I refuse to think about that. About what he might say about me and my family.

Elliot is worth it.

He's worth everything.

I make quick work of washing my hands and rinse my mouth with some mouthwash Elliot has, careful to return it to its place.

Elliot is so meticulous and tidy it makes me smile.

Such a complicated boy indeed.

I leave the bathroom only to find the bed empty. Frowning, I hover, unsure of what to do.

Before, I might have hid up here and waited for him to return. But I've made my choice.

It's him.

It was always going to be him.

Feeling a newfound confidence since facing Johnathon Eaton, I pull on one of Elliot's rugby hoodies and slip out of his room.

The Chapel, in all its ostentatious glory, still takes my breath away, and I run my fingers over the black gloss stair rail as I descend into the living room.

It's quiet. No sign of my friends and their boyfriends; and I wonder if they're still sleeping or whether Elliot told them all to scarper.

"I was bringing you breakfast in bed," he glances up from the kitchen island and gives me a lazy smirk.

"I missed you."

"You did, huh." His gaze darkens, tracking me as I make my way over to him.

My heart races in my chest, a delicious ache spreading through me.

I love the feeling, the way he makes me feel.

I never want it to end.

When I'm near enough, he hooks his arm around my waist and draws me close. "You look so fucking good in my clothes."

Gazing up at him, I frown.

"What?" he asks.

"You're a lot calmer about all this than I thought you'd be."

"Oh trust me, I'm furious that he came to you." Anger vibrates from every inch of him.

"Elliot." He glances away, his hand curling into a tight fist, and my heart sinks. "Look at me," I coax, brushing my fingers along his jaw.

His stone mask is firmly back in place, but I don't let it deter me.

"I love you. Nothing your father does or says is going to change that. You don't have to worry about protecting me."

"I could fucking kill him for—"

"No. No. I don't want you to do anything that could get you into trouble." I lean up on my tiptoes and inhale a shuddering breath. "I have money, Elliot. More money than I'll ever need. And the house—"

"No. Fuck. No." He holds me at arms length, staring at me with disbelief.

"If you're serious about breaking free from his control this is the easiest way. It doesn't have to be forever. Just until we figure things out."

"I'll figure it out," he says in that dismissive tone I know all too well.

"Okay. Maybe the guys will help—"

"I said I'll figure it out," he snaps, turning away from me.

It hurts but I know it's because he's used to being in control.

Elliot is used to holding the power.

Except when it comes to his future and his options.

"I love you," I stand my ground. "And I want to help. You can pay me back. You can—"

"What's up, lovebirds." The boys spill into the room, laughing and jostling each other. "That was some performance last night. Didn't know you had it in you, Abs."

A low growl rumbles in Elliot's chest, stopping them all in their tracks.

"Where are the girls?" I ask, sensing he needs a moment.

Maybe his best friends can talk some sense into him.

"They're over at Millie's," Theo mutters. "Boy troubles or something."

"Is she okay?"

"She'd better be," he spits. "Or I'll give that little shit something to –"

"Okay, Rocky." Oakley hooks him around the neck. "Why don't we all hit the gym. Looks like you and lover boy have some tension to work off."

"But breakfast," Elliot starts but I cut him off with a small smile.

"It's fine. Go with them and I'll go see the girls." I go to walk away but he grabs my hand and yanks me backward.

"Ell—"

"I'm sorry, Red." He lowers his head to mine. "This is all new to me and I don't like feeling out of control."

"I know. But we're in this together now. And I want to help."

His lips thin but his eyes soften. "I love you."

"I love you too. Go work out with the boys and I'll see you later."

"Okay." He steals a quick kiss, and somebody wolf

whistles. Elliot flips them off over my shoulder and soft laughter bubbles out of me.

"Have fun." I untangle myself from his arms and give the boys a small wave, before heading to get changed.

Silently praying he won't do anything stupid.

"How is she?" Tally asks Raine when she joins us in my dorm room.

I had gone straight to Millie's room only to find Tally and Liv lingering in the hall so we came up to my room to wait for them.

"First love sucks." She drops into my desk chair and lets out a weary sigh. "I've left her with a week's supply of chocolate and ice cream. That should do the trick for a while."

"She's a bright girl. She'll get over it," Liv says. "They'll probably be back on by lunch tomorrow."

"I don't know. She seemed pretty adamant it's over."

"They're still babies. How *on* can you be at that age?"

"Oh hush," Tally rolls her eyes. "Millie's feelings are valid. Even if he wasn't the one, break-ups are hard. At least she has you and Theo to pick up the pieces."

"If Theo doesn't leave him in pieces first." Raine frowns.

"I'm sure you'll convince him not to," Liv snickers.

"I'm sure you're right."

We all chuckle at that.

"And how are you, Abs? After almost setting the Chapel on fire with your little staircase tryst."

"I... I'd rather not talk about that."

"Babe." Tally eyes glitter with amusement. "You're

with Elliot now. The sooner you shed your innocence the better."

I let my hair out from behind my ears, desperately trying to hide the flush to my cheeks.

"You can't hide from us, Abigail Bancroft," Liv chuckles. "We all heard what you did."

"Okay, okay," I murmur. "Can we please stop talking about it?"

"Own it, babe," Raine says, offering me a knowing smile.

"Jokes aside, how are you feeling about everything?" Tally reaches for my hand. "I still can't believe his dad turned up here."

"I'm almost surprised it didn't happen sooner." Liv scoffs.

"Honestly, the only thing I care about is that Elliot is okay. Nothing Johnathon Eaton says or does can hurt me."

"I'm sure he was just all talk," Tally offers but I can tell from the worry in her eyes she doesn't believe her own words. "Do you want to talk about it... The other stuff."

"I..." God, I was stupid to hope they wouldn't have picked up on that. "I can't. Not yet. I love you all so much but I'm not ready."

"We understand," Raine says. "But whenever you are, just know that we're here for you, Abs."

"Thank you." A heavy silence falls over us and I hate it. So much I blurt, "I offered Elliot my money."

"What?"

"That's been the issue from day one, hasn't it? That Mr Eaton would cut him off? Well, I have money. More than I'll ever need. If it means he can make a clean break... What?" I ask when I realise they're all staring at me like I've lost my mind.

"You love him," Tally says.

"You really love him," Liv agrees.

"Well, yeah." I close in on myself, feeling vulnerable all of a sudden. "I love him so much. And I want to be with him. I want this to work."

"How did Elliot react to your... offer?" Liv asks, and I grimace.

"As well as you can imagine."

"Well, I think it's a great idea." Tally leaps up, grinning. "You can buy a cute little place together and Elliot can teach junior rugby at the local youth centre—"

"Elliot will be at university," I point out, and they all look at me again.

"If you think for one second Elliot is going to leave you, you're more deluded than we thought. Besides, attending SCU is his father's dream, not his."

"I guess I never thought about it like that."

"Clearly, the two of you have a lot to talk about."

We do.

Except, talking isn't exactly Elliot's forte.

Another awkward kind of silence descends over the four of us as the weight of what's to come settles.

I've made my choice.

Now Elliot needs to make his.

"Rise and shine, lovebirds." Someone bangs on Elliot's bedroom door, their laughter disappearing down the hall.

"Fucking idiots," he mutters, pulling me closer to his chest. "Morning." He nuzzles my shoulder, pressing a soft kiss to my neck.

"Good morning."

It's Monday and all my newfound confidence has evaporated. But I don't let him see that as I roll into his arms and cup his face in my hands. "No matter what happens, you need to keep a cool head today, okay?" I urge, needing him to remain calm.

"Yeah, yeah. I'm as cool as a cucumber," he grumbles.

"I love you."

"I love you too. But I really need to piss." He untangles himself from me and climbs out of bed.

I take a second to appreciate his very athletic, very naked body.

Despite things being a little tense between us yesterday, after me and the girls returned to the Chapel, we spent the day curled up on the sofa watching films with everyone. It was nice.

Normal.

A taste of what life might be like for us if things with his father blow over.

Elliot didn't mention my offer again and I didn't push.

But I'd be lying if I said I wasn't worried about what the day will bring.

The huge knot in my stomach tightens but I take a deep breath, reminding myself that I've got this.

That I can do this for the boy I love.

I just hope Mr Eaton doesn't push him too far.

29

ELLIOT

I don't hear anything from my father.

As far as I know, he isn't aware that I know about his little visit to Abigail.

My stomach twists, acid spilling through my veins at just the thought of him being anywhere near her.

She's too innocent, too pure to be subjected to his poison.

I fucking hate that I don't know what his next move is going to be.

Sure, he threatened to expose Abigail's secrets in order to keep her away from me. Did he really think that she'd agree with that and turn her back on me?

Who am I kidding, of course, he did.

True love doesn't exist in the world that men like Johnathon Eaton live in. Everything is a twisted business deal, corruption, and deception. There isn't space for the kind of connection that Abigail and I have found.

To him, love is a weakness. A distraction from what's really important.

Girlfriends and wives are just another transaction to him.

It's what Lauren and I would be.

A plan. A scheme. Probably a deception somewhere within their dark and twisted world.

A world I no longer have any interest in inhabiting.

"Come on, we need to go," Oak says after stuffing the last of his sweat-soaked kit into his bag.

The rugby season is officially over for us now spring is here. Everything we worked so hard for over the years is behind us.

We might not have ended the season where we were hoping to, but we've managed to find so much more than a trophy.

I stare up at one of my best friends, loving the happiness I see glitter in his eyes. In all their eyes.

I always thought they were happy, that as Heirs and rulers of this school, they were happy. I mean, they were, but seeing them now with their girls, it really puts it all into perspective.

We thought that hooking up with different Heir chasers every weekend was everything we could possibly want. I won't lie. It was good. Fucking epic some weekends, but it all pales in comparison to what we have now.

"Yeah," I mutter, already dreading what this day is going to hold.

There was a time when I thought that radio silence from my father was a good thing, but those days are long gone. I've since discovered that silence is more terrifying than anything else. It means he's making his moves shrouded in darkness, ready to strike when I'm least expecting it.

Shoving my feet into my school shoes, I shrug my blazer on and fix my tie.

Exams start next week, and despite all the revision I've been doing, I don't feel anywhere close to being ready. The only thing I can think about is Abigail.

Having her struggles out in the open is going to rip her apart.

It was hard enough for her to embrace her newfound fame when she became friends with the girls and began hanging out with us.

She was always the shy, quiet girl who hid in the corner in the hope of being ignored.

Embracing the change of being dragged into the spotlight has been hard enough but throw the loss of her father into that as well and… Fuck. I don't know how she's done it.

Sure, she has her vices. Ones that I completely understand. Ones that have helped her through. But they're meant to be hers. Her secrets, her way of coping with the bullshit life has thrown at her.

The thought of everything she's been through being public knowledge makes my blood boil.

I will do anything, fucking anything, to protect her.

But I fear that I can't win against my father.

He always gets his way and if he gets so much as a sniff that she hasn't followed his bullshit demands and broken it off with me, then he'll do exactly as he's threatened.

"Everything is going to be okay," Reese says, watching from the other side of the bench.

"Easy for you to say, your girl is safe right now."

"We're not going to let anything happen to Abi, Elliot," Theo assures me. "We're family. And no one, not even your cunt of a father, fucks with our family."

His words make my heart beat harder in my chest, and as much as I like hearing his sentiment, it doesn't exactly help right now.

"She's strong enough to fight for you," Oak says, just like he did at the weekend at the Chapel when we first learned of his threats.

"That's not the point. She shouldn't have to."

"You know, it might help if you told us what he's going to expose," Theo suggests.

And there it is. They all heard what she said the night my father paid her a visit. The threat he made. But we haven't talked about it, not yet.

I know Abigail wouldn't mind me sharing the truth with my best friends, but even still, the words refuse to fall from my lips.

Her issues are hers. Ours. No one else has the right to know what happens in our darkest hours.

"Elliot, you know we're not going to judge" Oak assures me.

"I know," I say, dragging my hand down my face. "It's just—"

"Not your secret to tell?" Reese answers, being unusually perceptive. Liv has definitely been a good influence on that motherfucker over these past few months.

They all study me as the rest of the team who turned up for a morning training session file out of the changing rooms.

"Shit has been hard for Abigail. She's been alone for a lot of what she's gone through, and—"

"She self-harms, doesn't she?" Oak asks quietly.

My brows pinch as my pulse begins to race.

I fucking hate that anyone knows my girl's weakness.

She'd hate it too, and all I want to do is protect her in any way possible.

I startle when his hand lands on my shoulder, squeezing tightly in support.

Silence surrounds us, his words echoing in the light breeze from the open door.

Sucking in a deep breath, I force my eyes to rise from the floor to find his. Compassion, understanding and empathy stare back at me.

He knows a little voice says in my head. *He knows you do it too.*

My hands tremble at my sides.

So much time and stress has gone into keeping my own secret from my three best friends over the years, it's been exhausting.

I never wanted them to know that I wasn't as strong as them. I was meant to be their leader, and yet I was crumbling under the pressure.

I should have been leading from the front. Standing tall and strong like my father requires of me. But while it might have looked like I was doing that, inside, I was dying and the second I got alone... Well...

"It's nothing to be ashamed of," Oak continues.

"He's right. She should be proud of everything she's overcome," Theo adds.

"I'm scared," I confess. "Scared of what the world knowing will do to her."

"She's fighting for you, Elliot," Reese states. "That is far more important to her than what a bunch of posh wankers think of her."

"Careful," Theo teases, "You're one of those posh wankers."

"Fuck off, I love Abi like a sister. Family, remember?" Reese says, reminding us of what Theo said only minutes ago.

"Yeah," Oak agrees. "Family. So shall we go and find them, support them?"

"Yeah, let's go find our girls," Reese agrees, looking like an excited little puppy despite only waking up to Liv less than two hours ago.

I shake my head, but as much as I might want to laugh at them, I'm exactly the fucking same.

Hiking my rucksack onto my shoulder, I follow them out and across campus to where our girls are having breakfast.

Just like always, almost every single student in the vast dining hall turns our way as we enter.

It's something that has become so normal to us now that I can't help but wonder what it'll be like when we embark on our new lives at uni.

Sure, we're all set to join the Scions at SCU, but we'll be at the bottom of the ladder. No one will give a shit about who we are until we prove ourselves.

Dread seeps through my muscles making each step forward harder than the last. I don't want to go through all that again.

I should. I should be fired up for the challenge, be ready for the stupid tasks and initiation bullshit that Scott and his elders will have concocted in an attempt to put us in our place.

But I'm not. I just... I don't care about any of it.

I want uni, sure. But I don't want the games, the expectation, the pressure.

I just want to be with my girl.

I want us to have a place where we can spend our spare time together studying. I want to hang out with friends. I want... I want to be a normal student. I don't want to be judged because of my surname.

I just want to be me.

Us.

The girl's faces light up as we move closer, but while Abigail might smile brightly at me, it doesn't meet her eyes and it only makes the dread coursing through me worse.

"Hey," I say, dropping onto the seat beside her.

We're still hiding our relationship, but honestly, it's getting harder and harder to do.

"Hi, good session?" she asks as the others fall into conversation around us.

"Missed you," I whisper, dropping my face closer to hers and studying her closely.

"Elliot," she chuckles, but still, it's not quite right.

"What's wrong?" I ask, my concern growing.

She smiles brighter, but it doesn't cover the darkness lingering in her eyes. "Nothing. Everything is fine."

I frown, searching her eyes for the truth. "My father... He hasn't—"

"No, Elliot. If he tries to contact me again, I'll tell you," she promises.

"Fuck," I sigh, letting my head fall back. "I fucking hate this, Red."

"It'll all work out," she says, sounding a lot more confident than I know she feels. "I refuse to let him win."

"I love you," I say under my breath so no one but her can hear the words.

"I love you too. You trust me, right?" she urges.

"You know I do."

"Come on, Eaton. I need fucking food," Theo says, dragging me from my seat so we can fill our stomachs.

My skin prickles with awareness as Abigail watches my every step towards the counter, and when I look back, she doesn't even attempt to hide her appraisal of my body.

Heat burns through me and I instantly wish I'd spent longer in bed with her this morning instead of going to train with these knobheads.

"She's got it bad for you, bro," Oak laughs.

"It's cute," Reese says before ordering one of everything available.

"Fucking pig," Theo teases, punching him in the arm.

I don't turn to look at them, I'm too enthralled with my girl, but she's no longer aware that I'm watching and the way her expression drops causes pain to slice through my chest.

She's more worried about this than she's letting on and I hate that she feels the need to be strong for us.

Unable to talk to her alone before our first class of the day, I'm forced to watch her go, being led away by Raine and Tally, while I go in the opposite direction.

All my morning classes pass as a blur. They're all last-minute revision sessions that I need to be listening to, but I can't get the image of my girl's sad face earlier out of my mind.

The second the bell rings for lunch, I stuff my things into my bag and storm from the room. My phone immediately begins vibrating in my pocket, but I don't pay it any mind. All I need is my girl.

"I always knew she was fucking weird," someone says as I pass. "Probably looks like a monster in the daylight."

The gossip continues as I make my way towards our table in the dining hall.

"Elliot," Oak calls when I've got the doors in my sight. "Wait."

I don't slow, but he still manages to catch up with me before I burst into the dining hall. His hand lands on my shoulder before he forcefully spins me around.

His frantic eyes find mine and it makes my heart kick up pace. "Fuck. Are you okay?" he asks, barely able to catch his breath.

"Y-yeah, why? What's happened?"

"She did it," he pants.

"Who did what?"

"Abi—"

"Did. What?" I spit.

"Released her own story. She beat your father to it. Everyone knows, Elliot. Everyone knows the truth."

30

ABIGAIL

"And it's... done." Tally hits a button on the computer in the student council office, and glances back at me, a look of pride shining in her eyes.

"Okay," I breathe. "Okay."

"It'll be okay, Abs." She squeezes my hand. "You'll see. But you probably need to find Elliot before he discovers it from somebody else."

"We're meeting for lunch."

"Then let's go find our guys." Tally laces her arms through mine and tugs me gently towards the door. "I'm so proud of you, babe. And I really think this could help a lot of people. But I can't help but think I should have realised—"

"No." I peek up at her. "We're not doing that. If I'd have wanted you to know, I would have told you."

"I know, I know. But what you've been through..." Guilt flashes in her eyes and for a second, I mirror her emotion. Because she's right, I didn't tell her.

But that's no reflection on our friendship.

"You're a good friend, Tally," I say. "I just hope this works."

The article had been my idea, but I knew she was the right person to help me pull it off. I just don't know if it'll be enough to get Mr Eaton to back off.

News travels fast because the second we reach the hallway leading to the dining hall students start staring and whispering and staring some more.

Tally gives my hand another reassuring squeeze. "Hold your head high, you've got nothing to be ashamed of."

For the first time in my life, I believe it.

Anxiety, depression, grief… They are valid feelings. Feelings so many of us—especially young adults—experience. But somewhere along the way, we're taught that it's better to keep those things inside. To put on a smile and pretend we're fine.

I'm not fine.

I haven't been fine ever since I survived the accident that killed my mum and turned my father into a shell of a man.

And yes, maybe I didn't deal with it all in a healthy way. Maybe losing my father was the catalyst that sent me spiralling into a dark, dark hole, but I survived.

I'm still here.

And I know that's partly thanks to Elliot.

My scars, my grief, the darkness that lives inside me didn't scare him away. Because he gets it. He knows what it's like to hide those parts of yourself. To go through the motions.

To pretend.

A smile graces my lips as I think about all we've been through. The things he taught me about myself, about what I'm capable of.

It's his acceptance, his love and friendship that makes me lift my head higher and meet their stares with my own.

"Go girl," Tally chuckles as the group drop their gazes and pretend to be talking about something other than the article.

"Oak." My friend lights up at the sight of her boyfriend heading towards us but his expression is anything but happy.

"What is it? What's wrong?" she asks.

But he looks straight at me. "I need you to come with me," he says grimly. "Now, Abs."

I nod, my heart plummeting into my toes as I rush out, "Where is he?"

Oakley leads us through the crowd gathered around the stairwell just past the dining hall just in time to see Elliot's fist fly straight into one of our classmate's stomachs.

"Oh, shit." Someone nearby lets out a low whistle.

"What the fuck did you say about her?" Elliot growls, all up in his face as he pins him to the wall.

"I-I... Come on, Eaton. It's all good. I was just—"

"Elliot, no!" I cry, hurrying over to them. His head twists and his eyes find mine. "Don't do this," I beg.

"Thank fuck," the boy breathes, relief skittering across his face as Oakley and Tally manage to disperse the crowd.

This is all my fault.

The thought hits me like a fist to the chest.

I didn't prepare him for the fallout of the article... because I knew if I told him my plan, he'd try and talk me out of it.

But I thought I could get to him, to explain before anything like this happened.

"Elliot," I say again, calmer this time, as I lay my hand on his arm.

A shudder goes through him as he shoves the boy away and grits out, "Get the fuck out of here and keep her name out of your mouth."

"Y-yeah. Of course, my bad, Abi." The boy gives me an apologetic half-smile as he scurries away.

Elliot's head drops in defeat, anger still rippling off him. I cast a wary glance towards Oakley and Tally and she grimaces. "Do you need us to—"

"No." I shake my head. "I've got this."

"You need anything, you let us know, okay." Oakley adds, and I nod.

"Thank you."

"Don't do anything stupid, big man," he adds before leading Tally away.

The corridor suddenly feels too small, the walls closing in around us.

"I'm sorry, I should have—"

Elliot grabs me and hauls me into his arms, his mouth crashing down on mine as he backs me up against the wall.

"Elliot," I breathe between kisses, so overwhelmed at the frustration and desire pouring off him in thick, angry waves.

"What the fuck were you thinking?" He presses his head to mine, trapping me in his icy gaze. "You shouldn't have done that."

"I did it for you. For us."

"But everyone—"

"I don't care." I slide a palm to his cheek and inhale a shaky breath. "I'm tired of hiding, Elliot. I'm tired of living in the shadows. For so many years, I thought my scars defined me. That my grief and pain made me different—

too different. The odd, shy girl who didn't know how to make friends or trust people.

"But the past does not define us. Our scars do not define us." I hold his face in my hands, willing him to understand.

To accept my decision to stand up for him.

To choose him.

"You know, it's supposed to be my job to protect you."

A soft huff escapes me. "Can't we protect each other?"

"I'm not... good at relinquishing control. When I heard that arsehole talking shit about you..."

"I should have told you, given you time to accept things."

"No, you're right, I would have tried to talk you out of it."

"I'm okay with everyone knowing my secrets, Elliot." Because you're more important, I swallow the words, unsure he's ready to hear them. "Besides, if my story can help just one person... That has to be a good thing."

He stares down at me, something warring in his eyes.

"What?" I ask, a little breathless at the intensity in his gaze. The admiration.

"You are one of the strongest people I know, Red. And does it gut me that you felt you had to do this, for me? Yeah, it does. But I'm in fucking awe of you." Elliot brushes a wisp of hair out of my face. "I love you."

"I love you too, so much." I press up on my tiptoes, brushing my lips against his.

This kiss is softer. Sweeter.

The tension slowly ebbs out of Elliot as he holds me close, holds me like he might never let me go.

And I don't want him to.

I want this—*him*—forever.

Forever.

The word clangs in my head, sending a spike of anxiety through me.

"What, what is it?" He breaks the kiss to search my face.

"Nothing." I smile. Because my thoughts, no matter how cruel and sabotaging, no longer hold sway over me.

Will a part of me always wonder if I'm strong enough, pretty enough, good enough to be with someone like Elliot?

Probably.

Do I intend on that stopping me from loving him? From choosing him? From fighting for him?

Never.

"Here she is." Theo grins as Elliot gently nudges me into the Chapel.

"Proud of you, Abs." Liv comes over and gives me a big hug, Raine not far behind her.

"What you wrote... You're made of strong stuff, babe." Raine offers me an understanding smile.

"Always knew you had it in you," Tally adds, and I'm sure I see tears glistening in her eyes.

"It was nothing, really," I murmur, not entirely comfortable with their attention.

The other students at school are one thing. I don't know them. But these people are my friends.

My family.

And now they know everything.

Well, not everything. I kept some small details out of the article.

A bolt of lust goes through me as I glance up at Elliot only to find him watching me intently.

"Want me to tell them all to fuck off?" he asks quietly, and I chuckle.

"Oh no you don't, Eaton," Reese says. "Abs is our friend too and you already stole her away for the afternoon."

It's true, he did.

After the incident earlier, we skipped afternoon classes and went for a drive. We didn't get very far before Elliot pulled over in a deserted rest area and put his mouth on me, but it was just the distraction I needed.

The boys all give me a knowing look and heat stains my cheeks.

"Quit it," Elliot barks. "I'll get us a drink." He drops a kiss on my head making a beeline for the kitchen while the girls herd me towards the sofa.

"I think you're Millie's new idol," Raine says. "She highlighted half your article and sent it to me."

"She did?"

Raine nods. "You made her feel understood, Abs."

"I... I wasn't really thinking about how people would react to it." I glance over at Elliot and the boys. "I just wanted to show Mr Eaton I'm not afraid. Struggling with mental health is nothing to be ashamed of."

"Did you and Elliot talk about what happens next?" Tally asks quietly.

"I think he's accepted I'm not walking away from this. But there's still things we need to figure out."

Like what if Johnathon doubles down on his threats? What if he completely cuts Elliot off financially and he still refuses to accept my help?

As if sensing my thoughts, Tally reaches over and grabs my hand. "It'll all work out."

"Yeah."

God, I want to believe her.

The boys join us and Theo switches the TV on, settling on some reality show about rich men and fast cars.

Elliot drops down beside me and drapes his arm along the back of the sofa, toying with my hair. "You good?"

I give him a reassuring smile.

"Fuck, exams start next week." Theo grumbles. "They came around way too quickly."

"Maybe if you actually revised during our sessions, you'd feel more confident about—"

"Hey, I revise."

Raine gives him a pointed look and everyone chuckles.

"Have you ever considered that you're too much of a distraction?" He throws back. "I can't help it if numbers and you get me horny."

"You should try Liv's trick," Reese adds. "For every question I get right, she rewards me with—"

"Don't you dare fucking say it." Oakley groans.

The two of them start arguing, the girls watching on with mild amusement.

"You really want to stay down here with these idiots when I could take you upstairs so you can help me revise?" Elliot leans in and nips my ear, sending a shiver down my spine.

"And how might I do that?" I simper.

"Well, for starters, you can—"

The doorbell rings out through the Chapel and everyone stops talking.

"Who the fuck is that? We're all here."

"Maybe it's Millie?"

"She's at therapy." He pads towards the door, disappearing into the hallway.

"Who is it?" Oakley calls but Theo reappears, his expression hard and unforgiving.

"You're not going to believe what the cat dragged in," he says, his eyes falling on Elliot.

Before anyone can speak, a hooded figure steps out from behind him and shoves his hood back, glaring in our direction.

"Hello, little brother."

31

ELLIOT

Fury floods through my system as Scott marches into the Chapel as if he still belongs here.

It might have been his home before it was ours, but his presence is no longer accepted.

Moving as fast as my legs will carry me, I stand in front of Abigail. There is no fucking way I'm going to subject her to any more of my family's bullshit.

She's already endured more than enough.

"Get out," I say, my voice making me sound way calmer and in control than I actually feel.

My entire body is already trembling with pent-up adrenaline from the past few days.

Unsurprisingly, Scott doesn't make any kind of effort to do as I say, instead, he widens his stance and lifts his chin.

"You're not welcome here," I try again.

"And yet, little brother, I seem to be standing right here in front of you."

My teeth grind in irritation as a smirk pulls across his lips. I startle when a warm hand lands on my waist before the heat of Abigail's body burns my back.

Her touch, her support, is everything.

But this isn't a fight I want her anywhere near.

"What do you want? I have nothing to say to you." I ask, moving forward, more than prepared to physically throw him out if I have to.

"I'm surprised you need to ask that question. I'm not the one who's playing stupid games, now, am I?"

I scoff. "I don't believe that for a minute."

As I close the space between us, he begins to shake his head. "I'm disappointed in you, you know that, little brother?"

"I don't give a shit what you think about me," I sneer.

"Giving it all up for a weak damaged girl like her," he says, his eyes shifting from mine to Abigail. "I always knew you weren't cut from the same cloth as me and Dad, but I didn't realise you were so fucking pathetic."

"Do not talk about her like that?" I warn, my fists curled at my sides, my mouth watering for the pain wiping that smug fucking grin from his face will cause.

It's been a few years since we really went at it, but I am fucking ready for it.

"Elliot," Oak warns.

"He's right, you should leave," Reese adds.

I sense all three of them step up behind me, also blocking our view from the girls.

"All as bad as each other," Scott muses. "Bunch of fucking pussies."

"That's enough," Theo barks.

"Oh no. After what this prick has done, it's not nearly enough," Scott announces, his eyes firmly locked on mine. "You're a disappointment, Elliot. You don't deserve to be a fucking Eaton."

"Fuck you," I spit, closing the last bit of space between us.

"She's fucked with your head, little brother. She's twisted everything up, and made you feel sorry for her with her pathetic stories and her ugly scars. She's—"

"Elliot, no," Abi cries before she suddenly appears between me and Scott.

"Aw, look. She's even trying to fight your battles for you."

"Abigail," I warn, reaching for her arm to pull her back.

I don't trust a single hair on Scott's head, I certainly don't want him within touching distance of my girl.

Throwing his head back, he laughs. "Do you remember how pathetic she looked that night in the pub? Fuck. I knew it was going to be good, but I never could have imagined that."

"Shut up," I spit, tugging Abi back towards me.

"Abs, it's okay. This is between the two of them," Oak says. "Tally?" he asks.

There's movement behind me but I don't turn to look, instead, I keep my eyes trained on Scott.

My chest heaves as I continue staring at him, my fists clenching and unclenching.

"No," my girl cries.

"It's okay. Let them do what they need to do," Raine says.

"You're going to regret this," Scott warns. "Eaton's don't give up their futures for a girl. Especially not one as pathetic as Judge Bancroft's daughter."

"Then maybe I'm not a fucking Eaton after all. Have it. All of it. I don't fucking want it," I shout.

"And what are you going to do? Live a quiet little life with your woman," he scoffs. "Please. That isn't a fucking life."

My nostrils flare with anger.

"Dad was right. He's been saying it since the day you were born. You're an embarrassment. A disgrace. We're better off—"

I move faster than Scott is expecting, and I catch him completely off guard as my fist collides with his cheek.

A loud crack rips through the air before Abigail screams behind me. Hearing her gives me pause and it's long enough to allow Scott to recover and retaliate.

His punch hits me square in the jaw, but I take it easily before launching myself at him.

"Elliot, stop," Abi screams, but her words barely register.

The red haze of anger has descended and the only thing I can focus on is hurting Scott.

I've hated him all of my fucking life.

Every single day he's looked down on me, belittled me.

I've always held back from doing what I really wanted to do for fear of the repercussions.

But now.

Now I don't give a fuck.

But for every hit I get in, he manages to one as well.

We've both trained for rugby all our lives and we're pretty evenly matched in height and weight. So as much as I might want to pummel him into the ground, he can hold his own.

Unfortunately for him, though, he doesn't have anyone to fight for like I do.

Sure, he has Zoey, but he doesn't really love her.

They're just putting on a good show because they have to. Just like I'd have been forced to do with Lauren if Abi didn't show me it didn't have to be that way.

"Stop it. Please," she begs as Scott stumbles back. His face is already swelling, blood trickling from both his lip and his eyebrow.

"I'm done," I shout, spittle flying everywhere as I wipe blood from my own chin. "I'm done with you. I'm done with him. I'm done with it all."

Scott glares at me. He looks like he wants to continue. He fucking can. I'll go all fucking night if he wants to. But something tells me that he already knows he's lost.

I hope it fucking hurts.

"You're going to regret this. You'll be a no one."

"Bring it fucking on."

"And these lot," he says, throwing his arm in the direction of my boys who are standing behind me. They might not have thrown any punches, but they're here to fight with me. Fighting for me. "They'll leave you. They don't want a friend like you. A friend who walks away from everything good in his life."

"No, they won't," I say confidently, and in silent agreement, all three of them stop closer. "They're my family. You're... nothing."

"No," a soft voice cries before footsteps move closer and a small body presses up against my side.

When I look over, I find all the girls have joined us.

A united force.

"We're family. All of us. And we don't need anything else," Abi says firmly, once again standing up for me without fear.

This girl.

This fucking girl. She's something else.

"Fine," Scott says, looking between each of us. "Fine. But don't say I didn't warn you."

Without another word, he spins around and stumbles away.

The sound of the front door slamming behind him rips through the Chapel a second before Abi falls apart.

"Shit," I gasp, wrapping my arms around her, I hold her

tight as pain sears through my body. "It's okay, Red. I'm okay."

Long minutes pass as she trembles and sobs against me.

Everyone else moves around us as if we're not there as they tidy up and get to grips with what just happened.

"Shh, everything is okay. It's over, baby. It's just you and me now."

It takes her a second to register the words, but the moment she does, she pulls her face from my chest and looks up at me through tear-filled eyes.

"Are you sure it's what you want?" she whispers brokenly.

I smile down at her, wincing when my lip cracks open. "More than anything, Red. I love you."

"I love you too."

"Okay, love birds. As cute as this is, someone needs to clean Elliot up before he stains his precious flagstone floor," Oak teases.

A frown appears across Abigail's forehead as if she's only just seeing me for the first time. "Oh my God, Elliot, your face."

"It's nothing. I can barely feel it."

"Liar," Reese coughs.

"Come on, let me clean you up."

Her small hand slips into mine and I'm powerless but to allow her to tow me towards the sofa where a first aid kit awaits.

Sitting back, I tap my lap, encouraging her to get as close as possible.

"Elliot," she warns. "You're hurt."

"And I need my girl. Straddle me, Red. Let me feel your hot little body against mine."

"Christ," Theo mutters.

I get it. They're not used to me being so tactile with anyone, but they're gonna have to get used to it.

This is it now.

Me and Abigail.

Us and our family.

A rush of unease goes through me as I think about what Dad's next move will be. But I figure that we'll handle it.

"What happens now?" Reese asks once they're all sitting back around us.

I shrug one shoulder as Abigail gently drags a wipe across my bottom lip. It stings like a bitch but I don't let them know it.

"I guess that's for me and Abi to decide."

"Do you really think your old man will just let it go?"

A bitter laugh spills from my lips, making Abigail tense on my lap. "Not a chance. But there's very little he can do at this point."

"What about uni?" Oak asks. "Will you still get into SCU without your connections?"

"I really fucking hope not," I confess.

"What is that supposed to mean?" Theo asks.

"It means…" I swallow nervously as they all stare at me. "It means that I'm not going to SCU in September."

"What?" Reese baulks. "But—"

"But nothing. My whole life has been dictated by him. By them. It's not anymore. My life—our lives—are ours to do with what we want."

"So what are you going to do?" Liv asks.

"Honestly, I've no idea. I still want uni, sure. But Abi isn't going next year, so maybe I'll wait for her. We can go together wherever the hell we want."

Silence follows my confession.

"You can't do that," she says quietly. "You've been working so hard and—"

"My results will still be there next year," I assure her, reaching up to cup her cheek. "And you'll be ready then too."

"But what will you do?"

"Get a job," I guess. "I'm pretty sure my trust fund just vanished before my eyes."

"We don't need their money," Abi assures me.

"I'm not taking your money, Red."

"We all have money," Oak says. "Scott is wrong, in case you wondered. We'd never abandon you."

"Guys, I appreciate it, but I don't need money from any of you. I'll figure this out. One day at a time, yeah?"

Silence falls between us, my words hanging heavy in the air.

It's Theo who finally breaks it. "Do you think…" He pauses, not wanting to continue with his question.

"Spit it out, Ashworth," Reese teases.

"Do you think you'll have to move out of here?"

His question hits me with the force of a baseball bat.

Ripping my eyes from Theo, I look around our home. Pain spreads from my chest at the thought of having to leave this place. But it's only a few more weeks.

"We had a good year, didn't we?" I murmur.

Besides, as sad as it is that this will all be over soon, there's excitement for the future.

My future with the girl I love.

32

ABIGAIL

"What did he say?" I shoot to my feet the second Elliot exits Mr Porter's office.

It's been two days since Scott turned up around the Chapel and it's been radio silence from Johnathon Eaton.

Until this morning when we arrived at college, and Elliot was summoned to the headteacher's office.

"As far as he's concerned, I'm to sit all my exams."

"So your father didn't—"

"He did." A pained expression flickers across his face. "But Oak's dad got there first. Said he'd take care of any financial issues."

"That's really nice of him."

"Yeah." Elliot grimaces, still not entirely happy with the thought of letting people help him.

Draping his arm over my shoulder, he pulls me down the emergency exit at the end of the hall.

"Uh, Elliot. We have class."

"Don't care," he murmurs, shouldering the heavy door and pulling me outside.

He wastes no time pressing me up against the wall and caging me there.

"You good?" I ask as he stares down at me, so much emotion warring in his eyes.

My savage, vicious boy has softened. All those sharp edges and jagged lines have begun to smooth out thanks to this.

Us.

Me.

"Not yet," he admits. "But I will be."

"Have you talked to her?"

His mum.

The one person he thought might help him in all of this.

He finally confessed that she never offered her support. That he lied because he didn't want me to worry.

"There's nothing to say. She made her choice, and it wasn't me." His icy gaze moves over my shoulder, and my heart breaks for him.

"Elliot." I palm his cheek, coaxing him back to me. "I love you."

"Love you too, Red. So fucking much." He lowers his face and brushes his lips over mine. Once. Twice. Teasing me in the best kind of way.

I try to get closer, to deepen the kiss and take what I want, but he hovers out of reach, a faint smirk tracing his mouth.

"Are you trying to drive me wild?" I ask, a little breathless.

"Always." He winks, and I swat his chest.

"Are you sure about this?" I ask, the air turning thick around us.

"What's that, Red?" he asks. Teasing.

Deflecting.

He's been doing a lot of that over the last two days. Trying to distract me. To reassure me that he's okay.

But I see past his act.

Elliot's future might have been decided for him by a man he hates but sometimes it's better the devil you know, and I can't help but worry that if Elliot gives it all up—SCU, moving on to the next chapter of his life with his best friends—he'll regret it one day.

"Don't," I said. "Don't do that. Not with me. If you still want to go to university—"

"I don't."

"But—"

"Look, I know I'm not good at this. At talking about shit and letting you know where my head is at, but let me be really clear about this... I choose this." He lowers his head to mine, trapping me in his intense gaze. "I choose you," he says with unwavering conviction.

"You think I want to be away from you for a year while you resist your exams? Not going to happen."

"I just don't want you to end up regretting anything."

"The only thing I regret is not standing up for myself a hell of a lot sooner."

"Why didn't you?"

"Because I had no reason to..." His fingers slide into my hair. "Until you."

"I hate that you've had to endure them." I wrap my arms around him and pull him closer.

"Good thing I don't have to anymore then," he says, stealing another kiss.

Someone wolf whistles and Elliot tenses.

"Relax, it's only some school kids," I say, watching the small group of boys jostle each other as they head towards the lower school building.

"We should probably go back inside," he says.

"Yeah, we should."

The air crackles between us. A veritable live wire ready to combust.

"Elliot," I breathe, my skin heating at the hunger in his eyes.

"Yeah, I know…" He exhales a steady breath, trying to compose himself. "Later," he says.

"Later." I nod.

Already counting the hours.

But our plans for later are ruined when we arrive at the Chapel after school.

"What happened?" Elliot asks a somber looking Oakley.

"It arrived special delivery an hour ago." He hands Elliot the A4 white envelope.

Elliot stares at it for a second and then tears into it, pulling out the thick pile of papers. He moves away from my side and a pang of dejection goes through me.

I know this is his burden to bear and that he'll come to me when he's ready. But it still hurts.

"What does it say?" Oakley asks, watching the boy I love with concern.

Elliot scans page after page before throwing them on the breakfast island and running a hand down his face.

"El—"

I startle as Elliot grabs the glass and hurls it against the wall, the thing shattering into a hundred pieces.

"That bad?" Oakley goes to him, but Elliot storms out of the Chapel, the door slamming behind him.

He picks up the letter and lets out a low whistle. "He did it. That motherfucker really did it."

"Should I go after him?" I ask, tears sliding down my cheeks as my gaze lingers on the door.

"Nah, let him cool off. I'll give the boys a heads up and message Tally to come stay with you."

"I feel so useless," I whisper, wrapping an arm around myself.

"You've been his rock, Abs. Don't let anyone tell you otherwise. What you did for him, laying yourself bare like that... It was fucking epic. But men like Johnathon Eaton have a way of getting into your psyche. Elliot knows his old man is an arsehole of gigantic proportions but it's still his dad. It's still his family. That shit takes time to come to terms with.

"You stay here, and I'll go find him, okay?" I nod, and he offers me a warm smile. "We've got this. Between you and me and the boys, we'll get him through this. I promise."

"People are wrong about you, you know." His brows furrow and I explain. "They think you're all just spoiled, entitled, rich boys. But you're so much more than that."

"We're not angels either, Abs."

"No, you're not. But you're family and that means something, Oakley."

He gives me a small nod. "I'll find him and bring him back to you."

"Thank you."

"No," he says. "Thank you. You saved Elliot from himself, Abs. You did that."

"Yeah." My chest tightens, my heart crashing violently beneath my rib cage as I whisper, "But he saved me too."

Hours pass and nothing.

Tally, Liv, and Raine have stayed with me, trying to distract me while their boyfriends are off trying to distract my boyfriend.

The letter disinheriting Elliot from the Eaton estate—*the family*—taunts me from the coffee table.

I want to burn the damn thing. Shred it into little pieces and post it back to Johnathon Eaton with a letter of my own.

But I know this is not my battle to fight, and all I can do is wait.

"Anything?" I ask Tally as she scrolls on her phone.

"Oak said they won't be long."

Long?

It's been hours.

I stand up, pacing, gnawing the end of my thumb because I hate this.

I hate it.

"You should have a smoke or a drink. Try to relax," Raine suggests.

"I.... No. I want a clear head for when he gets back."

"You know, it might be better if you're not here," Liv says, the pity in her eyes gutting me.

"I'm staying."

"Abs, I'm just saying—"

"I'm staying."

"Okay." She holds up her hands.

Silence falls over the four of us again as I continue to pace, wondering where they are and what they're doing.

When I finally hear a car pull up outside of the Chapel, I freeze, fear like I've never known plunking in my stomach.

And then he's there, standing in the doorway, dried blood on his knuckles, a nasty looking cut in his lip.

"What—"

"You said she wasn't here," he fumes, cutting Oakley with a look that could kill.

"I lied. Get over it."

The floor goes from under me, but I stand my ground, refusing to let him push me away because his father is an evil prick.

"You should go." Elliot pins me with a dark look.

"No."

"I mean it, Bancroft. I can't deal with this right now."

Me.

He means he can't deal with *me*.

I lock down the hurt and step towards him.

"We should probably give them some space," Oakley suggests.

"Don't," Elliot spits. But I give Oakley a nod.

"If you need us..." Tally adds.

"I'm fine. I've got this."

They clear out, leaving me alone with Elliot.

He narrows his eyes, so much pain and anger burning there. Then he storms over to the kitchen and pulls a bottle of vodka out of the cabinet, not bothering with a glass.

"That won't help," I say from behind him.

"And you think you can help me?" he sneers.

"Elliot." I move closer, laying my hand on his shoulder. "Talk to me."

"Stop," he says, knocking me away.

"But I want to help." I move around him, shoving myself between him and the counter. "Let me help, please." I gaze up at him with nothing but love and trust.

"Red." He inhales a sharp breath, his eyes shuttering. When they open again, I see a glimpse of my Elliot staring back at me. "I... I'm not in control right now. I need..."

"I know what you need, Elliot. And I want to help. I can handle it, I can—"

He jerks away from me, a caged animal fighting the urge to attack.

"Elliot." I take a step closer, taking the vodka bottle from him. I place it down, the air straining between us. "You helped me. You helped me so much… I'm here. And I trust you. You won't hurt me." I reach for him, silently pleading with him to let me do this.

To let me be his anchor.

"Elliot," I breathe, trying to keep a handle on the nervous energy rebounding through me.

"You don't know what you're asking for," he says in a low tone that sends a bolt of fear sliding down my spine.

But I'm not scared of him.

Never him.

I'm only scared of what he might do if he doesn't let me in. If he doesn't let me help.

"You should go," he snarls, trying to intimidate me. To push me away.

This— This is the cold, cruel Heir people know him to be. But it's only a mask. One he's been forced to wear to fit into his father's cutthroat world.

"No." I stand taller, lifting my chin in defiance. "I love you. I love you, Elliot. All parts of you including the ones you don't want me to see."

The air thins, my heart beating so fast I feel dizzy. But I refuse to back down.

I refuse to abandon him in his moment of need.

Elliot's expression darkens, anger radiating off him. But I don't back down an inch.

He needs this.

He needs me.

A beat passes. The room growing smaller around us as we remain locked in a standoff.

He thinks he'll hurt me.

He thinks I can't handle the darkness inside him.

He's wrong.

And I'm determined to prove it.

33

ELLIOT

My head and my heart war as I stare down at Abigail.

My Abigail. My sweet and innocent Abigail.

She looks up at me with wide, pleading eyes.

She so desperately wants to give me what I need. I think she understands what that entails as well. But the real question is, can I allow it to happen?

Since Dad cornered her in her dorm room, everything has been slipping away. The tight control I like to keep has been falling through my fingers like grains of sand.

All I want is to take care of her, to give her the kind of life she deserves.

But I have nothing.

Literally nothing.

The stack of legal papers sitting on the dining table behind me are evidence of that. My father, my own blood, has written me out of everything I was previously entitled to.

The only thing I have left is my surname because legally he can't take that.

My inheritance, my trust fund, my family... All gone.

Honestly, I don't really give a shit about the money. Sure, it's nice to have, but there are so many more important things in life.

I'll happily earn my own if it means I get to have everything else I've always been missing.

True love and real family.

Still, losing the only kind of life I've ever known terrifies me.

I have nothing to offer Abigail. I'm not even sure if the clothes on my back belong to me right now.

I wouldn't put it past my father to turn up here and demand I hand over everything that's been purchased by Eaton money.

If it weren't for Christian, I wouldn't have a school to attend or a place to live right now.

I didn't even know Oak had said anything to him, let alone got involved to help me out.

I suck in a breath and close my eyes, hating how I feel right now.

"Elliot, please," Abigail whispers. "Let me—"

Before I know what I'm doing, my hand slides against hers and my fingers grip tightly.

Her sharp gasp rips through the air but it's nowhere near enough to stop me as I move, dragging her behind me, focusing my attention on the door that leads down to the basement.

Many, many times over the past few weeks I've imagined bringing her down here. But never did I think the situation would be like this.

The heavy door slams behind us, echoing as we

descend the stairs before the sound of Abigail's heavy breathing takes over.

My skin prickles as the air cools around us.

Just being down here, I relax.

From the moment we stepped over the threshold, I was in control. Nothing beyond this basement matters.

It's just me and her.

As we emerge in the main room with a huge double bed in the middle, Abigail's hand begins to tremble in mine.

"You can say no," I tell her, giving her an out while I can.

If we get much farther inside, I'm not sure it's going to be possible.

"I'm here, Elliot. For you."

Her words gut me in the best possible way.

If she's expecting me to tow her towards the bed, then she's going to be disappointed.

Turning to the side, I march towards the closed door on the left.

There's a good chance that the girls have told her what's in here. And even if they haven't, Abigail has probably heard enough rumours to fuel her imagination.

But while what lies beyond this door might excite me, I've never brought a girl in here.

I've always been too terrified too.

Too terrified that I'll lose control.

And I can't fucking do that.

Not with a random girl who has no idea who she's dealing with.

I shouldn't with Abigail either... but...

Fuck.

I need it.

She knows it too.

"Oh my God," she whispers as I pull her to a stop beside me in front of the St Andrews Cross.

It's made of dark walnut with thick black chains hanging from each point.

I can understand why she's scared. Something tells me that she's not going to back down though.

"Last chance," I warn her. "You can walk out now or—"

"I'm not going anywhere," she says, walking in front of me and holding her arms out. "Do your worst, Elliot." She leans forward and stretches up on her tiptoes, her lips brushing my ear. "Make it hurt."

All the air rushes from my lungs as I reach out, curling my fingers around the bottom of her t-shirt and dragging it up her body.

Grabbing her chin, my fingers dig into her jaw as I hold her less than an inch in front of me. "You've no idea what you're asking for," I growl, my stomach a riot of excitement as the control I love so much slips back into place.

She smiles, or at least, as much as she can as I hold her.

Unable to stop myself, I lean closer and slam my lips down on hers. As our tongues duel, I unhook her bra and palm her breasts roughly in my hands. She moans desperately as I pinch her nipples hard enough to hurt.

"Elliot," she gasps the second I rip my lips from hers and drop to my knees, dragging her leggings and knickers from her body, leaving her beautifully bare for me.

The scar across her stomach calls to me and I lean forward, dragging my tongue up the length of it, revelling in the sweet taste of her skin.

My mouth waters for more, but then her fingers sink into my hair and I stop.

Sitting back on my haunches, I stare up at her, my heart thundering in my chest. "Go and stand in front of the cross, Red," I demand, my voice rough with desire.

Her neck and chest flush red and she hesitantly takes a step back. She might be nervous, but there is nothing but fire in her eyes.

A small gasp fills the air when she hits the cool wood of the cross.

I haven't moved, I'm still on my knees, worshipping her. "Spread your legs and put your arms up."

It takes her a second to convince herself to follow my order, but she does and pride washes through me.

Finally, I push to my feet and stalk over. Her chest is heaving, her eyes wide with apprehension and need.

"Good girl," I praise, loving the goosebumps that immediately erupt across her skin.

Reaching for her left arm, I wrap the soft handcuff around her wrist and secure it tightly.

She watches my every move, but I don't once look at her again. Instead, I focus on the task at hand and work in silence.

It only takes me a minute or two to have her bound to the cross and completely at my mercy.

Stepping back, I take my time getting my fill of her.

She's so incredibly beautiful. Her pale skin, her red hair, those rosy pink nipples. Her scars... Her strength.

She brings me to my knees.

Reaching behind me, I drag my shirt over my head, fold it, and place it on the dresser before pulling a drawer out.

Abigail's body flinches at the sound but she doesn't say a word as I study my options.

I don't need Abigail to tell me that this is her first time experimenting with this kind of thing to know that it is, and with that in mind when I reach for a soft leather flogger.

I glance up in time to see Abigail swallow nervously. I want to promise her that I won't hurt her, but I'm not sure I can do that. Also, I'm pretty sure she wants me to.

With my eyes locked on hers, I step up to her and drag the soft tails up her thigh. She shudders violently making the chains restraining her rattle.

"You're so perfect," I whisper before flicking the flogger against her thigh.

Her body locks up as she embraces the hit.

It's light. Just a taste of what it's capable of.

Her increased breathing becomes erratic as I drag it up her stomach and tease her breasts, her nipples puckering beautifully.

"More?" I breathe.

She nods, licking her lips hungrily.

I repeat my previous action with a little more force.

She squeaks as the tails hit her delicate skin and this time, I don't ask if she wants more, instead, I strike her again before moving to the inside of her thigh. Her skin is scarred and perfect.

My mouth waters with the thought of tracing each of those lines and marks with my tongue.

Soon.

"Oh God," she moans quietly when the leather catches her skin.

"So beautiful," I muse.

"Please," she begs, making me smirk.

"You'll get more when I think you deserve it," I say darkly. "I'm the one in control here, Red. You will do as you're told."

She nods before crying out when I strike her inner thigh again.

"And I want to hear you begging for me to fuck you."

Turning my hand, I flick the flogger again, only this time, I let the tails lightly graze her pussy.

"Elliot," she cries before I lift the flogger between us.

"Look at that," I muse, my dick harder than I thought possible. "Look how wet you are already, Red."

Her cheeks blaze so bright it spreads right down to her breasts.

"You won't come until I say you can. You got that?" I ask.

She nods. But it's not enough.

"Words, Red. I need your words."

"Yes."

"Safe word," I demand.

"Don't need one," she whimpers. "I trust you."

"You shouldn't. Safe word, Abigail."

She thinks for a minute before blurting, "Squirrel."

My lips twitch in amusement and my brow lifts in question.

"Elliot," she begs. "I need— YES," she screams as the tails land on the side of her breasts. "More. More."

Music to my fucking ears.

I work her over with the flogger, driving her to the brink of release over and over until her skin is red and glowing. Her thighs are soaked with her juices and her skin is flushed with sweat.

She's never looked more beautiful to me than in his moment.

Mine.

She is fucking mine.

"Oh my God," she screams, her body locking up as she fights against her impending release.

She's trying to follow orders, but she's barely holding on now.

Her cheeks are stained with the best kind of tears as she squeezes them closed, desperately trying to hold off.

Unable to torture her anymore, I drop to my knees, wrap my hands around her glowing inner thighs and suck on her clit. "Come, Red. Come all over my face," I demand.

It only takes one hungry lick of her pussy, and she quakes above me, screaming out my name as her body trembles violently.

The second she's done, I'm on my feet and releasing the chains holding her hands against the cross before fully releasing her legs. With my hands on her hips, I twist her around, letting the chains cross and tug her back, forcing her to bend over.

"Oh God, please," she begs as I rip at my trousers like a man possessed.

The second my dick is free, I fist it in my hand and run the head through her folds, coating myself in her arousal.

"Elliot," she whimpers. "I need—" her demand is cut off with a scream and I push inside her, unable to hold back any longer.

My grip on her hips is borderline painful but she doesn't complain. Instead, she takes every thrust of my hips as if she were made for me.

Her screams echo off the walls making me wish I could bottle them and listen to them every second of the fucking day.

Her body sucks mine deeper, squeezing me so fucking tight, it's all I can do to hold off until she falls over again.

Reaching around her stomach, I find her clit, rubbing her just like I know she likes.

Just like me, she's riding the fine edge of release and the second I pinch her, she detonates, taking me with her. Together, we free fall, our bodies and desire taking over.

With my arm banded around her waist, I hold her up as her legs give out. "I've got you, Red. I've always fucking got you."

34

ABIGAIL

"Was it too much?" Elliot asks, lifting his head off my stomach to look at me.

After uncuffing me from the cross, he had scooped me up in his arms and carried me into the other room and laid me on the bed while he fetched me some water and cleaned me up.

Aftercare, he called it.

"No, it was perfect." I run my fingers through his hair, loving how soft the strands feel against my skin.

I'm exhausted. Every inch of me is achy and sore but in the best way.

The fact that Elliot trusted me enough to bring me down here, that he finally bared himself to me, means everything.

"I'm sorry if I went too far."

"Elliot, stop." A contented sigh slips off my lips. "I wanted this. I want you. All of you."

"You really mean that, don't you."

The vulnerability in his eyes makes my heart squeeze.

"Yes, I mean it."

"They'll know," he whispers. "The boys and—"

"It doesn't matter." I brush my thumb along the curve of his jaw, gently coaxing him to crawl up my body.

Looping my arm around his neck, I pull him closer. Elliot leans in close, kissing me softly. A far cry from the boy who brought me down here earlier.

And I love it.

I love that I get to experience all his facets. Cold and dominant. Soft and vulnerable. Everybody might think he's the savage, vicious Heir but I know better.

Something I'll never take for granted.

"Do you want to talk about it?" I ask.

"There's nothing to say." He tries to pull away, but I anchor my hands around the back of his neck.

"Elliot..."

"He did it." His expression crumples. "He really did it. I mean, I knew he would, but fuck," he breathes. "I didn't expect it would hurt so much."

"I'm sorry."

"Not your fault, Red." He gives me a faint smile. "I guess I expected some big confrontation. I should have known he would cast me aside like I'm nothing."

Holding his face in my hands, I touch my head to his. "You are worth so much more than he'll ever know, Elliot. If you want to go and see him, talk it through, I'll come with—"

"No. No." His eyes shutter again. "I never want you anywhere near him again."

"Might be kind of difficult given we live in the same town."

"Actually, I was thinking about that. How do you feel about moving out of Saints Cross?"

"You want me to leave?" My heart tumbles.

"No, Red. I want you to leave... with me."

"Oh. Oh." Realisation hits, stealing the air from my lungs. "You want us to move in together?"

"Yeah, I do. Although given the fact that I'm as broke as fuck, I guess it will be me moving in with my very rich girlfriend."

"You want us to live together," I repeat, a slow grin breaking over my face.

"Yeah, I mean, if you want—"

"I want. I really, really want." I crush myself against Elliot and he rolls us back so we're lying facing each other.

"I'll get a job. Pay my way. I don't want—"

"Shh." I press a finger to his lips. "I don't care about any of that, Elliot. You being an Heir never meant anything to me.

"I love you. You."

A rare glimpse of emotion flickers across his expression. "I don't deserve you," he murmurs, brushing another kiss against my lips.

"Too bad because you're stuck with me."

"You and me, Red." He gazes at me with unwavering intensity.

"You and me," I breathe.

You and me against the world.

It's surprising how one minute your life can feel like it's teetering on a knife's edge and then the next, there's nothing but calm.

It's been a week since Johnathon Eaton served Elliot disinheritance papers.

One week since his Heir status was ripped out from beneath him. And yet, at school nothing much has changed at all.

Of course, the rumours were rife at first.

For the first time in my life, the whispers and stares have been aimed in a direction other than mine.

But Oakley, Reese, and Theo soon stamped out the gossip and chatter. Heir or no Heir, Elliot is still an Eaton by name and his reputation still precedes him.

"So I'm thinking end of exams party here at the end of June?" Oakley says as we laze around on the patch of grass outside the Chapel.

Elliot tightens his arm around my waist as I lean back against his solid chest, enjoying the mini-heatwave we've been having.

"No party," he grumbles, and Oakley rolls his eyes.

"Final party. It's happening. Get on board."

"I don't know, brother. He has a point. Do we even like anyone enough to invite them to a party?"

"It's not about liking them, dear sister." Oakley smirks at Liv. "It's about reminding them that no matter how much they try, they'll never be as cool or as epic as we are."

"Spoken like a true Heir," Tally mutters.

"You weren't saying that last night when you were riding this Heir's dick, crying for—"

"Pig," Liv scoffs right as Tally throws her empty can of Coke at Oakley's head.

"Ow, what the fuck was that for?"

"No party," Elliot repeats.

"We've got to do something to celebrate," Oakley complains.

"Can we tell them?" Elliot whispers against my ear, and I twist back to meet his heavy stare.

"You're sure?" I ask, and he nods.

"Okay."

"Actually, we might have a better alternative."

"If you're going to suggest we all pile down to the basement for—"

"Oakley!" We all grumble, and he grins.

"If everything goes to plan, we can celebrate at our new place," Elliot blurts, the slight quiver in his voice so adorable, I find myself smiling.

"What do you mean, your new place?" Theo frowns. "What—"

"Oh my God, you're moving in together?" Tally shrieks, and soft laughter spills out of me.

"If we can find somewhere," Elliot says, and I quickly add, "We'll find somewhere."

"Oh, how the tables have turned." Reese smirks.

"Don't even start." Elliot warns.

"Wouldn't dream of it."

Something about the twinkle in Reese's eye tells me the second me and the girls aren't around, they're going to give him plenty of crap about it. But I'm too happy to care.

Things are good.

Better than good.

Being with Elliot is... everything.

"All jokes aside, it's going to be fucking weird not having you start uni with us in September," Theo says, and the mood turns somber.

"I'll still be around to kick your arses," Elliot quips.

"Get in line." Liv flashes Reese a playful smirk and he grabs her arm and hauls her onto his lap.

"Something you want to say, sweet cheeks."

"Sister, wanker. That's my sister," Oakley protests, earning a round of laughter.

Family.

This is what family should be.

Love and laughter and unwavering support.

I never thought I'd find that in the halls of All Hallows' but here we are.

And I wouldn't change it for the world.

"At least we get to see out our school days here," Oakley says. "I knew Dad would come through."

"How did your old man wangle that?" Theo asks.

"He has his ways. Besides," his eyes flick to Elliot's, "old John boy isn't one for scandal and drama. He prefers to keep up appearances and letting Elliot stay here will soothe the rumour mill."

"Pretty sure everyone and their dog already knows that he cut me off," Elliot murmurs, tensing behind me.

"But as far as anyone knows, it's only rumour and conjecture."

"Scott's mangled face would say otherwise," Reese snorts, but no one laughs at that.

"Didn't you hear? Golden boy apparently got jumped by a couple of arseholes from Denton. Gave him a good hiding and sent him scurrying back to daddy dearest with his tail between his legs."

"Should have beat his ass in the cage if you ask me." Theo huffs. "He's had it a long time coming."

"I'm done, they can all rot in hell as far as I'm concerned," Elliot says, and that's that.

No one mentions Scott or Johnathon again, but I know the scars will stay with Elliot long after today.

Maybe even forever.

But I'll do my best to heal them. To soothe them when they hurt most.

Elliot taught me my scars don't define me. Now it's my turn to show him that his scars don't dictate who he is either.

Or the man he becomes.

SAVAGE VICIOUS HEIR: PART TWO

"What do you think?" I glance over my shoulder, hardly able to contain my smile.

"It's... small." Elliot huffs as he takes in the small two-bedroom cottage we're viewing today.

"I think it has character."

The second I saw the listing for the renovated cottage on the outskirts of Denton, I fell in love.

It's worlds away from the big house I grew up in. The house that became hollow and cold in the years after the accident, the years that slowly took my father away from me. Piece by piece.

"You know I have a lot of enemies in Denton, right?"

"Technically, we're not in Denton. And there's like five houses in the immediate vicinity. I think you're safe."

Elliot lifts a brow, but I don't let that deter me as I tiptoe towards him, and wrap my arms around his waist, gazing up at him.

"It's perfect for us. There's a secluded garden. The master suite overlooks the countryside. There's an amazing walk-in shower and—"

His lips slam down on mine, cutting me off. I slide my fingers into his hair and tug him closer, relishing the way his tongue tangles with mine.

"Hmm," I let out a contented sigh. "What was that for?"

"Wanted to kiss you," he says, taking my hand and pulling me through the house.

"Elliot, slow down. We haven't looked around properly yet."

But he doesn't stop, practically dragging me up the stairs and into the master bedroom.

The view is even better than the listing portrayed.

"Wow," I say, slightly awed that this might be ours.

Our home.

Elliot wraps me into his arms, my back to his chest, as we stare out of the large sash window.

"I get to fuck you here."

"W-what?" I breathe, pulse thundering in my ears as heat floods me.

"You want the house, I want you, pressed up against this glass, naked and ready for me."

"Now?" I whisper-shriek.

His lips brush my ear, sending shivers rippling down my spine. "Not right now, unless you want to give the estate agent a heart attack. But when it's ours."

"Ours?" I ask, hopeful, as I turn in his arms. "You mean…"

"As if I could ever tell you no. Besides, it's your money, Abi."

"But it's our house. Our home."

"Fuck, hearing you say that…"

"So I can tell him we'll take it?"

Elliot nods, swallowing over the lump in his throat.

"I love you." I throw my arms around him, so happy I could burst. "I love you so much. Let's go tell him. The sooner we get things moving, the sooner we get the keys."

It's my turn to grab his hand and drag him out of the room.

Towards a future neither of us saw coming.

35

ELLIOT

My footsteps thunder up the stairs as I go in search of my girl.

We moved into the cottage Abigail fell in love with on the outskirts of Denton a week ago.

I want to say that we're unpacked and totally settled, but that would be a lie.

No sooner did my exams end, did I embark on a new chapter of my life at Christian's law firm.

I'll never be able to thank him for everything he's done for me. Ensuring I still had a place at All Hallows' to sit my exams, and then offering me an unrefusable internship at his law firm for my gap year.

Thankfully, it's a paid position which means I'm able to contribute to our lives here.

I hate that Abigail had to buy the house alone. I hate that when we've gone out furniture shopping, it's been her who's been handing over her bank card to pay for it all.

I know it's not going to be forever, and I also know that she's more than happy to do it but... It still hurts.

I want to provide, and right now I feel pretty useless.

I don't regret it though.

Everything I've done, everything I've lost, it's all been worth it.

I always used to dream of what my life would be like without the pressure I always felt from my dad and Scott, but I never could have imagined it would be this freeing.

I am now surrounded by people who truly love me. They don't care about my status, my money, or my surname. They want me for me, and I'll forever be so fucking grateful for that.

"Red, are you nearly—" I stumble over my own feet as I cross the threshold into our bedroom. "Holy shit, you look — Fuck, Red."

Nervously, Abigail reaches up and tucks a lock of curled hair behind her ear.

My mouth runs dry as I take her in from head to toe. She's wearing a long, floral dress, but while it might hide a lot of her body, I think it might be the most revealing thing I've ever seen her wear. Two strips of fabric cover her tits and tie at the nape of her neck, leaving her sides and her back completely exposed. When she moves, I discover that the long skirt has a split that has to stop just shy of her underwear, assuming she's wearing any, of course.

Only a few months ago, she never would have worn something like this. She used to hide her beautiful body in the biggest, baggiest clothes she could find.

It was such a waste because she is fucking stunning.

And all mine.

"Is it too much?" she asks before chewing on her bottom lip.

"Red, it's... You look incredible."

"It's just a house-warming, I can change if—"

Stepping up to her, I wrap my hand around the back of her neck before dragging the fingers over my other hand up her exposed thigh.

"This dress isn't leaving your body until I unwrap you from it later. You look beautiful, sexy, and elegant."

She shudders as my fingers find the edge of her knickers.

"Elliot," she whispers.

"I was really hoping you were bare under here," I confess.

"They'll be here soon," she breathes, desperately trying to keep her head while my fingers glide over the soft lace covering her.

"They can wait. You're more important."

Her cheeks heat, turning them a burning shade of red that spills down her neck and onto her chest.

"I want you to feel as incredible as you look."

"Oh God," she moans as I rub her harder through the damp fabric.

"That's it," I encourage. "I want your scent all over my fingers while we hang out with our friends."

Her eyes hold mine as she sucks in ragged, hungry gasps of air.

"More?" I ask.

She nods eagerly, quickly forgetting any argument about why I shouldn't be doing this.

"Words, Red. Give me your words."

"Touch me," she whispers.

"I am." I smirk as I wait for her to be more specific.

"No, there's a barrier. Touch *me*."

I quirk a brow.

"Elliot," she breathes. "Just... put your fingers inside me."

My lips curl into a wicked grin.

"Now, that wasn't so hard, was it?"

She narrows her eyes at me as I tuck my fingers beneath her underwear and find her swollen clit.

"Oh shit."

"Better?" I ask, pushing lower to tuck two digits inside her.

Her head rolls back as a moan rips past her lips.

"So fucking tight, Red. Can't wait to fuck you later, feel you strangling my dick."

She swallows thickly as her body begins trembling with her impending release.

"You want that, Red? You want to feel me stretching you open, making you come all over my dick?"

"Yes, yes," she cries as I press my thumb against her clit, working her until she can't hold on any longer. "Elliot," she cries as the sound of the doorbell rips through the air.

Fuck them, though. They can wait until my girl's finished.

Once I'm happy she's ridden the whole thing out, I drag my fingers from inside her and push them into my mouth, licking them clean as her taste floods my tastebuds.

"Delicious."

Her cheeks blaze once more before she begins straightening herself up.

The doorbell rings again and she turns to rush out of the room.

"Wait," I demand, and she stops instantly, her hand curling around the door frame. Stepping up behind her, I grip her hip before spinning her around and crashing my lips to hers.

I kiss her as if no one is waiting on us, as if we have all the time in the world to enjoy each other.

I'm lost in her, letting her taste herself on my tongue

when our friends get fed up on the wrong side of the front door, and begin pounding on it.

"Stop fucking and let us in," one of them bellows.

Thank fuck we don't have any neighbours too close.

Our kiss ends with a laugh when they continue causing chaos.

"We need to let them in before they break down the door," Abigail says.

"Impatient arseholes. It's not like they've never made me wait for them," I sulk, rearranging myself as I follow my girl down the stairs.

The second she pulls the door open, they all barge inside. The guys carrying alcohol, the girls with bags of food.

"About fucking time. I thought Elliot was a two-pump chump," Oak mocks as he makes a beeline for the kitchen to abandon the crates of beer in his arms.

"Two? Don't give him that much credit," Theo adds, earning himself a slap across the head as he passes me. "Aw, what's wrong? Couldn't get it up?"

"Fuck you, Ashworth."

Taking the bags from the girls, I leave them to greet Abigail.

They all helped us move in last weekend, so it's not like they haven't seen the place, but still, they disappear off together as if this is all new and they need a tour.

"Fucking hell, this is mental," Reese muses as he rips the fridge open and begins loading it full of drinks. "You own a house and live with your girlfriend. Who'd have thought it."

I chuckle, but honestly, I've had the same thoughts.

"Wait now, Elliot doesn't own a house," Theo pipes up like an asshole. "His girlfriend bought it for him."

"Fuck off," I grunt, catching the beer that Oak throws me.

"Aw, leave him alone. It's cute."

"I'm not cute."

"Whatever. So how's it feel being my dad's little bitch then? Have you figured out how he likes his coffee yet?"

I shake my head. "My job is more important than that," I state.

"Oh yeah?" Theo muses.

Oak can take the piss as much as he wants, but the fucker spends his days in the exact same office I do. The only difference is that he's doing it because he wants to learn from his dad. I'm there because I need the money to provide for my family.

"Yep," I confirm before Oak pipes up with, "He has to do the Friday cake run as well."

"I fucking hate you all. I'm going to find the girls. They're nicer than you."

"Nah, you should know as well as us that they're not. They just hide it behind pretty faces and sexy bodies," Reese says.

"Truth," Theo mutters.

We spend a few minutes catching up on each other's lives before we grab the meat the girls brought and head out to the back garden to fire up the barbecue.

The hot summer sun blazes down and the trees and flowers filling the garden blow in the light breeze.

Happiness and contentment settle over me as the girls' voices float through the air from outside furniture we chose that now sits proudly on the large patio area.

The last year of our lives has been unexpected but in the best kind of way.

Only a few months ago, I never would have believed

that I wouldn't be heading to SCU in a few weeks with my boys. But it's the right thing to do.

I want to support Abigail through her second attempt at year thirteen. I also want to be here for Raine and Millie in Theo's absence.

Then next September, Abigail and I can follow them. Although, not to SCU. We've already agreed that we're going somewhere else. We're yet to decide where, but we'll figure it out.

There's no rush, and for the first time in my life, there is no pressure.

We can take life at a pace that suits us and allows us to navigate it as a couple.

"I need to take a piss," I say before pushing to my feet and heading inside.

Even after shutting myself in the bathroom, my friend's happiness and laughter float around me, and when I look up into the mirror as I wash my hands, I find myself smiling as if I don't have a care in the world.

I don't. Everything is fucking awesome.

Pulling the door open, I come to an abrupt stop when I find Reese loitering outside, obviously waiting for me.

"You okay?" I ask, not liking the crease between his brows.

"Yeah, um..."

"What is it?" I ask my heart rate picking up pace.

"Nothing. It's just..." He hesitates and I panic.

"Spit it out," I snap.

"Okay, so... I saw your mum."

My heart sinks.

There was a time after everything that happened when I hoped she'd reach out. There was no way she'd have agreed with how Dad reacted to my relationship with

Abigail. But I knew better than most just how much control he had.

"Right?" I ask coldly. It's been too long for her to try and reach out an olive branch now.

I'm done.

"She wanted me to give you this."

He pulls a small flat gift from behind his back. There's a card taped to the front with Mum's handwriting across it.

The sight of Abigail's name written by her makes my blood run cold.

Even that is closer than I ever want her to be to any of my family now.

"Not interested," I say, dismissing it and attempting to walk away just like she has.

"But—"

Spinning back around, I stare Reese dead in the eyes. "I don't give a fuck what it is, Reese. It doesn't have a place here. This house, it's for my family. She no longer counts."

Ripping it from his hand, I march into the kitchen and dump it into the bin.

"Okay then," he muses, watching my every move.

"I mean it. That part of my life is over. This," I say holding my hands out. "And everyone under this roof, that's all that matters now. My future is here."

Reese shakes his head, a smile playing on his lips. "I'm so fucking proud of you, man."

"Yeah, well, I'm proud of us all. We fucking killed it."

We walk out to the garden side by side. All eyes immediately turn our way as Reese rushes over and grabs a fresh drink and lifts it in the air.

"To our future reign," he says with a wild grin.

Abigail stands and rushes to my side. She wraps her arms around my waist as I pull her in as tight as I can.

"To our future," I repeat before ducking low and claiming my girl's lips.

Time for the next chapter of all our lives to begin.

Everything might be unknown right now, but one thing is certain.

Whatever it is, we'll all embrace it together.

As a family.

EPILOGUE

Abigail
One year later...

"Cheers." Tally hands me a champagne flute, and I take a sip, scanning the scene before us.

It's obscene. The huge black gazebo in Christian Beckworth's garden. The waiters all dressed immaculately in black and white. The flowers and balloons. The huge buffet table laid out complete with the biggest chocolate fountain I've ever seen.

No expense has been spared for the small, intimate celebration. Raine and I got our A Level results last week. We both passed with flying colours. Tally, Oakley, Theo, and Reese all survived their first year of university. And Elliot completed his internship, earning himself a promotion to junior paralegal.

We start at university next month and since it's only a

forty-minute journey, he's going to work part-time at the firm with Christian while doing his law degree.

I'm so proud of him, of the man he's becoming.

For a while, I worried that his father would make things difficult for us. But he didn't. He let Elliot go—disowned his own son—and never looked back.

We didn't either though.

We had a wonderful year of building a life together. Finding ourselves after years of pain and heartache. That's not to say there hasn't been ups and downs, there has.

For both of us.

But we give each other time and space and grace to make mistakes.

"Cheers," I say, meeting my best friend's smile. "This is… too much."

"Did you really expect anything less? You know how the boys can be."

Do I ever.

I glance over at the four of them, dressed to perfection in their suits. It's only been a year but they seem so much older. Mature in a way that comes from them being thrust into a world of money and power and influence from such a young age.

Christian approaches them, squeezing Elliot's shoulder as they shake hands. Tally's father joins them, clapping Theo on the back, and the six of them laugh at something Oakley says.

"You okay over there?" I ask Tally as she stares at them, an unreadable emotion on her face.

"It still feels too good to be true sometimes," she muses.

"Your father knows how much Oakley loves you."

"I know. I just never imagined… We're lucky, Abs." She grabs my hand and squeezes it. "I know things didn't end well with Elliot's family but—"

"It's fine. Johnathon and Scott aren't good people. We all know that." We've heard enough stories from the boys after their first year at SCU to confirm what a twisted, sick man Scott really is. "Do I wish that his family could support him, support us, yes. But they don't and so I'll love and support him enough to make up for it."

Her smile widens. "You're so different to the girl I met two years ago. I'm so proud of you, Abs. Of everything you've overcome." She hugs me tight, whispering, "He's watching you, you know."

Of course I know.

Elliot's intense gaze is like a permanent brand on my skin. Whenever we're in the same room but not together, I feel him watching. Feel the weight of his stare follow me.

But it doesn't make me shrink. It doesn't make me want to run and hide. It makes me stand tall. It lights me up inside and makes me burn.

Knowing that Elliot is always there, ready to fight my battles or stand at my side as I fight my own is more than I ever hoped for.

His love and understanding and encouragement has forged me into a strong, confident young woman who knows what she wants and what she's capable of.

"Enjoy the party, Abs," Tally says, giving me a knowing smirk as she walks off.

"There's my girl." Elliot slides his arm around my waist, pulling me in close. My hand goes to his chest as I gaze up at him. So giddy and full of love.

"Isn't this all a bit... much?" I arch a brow and Elliot lets out a small huff.

"You're one of the wealthiest girls in the county and yet a little luxury still offends you."

"It doesn't offend me, Elliot. I just don't need all this."

"Good thing it's not just for you then." He smirks, leaning down to brush a kiss against my lips. "I love you."

"I love you too. Can you believe we start uni next month?"

"Not going to lie, Red, never imagined I'd get to have this with you."

"Any regrets?"

His eyes darken, his fingers tightening on my waist. "The only thing I regret is the time we wasted. That I didn't make you mine sooner."

"Elliot..." I breathe, overcome with emotion.

"I need you, Red. Can we sneak away and—"

"Photo time," Fiona announces, and the rest of our friends crowd us as we stand and pose for Fiona and Christian and a few other adults invited today. Tally's parents, Maureen, and Theo's stepmum and sister Millie.

"Still can't believe you're not coming to SCU," Oakley grumbles.

"Seriously?" Reese says. "Elliot and Scott would destroy each other."

"Still fucking weird that he acts like you don't even exist," Theo adds, earning him an elbow in the ribs from Raine. "Ow, fuck, babe. What was that for?"

She shoots him an incredulous look and we all chuckle. Even Elliot. Because despite how things ended up with his family, he's happy.

He's finally free.

And family...

Well, family isn't always those you share DNA with.

Sometimes, it's the people you choose.

The people you love unconditionally.

And this group of Heirs and their girlfriends... are the only family we'll ever need.

Elliot

All afternoon I've watched my girl laughing and joking with her friends. She looks as beautiful as ever in her summer dress, her hair for once pulled back from her face, letting us see her.

My heart is fuller than I ever thought it could be. But something is missing.

Everything we've achieved this year has been incredible. More than I ever thought it would be. And I know that we've only got more of it to come.

I can't wait.

I want to experience everything with Abigail.

"You look like a love sick puppy," Oak says, stepping up beside me as I watch my girl laughing with his.

"I am," I confess without taking my eyes off her.

I get it, man. I fucking get it."

"Do you think about it…" His brows pinch as I trail off. "About the future?"

"Fuck, yeah. All the time. Graduating, our first jobs, our home," he says, getting this far off look in his eye.

"Y-yeah," I agree, but… Abigail and I have already kinda done that. Albeit a little backwards. Recently, I've been thinking about more than just that.

"Oh shit," Oak gasps, reading something in my eyes.

"What?"

"Are you gonna—"

"Excuse me," I say, interrupting his question and stalking towards my girl. "Sorry, Tally. I need to steal Abigail away for a few minutes."

Abigail stares at me, a frown forming between her brows as I take her hand and tow her away.

SAVAGE VICIOUS HEIR: PART TWO

"What's wrong?" she asks as we hurry around the back of the gazebo.

With my sights set on the summer house right at the bottom of the garden, I pick up my pace, forgetting that she's in heels.

"Jesus, Elliot. You need to slow— Fuck," she cries when I spin around and sweep her into my arms. "What the hell is going on?" she asks, staring up at me with a mixture of curiosity and panic in her eyes.

"I need a minute with you?"

"Why? What's happened?"

"Nothing," I say, hoping to reassure her.

The second we get to the summer house, I kick the door open and step inside.

"You're scaring me," she whispers as I set her back on her feet. "Why are you hiding down here?"

I stand before her, my eyes studying hers before I let my gaze drop down her body.

"I..." I start, although with the rate my heart is pounding, I struggle to conjure up any other words.

"You what, Elliot?" she asks, her eyes bouncing frantically between mine as she tries to read my mind.

"I was just talking to Oak, and I realised something."

"Okay," she muses, the frown on her forehead deepening.

"I love you," I blurt.

"I know. I love you too," she says, reaching out and gently cupping my jaw.

Her touch calms me, but not enough to stop my heart from racing and my hands from trembling.

"Elliot?" she questions again when I just stand and stare at her. "Seriously, you're freaking me— Oh my God," she gasps her hand lifting to cover her mouth as I suddenly sink to the floor, resting on one knee.

"I love you, Abigail. I love you so fucking much. You have given me the best year of my life. I want more. So much more. So..." She stares down at me with tears filling her eyes as I take her trembling hand in mine. "Will you marry me?"

"Oh my God," she gasps again.

"I didn't plan this. I don't have a ring, or some romantic speech. I just stood out there and realised that—"

"Yes."

"What?" I blink up at her, not believing what I just heard.

"Yes, Elliot. Yes, I'll marry you. A million times yes."

Her tears break free, spilling down her cheeks before she drops to her knees before me, wraps her arms around my shoulder and crashes her lips to mine.

Time ceases to exist as I lose myself in my girl, and when we part, we're both laughing deliriously.

"I can't believe you just did that," she giggles. There's so much happiness in the sound, on her face it makes it hard for me to breathe.

"Tell me about it," I mutter, shaking my head. "I think I might have lost control a little bit there."

"Aw," she soothes, gripping the back of my neck and pulling me closer. "I love it when you lose control, all kinds of magical things happen."

The twinkle in her eyes is nothing but pure mischief.

"Careful what you ask for, Red," I warn as I flip her onto her back in the middle of the summer house. "You know that I'll always deliver."

Looking for a new series? Meet Bexley in the Gravestone Elite series! **DOWNLOAD NOW**

SHATTERED LEGACY SNEAK PEEK
GRAVESTONE ELITE BOOK #1

Prologue
Mia

"You're not ready?" My mother freezes in the doorway, her expression slipping. "But we leave in less than an hour."

"Do I have to go?" I protest. "The whole thing seems like such a waste of time when we all know he's going to be paired with Brook."

Not that I would ever want to hear my name called. But at least if there was even a shred of mystery around which girl was going to be chosen as Cade Kingsley's prosapia, it would give the evening some entertainment value.

"Mia, sweetheart," she comes up behind me and places her perfectly manicured hands on my shoulders, "the Eligere is a rite of passage, you know this."

My stomach twists. "But it's just so... so archaic. Dressing us up like virginal brides in front of all those people…"

No, thank you.

"Mia, this isn't a punishment, it's a gift." She lets out a soft sigh. "I know Cade showed preference to Brook during the courting phase, but it doesn't mean anything. Only Quinctus can decide the fate of an Electi."

God, she makes it all sound so normal, when living in a town like Gravestone is anything but.

As soon as you start high school, you hear the whispers about this place, the traditions... the strange rules. And if you're lucky enough—or unlucky enough, as the case may be—to descend from one of the founding families, you get to reign supreme over the rest of us lowly folk, forcing us to partake in these ridiculous rites of passage.

Please. What girl with even an ounce of self-respect and aspirations wants to end up tied to one of the Electi?

The Chosen.

The heirs of Quinctus.

If you ask me, it's just a smokescreen for some really messed up arranged marriage scandal.

A scandal I have no desire to be a party to.

I want to escape this town and its fucked-up traditions... but part of me can't deny I am slightly intrigued. Nobody gets to know what happens behind the doors of Gravestone Hall.

And tonight, I have an open invitation.

"Please, Mia, don't make this any more difficult than it needs to be. Your father—"

"Yes, mother," I snipe. "I'll be ready."

Because that's what you do in a place like Gravestone. You follow the rules, smile where necessary, and always respect your elders.

Of course, it isn't like that for every teenager in Gravestone. Some have the luxury of moving into the area and having zero ties with the founding families. Unlike me. Our name, Thompson, descends from the Cargill line. My great grams was a Cargill until she married a Thompson... and here I am, bound to this strange life, expected to fall in line just because of my name.

"The car leaves in,"—she checks her diamond-encrusted Rolex, an anniversary gift from my father—"forty minutes."

"I said I'll be ready." It's not like I'm trying to impress anyone. The dress code for the Eligere is written in lore. All girls of age from the founding bloodlines—or verus line, as we call it—must enter the choosing at least once.

Although they are rarely picked.

My mother leaves me alone, and I begin to dress. The white gown flows over my slender form like a waterfall. I take my time braiding my dark blonde hair into a crown across my head and then pin the remaining curls into place with golden tipped pins. Adding a dusting of blush to my cheeks, I smear a lick of kohl liner under my eyes. The girl staring back at me in the mirror looks meek and innocent. A girl on the cusp of becoming a young woman.

In mere weeks, I will start college. But tonight, I will stand in front of Cade Kingsley as a prosapia.

A trickle of trepidation races down my spine. Everybody knows Cade and the Electi, even those who don't understand what it all means. He'll be a senior at Gravestone University in the fall, but I can still remember Cade as a senior in high school. I was in ninth grade, and he was everything I wasn't. Popular. Confident. Gorgeous.

Cade Kingsley, heir to the Kingsley line and notorious playboy, is finally going to discover the identity of his future wife.

And I am one of the offerings.

Gravestone Hall is the imposing gothic building that sits at the end of Prosperous Street. The entire town has been built leading toward it, making it the beacon landmark. The huge limestone bricks give it an eerie quality as shadows dance over the frontage.

"Ready?" my father asks me, squeezing my hand.

I give him a polite nod, unable to speak over the nervous energy pinging in my stomach. It's silly, really. We all know the outcome of tonight's Eligere.

The car pulls forward outside the steps leading up to the entrance, and the door opens. "Mr. and Mrs. Thompson, welcome," a young man says, reaching in to offer my mother his hand.

She climbs out elegantly, her silk gown swishing around her body. Temperance Thompson is always the picture of refinement. She thinks a woman's worth amounts to the designers she wears. It's something I didn't inherit. I did, however, inherit her hazel eyes and soft, dark blonde curls. Usually I wear them down, hanging like a cape over my shoulders. Tonight, however, they are intricately arranged on my head, leaving my shoulders and neck bare.

Tonight, I have no armor.

My lips curve grimly at the thought. I'm safe here. Cade didn't even attempt to court me. I know of at least four girls he took out on a date. Maisie Godiva told her friends at school that she gave him head in the cemetery. But I'm hardly surprised. Maisie gives out blowjobs like Santa gives out presents.

At first, I was relieved he didn't come for me. I have never had any interest in entering *their* world. But I'd be lying if I said it didn't sting a little. I know I'm a wallflower compared to most girls in this year's choosing. I'm pretty but not beautiful, slender but without those voluptuous curves guys seem to love so much, and I prefer lounge pants and leggings to dresses and stockings.

I have no desire to be judged on what's outside. A person can be beautiful to the eye but rotten to the core.

And a place like Gravestone... well, it's full of bad apples.

My father slides gracefully from the car and waits for me. I gather the dress in my hands and climb out, thanking the young man. His eyes skate down my body, lingering on my chest and the soft curve of my breasts. Heat rises inside me. I've never had a man look at me so brazenly before. It's both thrilling and terrifying.

Lowering my eyes, I push a loose curl from my face and offer him a small smile.

"Miss Thompson," he stutters over my name, "you look beautiful."

"Mia," my father barks, his expression displeased when I meet his eyes.

As we head inside, I feel the guy's hungry gaze follow me. Does he know why I'm here? Does he know what happens after the formal dinner ends?

The founding families—or Quinctus, as we call them—aren't stupid. They know how to cover their tracks and dress up their stupid traditions as celebrations and invite-only dinners.

Tonight is no different.

"He's watching her," I hear my father grumble.

"Relax, Garth. She looks beautiful. He'd be a fool not to look." My mother casts me a reassuring smile, but I avert my eyes.

When they talk like this, it makes me feel like I'm nothing more than a possession. A thing. It makes me feel like my life isn't my own.

I hate it.

I hate that I'm bound to these silly traditions. Suddenly, I want to run. I want to slip off my brand-new kitten heels and flee. But the minute we enter the Hall, all the fight leaves me.

"Wow," I breathe, taking in the vaulted ceiling and stained windows.

"I can still remember the first time I stepped foot in here." My mother joins me. "It's beautiful, isn't it?"

I nod, too awed to reply. Other families mingle. I spot a couple of girls from my school and we share an awkward wave. My father greets their parents, working the room like he was born to do it.

He wasn't.

It's my mother's bloodline that gives us the right to be here.

Right.

I swallow a derisive groan.

It isn't a right, it's an order.

"Come, Mia. Let's find our seats."

Of course, there's a three-course dinner to get through before the Eligere starts. I think it's just some kind of mental torture for the prosapia, but whatever.

The ballroom is a huge, elaborate room that has been dressed in white and gold. Flowers adorn the tables and huge floor-standing candelabras line the room. I pick out the other prosapia, six in total. Only Brook is missing. But she'll want to make a fashionably late entrance, no doubt. She was in my class, so we're the same age, but she's always acted superior. Probably because she's Phillip Cargill's stepdaughter. He's the town mayor *and* a Quinctus elder, one of the most powerful men in Gravestone. Brook was always full of herself, but the second her mom shacked up with Phillip, she became insufferable.

She honestly believes it's her right to be paired with Cade.

Good luck to her. Cade isn't exactly nice. Sure, he has those chiseled good looks and an arrogant charm, but there's something about him. Something dark lingering under the surface.

Something I want no part of.

As if I've summoned him from my mind, the room grows quiet and Cade and his posse make their grand entrance. Everyone—the other prosapia, the parents, even the servers handing out flutes of champagne—stops to watch them. The next generation. The Quinctus heirs... the Electi.

Cade Kingsley, Tim Davenport, Ashton Moore, Channing Rexford, and Brandon Cargill.

They move like a well-oiled machine, Cade slightly in front with Tim and Ashton flanking his sides, and Channing and Brandon coming up behind. They look ravishing in their matching black suits, although they all wear them in their own style. Channing has his collar unbuttoned, no tie. Tim looks the most clean-cut of the five, shirt tucked in and cuffs visible. Brandon's suit looks a little wrinkled, like he just rolled out of bed, or someone has been grabbing at the material. It wouldn't surprise me; rumor has it he's the biggest player of them all. It's easy to see why, though, with his easy smirk, bright blue eyes, and hair as dark as the night. Ashton has left his jacket off, draping it over his shoulder like he's in a photo shoot. And Cade... Cade looks positively breathtaking. His eyes catch mine, only for a second, and a shiver rolls down my spine. He knows who I am, but he doesn't *know* me.

Because he didn't give you a chance. I silence the little voice. I never wanted to be picked, I never wanted any of this... but I am only human, after all. An eighteen-year-old girl with dreams and desires. I press my thighs together. It's hard not to look at the Electi and imagine things... dark, sinful things.

But then a gong rings out and the spell is broken.

They are the Electi. The chosen. The future of Gravestone.

And me?

I'm no one.

Dinner is a total bore. I don't know what I expected, but it wasn't two hours of listening to various prominent residents of Gravestone giving speeches about the town's prosperity and bright future.

By the time Phillip Cargill steps onto the stage, I'm half asleep.

"Good evening friends." His voice echoes through the room. "Now that the formalities are out of the way, we can move onto more important things. Those of you here tonight understand the history of our great town, the importance of our heritage. Tonight, we will uphold one of our most sacred traditions: the Eligere." He takes a sip of his drink. "I now ask the prosapia and their fathers to join me in the Sanctuary for the ceremony."

My stomach flutters as my mother squeezes my hand. "Good luck, sweetheart. Remember, if you are not chosen, it doesn't reflect on you."

I barely refrain from rolling my eyes.

"Mia," my father says gruffly as he stands. I gather myself and accept his offer of help. The two flutes of champagne I drank with dinner rush to my head as the room grows small around me.

Everyone is watching, waiting with bated breath to know who Cade will emerge from the sanctuary bound to.

Of course, to anyone outside of tonight's ceremony, the engagement announcement that will follow the Eligere will be nothing out of the ordinary. Kids grow up, they attend college, date, and fall in love.

Only those with verus blood know the truth.

Everything is hazy as my father leads me out of the ballroom and down a simple stone hall. Maisie Godiva and her father are ahead of me. Her dress is slightly less demure than mine, cut low in the back and hemmed with pearls. It doesn't surprise me. Her mother is a bit of a show-off. Brook leads our quiet caravan. When she finally arrived, everyone had stopped to admire her dress. The prosapia are supposed to present themselves in a simple white gown, something pure and innocent to honor the union oath. But in true Brook fashion, her gown was something akin to a wedding dress, layered with lace and fine gold embroidery.

She is most definitely the sun, outshining the rest of us.

Eventually, we reach the Sanctuary, a place few people in Gravestone ever have the opportunity to visit.

"Ready?" my father asks me as we step inside.

"I guess," I murmur, wondering if anyone can ever be truly ready for something like this.

Candles flicker wildly in the cavernous room, bouncing shadows around the smooth limestone walls. It's simple in its decoration, nothing at all like the grand ballroom. But it only adds to the mystery and intrigue.

"Welcome to the Eligere." Phillip has slipped on a black robe that hangs to the floor. "Gentlemen, please present your daughters before the Electi."

I spot them then: Cade and his three sidekicks all standing poised and ready. Ashton isn't present because he isn't a true Electi. Of the four heirs, Tim is the only one already engaged. He and his fiancée, Fawn, were paired when he was just a freshman. But Channing and Brandon will both have to be paired eventually.

My father walks me to the line and kisses me on the cheek. "Whatever happens here tonight, I want you to know I love you, Mia."

My brows pinch, and I want to ask what he means, but he melts into the shadows.

"This is crazy," the girl beside me breathes. I've seen her around town, but she's older than me.

Phillip begins speaking again, regaling us with the history of the Eligere, the importance of unifying families and continuing to strengthen Gravestone's influence. But his voice becomes white noise to the blood roaring in my ears.

It's silly, we all know whose name is going to be pulled from the calix.

Cade and Brook are written in the stars.

"Maddoc." Phillip calls forward another robed man. I vaguely recognize him but can't place where from. My heart is pounding wildly in my chest, and the air in the Sanctuary is thick with anticipation. I can practically feel the other prosapia hold their breath as Phillip dips his hand inside the calix.

"Are you ready to meet your prosapia, Cade?"

Cade steps forward, nodding. "I am."

He's as cool as a cucumber, smug even, as if he's enjoying having eight girls lined up for his entertainment.

Asshole.

My teeth grind together behind pursed lips as I try to focus on something, *anything*, that will help distract me from the fact that this is fucking crazy.

Phillip pulls out the small slip of paper and unfolds it,

keeping his eyes on the prosapia. "Tonight, one of you will be chosen. It is a great honor, a great privilege, to be bound to an Electi." His eyes flick to the note, a deep frown marring his forehead. The blood drains from his face as he looks back to us. "I-I don't understand—"

"Spit it out, old man," Cade jokes, "we have a party to get to."

Oh goodie, the after-party. I can hardly wait for that.

"Ah yes, of course." Phillip clears his throat. "Cade Kingsley, on behalf of Quinctus, please step forward and accept Miss Mia Thompson as your prosapia."

I blink, certain I must have misheard him.

"Thompson?" Cade balks at the same time as Brook shrieks, "What the fuck?"

"Mia." The girl next to me jabs my ribs. "It's you," she whispers. "You need to go up there."

"W-what?" I croak, unable to process what's happening.

But then Phillip steps forward, commanding silence. "The calix has spoken," he says more firmly this time, as if there's no confusion, no mistake. "Mia Thompson is Cade's prosapia."

Oh, fuck.

DOWNLOAD NOW to keep reading Bexley and Mia's story.

ABOUT THE AUTHOR

CAITLYN DARE
DELICIOUSLY DARK ROMANCE

Two angsty romance lovers writing dark heroes and the feisty girls who bring them to their knees.

SIGN UP NOW
To receive news of our releases straight to your inbox.

Want to hang out with us?
Come and join CAITLYN'S DAREDEVILS group on Facebook.

ALSO BY CAITLYN DARE

Rebels at Sterling Prep

Taunt Her

Tame Him

Taint Her

Trust Him

Torment Her

Temper Him

Gravestone Elite

Shattered Legacy

Tarnished Crown

Fractured Reign

Savage Falls Sinners MC

Savage

Sacrifice

Sacred

Sever

Red Ridge Sinners MC

Crank

Ruin

Reap

Rule

Defy

Heirs of All Hallows'

Wicked Heinous Heirs

Filthy Jealous Heir: Part One

Filthy Jealous Heir: Part Two

Cruel Devious Heir : Part One

Cruel Devious Heir : Part Two

Brutal Callous Heir : Part One

Brutal Callous Heir : Part Two

Savage Vicious Heir : Part One

Savage Vicious Heir : Part Two

Boxsets

Ace

Cole

Conner

Savage Falls Sinners MC

www.ingramcontent.com/pod-product-compliance
Ingram Content Group UK Ltd.
Pitfield, Milton Keynes, MK11 3LW, UK
UKHW041308180625
6465UKWH00011B/30